PENGUIN BOOKS
Dying Scream

Mary Burton is the critically acclaimed author of *I'm Watching You*, *Dead Ringer* and *Dying Scream*, all set in Virginia, USA, where Mary lives with her family.

For more information about Mary, please visit her website: www.maryburton.com.

Dying Scream

MARY BURTON

PENGUIN BOOKS

PENGUIN BOOKS

Published by the Penguin Group
Penguin Books Ltd, 80 Strand, London WC2R ORL, England
Penguin Group (USA) Inc., 375 Hudson Street, New York, New York 10014, USA
Penguin Group (Canada), 90 Eglinton Avenue East, Suite 700, Toronto, Ontario, Canada M4P 2Y3
(a division of Pearson Penguin Canada Inc.)
Penguin Ireland, 25 St Stephen's Green, Dublin 2, Ireland (a division of Penguin Books Ltd)
Penguin Group (Australia), 250 Camberwell Road, Camberwell, Victoria 3124, Australia
(a division of Pearson Australia Group Pty Ltd)
Penguin Books India Pvt Ltd, 11 Community Centre,
Panchsheel Park, New Delhi – 110 017, India
Penguin Group (NZ), 67 Apollo Drive, Rosedale, Auckland 0632, New Zealand
(a division of Pearson New Zealand Ltd)
Penguin Books (South Africa) (Pty) Ltd, 24 Sturdee Avenue,
Rosebank, Johannesburg 2196, South Africa

Penguin Books Ltd, Registered Offices: 80 Strand, London WC2R ORL, England

www.penguin.com

First published in the USA by Kensington Publishing Corp. 2009
First published in Great Britain in Penguin Books 2011

001

Copyright © Mary Burton, 2009
All rights reserved

The moral right of the author has been asserted

Typeset by Jouve (UK), Milton Keynes
Printed in England by Clays Ltd, St Ives plc

ISBN: 978-1-405-91047-7

www.greenpenguin.co.uk

Penguin Books is committed to a sustainable
future for our business, our readers and our planet.
This book is made from Forest Stewardship
Council™ certified paper.

MIX
Paper from
responsible sources
FSC™ C018179

ALWAYS LEARNING   **PEARSON**

Prologue

Time had degraded the videotaped image of the cowering woman.

A line skimmed down the center screen now peppered with electronic snow, and a sallow haze paled the image's once vibrant colors.

As he'd made his movies over the last twelve years, he'd expected them to last forever. He'd never realized excessive viewing coupled with time would degrade the tapes of his three actresses and their final performances. The first tape wasn't a great loss. He didn't understand lighting, costumes, or camera angles. He'd been rushed and nervous. But as time passed, he'd gained experience and confidence and by the last tape, he'd honed his movie-making talent.

Remote in hand, he leaned forward and directed his attention to the most recent tape in his collection. He tuned out the annoying technical distractions and focused on the woman.

A pale satin slip, the shade of forget-me-nots, skimmed her full breasts and slim body and pooled over long legs tucked under her round bottom. A blond wig covered chestnut hair and accentuated a pale face and listless brown eyes underscored by smudged mascara.

Blue-black bruises darkened her cheeks. She stared sightlessly toward the ceiling, cradling the hand he'd broken the last time she'd resisted.

Off-screen a door opened and closed. Keys jangled. The woman straightened and tried to stand, but a waist-hugging chain forced her to remain on her knees. 'Hello?'

He'd never stepped in view of the camera lens. 'Sorry I'm late. I didn't mean to be gone so long.'

The woman's chest started to rise and fall in rapid, short breaths. 'I thought you weren't coming back.'

He'd been gone eighteen hours. 'I couldn't leave you forever.'

Over the last two weeks, he'd left her intermittently. Each time he made his exit, he threatened never to return as he shut the door. Then from a closed circuit television he watched as she begged him not to leave and yanked at her tether. Then after three, five, or ten hours, he'd return. Each time she wept, her expressive features reflected relief, horror, and flickers of anger. Slowly he'd been breaking her down, teaching her that her world revolved around him alone.

Now as she glanced up, she offered a smile both pleasing and desperate. 'Now are you going to let me go?'

'Not just yet.'

Her smile faltered. 'You said next time when you came back I could leave.'

'I've changed my mind.' He zoomed in the video image. 'I've enjoyed your performance so much I find I can't say good-bye.'

The close-up vividly captured expressive eyes that mirrored disappointment and a terrifying understanding. 'You're never going to let me go, are you?'

'Didn't I promise?' He sounded defensive.

Fresh tears rolled down her cheeks. Her lips quivered. She seemed to sense that this was the end. Game over.

Hysterically she started to yank the chain. Her breasts bounced delightfully as she struggled. 'Let me go! Why are you doing this to me!'

'I love you, Adrianna.'

'Let me go!' She all but howled the words.

'I told you that I loved you. What are you supposed to say?' The words dripped with annoyance. How many lessons would it take for her to play her part correctly?

'No, no, no! My name is Rhonda.' The silk under the chain had frayed and turned brown from the iron in the links. 'My name is Rhonda!'

'You are not Rhonda!' He snapped his fingers. 'Say the words like I taught you. Or I will get the cattle prod.'

Mention of the prod drained the fight from her eyes. 'Please. Please. Please.' The plea wound down to a hoarse whisper.

'Say it.' This would be their final scene together. And he couldn't hide the desperate anticipation from his voice.

The woman closed her eyes. 'I love you.' The faint whisper, void of feeling, tumbled out like rubbish from a bin. All the spirit and fight she'd had in the beginning was gone.

The words left him wanting. 'Say it again. And look at me when you speak.'

The woman looked directly at him. 'I love you.'

Better.

Nervously, she picked at the chipped red nail polish on her toenails. A ladybug tattoo framed her right ankle. 'Can I leave now?'

He ignored her question. 'Why do you have a ladybug tattoo?' These last two weeks he'd loved touching it. Kissing it.

Tears streamed down her face as if she realized her words had no effect on him. 'I told you a million times.'

'Tell me again.'

'It's a sign of good luck.'

3

His laughter rumbled rich and genuine. 'For me, it's good luck. Not such good luck for you.'

Her eyes flashed with sudden hot anger. 'Why do you keep doing this to me?'

'Doing what?'

'Playing games. Why don't you let me go? I've sworn that I'll keep this secret. I just want to go home. I want to forget. I want to live.' The camera zoomed and caught the beads of sweat on her forehead. 'I have done everything you asked.'

She tipped her head back and he could see her dark hair peeking out from under the wig. She was ruining the moment.

'Say it again.' His voice projected the annoyance he'd felt that day. 'And say it like you mean it!'

The woman dropped her gaze and fisted the fingers on her left hand so tightly her nails drew blood. For several long seconds, she remained silent.

The snap of the prod had her meeting his gaze. 'I love you.'

'What is my name?'

'Craig. Your name is Craig. I love you, Craig.'

'Again.'

This time she looked directly at the camera and nearly screamed the words. 'I love you, Craig!'

His erection hardened and finally he was able to take her. Though he'd been driven by powerful emotions, he was mindful of the all-seeing lens and careful to keep his face turned away from the camera.

She'd lain under him, the slip bunched around her waist, her body as still and cold as a lake in winter. His climax had come quickly, violently. He'd never felt so alive, so in the moment, and for those fleeting seconds the voices that always stalked him — told him he wasn't good enough — went silent.

4

Now as Craig viewed the tape for the hundredth time, the exquisite feelings he'd once enjoyed, like the tape, had faded.

The indefinable hunger that had tracked him for so many years had returned and the heavy weight of anticipation bore down on his chest. Lately, no matter how much he watched the tape, his darkest appetites clawed at his insides, begging to be satisfied.

'Damn.' He hit REWIND and replayed the last few seconds, his thirst desperate to be quenched. *'I love you, Craig. I love you, Craig. I love you, Craig.'*

Craig leaned toward the television and touched the image of her face. He traced her eyes and then her lips.

From the edge of the screen, the camera captured the tip of a gun barrel. The woman shrank back, trying to press herself through the wall.

Crying, she tried to crawl away, but the chain stopped her as he grabbed the wig and tossed it aside. He wrenched her upward. Her fingers clawed at his hand as she screamed and struggled to get free. He held on tight and raised the .38 to her temple.

He whispered, 'I love you, Adrianna.'

The revolver's bullet tore through her brain. Blood splattered his face. She slumped forward, dead. His heart raged in his chest like a tornado.

Then he released her, stepped back, and watched as she crumpled to the floor. A second passed before the recording ended and the image turned to static snow.

Now Craig understood how much he'd fed off her terror. Her panic and those of the other two had invigorated his blood like a narcotic.

'I shouldn't have listened. I never should have let you go.' He could have kept her tucked away down here for years.

If he'd known three years would pass until the next kill he'd have stowed her away and savored her all the more.

Stupid. Stupid. Stupid.

Frustrated, he shut off the television and turned his attention to the new digital camcorder he'd bought last week. It fit in the palm of his hand and had cost him a fortune but the kid in the electronics store had promised it would produce crystal-clear images guaranteed to last a lifetime.

'So clear you can see the pores on a face,' the kid had said.

Craig palmed the camera, amazed at its compact size. Technology was a wonderful thing.

Pointing the camera toward the empty basement corner with the wood panel and loosely coiled chain, he hit RECORD. The red light clicked on. He taped for a few seconds before stopping and replaying the image on the camera's view screen. The kid had been right. The clear picture caught the grains in the faux wood and the threads in the brown carpet.

Craig glanced at the newly purchased pink silk slip and blond wig. He set the camera down and picked up the wig. He stroked the strands of real human hair dyed just the right shade of blond.

Imagine what detail he would capture when he filmed the next one. This camera wouldn't miss anything, and the images would surely satisfy him for years.

This time, *this time*, he'd not be in such a rush. The next one, he'd savor.

Craig glanced at the pocket calendar taped to the side of his filing cabinet. Twenty-four red *X*'s marked through most of September. Anticipation burned like fire.

In just three days, it would be time again for hunting season.

In just three days, center stage would host a new actress to play his sweet Adrianna.

Chapter One

Tuesday, September 26, 7:15 a.m.

Adrianna Barrington ran down the center hallway of her house, keys clenched in one hand and a coffee mug in the other, as she wedged her feet in black leather flats and slid on a jean jacket. Fatigue-strained eyes had refused contacts, so she'd settled for tortoiseshell glasses. Breakfast was a banana muffin shoved in her purse. Make-up was simply mascara and lipstick.

Last night she'd planned to go to bed early. She wanted to be rested and ready to face this day. But an eleven p.m. call from the hospital emergency room derailed those plans. Her mother had arrived by ambulance and feared she was having a heart attack. Adrianna had dressed quickly and rushed to the hospital.

Over the last few years, Adrianna had seen the inside of too many hospitals. She'd grown to hate antiseptic smells, beeping monitors, and panicked visitors who endured endless waits for test results. She'd found Margaret Barrington in a back cubicle arguing with a nurse.

'Mom.'

Margaret Barrington's anger dissolved into tears. Adrianna glanced at the nurse, who'd made a quick retreat.

'It's okay, Mom. Don't worry.'

And so they'd spent the night, Adrianna sitting next to

her mother's bed on a round hard stool while her mother slept. And the unanswered question that they had argued about just two days ago remained wedged between them as it had these last nine months.

Why didn't you tell me I was adopted?

I don't know. I'm sorry.

At five a.m. the doctors had pronounced Margaret healthy and fit to go home. She'd simply had a panic attack.

Adrianna had taken her mother home where the waiting home nurse had put her to bed. By the time Adrianna arrived home and showered the grime and smells of the hospital from her skin and hair, it was nearly seven.

And now she was late.

She scooped up her oversized Coach bag from the entryway table and yanked her black lacquered front door open. Temperatures for this Indian summer morning already nudged seventy degrees, and humidity left the air thick and sticky. Browns and golds were slowly replacing summer's green leaves on the one-hundred-year-old oak in her yard.

Adrianna closed the door with unintentional force that made the brass lion-head knocker clank. She dropped her keys into her free hand and dashed down the front steps to her Land Rover, sloshing coffee. She had a little over forty-five minutes to make a fifty-minute drive in rush-hour traffic.

Always late. Always overscheduled. Always looking for the next project to keep the bills paid.

Adrianna rushed past the FOR SALE sign in her front yard to her car parked by the curb. She opened the door, tossed in her purse, and slid behind the wheel. As she raised her cup to her lips for a quick sip, she noticed the card under her windshield.

Groaning, Adrianna set her cup in the holder, got out, and plucked the rich linen envelope free. Her name was written in a bold, thick handwriting. *Adrianna Thornton.* Her married name, a name she'd not used in two years. She ripped open the back flap and pulled out the card.

Happy Third Anniversary. Adrianna, you are mine forever.

Love,
Craig

Craig.

Her husband.

The unexpected endearment sent a bolt of fear and pain through her body. Her heart pounded.

You are mine forever. Craig.

Time stopped. Remorse broadsided Adrianna as she traced a thumb over the embossed CRT at the top of the card. The initials stood for Craig Robert Thornton.

Good God, she'd forgotten today was her third anniversary. How could she forget?

This was the kind of note Craig would have written her. Simple. Endearing. Heartfelt. He'd always been writing her notes. *Love you, babe. You're the best. Always yours.*

But her husband couldn't have written this endearment.

Craig Thornton was dead.

Tears burned in her eyes as she stared at the bold script. Her hand slid to her stomach, hollow and empty.

Who could have left her this?

She glanced around at the University Drive neighborhood's neat brick one-level homes and well-manicured lawns half-expecting – *even hoping* – to catch someone staring. In this moment, she'd dearly have loved to channel her pain into a fight.

A Prada-clad neighbor dragging a green recycling bin to the curb; an older man juggling a coffee cup and briefcase as he lowered into his Lexus; and a thirtysomething mom hustling elementary age kids into a van for the morning trip to private school. It was business as usual. Painfully predictable. Nothing out of place.

There could be only one explanation for the card. It was a coward's attempt to frighten her and throw her off balance because she was selling the Thornton land and estate she'd inherited from her husband. The Thornton estate, called the Colonies, was a brick antebellum home in eastern Henrico County that sat on twenty acres of prime riverfront property. It predated the Civil War and was revered by historians. Selling the Colonies would drag this forgotten pocket of land into the twenty-first century. And there were some who didn't like the changes on the horizon.

Today not only was it her wedding anniversary, it was the day contractors were scheduled to move the eleven Thornton family graves from the estate. The land had been sold, and all that was left was to move the graves. By day's end her ties to the Thorntons would be forever severed.

When she'd filed permits with the state to remove the graves, she'd expected and braced for angry words, protests, and even lawsuits. But she'd expected nothing like this.

'Jerk.'

She marched around the side of the house, opened the lid to a trash can, dumped the note in the bin, and slammed the metal lid down. The clang reverberated up her arm.

Adrianna turned her back on the trash and moved forward. 'I am not going to be scared off by a bunch of cowards.'

Happy Anniversary.

Stillness sank into her bones and she felt sudden hot tears burn her eyes. She tipped her head back, willing the sadness to vanish. 'It means nothing. Someone is just messing with you.'

Happy Anniversary.

And yet the simple words scraped open old wounds she'd prayed had healed.

Adrianna's still damp hair brushed her face and clung to her skin like a spiderweb. Suddenly she didn't have the patience for the thick mane. She combed her fingers through her hair until it was off her face and tied it back with a rubber band.

A measure of control returning, she got into her car, locked the doors, and clicked on the radio. She cranked a Sheryl Crow tune. The singer's words and melody rolled over her and coaxed away her fears. She wouldn't think about the damn card. Her only priority today was getting the graves moved.

Adrianna fired up the engine, backed out of her driveway, and soon was skimming east down I-64. She elbowed aside thoughts of the note and used the drive time to call clients on her cell.

She owned Barrington Designs, an interior design business that specialized in home décor. A business that required not only an eye for design and color, but a talent for managing thousands of details that fit together like the pieces of a puzzle. Fabric colors. Shades of tile. Hardware. Furniture selection. All had to be considered, chosen, and monitored. It took endless follow-up calls to keep her projects on time and budget.

By the time Adrianna exited the interstate and wound down the old country roads to the estate, she'd contacted two painters, a wallpaper hanger, and a furniture company in North Carolina. She concluded her last call as she reached the estate's white brick pillars.

The grass by the entrance was overgrown. The paint on the estate's columns was chipped and several of the top bricks were missing thanks to age and a hurricane that had hit the county in late August.

A savvy seller in this slowing real estate market would have worried about curb appeal, but the estate had sold within hours of being listed. The buyer, William Mazur, was a powerfully built, fortysomething man with buzzed hair and sun-weathered skin. He had explained that he had always loved the property and had dreamed of owning it since he'd first moved to the area. He'd paid her asking price and his only stipulation was that she remove the family graveyard from the estate. Having graves on the property was too unsettling for his new wife. She'd agreed immediately.

Now as she drove through the pillars toward the house, she fended off jabs of guilt. The Thorntons had treasured the Colonies. So much family history. So much tradition. And she was selling out.

Her mind drifted to the last time she and Craig had

visited. Just a week before their late September wedding, her mother-in-law-to-be Frances Thornton had asked the couple to travel to the estate and place flowers on the graves of the departed Thorntons. Frances and Adrianna's own mother Margaret Barrington had been friends since college and Adrianna had grown up loving Aunt Frances and would have done anything for the woman who by then was weeks away from losing her battle with cancer.

'Craig, you really need to take this seriously,' Adrianna had said as she'd knelt in front of the grave.

Craig's thick blond hair hung restlessly over crystal blue eyes and he reminded her more of a boy than a man. He wore khakis, a white polo, and Italian loafers with no socks. 'I am taking this seriously, babe.' He checked his Rolex watch. 'How long do you think this is going to take?'

'I don't know. We're supposed to put flowers on each grave and have a moment of silence.'

'What's with the moment of silence?'

'I don't know. This is your family tradition, not mine.'

Adrianna laid the lilies on the grave and rose, brushing the leaves from her designer jeans. 'Now take my hand and let's bow our heads.'

His smile was loving, indulgent. 'You worry about the details so much, Adrianna.'

And he never worried. 'Traditions hold families together.'

'They suffocate me.'

'Craig.' The warning note in her voice reminded him that she'd broken their engagement last summer. She'd grown tired of the parties and the glib jokes. She had needed a man, not a boy. Only a great deal of pressure from her mother and his mother had brought her back to him at summer's end. This was their second chance.

Craig straightened his shoulders and his expression became somber. 'Okay, I'll be more serious. I promise.' He wrapped long fingers around her smooth, soft hand.

Placated, she smiled. 'Just stand here for a minute in silence.'

They stood in front of Craig's father's grave: Robert Thornton, devoted husband to Frances and loving father to Craig. She bowed her head and said a silent prayer for the Thorntons and for the marriage she was about to enter.

Within seconds Craig started to squirm and tap his foot. She opened one eye and peeked at him. 'Didn't your dad ever talk about this ceremony?'

Craig tossed her a rueful grin. 'You knew Dad. He wasn't the talkative type.'

Robert Thornton, unlike his only son, had been a serious, stern man. 'He had to have said something.'

'Dad wasn't as much into the family legacy thing as Mom was. You know how obsessed she is with the family. Especially now.'

Adrianna desperately wanted Craig to take charge of this moment and be a man worthy of her sacrifices. 'And?'

He gave her a good-natured smile. 'I honor the Thornton family and the privileges they've bestowed. And into the family welcome my new bride. We will be forever and always together.'

She lifted a brow. 'That's what you're supposed to say?'

He leaned forward. 'Close enough. And we're supposed to kiss.'

'Really?'

'Really.' He winked as he kissed her warmly on the lips. 'Now, I have a lovely bottle of Chardonnay and a picnic lunch in the trunk of my car. Let's enjoy this day and leave the dead in peace.'

She let him wrap his arms around her and she sank into the warm embrace, savoring the scent of his cologne. 'Do you take anything seriously?'

'I take you seriously.' Genuine emotion punctuated the words. 'I love you. I never want to lose you again, Adrianna.'

The rapid beat of his heart drummed against her ear. Craig did love her. And she cared deeply for him. She just hoped it was enough and that marriage would help him settle down and mature.

'I'm pregnant.'

He hauled her back and stared into her eyes. 'What?'

She nibbled her bottom lip, now afraid that he wouldn't want the child. In so many ways he was a child. 'Four weeks.'

Craig's mouth rose into a genuine smile. He hugged her close. 'Babe, this is great!'

'You're okay with this? I know it wasn't planned.'

He chuckled warmly. 'It's the best news I've ever heard! Life is going to just get better and better.'

Two months later a drunk driver had broadsided their car. She'd miscarried and Craig had suffered irreparable brain damage. He'd languished in a coma for two years before he'd died last December.

A twin pair of cardinals flapped across the drive, start-ling her and closing her mind to the memories that only made her miserable.

A deep breath loosened the tightness in her chest as she drove the half mile down the gravel driveway, which flowed into the circular loop by the old house's front door. Out of the car, she glanced at her watch. With minutes to spare before the scheduled meeting with the grave excavation team at the cemetery, she had time to check on the progress in the house.

The place had been a showpiece just fifteen years ago, and had hosted some of the state's most powerful and rich. She'd attended parties here as a teenager. Frances had even hosted her sixteenth birthday party in this house.

But over the last few years, she'd not visited the property. Her neglect showed in the rot that had eaten away at the rounded columns, the mold that had dulled the white-washed clapboard, and the missing shingles damaged in the August storm.

Adrianna climbed the front steps and moved into the central foyer that led to a wide staircase and a long hallway that cut through the first floor. Open doors leaked light in from the side rooms to the hallway.

'Mrs. Wells,' Adrianna shouted.

Mrs. Wells peered out the front parlor. The house-keeper was a sixtysomething woman with short curly red-gray hair and a plump frame that filled out her blue sweatshirt and faded jeans. She and her husband, Dwayne, lived just miles from here and had looked after the estate for forty years. The woman dabbed red-rimmed eyes. 'Yes, ma'am.'

Concern gave Adrianna pause. 'Is everything all right, Mrs. Wells?'

Mrs. Wells sniffed. 'Yes, yes, I'm fine. It's just so emotional closing up the old place. So many memories. Thank you for asking, Mrs. Thornton.'

Adrianna tensed. 'Please, just call me Adrianna.'

Mrs. Wells offered a lopsided smile. 'It just doesn't feel right calling you by your given name.'

The housekeeper was over thirty years Adrianna's senior. 'This isn't the nineteenth century, Mrs. Wells.'

A hint of humor sparked in pale green eyes. 'Now that depends on who you ask. Some folks around here would strongly argue that point. Fact, I suspect some are still thinking the Confederacy will again rise.'

'I suppose you are right.' Adrianna smiled, following her into the parlor.

White sheets covered the furniture and carpets had been rolled. The furnishings would go with the house but the twenty-three paintings, which now were crated and tilting against the walls, belonged to Adrianna. They awaited transport to the auction house where they'd be sold in a week. Auction proceeds would be donated to the new Thornton Neonatal Unit at Mercy Hospital.

'It looks like you've made headway downstairs.'

'All the furniture has been polished and covered in the front two rooms. I've still to do the rest of upstairs furnishings.'

'Are Dwayne and Ben coming today to move the furniture to the warehouse?' Mrs. Wells's husband and son, Dwayne and Ben Wells owned a successful moving company that specialized in antique furniture and artwork. Adrianna had used them on several Barrington Designs jobs.

'Ben said to tell you it would be first thing tomorrow.

They had another small job today. I think antiques to a dealer.' She smiled. 'The paintings will go to the auction house tomorrow as well.'

'You'll have each piece cleaned by then?'

'Yes, ma'am.'

'Great. The new buyer, Mr. Mazur, has insisted the home's interior be pristine.'

'Excuse me for asking, but isn't Mr. Mazur bringing in contractors to renovate the wiring and plumbing?'

'He is. And you're right, the contractors are going to tear the place up when they modernize. Why Mr. Mazur wants the house cleaned before a renovation is beyond me. But he is the buyer.'

Mrs. Wells nodded. 'Will do.'

She checked her watch. 'I've got to get down to the gravesite.'

'I saw that Dr. Heckman headed that way.'

Adrianna's lips flattened. 'No doubt he saw the public notice in the paper.' The notice had been required by the state.

Dr. Cyril Heckman had been a friend of Frances Thornton for many, many years. During the last years of her life they'd grown close. He now saw it as his personal mission to maintain the Thornton estate as it had been for generations. He'd filed suit in the spring to stop the sale but Adrianna's attorney had had it dismissed.

'You want me to call Dwayne or Ben and have them run him off?'

'Tempting, but I can handle him.'

Mrs. Wells blew a strand of hair from her eyes. 'I don't like the man and I don't care that Miss Frances was partial to him.' Mrs. Wells was intensely loyal to Frances Thornton's memory. Frances had left Marie Wells the caretaker's cottage and surrounding land in her will.

'Once the furniture and paintings are gone, have Ben bring the old drums up from the basement,' Adrianna said.

'Why do you want to fool with them? Let me go through them and save you the trouble.'

'I think it's best I do it.'

'Must be three generations' worth of stuff shoved in those bins. Good Lord, there is no telling what you'll find.'

'Yeah, no telling.'

Chapter Two

Anticipation and determination congealed in Detective Gage Hudson's gut as he drove down the rural road toward the Thornton estate.

'Hudson, Thorntons are practically Virginia royalty, and let's face it, sport, you're a good ol' boy from southwest Virginia.' The comment came from homicide detective Nick Vega, who propped his arm on the front seat of the Crown Vic. Perfectly relaxed, he didn't seem to have a care in the world even as Gage pushed the speedometer higher and maneuvered around a pickup truck.

Hudson was the lead detective in the missing persons division and more often than he'd have liked, his cases resulted in death. He'd consulted with Vega and the other members of the homicide team over the years and had gotten to know work styles and some habits. Vega's jabs and digs were as much a part of him as his love of cigars and jazz music.

'Didn't you hear my briefing to the homicide team?' His southwest Virginia accent deepened when he was under stress.

Vega shrugged wide shoulders honed by regular body-building and amateur league baseball. About thirty, he had olive skin, ink-dark hair kept short, not shorn. He preferred casual open collars, loose pants, and bad jokes that disguised a lightning-quick mind. 'Had to take a call. Missed the big finish.'

Gage tapped his thumb on the steering wheel. He wasn't accustomed to repeating himself. He'd been a cop for twelve years and in missing persons for six. He was considered tenacious when it came to finding the missing; some went so far as to claim he was part hound dog.

No one questioned Gage's competence, but many had wondered why he'd chosen police work when he'd had a promising football career.

Football – specifically quarterbacking – had set him apart since he'd played peewee ball. A strong work ethic and raw talent earned him the starting spot on the high school team and eventually a scholarship to Virginia Tech. Freshman year, he was a standout in the thirty-thousand-plus student body and by sophomore year a genuine star after a big win at the Sugar Bowl. Then came a quick marriage to the head cheerleader and a draft by the Atlanta Falcons. For a brief time he was bulletproof.

Two weeks into training camp, he'd taken a hard tackle. Tendons and bone in his shoulder had ripped and he'd ended up on the injured reserve list. While his wife remained in Atlanta, he'd returned to the home he'd recently purchased for his parents and siblings to mend. He'd been dozing one afternoon when his mother woke him up and asked where she could find Jessie, his ten-year-old sister. She was three hours overdue. He'd rattled the fog from his brain and started calling around. No one had seen her.

And then the grueling task of searching for Jessie had begun. For three days he didn't sleep as he searched the woods.

And then on the fourth morning he had found Jessie in a dilapidated cabin. She'd been tied to a chair. Drugged. Covered in dirt. Scrapes on her legs. One shoe missing.

Jessie had looked up at him with hazy eyes. 'Gage.'

Even now the memory choked the breath from his lungs. He'd rushed her to the emergency room and the doctors had confirmed his worst nightmare. She'd been raped.

That day had changed the course of his life. He'd resigned from the Falcons and joined the police department.

That's when he'd learned how much others had been so emotionally invested in his football career. Townfolks, his parents, and his wife all resented the decision and eventually abandoned him in some way. But Gage had never looked back. Never regretted the move.

Gage cleared his throat. 'Three years ago, I worked the case of a missing woman. Her name was Rhonda Minor. She was supposed to meet her brother for a drink one Friday but she never showed. The brother called her cell phone repeatedly, tried to figure out where she'd gone, but she'd vanished along with all of her stuff. Her brother said she was a hardworking, good kid. He admitted that they'd fought a few days before but it wouldn't be like her to just leave. I spoke to neighbors, roommates, and friends, and each said the same thing – she wanted to move to Italy to study art.'

All hints of humor vanished from Vega's eyes. 'Is that what she and her brother fought about?'

'Yeah. He didn't like the idea of her leaving. Said her boss had put fancy ideas in her head.'

'And her boss was?'

'Craig Thornton.'

Vega whistled. 'Craig Thornton of *the* Colonies.'

'Right. Rhonda worked at the Thornton Art Gallery as an administrative assistant. She had a degree in art from Virginia Commonwealth University and was looking to get gallery experience. Apparently Craig kept telling her how good she was and that she should paint full-time.'

'That gallery's been around forever.'

'Eighty-one years.' Gage's jaw tightened a fraction.

'So what happened? Was Thornton any help?'

Gage tightened his hands on the wheel. 'No. The guy was a glib son of a bitch, who acted like it was all a joke. The instant I laid eyes on Thornton I suspected he was hiding secrets. He even showed me a postcard she'd mailed from New York City. It said: *Thanks! Ciao.*'

Rain had pelted the city that October afternoon when Gage had gone to see Craig Thornton. He'd been in a foul mood and itching for a fight. Gage had dated Thornton's new wife Adrianna Barrington the summer before. Adrianna had broken up with Craig and said she'd been ready to move on with her life. Dated. Shit. Who was he kidding? The affair had been hot and soul searing. Gage had dreamed of a future with Adrianna. And then he'd been pulled into a case midsummer. They'd not seen much of each other in those last weeks of August. He kept promising himself he'd make up for his long hours after the case was solved. And then she'd told him she was leaving him, returning to her ex, Thornton.

When Gage had walked through the doors of the Thornton Gallery, those intense feelings for Adrianna still smoldered in his belly like ashen coals.

Over the last four years, he'd trained himself not to dwell on what he'd had with Adrianna. What he'd lost. Most days he had no regrets.

'Thornton offer any kind of help?'

'None. And there was something else about him that didn't set right. A vibe. A sense that there was more between Rhonda and him. I asked him if his wife had met Rhonda.'

Vega arched a brow. 'And?'

'His face tightened a fraction and he said Adrianna didn't mix with his employees. She had her hands full with her new interior design business and the new baby on the way.' Baby. That had been a kick in the gut for Gage.

Gage tightened his hands on the wheel. 'I'd have bet money that Thornton was having an affair with Rhonda.'

Vega grunted. 'Why do you say that?'

'Something was going on between them. I just couldn't prove a connection.'

Vega opened the worn manila folder marked *Minor* on the tab. He flipped open the front to a photograph stapled to the inside flap. Dark brown hair, lush blue eyes, bright smile, and cleavage that had him whistling. 'Damn.'

Gage glanced down and back at the road. 'Yeah. She was stunning.'

Vega started to flip through Gage's notes. 'You save files on all the cases you don't solve?'

'The ones that bother me most.'

Vega nodded, accepting, not questioning Gage's motives. 'So what happened?'

'I started doing a little digging. I didn't have cause to get his financial records but I started poking around in his past. Rhonda wasn't the first woman he'd known who had vanished. His prom date had gone missing, but in her case no evidence linked Thornton, who was out of the country when her report was investigated. But the guy was hiding something. No links and a well-connected family meant no arrest.'

Vega frowned. 'Didn't Craig Thornton have some kind of car accident?'

'Yeah. It was about six weeks after I interviewed him. Blindsided by a drunk driver. Really a freak accident. Impact smashed in his skull. Banged up his wife pretty badly.'

'He didn't die right off, as I remember.'

'Languished in a coma for over two years. He died last December.'

Vega nodded as if the details were coming back. 'The woman driving ran a red light.'

'She blew a .26 when the officer at the scene checked her blood alcohol.'

'Shit. It's a wonder she could stand, let alone drive a car.'

'She was convicted of drunk driving. It was her third DUI conviction and she's in jail now. Serving a three-year sentence.'

Vega arched a thick brow. 'You know a lot about this family.'

'I don't like unsolved cases.' He kept his tone steady, his gaze ahead, his body relaxed. However, relaxed wasn't close to what he was feeling.

Gage had kept up with Adrianna through the papers. Notices about her business. Her accepting the chair of the pediatric clinic fund-raiser. The funeral. The public notice announcing the land sale and grave relocation.

'So why are we headed to the Thornton estate?'

'Adrianna Barrington, Thornton's widow, has sold the estate, according to the public notice in the paper. As a condition of the sale, she's moving the family graveyard and clearing the old house.'

'Okay . . .'

'Two missing women. What better place to hide them than in a private graveyard?'

'You're stretching this, aren't you?'

Gage had asked himself that question a lot in the last few weeks since the notice appeared. Maybe he was. 'I don't think so. I wanted to search the land three years ago but Thornton refused. His attorney made sure I stayed out of his business.'

'That doesn't prove anything.'

'I know.' He shrugged. 'Just seems to me when you start moving rocks something is bound to crawl out.' He ran his hands over his shorn black hair. 'At the most, it'll cost us a morning of our time.'

Vega rubbed his hand over his freshly shaved chin. 'You know Adrianna Barrington is Detective Warwick's sister-in-law.'

That bit of information caught Gage short. 'Detective Jacob Warwick?'

'One and the same.' Warwick was an ex-boxer and former army sergeant who'd proven himself a shrewd investigator that tolerated little bullshit. He'd shocked everyone this past winter when he and the metro area's leading reporter had married in a quiet ceremony.

So much he didn't know about Adrianna. 'You're talking about Kendall Shaw Warwick, the former news reporter with Channel 10.'

'Yeah. They're sisters. Just found out about each other. Both adopted out as very young children.'

'That's the first I heard it.'

'You know Warwick. He plays it close to the vest. And I think Kendall asked him to keep quiet. She called in favors within the media so the story never made it to light. Apparently no one ever told Adrianna she was adopted. Kinda threw her for a loop when she found out last winter.'

A kick in the teeth was more than likely. 'Why the big secret about the adoption?'

'The Barringtons had another daughter almost exactly Adrianna's age. She was also named Adrianna. She died and the Barringtons just replaced her.'

'Damn. What happened to the other daughter?'

'The family doctor testified the kid died of crib death.'

'Where was she buried?'

'Never found the baby's grave. The burial was just as secret as the adoption. In the end there wasn't evidence for the commonwealth's attorney to prosecute.'

'A doctor's twenty-seven-year-old testimony and no body to examine,' Gage said.

'Just enough evidence to close the case but not enough to solve it.'

'Explains the physical resemblance between the women.' When he'd first met Adrianna, he'd joked with her about the likeness. She'd said she heard the comment a lot.

'When did you meet Adrianna Barrington?'

'I spoke to her after the car accident. I hoped Craig had

told her something about Minor.' His relationship with Adrianna was ancient history and as far as he was concerned didn't impact the case, so he kept it to himself.

The Minor case had been the excuse Gage had given the department, but in truth he'd needed to know Adrianna was okay.

When he'd found her, Adrianna had been standing at the glass window of the small neonatal unit at Mercy Hospital staring at the babies. Thick blond hair swept over straight narrow shoulders and accentuated a high slash of cheekbones bruised by the air bag. She'd worn a robe. Her face was scrubbed clean, pale.

Gage cleared his throat. 'Adrianna?'

Adrianna didn't look up at first.

'Adrianna?'

Sharp sapphire eyes met his and then darkened with confusion. 'Gage? What are you doing here?'

The nurses had told him she'd been three months pregnant and had miscarried after the accident. Despite their history, his heart ached for her. 'I'm here on police business. Your floor nurse said I could find you here.'

'Oh.'

'What are you doing down here?'

'Looking at the babies.' Adrianna glanced back at the infants on the other side of the glass. She was tall for a woman, maybe five foot eleven. Her straight-backed posture telegraphed her pain.

He slid his hand into his pocket so he wouldn't be tempted to touch her. 'I heard about the accident. The baby. I'm sorry.'

For a brief instant, pain glistened behind the ice.

'How are you doing?'

'I'll survive,' she whispered.

He searched for something comforting to say but feared any words would sound ham-fisted. 'What do the doctors say about Craig?' He couldn't bring himself to say 'husband.'

Adrianna turned her gaze back to the infants. 'I'm waiting on the last round of tests.'

'I know this must be tough.'

'Tough?' A bitter smile twisted her lips and for the first time he glimpsed the anger and fear behind the facade. 'I lost my son. My husband is hooked up to a breathing machine and God knows how many monitors. I'm waiting for the doctor who is supposed to tell me if Craig is going to be a vegetable or not. Tough? Yeah. It's tough.'

Gage's arms ached to hold her but remained at his sides, stiff and tense.

Adrianna's fingers clenched a shredded tissue in a white-knuckle grip. The nurses had said that some of Craig's friends and associates had drifted through but none had stayed long, and they'd sensed Adrianna was more of a comfort to Craig's friends and coworkers than they to her.

'Do you have any family or friends that can come sit with you? Your mother?'

Adrianna sighed. 'Thank you for asking, Gage, but I'll manage.'

In that moment the barriers dropped. Tears brimmed in fragile eyes and spilled down her cheeks. And whatever anger or chip he'd carried washed away. He leaned into her a fraction and in an even voice whispered, 'You don't look so fine.'

His tone was riddled with pity and sadness. And that had her swiping away the tears. 'It's one foot in front of the other now.'

There was no self-pity in her voice. And that was what got to him. 'When's the last time you ate?'

A half smile was weak and apologetic. 'I don't remember.'

'Let me get you something. There's a coffee shop in the lobby. Let me help.'

As if she'd realized how close she'd been to surrender, she stiffened. The ramparts slammed back in place. 'No, I'm fine, Gage. Please just leave. I don't want your help. You don't belong here.'

Behind the nursery's glass walls a baby began to cry. Adrianna turned from him and looked through the glass.

Forcing his mind to business, he cleared his throat. 'I'm investigating the disappearance of a woman. Rhonda Minor. She worked for your husband. She's been missing a couple of months.'

'Craig told me that you'd been stopping by the gallery a lot lately. That you kept questioning him about one of his employees.'

He'd been on a mission to solve this case and he believed Craig was the key. 'That's right.'

'You could have saved yourself a trip. I don't know much about my husband's business. He doesn't talk about it and I don't ask questions.'

Gage reached in his coat pocket and pulled out a photograph of Rhonda Minor. 'Do me a favor, take a look at her picture.'

She didn't touch the photo, or move closer to him, but

glanced down. She studied the image. 'I knew her. We met at a couple of office parties. I said hi but we never really talked.'

'Take another look. Think. She's twenty-three. An artist. Wants to be a painter. Was there anything that she said or your husband said that would have seemed off to you?'

Adrianna glanced down a second time. 'I'm sorry, I don't know anything. Honestly.'

'Do you know Jill Lable?'

She shook her head. 'No. And I'm not in the mood for a guessing game. Who is she?'

'She went to high school with Craig. She's been missing for twelve years.'

'What are you saying, Gage?'

Gage chose his words carefully. 'Just following leads on two women who were acquainted with your husband and are now missing. I was hoping he might have said something. Men tell their wives all kinds of things.'

'Like murder?'

He shrugged.

'Craig had his share of faults, but he was no murderer.'

'I'm not so sure.'

Adrianna's eyes flashed. Too much class kept her from telling him to fuck off but her expression communicated the sentiment. 'I don't know anything. Now please leave.'

After that all leads had dried up. And then he'd read the legal notice in the *Richmond Times-Dispatch* announcing the removal of the Thornton family graves. He'd been given a second chance.

Gage maneuvered around a more slow-moving van.

Vega rested his arm on his car door and tapped his thumb. 'You think Rhonda Minor is dead?'

'Yes. I think she was dead before Craig Thornton's accident. But I've never proven it. I never found that other woman. But I promised myself I'd never stop looking.' Uncertainty could tear a family in two. 'Rhonda's brother still calls me about once a month to check and see if there is any new evidence.' Last time Fred Minor's voice had cracked with anguish. September second would have been Rhonda's twenty-sixth birthday.

'Your turn is coming up,' Vega said.

Gage glanced at the green road sign ahead that read: HONOR. 'Right.'

He took the next left and wound deeper down the country road. Unlike the west end of Henrico, the east end was relatively undeveloped and rural.

Gage slowed as he drove through Honor. Dried up and forgotten, Honor wasn't more than a collection of antique stores and novelty shops. A gas station. These days it was a bedroom community to the city of Richmond.

Following the twenty-five-mile-an-hour speed limit, he passed through town and down Route 60. Two miles beyond the town limits, he spotted the long dirt driveway marked by twin white pillars. The sign out front read: THE COLONIES.

'Imagine, being rich enough to have your own graveyard,' Vega quipped. 'Man, that's living.'

Gage reminded himself to take in air. To relax. 'We can all hope to aspire.'

Vega surveyed the wooded terrain. 'Makes sense that if

Thornton killed those women he'd bury them here. It's remote and would have been his home turf.'

'Yeah.'

The car bumped and rocked when he turned down the furrowed road that led them through tall oaks. When they hit a clearing, it was easy to spot the collection of pickup trucks and the yellow backhoe, which sat silent by the cemetery shaded by an old tree.

Gage put the car in PARK and shut off the engine. As he got out of the car, tension knotted his gut like it had before a big game in college. He fastened his collar, tightened his tie, and shrugged on his suit jacket as he scanned the crowd. No sign of Adrianna. He wasn't sure if he was more relieved or disappointed.

The memory of those three days Jessie had been missing had branded him. Forever and always the case would always come first. He'd remain vigilant until every grave was excavated and every missing woman found. And any personal feelings he had for Adrianna Barrington would stay buried.

Chapter Three

Tuesday, September 26, 8:30 a.m.

The Thornton family graveyard was located in a small field near a stand of woods. A chipped black wrought-iron fence, partly shaded by a hundred-year-old oak, encased a hundred-foot-patch of land and eleven gravestones. Most were weathered, worn by wind and rain, but the three graves that stood apart from the others belonged to Adrianna's late husband and his parents. Their marble headstones had crisp clear lines and the brass plaques remained clean and bright.

Adrianna had not realized last December when she'd buried Craig she'd ever have to move his grave. Mountains of debt had a way of realigning priorities.

She pulled off the dirt road, noting the collection of vehicles parked on the grassy field: construction trucks, the backhoe, the white Mercedes, the old Toyota, and the dark sedan. The trucks belonged to Miller Construction, the Mercedes to the land's buyer, William Mazur, and the old car to Dr. Cyril Heckman. He held a handmade poster that read: SAVE OUR DEAD. Thankfully, Dr. Heckman hadn't stirred media attention.

The one car she didn't expect was a dark sedan. Parked away from the other vehicles, it lingered on the sidelines like a spider viewing prey.

As she approached the site, two men in dark suits moved around the front of the sedan. One wore scuffed cowboy boots. Their backs faced her, but she didn't need to see faces to know the taller man. Gage Hudson. She recognized his braced stance and broad shoulders that reflected confidence almost to the point of arrogance.

Tension prickled her spine. What was Gage Hudson doing here?

'Damn it,' she muttered. The regrets she had in life were few, but Gage Hudson topped the list. Her thoughts turned to their last meeting and the questions he'd asked her about Craig. This visit was not social or coincidence.

Squaring her shoulders, she made a direct line toward Gage, opting not to run from trouble. Better to rip the proverbial Band-Aid off in one quick jerk than peel it off slowly. Less pain. She hoped.

'Detective Hudson.' Thankfully, her voice sounded clear and direct. 'What brings you out here?'

Gage's mirrored sunglasses tossed back her reflection. The subtle stiffening in his shoulders hinted at his dislike of her formal address. She sensed gray, accessing eyes narrowed. So be it. It was better this way.

'*Ms.* Thornton. I hope you don't mind, but my partner here – Detective Vega – and I wanted to observe the grave relocation.'

A hacksaw wouldn't cut through that southwest Virginia drawl now. 'The name is Barrington. Why?'

He moved toward her with intentional slowness. 'I think you know why, *Ms.* Barrington.'

The two missing women he'd mentioned during their last visit. He believed those women were buried out here. And the fact that he'd not called ahead to announce his visit told her he didn't trust her. The sting of that realization had her firing back before she thought. 'Do you have a warrant?'

Gage shook his head slowly. 'No, ma'am, I don't. I'm just here for a casual visit. Do I need a warrant?'

Menace reverberated off the words like a flashing yellow light. If she had a bit more equilibrium where he was concerned, she'd have recognized that he was just doing his job. This was business. It wasn't personal.

But it felt deeply personal, just like the questions he'd asked her in the hospital a couple of years ago. As she had then, she felt under attack.

Aware the gazes of Mazur, Dr. Heckman, and the construction crew rested upon her, Adrianna managed a smile that generally disarmed most. She'd eat dirt before she showed him any sign of weakness. 'No. You're free to observe. Just don't get in the way of my crews.'

A hint of a smile tugged at the edge of his lips. 'Oh, I'll do my best to stay out of the way, Ms. Barrington.'

The honey coating didn't mask the underlying message. Gage Hudson would do whatever he pleased, whenever he pleased. 'Thanks.'

Adrianna turned toward Mr. Mazur and the six-man construction crew. Under Mazur's paper-thin calm simmered a dark intensity. Built like a medieval knight, he had come up hard and made a fortune in real estate, she'd been told. Ruthless was how her own attorney had described Mazur. 'Not the kind of guy you want to do business with,' her attorney had said. 'Buys his land tracts from the dead and dying.'

But beggars couldn't be choosers.

Adrianna moved toward Mr. Mazur, smiling as she

extended her hand. 'This is a pleasant surprise. I wasn't expecting you.'

He took her hand, squeezed a bit too hard. 'I told you I might come. Why aren't your men digging?'

'I don't know. They should be working.' Calmness in a storm was her specialty. Later, when she was alone, she'd lower her guard and allow tears and fear. 'Mr. Mazur, you could have saved yourself the trouble of driving out here. I would have given you a full report.'

He didn't seem taken by her smile either. 'I like to see things for myself.'

'I see.' Like Gage, Mazur somehow expected her not to come through. 'Well, you are welcome to stay as long as you wish. Now if you don't mind, I'll talk to my construction crew and see about that holdup.'

'I asked but the foreman wouldn't say. Said he worked for you.'

Points for Mr. Miller. 'I'm sure it's nothing,' she said, hoping she was right.

'That Dr. Heckman has been lurking around all morning with that damn sign.'

'He's harmless. I'll handle him.'

'He says he's going to call the press.'

'He's tried several times. No one cares.' Adrianna moved over the uneven land, but made it just a dozen steps before Dr. Heckman cut across her path.

'Mrs. Thornton.'

She bristled. 'The name is Barrington. What are you doing here, Professor?'

'Looking out for the dead.' He wore a tweed jacket with patched sleeves and what looked like a tea stain on the lapel. Dark pants, rumpled white shirt, and tennis shoes completed the perfect stereotype of an eccentric academic. He smelled of mothballs and peppermint.

'They're just fine without you.'

He tucked his poster under his arm and rubbed long, thin hands together. 'You are desecrating the memory of this grand family.'

'I don't look at it that way.' She'd paid more than she should for the gravesites in a lovely church cemetery down the road. Moving these graves was the only way she could save them. 'Professor, if you'll excuse me. I need to talk to my foreman.'

A frantic energy radiated from his blue eyes. 'You can't do this.'

'I can.'

'I will throw myself on the graves.'

'My foreman will throw you off this land if you so much as make a move.' If Mazur weren't here, she'd have done it already.

Billy Miller, the grave removal company's owner, was a tall man with a broad chest and a big belly that hung over his belt. Puffy cheeks and a ruddy complexion made him appear older than his thirtysomething years. He'd come highly recommended by several properties in Maryland and Northern Virginia and could handle the logistical tangles of moving old graves.

'What's going on, Mr. Miller?' she said.

'We might have a problem.' Miller chewed gum constantly, which was an alternative to his former two-pack-a-day cigarette habit.

Adrianna felt Gage's sharp hungry gaze. 'What is it? Permits? Do the Feds have more questions about protecting groundwater contamination?'

Miller glanced toward the men behind her and frowned. 'It's a little more complicated.'

The growing tightness in Adrianna's chest threatened to cut off her breath completely. 'Explain.'

Miller drew Adrianna away from his crew, Dr. Heckman, and the cops before he spoke. He glanced back to make sure no one had followed. Satisfied, he planted his hands on his hips and kept his voice low. 'I swept all the land inside the cemetery fence with ground-penetrating radar just like you asked.'

A cool breeze blew on her face. 'Okay.'

'I found some irregularities in the soil in the corner nearest the river.'

'What does that mean?'

'Means I might have found something we weren't expecting.' Gum snapped in his mouth.

'Like what?'

'Might be nothing.'

'Then why are we having this discussion?' Her words rang brittle and impatient.

Miller looked surprised. Up until now, she'd been calm and reserved during their few preliminary meetings. He glanced around again to make sure no one was in earshot. 'I think I've found additional graves.'

A jolt of fear hit Adrianna. Temptation prodded her to see if Gage was watching. But she didn't. Instead of looking at him or the cemetery, she glanced toward the band of trees that ringed the field. The woods were thick and the underbrush overgrown. 'Where?'

'In the cemetery corner closest to the river.'

She turned slowly and studied the southeast section of the family graveyard shaded by the thick leaves of the oak tree. 'I don't see anything. It looks perfectly fine to me.'

Miller's voice was patient. 'That's because you don't move graves for a living. When a body decomposes, it shrinks and the soil on top of it collapses a little. The vegetation also grows back unevenly.'

'Is it a child's grave?' She rubbed the back of her neck with her hand, wishing she could ignore her worries.

'No. Too large.'

Relief eased some of the fear she'd been holding. She'd often thought that this cemetery could be the place where her mother's first daughter could have been buried. Frances Thornton would have been the one her mother would have called in a crisis. 'Okay.'

Gum snapped as Miller shook his head and raised a slim T-shaped instrument that he'd been holding, which until now she'd not noticed. 'This is a T-bar. I use it to take soil samples. By looking at the sample I can tell whether the soil has been disturbed or not.' The end looked like a cookie cutter, and showed her a cross section of dirt. 'The radar and T-bar suggest something is buried in that spot.'

She thought about the reason for Gage's visit. 'I've read that families like the Thorntons buried servants close. A wooden marker would long have been eroded by the elements.'

Miller shook his head. 'These sites aren't that old. They're less than a decade old.'

A decade. Was Gage right about Rhonda?

She pulled off her sunglasses. From the corner of her eyes she saw Gage by his car staring right at her. Damn. She'd heard once the guy had a freaky talent for finding the missing.

Miller leaned closer. 'This is the country, Ms. Barrington. It's the perfect place to stash a body. I saw it up in Maryland. We was doing a job and found the body of a missing child.'

Her heart tightened. 'A child. You said this grave wasn't a child's.'

'Yeah, it's not. I was just talking about an old case.'

Adrianna nodded. 'Do you have any idea what or who is down here?'

'I'll have to open it up to find out. And to do that I need your permission.'

God, this was not happening.

Miller glanced toward the wrought-iron fence. 'There is something else to consider. You can go ahead and excavate the family plot and then dig up the unknown sites later. That way, if you actually find something – someone – then the other work will already be done.'

Adrianna saw his logic. It would be easy to take care of business first.

'What would be the harm?' Mr. Miller said. 'Three or four days at most and you can do the right thing. No harm, no foul.'

So tempting, it would be easy to justify financially. But morally? She remembered the picture of Rhonda Minor – she'd had a bright, pretty smile. Dark hair. A dimple on her right cheek.

Miller took Adrianna's silence for agreement. 'So we go for the old graves first?'

Four days and the graves would be gone and she'd be free of this place.

Four days hardly mattered at all.

Four days was nothing in the big picture.

But now they seemed to mean everything. If that was Rhonda Minor in the ground, she'd not let her linger another day.

She relented to her conscience. 'Dig the mounds up first.'

'You sure?'

'Yes.' Her stomach growing queasy, she slid her long fingers into the front pockets of her jeans. 'But do me a favor. Be subtle. I've got two cops watching, a fanatic, and the new landowner. I don't want to sound alarm bells unless I have a problem.'

'Will do.'

Miller nodded and turned and shouted to one of his men. When the guy approached, he said, 'Smokey, get a shovel and start digging on that first site.'

Smokey, a willowy man, wore jeans, workboots, a black NASCAR hat and T-shirt with the number three on the front. He tossed the cigarette in his mouth to the ground and ground it out. 'Okay.'

'This is above and beyond my bid,' Miller said.

'It's my time and my money, Mr. Miller,' Adrianna said. 'I can waste it however I wish.'

Since Craig's accident, she'd made hundreds of decisions she'd not wanted to make. Some had turned out for the best, others had not. But good or bad, she'd learned to get the job done no matter how dirty.

Adrianna watched as Smokey grabbed a shovel from the bed of a red pickup truck. He sniffed and ambled as if he had all the time in the world. 'Mr. Miller, do you think your man can move a little faster?'

Miller stiffened. The foreman didn't like taking orders from a woman. 'Smokey, get a move on.'

Smokey shuffled a little faster through the men and positioned his shovel. He put a mudded boot on the edge and shoved his weight forward. A wet summer and fall had left the ground soft and the shovel slid in like a hot knife into butter.

Adrianna nibbled her bottom lip. She wanted this to be nothing more than a simple delay.

Smokey dug out a few more shovelfuls of earth. The entire crew had stopped talking and all were watching as Smokey dug deeper. The shovel clinked against a hard surface. 'I hit something.'

Her thoughts tripped and her stomach twisted into a knot. The workmen immediately circled around trying to get a better look. Miller got a flashlight from his truck and shone it down the hole. She heard a few gasps and muttered oaths.

Adrianna pushed through the ring of men who encircled Smokey and his find. They all smelled of sweat and tobacco.

Miller blocked her path. 'Maybe you best let us take care of this.'

'What did you find?'

His haggard features struggled to remain stoic. 'Let us worry about it.'

A couple of years ago, Adrianna wouldn't have worried

about it. She'd have let him take care of it all. That's what she'd always done. Her father and then her husband had taken care of the important details.

And where had it gotten her? Knee deep in debt, with the cops, an eccentric, and an angry buyer breathing down her neck.

'Step aside.'

Miller pursed his lips and appeared to count to ten. 'Suit yourself, Ms. Barrington. But I really don't recommend you looking.'

She pulled in a steadying breath. 'I'm a big girl, Mr. Miller.'

He shook his head.

Adrianna peered down the hole. What she saw nearly took her breath away.

Protruding from the ground was a human skull.

Chapter Four

The instant Adrianna turned and moved toward the cemetery's corner, Gage suspected that there was a problem. Her stiff back and tilted chin reminded him of the day she'd left him. Something had upset her.

The crews had found something.

Gage couldn't suppress the rush of exhilaration and despair. He'd bet his last dollar they'd found Rhonda Minor. 'Something's happening.'

Vega nodded. 'You saw the T-bar as well?'

'Yeah. Let's head over.'

'Sure.'

They'd not taken five steps when Gage's cell rang. Not breaking stride, he pulled the phone from its holster and flipped it open. 'Detective Hudson.'

'What's your status?' Homicide detective Jacob Warwick rarely took time for pleasantries.

'I'm on the Thornton property. And I think they've found something.'

'What?'

'That's what I'm going to find out. But I can tell you the foreman was carrying a T-bar and motioning toward the ground.'

47

'A body they weren't expecting?'

Gage pictured Warwick standing not sitting behind his desk. 'We'll see. It might be nothing.' As much as he liked to win, he took no pleasure unearthing the dead and telling a family their loved one was dead. 'I'll call you back as soon as I have something.'

Warwick hesitated. 'You've heard about Ms. Barrington's connection to my wife?'

Gage glanced at Vega. 'Yeah.'

'My wife wants to build a relationship with her sister. But I don't want my wife hurt. Kendall is a smart woman, but she has blinders on when it comes to her birth sister. She wants their relationship to work. But if Adrianna Barrington is involved in something illegal, I don't want you to hesitate to investigate.'

'Her relationship to your wife has no bearing as far as I'm concerned.' And it didn't.

'Good.' Warwick clicked off.

Vega raised a brow. 'Nothing like telling a coworker you'll arrest his family. Sets the tone for a good working relationship.'

'Warwick would do the same.' Gage grinned. 'And I'm the first to admit I have more balls than brains.'

Vega laughed. 'Now, on that I do agree.'

Adjusting his cuffs, Gage strode toward Adrianna. He stopped a few feet behind her. 'What's going on?'

The sound of his voice startled her. She turned and looked up at him with a direct clear, if slightly pained, gaze. He sensed that her nerves were so tight they could snap. 'They've found a skeleton.'

'Does Miller know if the remains are human or not?'

Her chest rose and fell in deliberate breaths. He sensed dogged determination kept her from running. 'Human.'

Even though she looked like she could use a friend, comforting her was not an option. He owed it to two missing women to be only the cop.

Gage glanced past her to see a young guy with a NASCAR shirt drive the shovel into the grave. 'Stop!'

The kid looked up and frowned. 'Who the hell are you?'

He pulled his badge from his pocket. 'Police. And from this moment on, consider this job site closed.'

An hour later Adrianna leaned against her car watching as the county forensics crew strung yellow crime scene tape around the trees isolating the mounds Miller had found.

The last few years, she'd learned of her husband's disastrous financial decisions. Arrogance and foolishness had been his undoing. But she refused to believe that he'd killed Rhonda Minor.

Mazur, who'd been on his phone most of that time, finally approached her. The sour frown on his face didn't bode well. 'Have the police reported anything new?'

Even as an oily sickness coiled in her stomach, she smiled. 'No, but I'm sure they'll wrap up their investigation quickly. Detective Hudson is efficient.'

Mazur clenched his jaw. 'I don't like this.'

'Don't worry. I'll have the graves removed. And you can take over as planned.'

'I've got a lot of money riding on this property. And the last thing I want or need is a long legal battle to get a bunch of bones out of the ground.'

She glared at him. 'I'll take care of it, as I promised.'

He reached in his pocket, pulled out a cigar, and lit it. A few puffs and white smoke billowed upward. 'You do that, because I've paid you a lot of money and I'll want every damn dime back plus interest if this doesn't happen.'

It always came down to money. 'I can assure you that I need this sale as much as you. Maybe more.'

He puffed his cigar. 'If I get fucked, I'm taking someone with me. And that's going to be you.'

His words struck her like a hard slap. 'Don't worry, Mr. Mazur. The graves will be gone soon.'

'Good. Call me in a couple of hours with a report.'

'Sure.'

Adrianna watched him saunter to his white Mercedes. Behind the wheel, he snapped open his cell phone and then drove off.

For an instant she closed her eyes and let her mind drift. Soon the land would be gone. Her house would be sold and she'd be managing her business from somewhere far away. Just a little longer and she'd sever her ties with the past.

Soon. Soon. Soon.

Calmer, she turned back to see Dr. Heckman rushing her way. He tugged nervously at a loose thread on his coat pocket as his short, quick strides ate up the distance. 'Mrs. Thornton?'

Adrianna tensed, forced herself to smile. 'It's Barrington, not Thornton, Dr. Heckman.'

'Right. Yes, you've told me that.'

'What can I do for you?'

'The crews aren't digging. What is going on? I've been asking but no one is talking.'

'There's a delay.'

Dr. Heckman clapped his hands together. 'What kind of delay?'

'Nothing she can discuss.' The answer came from Gage, who'd approached without her noticing. Gage towered over the doctor like a mature oak over a sapling.

Adrianna had been patient with the man, but his constant e-mails and pestering over the last few weeks had thinned her patience. 'You're trespassing, Dr. Heckman. Please don't try what is left of my nerves.'

His eyes narrowed to priggish slits and for a moment he looked ready to rebut. 'You have no right to move those graves. This is an abomination.'

Gage watched the older man march off. 'Who the hell is that?'

'A professor who sees it as his personal mission to keep those graves from being moved.'

'What's he doing here today?'

'I don't know. Someone must have tipped him.'

'And that other guy – the one in the Mercedes?'

'The man who is buying the land. William Mazur.'

'He looked pissed when he spoke to you. What was that about?'

It surprised her he'd noticed the exchange. 'That he really, really wants those graves moved off his land.'

Gage's gaze bored into her. 'It appeared to be more than that.'

'Money has a way of churning up emotions.' After what she'd done to Gage, he would be the last person she'd ever run to for help. 'Don't worry about it.'

He hesitated as if he wanted to say more but reconsidered. 'Have any idea who the victim might be?'

'No, but you believe the body belongs to Rhonda Minor or that other woman you asked me about.'

Bitterness tightened his smile. 'I'm surprised you remember.'

'I remember.' Her calm voice hid a reeling mind.

'Do you think it's Rhonda Minor?' Behind the dark glasses she sensed his gaze absorbed every one of her expressions.

'I don't know.' She spoke clearly, directly. 'I haven't visited this property for a couple of years.'

Gage nodded slowly. 'You live in Richmond?'

'Yes.'

'Still on Riverside Drive?'

He'd known where she and Craig had lived. 'No. I sold that house a couple of years ago. I'm closer to the university now.' Sale of the Riverside house had paid for Craig's first year in the nursing home.

'And I suppose you inherited this land from your late husband.'

'That's correct.'

'Been in the Thornton family a while?'

'Don't play games. You know more about this family than I do.'

'Do you still own your design business?'

'Yes, I do. Why are you asking all these questions? You know the answers.'

He shrugged. 'I like to double-check.' He glanced around the clearing and the woods that ringed it. 'Anyone live on the property full-time?'

'No. But Marie Wells checks on the property regularly. She lives a couple of miles from here and is a part-time caretaker of sorts; lets me know if there's a problem. When we had the hurricane damage she was the one who came out here first and inspected the property before calling me.'

'You get a lot of damage in the storm?'

'Not much. We were lucky. Mostly erosion. Some damage to the house's roof.'

He pulled a small spiral notebook from his breast pocket and flipped it open. 'Any odd people on the land?'

'None I know of. Ask Marie.'

'I will.'

'She's up at the main house. Her husband Dwayne should be here soon as well.'

He clicked the end of a ballpoint pen. 'You said his name was Dwayne. Dwayne Wells?'

'That's right. He and his family own a moving company. He'll be by later today to start clearing the main house of the paintings. I'm having them taken to Mooney's Auction House for sale.'

Behind his dark glasses she sensed that his gaze roamed up and down her body. The look didn't feel sexual, but analytical. He was trying to figure her out, as if she were a puzzle.

'So how did you hook up with Dr. Heckman?'

'He's been associated with the family for years. He's written several papers on the Thornton family. My late mother-in-law held him in high regard.'

'What do you know about this guy?' That question came

from Gage's partner. The guy was dressed more casually and stood a couple of inches shorter than Hudson.

'Not much. Only the few bits of information Frances mentioned. And your name is?'

'Detective Nick Vega.' Vega pushed his Ray-Ban sunglasses up on his head. 'Why not just hang on to the land? Why sell?'

'It doesn't make sense. I live in the city and have no need for a country house.'

'You're selling the entire tract?' Gage said.

'Yes. That includes the main house and the surrounding twenty riverfront acres.'

Vega nodded. 'Mazur must be paying a fortune.'

Adrianna wasn't fooled by Vega's casual dress and manner. Like Gage, she suspected his mind was razor sharp. 'Mr. Mazur paid my asking price.'

'Well, that is something in today's real estate market,' Gage said. 'Fact, it's mighty lucky.'

'Yes, it is.'

'The sale's going to make you a rich woman,' Gage said.

'Not really. Go to the county tax office and look up this estate. Have a look at the check I just wrote for back taxes, which haven't been paid in a decade.'

'That's got to be millions,' Vega said.

'It is. No one is getting rich on this deal.'

Gage gave no hint to his thoughts. 'Who has access to the land?'

'The front gate remains locked when no one is here, but as you can see, the fence around the property is in bad shape. I suppose anyone could drive onto the land at any time.'

Miller approached, looking nervous, clearly unhappy

about the entire situation. 'I hear you want to talk to me, Detective.'

Gage nodded. 'You move graves for a living?'

Miller shrugged. 'Nearly twenty years now. Got offices in Richmond and Alexandria. I'm based in the Richmond office.'

'Moved a lot of graves?' Gage said.

'More than I can count. It's big business to relocate the dead to make room for the living.'

'What ever happened to a final resting place?' Vega said.

Miller shook his head. 'If you get a couple of hundred years in the ground you're doing well these days. There's always someone that wants to move you.' A hint of red warmed his face as he glanced at Adrianna. 'No offense intended.'

'None taken,' Adrianna said. 'I've heard enough cracks and comments about this grave relocation to fill a book.'

Gage glanced at her. 'From who?'

'The people who live in the area.'

'You're getting opposition to the sale?' Gage said.

'The sale. The graveyard relocation. The buyer's plans to build thirty homes. No one is happy with most of the changes.'

'Any threats?'

She thought about the card signed *Craig*. 'No threats, exactly. Mostly vague warnings that I'm committing a sin by moving the graves. One guy in Honor suggested that I'm going to hell. I just make it a point not to stop in Honor anymore.'

'You call the police?'

'And tell them what? I'm unpopular with the locals?

That's the story of my life. And like I said, there were no out-and-out threats. No property damage.'

'If something like that happens again, call me.' Gage had issued an order, not a request.

Adrianna bristled. 'Hopefully, by this time next month I won't have this to worry about.'

'A lot can happen in a month,' Gage said.

Adrianna glanced toward the edge of the cemetery. The image of the skull wasn't easily forgotten.

'We're going to have another look at the graves.'

'I understand.'

'Don't leave the property without checking in with me.'

Resentment bubbled. 'If I'm not here, I'll be at the main house.'

Gage studied her a beat and then turned and left her to watch Vega, Miller, and him move away toward the edge of the woods. They didn't pass beyond the yellow crime scene tape.

Crime Scene. 'God, how did this day go so wrong?'

'You doing all right?'

Mrs. Wells's voice came from behind Adrianna. Recovering, she smiled with relief. 'Yes. I didn't see you come up.'

'Just got here.' She looked a bit desperate to do something, anything that might smooth out this situation. 'Figured my time was best spent at the main house working than standing around here. But then I just couldn't stay away anymore. So how are you holding up?'

'Considering we have an unknown body on the property and the excavation is delayed indefinitely, I'm hanging in there.'

Mrs. Wells glanced toward the police. 'When I rolled out

of bed this morning, I expected that my biggest challenge was going to be getting those upstairs curtains down.'

Adrianna smiled. 'I was worried that I'd be late for a five o'clock charity meeting. Now I feel like a fool for worrying over something so small.'

'We all get caught up in the little things until something big happens.'

'I suppose.' She glanced toward Gage, who stood near the lip of the woods. 'Do you have any idea who could be buried over there?'

Mrs. Wells followed her gaze. 'None. When Miss Frances got sick, she came out here less and less. Could be anyone.'

Adrianna let out a breath. Dread crept through her bones as she stared at the billowing yellow tape.

Mrs. Wells followed her line of sight. 'There's plenty of work up there for you to do and it's clear these graves aren't going anywhere today. Busy hands will keep your mind from worrying.'

'Me, not worry?' A smile lifted the edge of Adrianna's lips. 'Worry is what I do best.'

Mrs. Wells's surprise appeared genuine. 'You're as cool as a cucumber.'

That made her laugh. 'Don't believe it. I'm a worrier. In fact, I can easily stay very busy and worry at the same time. A multitasker at heart.'

Mrs. Wells patted her on the shoulder. 'Well, at least you'll be getting something done if you do your fretting at the main house.'

'You're right.' And honestly, she just wanted to get away from Gage. 'If anyone needs me, just tell them that I'll be at the main house. Or they can call me on my cell.'

'Will do.'

Adrianna thanked Mrs. Wells and got into her Land Rover. She started the engine and backed up. When she put the car in drive, she glanced up and realized Gage had turned from the crime scene and was staring at her.

Chapter Five

Tuesday, September 26, 9:40 a.m.

Adrianna's Land Rover kicked up dust and gravel as she drove off toward the main house. When her car rounded the corner out of sight, Gage let out a breath, which he felt like he'd been holding since he'd first seen her.

She was just as stunning, just as poised, and just as elusive as he remembered. This was the first time he'd seen her in glasses with little make-up. And each time he'd seen her before, her hair had been blown dry, straightened. Today the unexpected waves made it look a bit wild.

For a split second, the last four years melted. Pain and anger receded. His body hardened at the sight of her until his gaze caught the wink of gold and diamond on her left ring finger. And in a rush, he remembered what had slipped through his fingers.

'She's wound tighter than a bowstring,' Gage muttered.

'Makes you wonder if there was something else chewing at her?' Vega said.

Like facing off with an old lover? 'Maybe.'

The detectives moved toward Mr. Miller, who frowned over a clipboard. When they approached, he lowered it and tried out a smile that didn't quite work. 'Detectives.'

Gage slid his hand into his pocket. 'Something's been

bothering me since I arrived. Why did you search the land around the graves? Is that standard procedure?'

'Ms. Barrington asked. She said she'd done research on this kind of work and said that old cemeteries often had other unmarked graves. She didn't want any surprises.'

'Really?'

'Said a little extra time now could save her big trouble down the road.'

'Speaking of time, she was late this morning,' Vega said.

'She called me around seven thirty. Had to take her mom to the emergency room last night. Turns out the old lady was fine. Ms. Barrington drips with stress but does her best not to show it.'

'Other than her mother, why is she stressed?' Gage said.

'I've not met anyone that likes moving graves. Messing with the dead doesn't sit well.' He shrugged. 'Hell, you'd know better about that than anybody.'

Vega took that one. 'Death is the ultimate deadline. And nobody likes to be rushed.'

Miller nodded. 'I hear ya.'

'You ever had surprises like this on a job before?' Vega was good at relaxing people, getting them to drop their guard and reveal more information than they'd originally intended.

'I found an infant's body outside of Bethesda, Maryland, on a job once. That caught us off guard. I told Ms. Barrington. Mention of the baby spooked her.'

A dead child upset most folks. Adrianna would be more susceptible considering she'd lost her child in the car accident. There was also the child that had died twenty-seven years ago – the child she'd been intended to replace.

Frances Thornton and Margaret Barrington had been friends back in the day. Interesting.

'What are the chances that you'd find a grave out here?' Vega said.

'Slim,' Gage said, rising. His knees ached, a holdover from too many tackles. 'Even just fifty feet from the other graves the bones could have been missed. I've worked a missing persons case a few years back. Serial rapist killed a twelve-year-old girl when she fought back. He buried her in the woods. We traced the evidence found in his pickup truck to the girl. He confessed and told us where the body was buried. Still took us five days to find it.' He glanced around the field. He'd not had his share of good luck in his life and always questioned it when it found him. 'Miller, how the hell did you find this?'

Miller pulled off his hat and scratched his bald head. 'A radar blip and then we spotted the mounds.'

'Find anything before that? Something else that might have caught your eye?'

'Funny you should say that. There was an old bandana tied to the fence. Old, torn, and blowing in the wind.'

'A what?' Gage said.

'Bandana.' He reached in his back pocket. Sunlight and time had faded the red dye and frayed the edges. 'Until you asked, I forgot all about it.'

Gage frowned. The bandana had been contaminated. Miller's clothing fibers and DNA would be all over the damn thing. Gage reached in his coat pocket and pulled out a plastic bag. 'Put it in here.'

Miller glanced at the fabric before dropping it in the bag. 'It's just a damn bandana.'

Vega released a breath, muttering, 'Shit.'

'It might be a private marker that only the killer would recognize. It's not uncommon for a killer to return to a burial site,' Gage explained.

'Why would he come back? You'd think they'd just stay clear.'

'They come out of remorse or even to relive the thrill of death.'

'Damn, didn't think it was anything more than a bit of trash.'

Gage sealed the bag. 'That just happened to be next to an unmarked gravesite?'

'Yep.'

Gage shook his head. 'You find anything else in this area?'

'Nope.'

'What about your men?'

'Doubt it, but go ahead and ask. They're getting paid to do nothing right now.'

Gage glanced at Vega. 'You mind?'

'No, I'll go talk to them.'

'Who from forensics is coming?' Gage asked.

'Tess Kier,' Vega said.

'Good.' Tess Kier had worked on the forensics team for the last three years. She was sharp. All business. She had a brother on SWAT and another on the homicide team. Normally, forensics was first on the scene. Homicide followed hours later. Tess would be irked that they'd gotten here first.

Miller planted scuffed hands on his wide hips. 'Don't suppose if I stay out of your way I can get to work on the Thornton cemetery?'

Gage smiled at the guy, admiring his balls. 'No. You're closing up shop today.'

'Figured as much.'

Gage pulled off his sunglasses and studied the disturbed earth. 'You said you found two mounds.'

'That's right.' Miller stretched out his thick arm. 'See the land just about three feet to the left of the hole?'

'Yes.' Gage could make out a rectangular patch that was just a few inches deeper than the land around it. There was also a second depression in the center.

'When a body is put in the ground, it's solid. As it breaks down, decomposes, the flesh that had been supporting the soil vanishes. So the soil drops. And see in the center of the rectangle the soil is compressed even more?'

Gage nodded. 'That's the belly. It expanded upward with the decomposition gases and then collapsed.'

'Right, I guess you would know about that.' All that shifting up and down cracked the earth. A body also affected the vegetation, which tended to be weedier and thinner in the decomposition zone.

'And you searched this entire area?' Vega said.

'I searched along the fence and the open area twice.'

'What equipment do you use?'

'A little ground radar. Handheld stuff.'

'And nothing unusual?'

'No. I found eleven bodies, as expected.'

'Even the oldest graves? I'd have thought by now they'd have disintegrated.'

Miller nodded. 'Would be true for a wooden coffin. But these folks had money. Coffins are iron. Intact.'

Gage slid his hands into his pockets. The guy was pretty damn thorough. 'That it?'

Miller pulled off his hat and drove his round fingers through his thinning red hair. 'I better go talk to my men and then talk to Ms. Barrington.'

'Don't worry about Ms. Barrington. I'll fill her in on the situation.'

Miller nodded. 'Sure.'

Gage watched the man walk away. Miller reminded Gage of his own father: small town, knew all his neighbors, and had no desire to ever leave.

'You think it's Minor?' Vega spoke loud enough for only Gage to hear.

Gage glanced toward the road that led to the main house. 'Assuming always gets me into trouble. Let's wait for some facts before we start theorizing.'

The crunch of tire over gravel had them all turning to catch the arrival of the Henrico County white forensics van, which parked just beyond Gage's car closer to the site.

The driver's side door opened and a leggy brunette slid out. Tess Kier. She wore a blue jumpsuit and her hair in a loose ponytail.

Vega stared at Tess, his admiration clear.

'She moves like an athlete,' Gage said.

'She was a swimmer in college. Division one. Qualified for the U.S. Olympic team.'

'Impressive.'

'Smart as hell, too, but don't tell her I said that. I try to be obnoxious. I want her to think I don't like her.'

'Vega, this isn't middle school.'

Vega shrugged.

Tess moved toward them with purpose. She had a straightforward attitude that had won her a good deal of respect. Meticulous, she protected her crime scenes like a mother hen.

'So what do we have?' Her voice was husky. 'I hear you have a skeleton.'

Vega nodded. 'Maybe two.'

Gage always knew where he stood with Tess. It was black and white with her. He didn't always like what she had to say, but he respected her. Adrianna Barrington was a different matter. She was awash in grays and he suspected kept many secrets locked away. 'Let me show you.'

Tess grabbed her camera from the van and snapped pictures as she closed in on the site. 'I'm gonna need a list of people who've been around the grave.'

'Can do,' Gage said.

'That includes shoe imprints, fingerprints, maybe even hair samples.' She snapped more pictures and then peered into the hole. 'Human. Who dug it up?'

Gage gave her the recap.

Tess frowned, her displeasure clear. 'That's too bad.'

Vega folded his arms over his chest. 'If not for them, we'd not have anything.'

'Yeah, I know.' But she didn't look appeased. 'I'm not an expert on this but I do know that excavating a body is a slow process. Hand shovels and small brushes kind of slow. God only knows what they've wrecked with their boots and shovels.'

'You think you can handle this job?' Gage said.

Tess shook her head. 'Honestly? No. I've never done it

65

before and you're better off with a forensic anthropologist like Dr. Alex Butler.'

'He works in the medical examiner's office,' Vega said.

'Yeah. But he's got more degrees than I can count and worked in Hawaii with the government identifying the remains of U.S. soldiers. Long story short, he knows this kind of stuff.'

Gage reached for the cell clipped to his belt. He dialed the medical examiner's office and within minutes was connected to Dr. Butler. He explained the situation, heard the rustle of papers and finally Dr. Butler's commitment to be there as soon as he could.

He closed his phone. 'I'm anxious to get the body excavated. It might connect to a missing persons case I worked a couple of years ago. And if not mine, someone else's.'

'We'll move as fast as we can.' But she didn't look the least bit rushed. 'As soon as I shoot the area and check the immediate crime scene for anything out of the ordinary, Dr. Butler should arrive. But I'll warn you again, it's going to be a slow process. I don't know what we'll find when he starts stripping away the dirt. Better to treat this like an archeology site.'

Gage thought about the bandana and held it up for her. 'This was found hanging on the fence by the grave.'

Tess's lips flattened. 'And handled by how many people?'

'Just the foreman, Billy Miller, from what I can tell.'

'Great.' She took the plastic bag.

Tess shot dozens more pictures from multiple angles. She pulled out her sketchpad and did a rough drawing of the area.

Gage scanned the crowd of construction workers. His

gaze landed on the slight man who stood hovering by a tree. Dr. Heckman, who had a keen interest in the whole process. Gage moved toward him. 'What are you still doing here, Dr. Heckman?'

Dr. Heckman flipped a silver coin in his hand. 'I wanted to be sure I didn't miss anything.'

'Like what?'

'I want to make sure those graves stay in the ground.'

'That so?'

'Andrew Thornton, who is buried in that cemetery, was a colonel in the Confederate Army. He died at the battle of Chancellorsville, 1863. Great, great man. I've read diary accounts of his funeral and we believe he was buried in an iron coffin. Next to him will be his wife Eleanor. Another accomplished woman. They deserve to be left in peace.'

Gage rested his hand on his hip. 'I never did like the idea of messing with the dead. Leave 'em in peace is what I say.'

Dr. Heckman arched a brow. 'My thoughts exactly. I just wish I could convince Ms. Barrington that what she's doing is wrong.'

Gage kept his tone even. 'I'd hate to think someone was going to dig me up one day and poke around my remains. I say, just leave me the hell alone.' He reached in his coat pocket and pulled out a pack of gum. He offered one to Dr. Heckman and when he declined, unwrapped a piece as he slid the package back in his pocket.

Dr. Heckman bristled. 'That's what I've been telling her.'

Gage noted the way the man fiddled with the coin. 'So how long have you had an interest in this property?'

'Since I met Mrs. Thornton, Mrs. Frances Thornton,

about ten years ago. I shared her love of this family. She'd be ill if she saw what was happening here today.'

'Mr. Mazur wants the graves removed.'

'She didn't have to sell to him.' There was menace behind the mothballs.

'You think Ms. Barrington has any idea who is in that grave?'

'I think her conscience is troubled.'

'Really?'

'Yes.'

'You've noticed a lot about Ms. Barrington.' Gage kept his voice even, but he could see that the guy had a thing for Adrianna.

Dr. Heckman straightened. 'She's a beautiful woman. She's an easy woman to watch.' He flipped the coin faster in his hand.

Gage grinned. 'Do you stare at her a lot?'

He nearly nodded and then stopped. 'No, not really. No. What are you suggesting?' The coin flipped faster.

'Who did you say you were with?'

Dr. Heckman gave him a look that told Gage the professor had pegged him a hayseed. 'The Virginia Cemetery Preservation Society.'

Gage studied the card. 'I'm going to need more information. Contact name of your boss.'

'Why? I'm here as an observer.'

'Still. I'm gonna need that name. Then I'm gonna need you to leave.'

'Why?'

'No one in that cemetery is getting dug up today,

Dr. Heckman. Your graves are safe. This is now a crime scene.'

Dr. Heckman shook his head. 'I won't get in the way. I will stay back and just watch.'

'Can't have that, I'm afraid. You're going to have to leave. We are going to get mighty busy around here. Time for you to go.' He made a note to do some checking on this guy.

'I will have a word with Mrs. Thornton about staying.' The guy stuck his chest out for extra emphasis. 'This is still her land.'

'Her name is Barrington.' Gage leaned toward him. 'And it's my crime scene. I'm running this show now.'

'You can't do that.'

Gage chewed his gum, his jaw working with each bite. 'Leave or I'll have you arrested for trespassing.'

The professor's eyes narrowed. 'I don't like you, Detective Hudson.'

'Can't help that now, can I?' Gage leaned forward using his size to intimidate. 'Now get going.'

The man's face paled slightly but he held his ground for a second or two longer before he lost his nerve and scurried toward a beat-up old Ford. Gage watched as he drove off.

'Creepy bastard,' Vega said.

'Yeah.' He glanced toward the body. 'But the one that really bothers me is Mazur.'

Vega raised a brow. 'Looked like he was getting into it with Adrianna.'

Gage curled his fingers on his right hand into a fist. 'Yeah.'

Tess had extended the yellow crime scene tape around a more generous area. She'd started to sketch the scene. 'This is going to take a while.'

'Looks like it.'

'Do me a favor and talk to the men on the construction crew. And make sure Dr. Heckman really leaves. I'm headed up to the main house to have a chat with Mrs. Wells and Ms. Barrington.'

Chapter Six

Tuesday, September 26, 12:45 p.m.

Adrianna had pulled out all the leather-bound household ledgers from the Chippendale desk in the study and piled them on top. Knowing the furniture was going to Mazur, she'd been careful to go through every drawer in every stick of furniture in the house to make sure all Frances's papers had been collected. The desk was her last to empty out. She dumped the papers and ledgers in a plastic bin. Later she'd go through them.

Adrianna picked up a ledger and thumbed through the pages. After Craig's accident and her miscarriage she had had to go through Craig's papers in search of insurance and financial documents. Nearly every sheet had been marked with his thick dark handwriting or the lingering scent of his aftershave. The process had been more emotionally draining than she could ever have imagined. In those days, she'd thought of Gage a lot and so many times had been tempted to call him. Several times she'd even picked up the phone and dialed half his number before she'd slammed the receiver down.

A heavy weight settled on her chest and for a moment she had to remind herself to breathe. *Hang tough.* One foot in front of the other. *I can do this.*

The sound of heels clicking down the center hallway had her hustling the last of the papers in the bin in case Dr. Heckman had come to pester her again. She secured the lid on the top.

'Adrianna! Where are you?'

Kendall Shaw Warwick's voice had Adrianna rising. Kendall. Her sister. *Sister*. God, that still sounded weird. Could this day get any more complicated?

'Kendall, I'm in here.'

Kendall appeared in the doorway, all long legs, sharp cheekbones with a slender frame so much like Adrianna's. Kendall wore rust-colored suede pants, a cream silk blouse, high heels, and her long dark hair loose around her shoulders.

For years Adrianna had been told that she looked like that reporter on Channel 10. Even Gage had mentioned it when they'd dated. But she'd brushed off the comments. Everyone had a lookalike. The farthest thought from her mind was that they were sisters, both adopted out in closed proceedings as young children to separate families.

'Good, I found you!' Kendall grinned.

Adrianna crossed the room and Kendall wrapped her in a warm embrace. Adrianna felt stiff, tried to wrestle the awkwardness from her body and when she couldn't, smiled to compensate.

The two women had forged a shaky relationship since they'd discovered they were full-blooded sisters nine months ago. It had gone well enough initially, but after a few months Adrianna had backed away. Kendall was doing her best to be a good older sister, but Adrianna was on sensory overload. With all that she'd had going on in her life, she didn't have the energy to invest in a new family, especially when all the old ones had ended up so broken.

Adrianna managed a bigger smile for Kendall. 'What brings you out here?'

'The last time we had lunch you said the cemetery was being moved on the twenty-sixth.'

'That was a month ago. I'm surprised you remembered.'

'Once a reporter, always a reporter.' Six months ago, Kendall had left Channel 10's top anchor spot and opened her own public relations firm. In those few short months she'd landed several key accounts and was on her way to running a successful business. The move had shocked many, who'd expected the anchor to take a national job, but Kendall didn't want to move and privately admitted to Adrianna that she no longer had the stomach to cover death after nearly dying at the hands of two serial killers.

'Remembering facts is my stock in trade,' Kendall said. 'Was that a forensics van I saw through the trees?'

Adrianna almost laughed. 'Your husband didn't tell you about this?'

'Jacob and I share many things. But he never discusses active investigations. I always ask, because I'm too nosy for my own good, but he never tells.' She studied Adrianna with a critical eye. 'I'm out here just to check on you.'

Adrianna ran a hand through her hair. 'You picked a hell of a day.'

Kendall's eyes brightened with interest. 'I'd be lying if I said this kind of event doesn't make me salivate. I suspect it's one hell of a story, and if I were still on the job I'd be on the phone with my crew right now.'

'This isn't a happy story.' She recapped the gruesome details.

'Who's the detective?'

'Gage Hudson.'

Kendall nodded. 'Good cop. Tenacious. Jacob respects his work.'

For an instant, Adrianna wanted to tell Kendall about her former relationship with Gage but just as quickly rejected the idea. She and Kendall shared the same birth parents. But trust came with time, not biology.

'The body was just found?' Kendall said.

'Couple of hours ago.'

'So no press yet?'

Adrianna cringed. 'No, thank God. But I think they're not here because I took your advice and gave that mini press conference last week. Gave the grand tour, explained what we were doing. I demystified the whole thing.'

'I saw the news reports and read the articles. You did a good job.'

'Thanks.'

Kendall shook her head. 'Today's discovery is going to change everything. Unidentified dead person discovered in an unmarked grave. This is the kind of piece my old boss Brett would be all over. He'd have had me out here reporting the story ten minutes ago.'

'Channel 10 was the only station not at my press conference.'

'That's because my old boss would eat dirt before he'd ever do me a favor. You don't want him to get wind of this story.'

Adrianna dug her fingers through her hair. 'I don't need curiosity seekers.'

'I understand, I do. But you are going to have to tread carefully. Reporters at all the stations have their sources in the police department. Someone is going to talk, and when they do it'll be all over the media.'

'Detective Hudson wants this kept quiet.'

'I'll bet. I know I could be a real pain in the ass for the cops when I was on the job.' Kendall's gaze turned sympathetic. 'But if anyone can keep it quiet for as long as possible, it's Hudson and my husband.'

Adrianna lifted her chin. 'If anyone had to cover the story, I'd rather it be you.'

The statement softened Kendall's gaze. 'That means a lot.'

'I mean it.'

'Well, I wouldn't take the story.'

Adrianna raised a brow. 'If I know anything about you, Kendall, it's that you love a good story. I'll bet your heart is racing right now just thinking about it.'

Kendall shrugged. 'It's beating a little fast. Old habits die hard. But I value you more than the story.'

Unwelcome emotions rushed through her limbs. 'Thanks.'

'So what are you doing here?'

'Going through my mother-in-law's papers. This is the last piece of furniture I have to clear out.'

Kendall glanced at the ledgers. 'What are you looking for?'

'If there is anything of historical value, I'll pass it on to the buyer. If it's personal, I'll destroy it.'

'That's gracious.'

'I'm not as selfless as you might think. Frances and Mom were friends since college and even though I do feel an obligation to keep her papers private, I'm hoping there's something in here that'll tell me about my adoption.'

'We have all the answers about our birth family. What could you be looking for?'

'Information about my parents' first daughter.'

'Your mom still hasn't told you what happened to her?'

'No. And each time I bring it up, she ends up in tears. Yesterday we talked again. I told her about the grave removal. Last night she landed in the ER with phantom chest pains.'

'I'm sorry.' Kendall frowned. 'Adrianna, why do you care so much about that child?'

'I don't know exactly. Maybe because I lost a baby. Maybe no child should be forgotten. I do know I'll go through every box and slip of paper in this house looking for any clue that might tell me what happened to her.'

'Can I help?'

'Thanks. Really. But I've got to do this on my own.'

Gage got into the car, backtracked to the main house, and stopped behind an Audi parked behind Adrianna's Land Rover. He scrutinized the extra car. The last thing he wanted was more people on the property.

Sighing, he shifted his gaze to the house. It wasn't large by today's standards but despite the neglect, it was built well, no doubt the nails handmade and the support joists notched individually. Quality. Simple lines like he preferred.

Lots of overgrown plants crept up the brick and mortar and a couple of windows on the top floor had been knocked out with rocks. The place looked like it had been vacant for years and in need of attention.

As much as he admired the construction, places like this made the muscles in his back tighten. Maybe because when he'd been a kid in the trailer park, he'd once dreamed of having a fancy house. Maybe because when he'd signed with the Falcons he'd just placed a bid on a fine house he would later relinquish. Shit. Maybe he just didn't trust the types born with silver spoons. They liked to believe they lived by a different set of rules. That consequences didn't apply.

Adrianna Barrington Thornton was from the silver spoon world. He doubted she'd ever broken a sweat or one of her pretty nails.

Gage climbed the front steps, noting the way the boards creaked. He crossed the wide front porch to the door, which was ajar. Instead of knocking, he walked into the foyer. The place smelled of mothballs and dust, and though the windows were open, the poor light and dank feeling made it easy to forget that it was a sunny day. Like a damn morgue, he thought as he moved down the center hallway and his polished boots creaked on darkened pine floors.

He glanced in the first big room on his right. It was a parlor. Sheets covered the furniture, and the portraits that had hung on the walls had been removed. The only traces of them were the faded outlines on the walls. Somewhere a clock ticked.

He moved into a room on the left and saw that the pictures had been moved in there and crated. Gage sauntered out of the room and down the center hallway. When he reached the door he peered inside and saw Adrianna speaking to another woman. 'Excuse me.'

Adrianna and the woman turned. He swallowed a curse when he saw Kendall Shaw Warwick's face. Boss's wife. Ex-reporter. Trouble. His emotions must have registered on his face because Adrianna's pale eyes mirrored faint amusement.

'Detective Hudson. You know my sister, Kendall Shaw Warwick.'

Seeing them together, the family resemblance was unmistakable. Kendall's coloring was darker, her skin tones more olive. Adrianna was blond, her complexion as pale as cream. Kendall was a knockout but Adrianna was the one that ignited his blood. 'Ms. Warwick.'

'Detective.'

'Ms. Warwick, if you don't mind, I have a few questions for Ms. Barrington.'

Adrianna shifted, her amusement vanishing. 'Sure.'

Kendall picked up on the shift in her sister's mood and her gaze glanced quickly between them. She seemed to detect a crackle of tension that extended far beyond this case. 'My, my.'

Adrianna shot Kendall an embarrassed glance that warned her to be quiet.

Kendall smiled. 'Adrianna, if you're okay, I'll leave you two alone.'

'Thanks, Kendall. I'm good.'

'Too bad I'm not a reporter anymore, Detective Hudson.' The comment was designed to rattle. 'I'd take this story national.'

Gage blocked Kendall's exit. 'This stays under wraps for now, Ms. Warwick.'

Kendall's gaze didn't waver. 'That an order?'

Gage held her glare, willing to go toe to toe with her. He didn't care if she was the president's wife. 'A request, ma'am.'

Kendall lifted a brow, not the least bit intimidated. 'Not to worry, Detective. I promised Adrianna I'd keep silent and I will. I'll call you later, Adrianna.'

'Let me know if anyone picks up the story,' Adrianna said.

'No one's going to,' Gage said.

Kendall shook her head. 'They won't hear of it from me, but I promise you this is going to leak out within seventy-two hours.'

He couldn't deny the truth of her words. 'Just do your part.'

'Oh, I will.' Kendall tossed another assessing glance at Gage that said *Hurt my sister and you'll have me to contend with* and left.

Gage shoved his hands in his pockets and listened to the click of heels as she moved down the hallway and out the door. When her car fired up, he turned to Adrianna. 'Let's hope the story comes out later than sooner. Not just for your sake or mine, but for the victims'.'

'We are on the same side in this matter, Detective. I want the graves relocated. Bad press could mess all that up.'

Formal. Reserved. And it galled him. With an effort, he shifted his attention from her to the desk behind her. Stacks of ledgers covered the antique finish. 'Looks like you've got some reading.'

'Just old papers I've got to dig through.'

He struggled to relax his stance, wanting to defuse their rippling tension.

'Looks like you've got your work cut out.'

Long hands smoothed over jeans that weren't everyday jeans, but designer. Expensive. 'Nothing I can't handle.'

'Your husband didn't have brothers or sisters?'

'No. He was the last of his line. There's only been one male heir for the last several generations.'

Gage glanced around the room, studying the heavy wood paneling and the empty floor-to-ceiling bookcases. 'This place is chock full of history and secrets.'

'More than I'll likely ever know.'

He moved to a bank of dusty shelves recently stripped of books. 'Is the money from the land sale going to your bills? I mean, the nursing home must have been real pricey.'

'If I'm lucky, I'll clear all the debts.' The topic seemed to make her uncomfortable. 'Is there something specific you'd like to ask me? I've got a lot of work.'

'Just came to tell you we'll be on-site for a while.' He'd tear this whole damn place apart if that's what it took to find out who was in that grave. 'The work at the cemetery is suspended until I say otherwise.'

Full lips flattened. 'How long will that be?'

'Until the job is finished.'

'I've got to finish that grave relocation within thirty days or the land sale is void.'

'We'll be done when we're done.'

Annoyance flashed in her eyes. 'I'm calling my attorney today. He'll ensure you don't dawdle.'

The knocks Adrianna had taken over the last couple of years had transformed her unsure, wide-eyed innocence into leveled confidence. This Adrianna wasn't afraid to roll up her sleeves and fight. Good. He preferred her this way. Mentally he stripped off the gloves.

Gage leaned forward. 'You sure you don't have any idea who might be in that grave?'

Her long fingers curled into fists. 'I really don't know.'

'Why'd you ask Miller to sweep the land inside the cemetery with radar?'

'It seemed prudent. I was worried there'd be some kind of surprise that would void the land sale.'

'Like a dead body?'

'I had no idea what Miller would find today.'

He studied her face closely. 'Now, why don't I believe that?'

She arched an eyebrow. 'I don't know. Maybe you're paranoid.'

'That's part of the reason the county pays me, ma'am.'

They stood there a moment, the heavy divide between them widening. 'Well, if anything should come to you that you think I should know, you'll call, won't you?'

She drummed her fingers on her thigh. Again, gold and diamonds flashed. 'I have a consultation in New York. It's a good client and I've got to be there for a meeting on Friday.'

'Well, I guess you're going to have to cancel.'

Exasperation lit up her eyes. 'I don't trust your agenda, Detective. You hounded my late husband. He thought you were out to get him. Maybe you still are.'

In a blink, mildly annoyed morphed to pissed. 'I had

questions that *he* refused to answer. That combination never sets well with me, ma'am.' His left hand slid into his pocket and rattled loose change. 'You jerk me around like he did and I'll be after you just as fast.'

Adrianna didn't flinch. 'You play fair and so will I, Detective.'

'Why'd you have Miller sweep that land?'

'Like I said, to cover my bases.'

Gage shook his head. 'I don't believe you.'

'I can't help that.'

He removed his hand from his pocket and waggled his index finger slowly, deliberately. 'You know what, Ms. Barrington, if you've got something to say that I need to hear, you best say it.'

'I've nothing to say.'

'You're not protecting your late husband?'

'No.' Unconsciously, her thumb fidgeted with her wedding bands.

'You can try to run from the past but you won't escape it. Fact, I'm willing to bet it's about to rear its ugly head and bite you in the ass.'

Chapter Seven

Dr. Alex Butler had been on his feet for sixteen hours when he got the call about the partly unearthed skeleton at the Thornton estate. His lower back ached from standing over the autopsy table and his feet hurt.

Alex rarely wasted time worrying about what couldn't be fixed. It was an illogical use of time. So accepting that the aches and pains would remain until he could get some rest, he focused on what he could fix: the hunger chewing at his gut. He'd stopped to grab six turkey club sandwiches, a few waters, and a half dozen apples en route to the crime scene. He'd eaten two sandwiches as he drove and stored the remaining food in a cooler that he always kept in his car. It had been his experience that jobs like this took a long, long time. Hunger was a distraction he didn't wish to factor.

Dr. Butler was tall and lean and had thick blond hair that swept over brown eyes. A quick gait added to a youthful appearance that made it easy to assume he was much younger than his thirty-three years. Youth. It had stalked him since he'd entered high school at age ten, graduated from medical school at fourteen, and been awarded a PhD in anthropology at twenty.

For as long as he could remember, he'd wanted to look

older. Be older. And his prayers had earned him a baby face.

His intelligence set him apart and made others uncomfortable, angry sometimes. Logic dictated if he were kind and helpful, he'd be accepted. But his two hundred plus IQ intimidated most and kept them at a predictably polite distance. Consequently, most of his spare time was spent alone.

Having little success with the living, he'd narrowed his focus in on the dead. But lately, the dead had become as predictable as the living. Two years in the medical examiner's office had been fascinating, but in recent months, he'd toyed with the idea of contacting his old boss in Hawaii and rejoining the search for MIA soldiers. There was also an offer from Boston's medical examiner's office. It paid well and the change of scenery would interest him for a time. However, experience suggested the inevitable ennui would return and with it bring the restless energy he found maddening.

Alex parked his state-issue four-door sedan behind the forensics van and grabbed his notebook. Closing the door, he pressed Lock on the keyless entry and then tugged the handle for good measure. Six patrol cars were parked on-site as well as a couple of unmarked police vehicles. This case had piqued the interest of quite a few officers.

Alex spotted Tess standing inside the yellow crime scene tape sketching the layout. A blue jumpsuit skimmed narrow hips and mud-coated scuffed boots. Ink-dark hair twisted into a topknot skewered by a pencil. She was frowning. Always frowning.

It was never easy or predictable with Tess. She rarely

84

minced words and was quick to launch verbal strikes if she suspected a screwup. She reminded him of a tornado or hurricane. Magnificent. Wild. And a man could study both all his life and still not know what it would spare or ravage.

A smile tipped the edge of his lips. He liked that about her. Liked her passion. Her volatility.

Alex spotted Hudson and moved toward him. 'Detective.'

Hudson shook his hand. 'Dr. Butler. Thanks for coming so quickly.'

'Alex.'

'Right.'

Alex had only crossed paths with Hudson a couple of times. Hudson was good at playing the hick, but that good ol' boy demeanor hid a sharp mind. Hudson also had one hell of a work ethic and like a dog with a bone, didn't let go of a case until it was solved or there was nothing left to pursue. Alex's dad had once scrounged an old *Sports Illustrated* and shown him an article about Hudson's football career. His early retirement had been a shock to all.

'Tell me what you have,' Alex said.

Hudson shook his head. 'All I know is that I have a partly unearthed skull. Tess didn't want to open up the grave until you got here. Said you know about this kind of stuff.'

Alex nodded. 'That was smart. The excavation has got to be done right or evidence could be lost.'

Hudson didn't seem pleased. 'That sounds like it's going to take time.'

'It will.'

'How fast can you do this?'

'I don't know.'

Hudson rested his hand on his hip. 'Doc, I've got to tell you, I'd love to see this done by yesterday.'

'That's impossible.'

Even white teeth flashed conjuring images of a lion on the hunt. 'I know. What I'm saying is when can you give me some information?'

'I've got my brushes and small trowels in my trunk. Let me check in with Tess and we'll get started right away. As soon as I know something, I'll let you know.'

'Thanks, Doc.' Hudson rubbed the back of his neck. 'Be warned, Tess is in a foul mood.'

Alex raised a brow. 'Why?'

'Pissed that the construction crew trampled her site.'

Alex pulled rubber gloves from the pocket of his khakis and slipped them on. 'Never a dull moment with Ms. Kier.'

Hudson chuckled. 'No, siree. Never dull.'

Alex moved toward the yellow tape. 'May I enter?'

Tess's gaze swung around and for a moment murder flashed in her blue eyes. When she recognized him, the look softened only a little. 'What took you so long?'

'Work. Traffic. The usual. Mind if I approach?'

'Go ahead. I've photographed and sketched all that I can.' He ducked under the tape and together they walked to the earth mound.

Alex squatted, pulled wire-rimmed glasses from his breast pocket, and studied the site as a whole and then started to key in on specific details. 'Do you have a flashlight?'

She pulled a small flashlight from the pocket of her jumpsuit and tossed it to him.

He caught it easily and clicked it on. Peering down the

hole, he studied the skull. 'Looks like it's down about eight inches to a foot.'

Tess knelt beside him and a slight breeze caught her scent. Soap. Clean. Surprisingly floral. 'What's the protocol when digging up a site like this?'

'We'll start excavating around the head and upper torso first.'

'Why not the whole body at once? I take the top, you take the bottom.'

'We don't know the bottom's exact location. Body could be flat or angled. This way we'll have an idea about the position before we move to the lower part.'

'Right.'

'I'll pull soil off in layers, give it to you, and you can sift and search for artifacts, bone, et cetera.'

'All right.'

'I hope you've eaten. It's going to take a while.'

'I'm fine.'

He rose and clicked off the light. 'Is that a yes or no?'

Standing, she brushed the dirt from her knees. 'A no. But I'm fine.'

'How long do you believe you can function on an empty stomach?'

Tess's chin jutted out a fraction. 'Is this a quiz?'

'It's a straightforward question.'

'Then I'd say as long as I need to, *Alex*.'

Her tone puzzled him. 'Are you always this defensive?'

Her gaze narrowed like a boxer entering the ring. 'I am not defensive.'

'Stubborn, then? Afraid to show weakness?'

'I'll admit to stubborn. But I've no weaknesses.'

The illogical nature of the statement made Alex laugh. The day was looking up. 'We'll see.'

Gage and Vega found Mazur on the site of his latest road project, standing on the five-foot-tall wheel of a Bobcat talking to its operator. He wore construction boots, beat-up jeans, and an old, dirt-smudged shirt. Wind-tossed hair accentuated the lines deepened by the sun. If the foreman hadn't pointed him out, Gage wouldn't have pegged him for the decked-out guy he'd met this morning.

He waited for Mazur to wrap up his instructions to his driver before calling out. Mazur turned, his frown deepening. He hopped to the ground and strode toward them. 'Detective Hudson. You must be here about the graves.'

'Right.'

'It's a real pisser.' Mazur's accent, Chicago maybe, sharpened the words. 'Last damn thing I expected.'

'I'd say that's true for everyone, including the families of the victims.' Gage's temper railed against its leash.

Mazur looked bored. 'Look, I've got work. Ask me your questions and leave.'

Gage leaned forward, his frame rigid and uncompromising. 'What were you doing on the estate?'

'Protecting my investment. I've paid a lot of money for that property. I wanted to make sure the job was done right. I want those graves removed from my property.'

'Why do you want the graves moved?'

'I just got married and my wife doesn't want dead bodies on the land.'

'You're a hands-on kind of guy,' Vega said.

'That's right. Want it done right, do it yourself.'

Gage rested his hands on his hips. 'Then why have Adrianna Barrington move the graves? Why not handle the job yourself?'

'A guy moves to a conservative Southern state from the North and buys an old house beloved by all. And then he announces he wants to dig up the family graveyard. You know what that equals?'

'What?'

'Legal issues up the ass. But if the heir's sainted widow moves the graves, there's less fuss. People feel for her and they let her do the job. So far she's only had that nut Dr. Heckman to handle.'

'You put Ms. Barrington in a tough spot.'

'She's a big girl who negotiated a good price and insisted we close the sale immediately.'

'When did you close?'

'Early February. And she didn't waste a day cashing my check.'

Vega rested a tanned hand on his hip. 'Why the delay?'

'State regulations. Even a saint has to jump through hoops when she wants to move a grave. Once she received approval, our deal was she had thirty days to finish the job or give the money back.'

'Any idea who those unknown graves might belong to?'

That seemed to amuse him. 'How the hell would I know? I bought the property, not the history.'

'Why buy it?'

'Great piece of land. Location. The river. It doesn't get much sweeter.'

'I understand you made an offer to Adrianna Barrington a month before her husband died.'

'I read the papers. According to the newspapers, Thornton was in an irreversible coma. I did a little digging and found that he had no other blood family. A young wife with no lasting ties to the Thornton family was the sole heir. Expensive nursing home. Family debts. All added up to a sale. The problem was she couldn't sell while her husband was alive.'

'And he died a month later.'

'Lucky for us all.'

'You're keeping the house?' Vega said.

'If it were up to me, I'd bulldoze the place, but my wife has an idea to restore it. She has a vision of landing a spread in *House and Garden*.' Mazur rested a manicured hand on a worn belt. 'And I've got to admit that living in that house gives me a measure of satisfaction.'

'Why's that?'

'Poor kid from south side of Chicago makes good. Has the fancy old house and young hot wife to prove it. I plan to rename the place and start my own dynasty.'

Gage sniffed. 'You aren't fond of the rich, are you?'

'Everything I have, I took for myself. No one gave me shit, parents included.'

Six hours later the sun had sunk in the sky and the police had turned on portable floodlights, powered by a generator, knowing darkness would soon follow. Tess's back ached. And her stomach grumbled painfully for food.

She and Alex had been working over the burial site, meticulously removing and sifting through dirt. They'd excavated about twenty-five inches around the top portion of the skeleton. The body now appeared to rest on what looked like an earthen platform.

The remains were completely skeletonized. All the flesh had decomposed. With the head, shoulders, and torso now exposed, Alex theorized that the body had been buried on its back, legs extended, left hand positioned over the chest, and the skull turned to the right.

Tess rose from her knees and stretched the soreness from her lower back. A touch of resentment burned as she watched Alex hunched over the skull. She was running on empty while these long hours had energized him.

God, but she'd kill to escape to the forensics van to make a hot cup of coffee and grab a handful of crackers. However, to admit she couldn't keep up with him was galling.

'How about a break?' His gaze remained on the bones.

Okay, she could add mind reader to his list of annoyances. 'Nope. I'm good. I can keep going.'

'I'm starving.' He laid his trowel down, mentally seemed to note its position, and rose.

On cue her stomach grumbled. 'If you insist. The closest place to get food around here is ten miles down the road.'

'I brought a cooler.'

She raised a brow, not sure if she was impressed or annoyed. 'You think of everything.'

'Usually.'

Tess and Alex walked in silence to his car. He popped the trunk. The contents were all neatly organized: blanket, cooler, change of clothes, MREs, even a couple of large flashlights. 'Looks like you packed for a camping trip.'

He reached past her, his shoulder brushing her arm as he pulled out the cooler. 'I never know how long I'll have to remain in the field.'

'Let's head to the forensics van. I can make us hot coffee.'

'Excellent.'

They climbed in the back of the van. It was six by twenty and looked like a mini command center with cabinets on either wall, counters to process evidence, and a television mounted behind the front cab.

Alex's blond hair was in need of a trim and the bangs drifted over his forehead into his eyes, which forced him to push it back with his long fingers every few minutes. He wore a white button-down, pressed khakis, and of all things a pocket protector that held three ink pens. His body was lean and muscled, signs he kept himself in shape.

Tess pulled coffee from the cabinet, filled the coffee machine filter, and poured water from a gallon jug. Within seconds, the coffee perked.

Alex handed her a sub sandwich wrapped in wax paper. 'It's turkey on whole wheat, no mayo.'

Her stomach growled painfully and she had to laugh. 'I'd eat bark off a tree right now.'

'I thought you weren't hungry?'

'I lied.' She bit into the sandwich. It tasted like heaven. She ate half of it before she stopped and poured coffee for them both. With a little food in her belly and hot coffee in hand, she felt almost human. 'So how much longer is this going to take?'

'We should have the second half of her removed in the next few hours.'

Tess tensed. 'You said *her*.'

'Yes. Definitely female.'

Tess picked at the rim of her Styrofoam cup. Up until now she'd not asked for his opinion so that he could focus on his work. 'What else can you tell so far?'

'At this point beyond sex and race, it's just going to be the basics.' He sniffed and took another sip of coffee. 'Good coffee.'

'Other than toast, my one culinary talent.'

Alex, she sensed, catalogued the detail in some dusty corner of his brain along with the trillion other facts he had stored. 'Miller's guys took a chunk out of her skull when they dug into the site.'

Her nerves settling thanks to more food, her sense of control grew. 'How can you know that?'

'By the bone. The edges are white, freshly cut. If the cut had been old they'd be discolored like the rest of the body.'

Tess could count on one hand the facts she'd confirmed about Alex Butler. *One*. Alex despised unanswered questions. *Two*. His quest for truth bordered on obsessive. *Three*. One and two made him one of the best medical examiners in the country. *Four*. She realized there was no four. That's all she knew about him. 'How do you know the body is female?'

'Based on the skull.' He sipped his coffee. 'The brow ridge isn't as pronounced or as thick as a man's. We menfolk are a little more Neanderthal than you gals.'

She picked a stray piece of lettuce off the waxed paper and ate it. 'My ex-boyfriend proved that theory.'

'An ex-boyfriend? Now that's a first.'

'What do you mean?'

'All you ever talk about is work.'

93

'It's about all I do these days.' She tipped her cup toward him. 'No one's heard many details about you.'

Alex shrugged. 'What do you want to know?'

'Wives? Exes? Kids?'

'None of the above.'

Pleased for reasons she couldn't explain, she set her sandwich down. 'So what do you do for fun? You can't be all work and no play.'

'I hike. I hang with my brothers. Watch old movies.'

'You have brothers?'

He lifted a brow. 'I wasn't hatched in a lab, Tess.'

The hint of humor had her cringing slightly. That had been one of the theories she'd floated around about him at the Christmas party last year. Had it gotten back to him or was the word choice a coincidence? She cleared her throat. 'Your brothers live around here?'

'Sure do. All three are with the FBI.'

'All as smart as you?'

'They're smart enough.'

'Your kind of smart?'

'Close.'

'So do you all read math and physics books for fun?'

'Sometimes.'

A joke danced on the tip of her tongue, but she decided against sharing. She was beginning to feel a little comfortable around him and that was just too weird for words. She shifted back to work. 'What else about the victim?'

'She was Caucasian.'

'You know this because?'

'The bones between the nose and chin are flat and the nasal tall and narrow. If she'd been African American, her skull would have been more rounded. And if she'd been of Asian descent the face would be wider, flatter, and the cheekbones would be more prominent.'

'What about her age?'

'Rough guess . . . and I do mean rough, I'd say late twenties. The fusing of the cranial bones is almost complete but not as complete as someone in their late thirties.' He drew his finger along the top of his own skull to demonstrate. 'I'll know more when I get the rest of her unearthed.'

'How?'

He pushed off from the counter. This close she could smell the earthy blend of dirt and his clean scent. 'The pubic symphysis, the point where the right and left portions of the pubic bone meet, undergoes gradual and subtle changes as we age. It's bumpier during the teen years and smooths in the twenties. By forty it erodes.'

All his description started to paint a picture of the victim in her mind. A twentysomething female. She wondered what her hair color might have been or what she did for a living or for fun. 'How long has she been in the ground?'

'Not more than a few years.'

'So she's definitely not some kind of servant from the past that might have worked for the Thorntons.'

'Definitely not. The bones still have a greasy feel. We call that green bone. If she'd been belowground a hundred, fifty, even twenty years, the bone would have been drier.'

'How long does green bone last?'

'If she were on the surface, a year or less. But she was about twelve inches belowground, so a couple of years would be reasonable.'

'There's an odor. Like candle wax.'

95

'That's residue from the bone marrow. That can last several years.'

Tess tapped a long index finger against her coffee cup. 'So we have a white female, late twenties, dead less than five years, and I'd say she was, what . . . five-six?'

'Give or take.'

'Cause of death?'

'That I'm not certain. Miller's men cracked the side skull up pretty bad. But I did try to put the pieces together and I think there's a bullet hole. I'll figure that out at the lab.'

'I've sifted every inch of dirt you've given me. No bullets so far. But it could very well be under the body.'

'We'll know when we get the bones removed.'

'I'd like to stay close to this case. You know bone better than most and I'm curious.'

'Sure.'

She gulped the last of her coffee. 'Do you think there is a second body?'

'Definitely.'

She bit into her sandwich and let her mind wander to the killer's motivation. 'God, why bury them out here?'

'Logical. Three to five years ago, this land was deserted, and the chances of it being sold minimal.'

She set her half-eaten sandwich down. 'I wonder if he shot her here.'

'Hard to say.'

Tess stared out the open back door of the van into the dark. 'She must have been terrified.'

'No doubt.'

'Don't you ever think about the victims? The people they were before death?'

'I may consider habits or behavior as it relates to the cause of death, but beyond that, no, I don't think about them. It's pointless.'

Dr. Butler's logic was useful but often annoying. 'Do you ever try to put yourself in the victim's mind? See what they saw last?'

Alex's gaze settled on her. 'The bodies, these bones – they're just evidence. To think of them as people is not productive.'

'I know that. And I tell myself that a lot.' She picked at a piece of sandwich crust. 'But I can't think that way.'

'You better or you'll go insane.'

Chapter Eight

Tuesday, September 26, 9:00 p.m.

Gage closed his phone and he turned down the tree-lined driveway that wound into the woods toward the Wellses' house. He'd called Dr. Butler and gotten an update on the body. The skeleton had been excavated and was now being moved bone by bone to a collection of bags. No bullets had been found and Alex and Tess were calling it a day in the next hour. A little rest and both promised to return first thing in the morning.

Gage drew in a breath. He'd told Vega not to assume they'd found Rhonda Minor, but right now he'd bet a paycheck they had. More than ever, he believed that Rhonda and Craig had been having an affair, she threatened trouble before the wedding, and he killed her. The trick was proving it. Thornton was dead and there'd be no trial, but solving this case would give Rhonda's family some measure of peace.

Losing someone hurt like hell, but the not knowing *was* worse. Those four days Jessie had been missing had been the worst in his life. Each moment of each day his gut turned as if he'd swallowed cut glass and his head pounded as if an anvil kept striking. There'd been no sleep. No eating. No peace.

Even now, remembering made his insides clench.

He parked on the street in front of a neatly kept white trilevel and checked the address in his notes. This was the home of Dwayne and Marie Wells. He'd called ahead and asked if he could interview them and they'd readily agreed.

Gage moved to the front door, lighted by a single bulb that sent light pooling on the stoop. He rang the bell.

Seconds later the lights in the living room clicked on and the door pulled open. The man standing on the other side of the screened door was in his midsixties and had a potbelly and gray hair cut in a crew cut. He wore jeans and a thick blue sweatshirt.

Gage pulled out his badge. 'I'm Detective Hudson. I called earlier.'

'Yes, sir,' the man said, nodding. 'I'm Dwayne Wells. Please come in.' He pushed open the door.

Gage stepped inside to a neatly kept living room furnished with a green tufted sofa, matching wing-back chairs, and an upright piano. From the kitchen, the sound of water running in a sink stopped and a woman appeared in the kitchen door wiping her hands on a checkered cloth. 'Ma'am.'

Dwayne held out his hand, inviting Gage to sit. 'Detective, this is my wife Marie.'

He nodded. 'We met at the Thornton estate today.'

Marie came into the room. 'Can I get you a cola or some sweet tea?'

Gage nodded his thanks. 'I appreciate that, but no, thank you.'

'Water?'

'No, ma'am.' Marie reminded him of his own mother. She'd keep offering until he accepted something.

She looked disappointed and moved into the living room to stand beside her husband. 'It's just awful what they found out there today. Just awful.'

The three sat, the Wellses on the sofa and Gage across from them in a wing chair.

'So you've known the Thornton family long?' Gage said.

'Since we were both teenagers. My first job was tending the property. Marie got her start there cleaning for the family. That's how we met.'

'And you own a moving company?'

'That's right, with my boy, Ben. We do mostly specialized work now. Move art and fine antiques. Travel all up and down the East Coast. My boy oversees most of the day-to-day operations. I'm doing the paperwork these days. Ruined my back about five years ago.'

'How'd you get into that line of work?'

'Through the Thorntons, of course. The old man brought me to work in his gallery. Art needed to be moved and I learned how to do it right. From there the business just grew.'

'That specialized work keep you busy?'

'We do just fine. In the last year it's been a bit slow – the new owner of the Thornton Gallery is farming work out to other companies. But Adrianna started calling us to do some work for her clients. Most of them are rich folks and the furniture they have is expensive, almost like art in some cases.'

Gage flipped open his notebook. 'What can you tell me about the Thornton family?'

Dwayne and Marie looked at each other, their eyes softening with clear fondness.

'They was kinda like local royalty,' Dwayne said. 'The family's been in the county for a century and a half. And as I recall, that house was built on tobacco money. Later they switched to banking. Then Robert Thornton's daddy got them into the art business.'

'Rich folk from way back,' Gage said with a grin.

'You bet,' Dwayne said.

'What do you think about Adrianna selling?'

Marie sighed. 'I don't think she had much choice. She hasn't said anything, of course. She's too loyal to the Thorntons, but the last couple of generations haven't been the best or smartest workers. Craig, his father and grandfather liked to throw parties and live it up well. Craig and his daddy didn't always choose wisely when it came to art and ended up selling many pieces at a loss.'

'How do you know?'

'They talked. I listened.'

Dwayne shook his head. 'Robert did his best to make that boy in his image.'

Gage flipped the pages of his notebook. 'What can you tell me about Robert Thornton?'

'Well, he was book smart. And like I said, loved art,' Dwayne said. 'Stayed in the city a lot while his wife Frances stayed on the estate. She liked to garden and have friends up for long weekends.'

'Craig their only child?'

'Yes. Born to them after they'd been married about eight years. You never saw a daddy as proud as Robert Thornton when Craig was born. That boy never did without once.'

Marie smiled. 'He threw a big party to celebrate Craig's birth.'

Gage noted Dwayne's frown. The man had something on his mind regarding Robert Thornton. He paused, believing the man had more to say. He did.

'Thornton's spoiling just about ruined that boy. I can't tell you how many late-night calls I got from Craig asking if I could pick him up from a party because he'd been drinking too much.'

'Why didn't he call his father?'

'Didn't want to disappoint him, I guess. And I was kinda like a Dutch uncle to Craig. A few times I tried to speak to him about his partying ways, but he wasn't listening. Shame. The boy had so damn much potential.'

Marie shook her head. 'And then he gets killed by a drunk driver and Adrianna loses her baby. Fate can be so cruel.'

Gage thought about the accident photos. His blood ran cold each time he thought of Adrianna encased in twisted metal. 'What happened after Craig's accident?'

Dwayne's eyes darkened, his anger almost palpable. 'You never did see a better wife than Adrianna. She stuck by Craig, even when doctors said he'd be in a coma forever. No better wife.'

Gage wrote *Adrianna* on his notepad and circled it three times. 'Do you have any idea who might be buried on that property?'

Both shook their heads but Marie was the one that answered. 'It's caught us all by surprise. We're all just sick about it.'

Dwayne shook his head. 'Hell of a way to end up. Too bad. But the timing couldn't be worse for Adrianna. Poor thing just wants to be done with the place.'

'You like Adrianna?'

Dwayne nodded, unapologetic. 'Kind of like a daughter to me. I've watched her grow up. Handle some nasty stuff with her folks.'

'Such as?' His own curiosity about the woman prompted the question.

'Her mother suffered from all kinds of health issues. She's kind of fragile. And her dad didn't have much use for either one of them.'

Marie interjected, 'Mr. Barrington was always working.'

'How do you know that?'

'Miss Frances and Miss Margaret talked. Hard not to hear.'

'Who else did Craig date other than Adrianna?'

Dwayne looked puzzled, shook his head. 'A few girls in high school, maybe one or two in college. He and Adrianna didn't get serious until his junior year of college.'

Marie answered, 'Once he and Adrianna got together I don't think he looked at other women.'

'No one from work?'

Dwayne shook his head. 'No. He was dedicated to Adrianna. Fact, there was a time a few years back they broke up for the summer. He was a wreck.'

'Why'd they break up?'

Marie frowned. 'Truth be told, Craig did have some growing up to do. And I think he did a lot that summer. Losing Adrianna was like a bucket of ice water on his head. He straightened up. And in the end Adrianna saw that and came back to him.'

Gage cleared his throat. 'While they were apart, did he date anyone else?'

Dwayne shook his head. 'That I don't know.'

Marie shook her head. 'He was so sad during that time. If he did date anyone, it wouldn't have been serious. He wanted Adrianna back.'

Gage let the comment pass. 'Have you seen anyone on the property lately that didn't fit?'

'I'm not there every day, but when I am it's quiet.' Marie snapped her fingers. 'I did see that Mr. Mazur on the property last fall, right before Craig died. I asked him what he was doing here and he said he'd always admired the place. He was just walking the property. Left without a word.'

'Anyone else?'

Marie shook her head. 'No. Like I said, the place is quiet since Miss Frances died. There is that Dr. Heckman fellow. Creepy. Always manages to be here when Adrianna visits. He carries his signs and shouts for her to leave the dead in peace.'

'Did he ever threaten her?'

'Not that I've heard. Reminds me more of a buzzing fly. An annoyance.'

Maybe. Or maybe Dr. Heckman was more of a threat than anyone thought. The mild mannered could kill as easily as anyone else.

'What do you think about the land sale?'

Dwayne and Marie looked at each other.

'Got to be done,' Dwayne said.

Gage sensed some disapproval from both. 'You're sorry she's selling.'

Marie nodded. 'I understand why the place has to be sold, but it still hurts to see it go.'

Dwayne flexed his weathered fingers. 'Change can be unsettling.'

Gage pulled business cards from his pocket and handed one to each. 'If you think of anything else, you'll let me know.'

Nodding, Marie glanced down at her card. 'I sure will.'

Dwayne tucked the card in his breast pocket. 'We want this case solved so Adrianna can get on with her life. She deserves to be happy.'

'Thank you for your time.' Gage rose.

Dwayne stood, moving slowly as if his bones ached. Gage noticed that arthritis had started to deform his hands.

Thanking them again, Gage got into his car. He fired up the engine and pulled onto the street.

The Wellses had painted Craig as a saint. As far as Gage was concerned, the guy had been a royal prick. And likely, the truth was somewhere in between.

Instead of going home, Gage opted to return to the Thornton estate. He wanted to see with his own eyes how the work had progressed.

A half hour later he arrived at the yellow crime scene tape, which corralled a collection of paper bags lined up beside the empty grave.

Tess moved toward the tape. Wisps of hair had escaped her ponytail and dark circles hung under her eyes. 'So what brings you out here?'

'Just having a look.' Gage doubted he'd sleep tonight.

'As you can see, we've almost bagged all the bones.' The bones were in paper bags because plastic trapped moisture and caused mold growth, which contaminated evidence.

'Don't let me stop you.'

Tess nodded and turned back to her work. Alex raised his gaze from a bag and acknowledged Gage's presence with a nod but went right back to work.

Gage watched Tess and Alex's painstaking process, frustrated that there wasn't more he could do to help them right now. His turn would come as soon as Dr. Butler identified the body.

The two moved slowly, their deliberate movements a sign exhaustion had taken root.

Tess reached for her camera and shot more pictures to document the empty gravesite. 'I sifted through this soil and didn't find any evidence. No bullet, jewelry, or anything that might help with identification.'

'The bones will tell me more,' Dr. Butler said.

'When do you think you can open the second mound?' Gage said.

Dr. Butler considered the question. 'I should return tomorrow by early afternoon.'

Tess wiped sweat from the back of her forehead with a hand that trembled with fatigue. 'That late?' Tess said.

'I won't be any good to anyone if I'm exhausted. Neither will you,' Dr. Butler said. 'Do us both a favor and get some rest tonight.'

Gage nodded. 'I'll post uniforms to watch the area.'

'Good,' Alex said. 'I don't need any curiosity seekers digging into the mound and destroying evidence.'

Gage slid his hand into his pocket and rattled his keys. 'I have a theory about this body.'

He arched a brow. 'Really?'

'A missing persons case I worked a couple of years ago. She knew the Thorntons.'

Tess folded her arms. 'Really?'

'I've already spoken to her dentist. He's sending you dental records in the morning.'

'Then I'll check to see if you're right or wrong,' Dr. Butler said.

It was nearly midnight when Adrianna set down the bin of journals and reached for the front door of her house. She dug her keys out of her purse and slid her key in the lock. To her surprise it was unlocked. She paused. Damn. Had she forgotten to lock the door this morning? Maybe a realtor had stopped by and shown the house? Whatever the reason, an unlocked door jangled her nerves.

She hesitated. Listened. There was nothing. Shaking off the jab of fear, she pushed open the door and pulled the bin inside to the foyer.

Her home was older, built in the forties, and by Thornton or Barrington standards it was barely a cottage. But she loved the place from the moment she'd first spotted it one Sunday afternoon. Plaster walls, arched doorways, and hardwood floors flowed throughout the house. It was loaded with charm.

She'd bought the house using a small inheritance from her father after she'd sold the Riverside Drive home she'd shared with Craig. When she'd moved in, Craig had been in the nursing home for six months. She'd needed a distraction so she'd set her sights on the house. Not only did she gut the kitchen, but also she had all the hardwood floors sanded and the walls painted a soft yellow.

She'd not had the money to buy new furniture so she'd started scanning antique markets and yard sales. Each

Saturday morning she'd risen before dawn and hit the circuit. By ten she was at the nursing home where she spent the rest of her Saturdays sitting in Craig's room and reading articles from his favorite magazines.

Often after a visit to Craig's bedside, she'd return home and spend endless hours stripping paint from the stone fireplace or sanding woodwork.

She'd turned an outdated, dark house into a sanctuary that had become an island of sanity. Leaving this house would be hard because it had been her sole haven for the last two and a half years.

Beside the black lacquered front door was a large cast-iron kettle filled with red and purple winter pansies and cascading ivy. She retrieved her mail from the brass box by the front door and slowly flipped through the envelopes.

Bills. Always bills. She'd called her New York client, Pauline Collins, and told her she'd not be able to make their appointment. She'd spent the better part of the next half hour convincing the woman that the colors that she'd chosen would be perfect.

She moved through the house flipping on lights as she made her way to the kitchen. A gray slate floor and buttery yellow walls accentuated honey maple cabinets, granite countertops, and stainless steel appliances. In the center of the room was an island and above it a pot rack filled with well-worn stainless steel pots. It was a cook's kitchen, one she'd spent hours in, baking when she felt stress or tired.

The last envelope was hand addressed to her and had a standard Forever stamp in the corner. Curious, she tore open the back flap and pulled out a coupon for cologne. The information was ordinary and not very interesting but it was the scent on the card that hit her. *Armani*. Craig's aftershave. The hairs on the back of her neck rose. She raised the card to her nose. She inhaled.

The scent was unmistakable.

How many times had his aftershave clung to her body after they'd made love? To his clothes? His pillow? After the accident, she'd not been able to launder his shirts because she'd have lost the scent that had comforted her so much.

Now, it brought no peace. Only sadness and loss.

Adrianna took a step back, her throat burning with unshed tears. What were the chances of receiving this?

A few days ago, she'd not have thought twice about it but after the anniversary card, and the unlocked front door, she couldn't help but wonder if this was another anonymous cruelty.

That had to be the explanation. She glanced at the kitchen counter and searched for a business card that signaled a visit from her realtor. It was there. By the stove.

She grabbed the kitchen phone and dialed. Voicemail picked up immediately. 'Catherine, this is Adrianna. Just checking to see if you showed the house today? You left the house unlocked. Please be more careful. Thanks.'

She moved to the back door that led to a small patio and opened it. Cool night air swirled inside. The breeze carried the scent of the aftershave from the card and soon the fragrance had vanished as if it had never been there.

Adrianna tossed the card in the trash can outside and

rubbed her hand over the goose bumps on her arm. Nervous laughter bubbled in her chest. 'It's a freaking perfume advertisement. Get a grip.'

The day's nightmarish events had clearly taken their toll.

As she shrugged off her coat, the cell phone in her purse rang. The sound made her jump. 'Idiot.' She laughed as she dug it out of her purse.

Expecting to see her realtor's number, she was disappointed to see her mother's number. Squaring her shoulders, she flipped open the phone. 'Hello.'

'Adrianna.' There was no missing the trademark panic in her mother's voice. Ever since Adrianna could remember, there was always some crisis to be managed.

She pressed her fingers to her forehead, too tired to rehash last night. 'Hey, Mom.'

'I'm sorry about last night.'

'That's okay.' She moved to the fridge and pulled out a half-full bottle of Chardonnay.

'I've been so worried about you. I'm sorry we fought yesterday morning.'

'Me, too, Mom, me too.'

'You went to the Thornton house today?' Tension etched each of Margaret's words.

'Yes. And it all went fine.' No good would come from telling her mother about today's discovery at the Thornton place. Last night's trip to the ER affirmed that her mother didn't handle conflict well.

'You would tell me if things weren't good.' Worry dripped from each word.

Despite all their problems, her mother did know when she hedged the truth. If not blood, a lifetime of memories linked them forever. 'Yes, of course,' she lied. 'There's nothing to worry about.'

She pulled a glass from the cabinet, uncorked the bottle, and poured herself a glass.

'When are you coming to see me again, Adrianna?'

'Soon, Mom, soon.'

'When?'

'I don't know, Mom. Soon. There's a lot to wrap up with the land sale and I've got a lot of work at the shop. I'm just swamped right now.'

'I miss working at the shop. We had such fun working together.' She added an inflection to the end of the sentence, a clear cue she needed reinforcement.

'I know.' Adrianna had suggested they open the store together after her father had died four years ago, fearing her mother would slip into another deep depression. Margaret was an artist at heart and the interior design shop appealed. No denying the woman had an excellent eye for color and detail.

Initially, both had worked hard to launch the business and the shop had soared, but Margaret had started to fade after about eight months. The day-to-day pressures of work had gotten the better of her and she'd retreated for a time. During Margaret's hiatus, the brunt of the business had fallen on Adrianna's shoulders, and that coupled with Craig's accident had meant long days. Her mother had managed to get herself together after about a year and returned to work for a while, but in January the adoption mess had been exposed and Margaret had suffered a major setback.

If Barrington Designs was going to survive it would

have to be without Margaret. In February, Adrianna had hired help.

'I want to come back to work.' Her mother's voice shook with emotion.

Adrianna gripped the phone. Now wasn't the time to have this conversation. 'What does your doctor say?'

'He said maybe next month.'

'Then let's give it more time.' She took a sip of wine, savoring the cool flavor in her mouth.

'But I can come back?'

'It depends. I've told you I might not keep the store.'

'That's right. But I was helpful with your designs. I'm good with colors.'

'You are. And if you can help, that would be great.'

'Thank you.' Margaret paused. 'Adrianna, I love you.'

The words cut into Adrianna. *Then why did you lie to me all those years?* She closed her eyes. As angry as she was at Margaret, she couldn't be cruel by denying her a response. 'I love you, too, Mom.'

'I pulled out your wedding album today. You were so beautiful and Craig was so handsome.'

'What made you look at the album?'

'You haven't forgotten your anniversary, have you? It's today.'

'No, I didn't forget.' A thought occurred to her and before she thought she said, 'You didn't send me an anniversary card, did you?'

'No. Did you get a card?'

'I think it was just a mistake. Nothing to worry about.' *Love always, Craig.* It had been a cruel joke.

'You're sure?'

She regretted opening this can of worms. 'Yes. Really. Hey, I've got to go. I've an early wake-up call.'

'Of course. You will come and see me soon?'

'Yes. I promise.'

Adrianna hung up. The second and third sips of wine eased through her body, warming her. Twelve twenty-one. It was after midnight.

It was September twenty-seventh.

Her anniversary had passed.

Adrianna pressed the cold glass to her temple.

She'd survived another painful milestone. 'Thank God.'

Craig sat in his car across the street from Hudson's house eating one of the cookies he'd snagged from Adrianna's kitchen. In the last few weeks, he'd taken to entering her house when she wasn't there because he loved touching her things. This time, he'd left the card in her mailbox and intentionally left the front door unlocked. He wanted her to have a hint of his presence. 'Soon, my love.'

To think, just three years ago before the accident, he'd not have had the stones to do half the things he was doing today. In the pre-accident days he was so weak, so ineffective. So worried about what people thought of him. So spineless.

But no more. The accident had obliterated the wimp he had been and transformed him into a better, stronger *man*. Now there was only the newer, stronger Craig who took charge of situations. He no longer wrung his hands and worried about rules or the law. He did what needed to be done. He took charge.

Like now.

Bright moonlight filtered through the trees as Craig watched Hudson's house. It was bungalow style with a stone façade, thick porch supports, and a low-pitched roof. The flowerbeds were empty but the lawn neatly trimmed. The lights in the downstairs living room were on and Hudson's car parked in the driveway.

Night air, damp with humidity made the car's interior hot. God, but he couldn't wait for winter and the cold, dry weather to arrive.

Craig watched as Gage moved through the rooms on the first floor of his house. The cop had taken off his coat jacket, loosened his tie, and rolled up the sleeves of his white dress shirt. He paced, as if waiting for someone.

Craig curled calloused fingers into a fist. Adrianna had never told anyone about her affair with Hudson, but he had known. One Sunday afternoon, he'd accidentally seen Adrianna walking hand in hand with Hudson. Rage had rolled over him like a tidal wave even as sadness banded his chest like a vise.

He hadn't wanted to watch. But he had.

He had hated the idea of them together. And he knew nothing he could have said to her would have changed her mind about Hudson. So he'd gone to Margaret Barrington and told her about his chance sighting. And she'd done as he'd expected. She'd convinced Adrianna to return to the life she was intended to lead.

Now Adrianna was getting her life back on track and he was preparing to show her how he'd changed. This was supposed to be their time. He wanted to tell Adrianna about the women in the graves. How he'd killed them all for her. Now was time for all the secrets to be revealed to Adrianna and the world.

But Hudson had returned and threatened to ruin it all. *Bastard.*

Craig glanced down at the gold signet ring on his left pinky. The tarnished gold band squeezed his finger, begging to be resized. Still, he loved the ring and all that it symbolized. He traced his thumb over the letter *T* etched into the top.

A VW bug pulled into Hudson's driveway and rumbled to a stop. A young woman got out. Craig leaned closer, narrowed his gaze so that he could see better. The woman was Hudson's sister. Jessie. A college student.

The girl hurried to the front door with a basket of dirty laundry. As she fished a key from her pocket, Hudson moved to the door and opened it. He took the basket from her and said something that made her laugh.

Jessie was a pretty girl. Her hair was too dark for his tastes but hair was easy to change. What he liked about her was her spirit. She was a fighter. A bolt of restless energy surged through Craig and his body hardened.

He thought about touching Jessie's skin and of using his new camera and putting her in his next movie.

Despite the urge, he kept his desires at bay. It was enough now to know that he could take Jessie whenever he wanted.

And as long as Hudson left his Adrianna alone, he'd leave Jessie alone.

With the Thornton land nearly sold and the bodies gone, there was nothing now that anchored him to the past. There was only the future.

In his future he saw Adrianna.

Sweet, sweet Adrianna.

When they finally reunited, the moment would be so perfect.

'Soon, Adrianna, soon. One more actress to take my stage and then it will be your turn.'

Chapter Nine

When Gage arrived at the state medical examiner's office, his eyes itched with fatigue. His sister Jessie had been running late last night and hadn't shown up until after midnight. Extra hours at the hotel, she'd explained. 'Can't say no to the hours, bro. Money is too good.'

He didn't like her working so hard. It was his job to put her through school, his job to worry. But Jessie had come wired like him and no amount of coaxing or prodding had convinced her to give up her job in the Madison Hotel's catering department.

Pride welled.

Gage liked seeing her, if only for ten minutes. He was far too protective, worried more than he should, but he did his best not to let his fears show. And after the grave excavation yesterday, that had been a feat unto itself.

He rubbed the back of his neck as he moved down the tiled hallway. The place had a sick sweet smell that the antiseptic didn't quite eradicate.

After he'd touched base with Jessie, he'd pulled out his files and notes on the Rhonda Minor case. He'd paid particular attention to the notes he'd taken on his interview with Thornton. In the bottom right margin of the notes he'd written the word *Slick* and had circled it several times.

He pushed through the metal doors of the autopsy room. Tiled floor to ceiling, the room had several large metal sinks with spray faucets on one wall and on the other metal counters filled with a variety of instruments.

A body, draped in a white sheet, lay on the medical examiner's stainless steel table positioned in the center of the room over a floor drain. Behind the table stood Dr. Alex Butler. Across from him was a heavyset young woman who wore her sandy blond hair in a ponytail. Her name was Kate, Gage remembered. She was another one of Dr. Butler's assistants. Apparently, it took several assistants to keep up with his pace.

Dr. Butler glanced up over wire-rimmed glasses as the door whooshed closed behind Gage. 'I'll be with you in a moment.'

Gage slid his hand into his pocket, annoyed that he'd have to linger in this room. 'Sure.'

Dr. Butler, with a gloved hand, reached into the water and pulled out what looked like a second glove. But it wasn't a glove. It was skin from a body.

Gage's stomach rolled. 'What the hell are you doing?'

'I've softened the skin from a dead man's hand in fabric softener. With luck, I'll be able to slip it on my fingers and get a print.'

Gage watched as Dr. Butler maneuvered his own hand into a dead man's skin as if it were a glove. He could see that Kate had set out an inkpad and a fingerprint card. She came around the table and gently guided Dr. Butler's hand to the inkpad and carefully rolled a print in the pre-printed box. She repeated this with each finger.

'Prints any good?' Gage said, glad now he'd only had coffee for breakfast.

'Looks like it might work.' Dr. Butler glanced at Kate as he pulled the second skin off his hand and dropped it in a stainless steel bowl. 'Kate, can you get those sent off for me?'

'Will do, Doc.'

Dr. Butler washed his hands in a large galvanized sink. 'Well, you were right.'

'How's that?' Hiding the snap of irritation, Gage moved across the tile floor, stopping inches short of the autopsy table.

'Vega dropped off Rhonda Minor's dental records about an hour ago. The bridgework and the fillings in my Jane Doe match Rhonda Minor's perfectly.'

Gage didn't feel any sense of triumph, only a grim sense of relief. Having a name for the victim put him one step closer to nailing Thornton. 'All right.'

'I'm headed out to the Thornton estate in about an hour. Should start work on the second grave by noon.'

'Good.'

The doors opened with a jerk and Gage turned to see Vega. The detective couldn't have gotten more than a couple of hours' sleep but the guy looked bright-eyed and ready to go. He had a to-go tray holding three coffees in his hand. 'Got that ID?'

'Doc just confirmed it's Minor,' Gage said.

'No food in the lab,' Dr. Butler said. 'Back in the hallway.'

Vega glanced at his coffee cups as if he were sending

old friends away. 'Sure thing, Doc.' He left, returned seconds later empty-handed.

Dr. Butler nodded. 'Thanks.'

Vega shook his head. 'You're a hard man, Doc, separating a man from his coffee this early in the morning.'

Gage drew in a measured breath. 'So you think a gunshot to the head killed her?'

Dr. Butler nodded. 'I had a look at the bones last night. As you know, the skull was shattered by Miller's shovel. I pieced it back together and it appears one gunshot entered her brain at the base of her skull and came out of her right eye socket. She was dead before she hit the ground.'

'Tess didn't find a bullet,' Gage said.

'No. Likely it's lodged in a wall or tree near where she was killed.'

Vega rolled his shoulders to release tension. 'No soft tissue remains.'

'None,' Dr. Butler said.

'That unusual?'

'Not considering the hot, moist summers we've had the last couple of years. Perfect conditions for decomposition. It's impossible to tell if any kind of sexual assault occurred. I can tell you that her right hand was broken. It was a significant break that probably happened a few days before her death.'

'How can you tell?' Gage said.

'Signs that the bone was healing and starting to knit.' He moved to the top of the table where the body lay and reached for a saw. 'As you can see, I'm backed up and I've just not had a chance yet to do a thorough workup.'

Gage shifted his gaze away from the saw. 'Tess has called me twice this morning. She's anxious to begin work.'

'So am I. I'd have been out there at first light if not for this autopsy.'

Gage noted the bags under Dr. Butler's eyes. 'When is the last time you had a full eight hours?'

Dr. Butler scrunched his face in thought. 'High school. No, elementary school, I think.'

Adrianna arrived at the Thornton estate just after eleven. She'd spent part of the night arranging Frances's ten ledgers in chronological order and leafing through the yellowed pages of the first and second ones, which dated back almost forty years. In a neat, controlled handwriting Frances had kept meticulous details of the daily expenses of the estate. *Fresh flowers. Robert's favorite wines. Art. Painting. New furniture.* The only thing she'd gleaned from those first two ledgers, which spanned five years, was that Frances and Robert had expensive tastes.

After reading until one, she'd turned off the light and fallen into a hard sleep. The alarm had gone off at five and she'd forced herself out of bed and into the shower. After coffee and an omelet, she'd headed to the office, cleared up a few details, and then headed east to the estate.

As she pulled through the front gates of the Colonies, she realized just how hopeful she'd been yesterday morning when she'd driven out here. The house and land were sold and still the Thorntons had found a way to hold on to her.

The honk of a horn had her starting and looking in her rearview mirror. A Wells Moving van pulled up behind her car. She smiled, instantly relaxing.

Ben and Dwayne Wells got out of the front cab. Both were tall burly men – like father like son. Ben wore his dark hair slicked back and a goatee accentuated his full face. He had thick forearms and a chest that stretched under a yellow Wells Moving T-shirt.

Dwayne was in his sixties and an older version of his son. 'Good morning, Adrianna. How are you doing after yesterday's excitement?'

She grinned. 'Excitement. Dwayne, I can always count on you to put a positive spin on things.'

Dwayne laughed. 'I do try. Cops said anything more to you?'

'Nothing.'

'They came by and talked to Marie and me last night. We had nothing but good things to say about you and Craig.'

'Thanks, Dwayne.'

Ben held out his hand to her. 'Morning. Good day to move some art.'

She accepted Ben's hand, noting his strength. 'Hey, Ben.'

'So,' Dwayne said. 'You want the art moved to the auction house?'

'That's right. After that you can get the furniture to Mazur's storage facility.'

'Cops give the all clear?' Ben said.

'They haven't secured the house and didn't say I couldn't move furniture.'

'Better to get forgiveness rather than permission, I always say,' Dwayne said.

Adrianna suspected Gage was just as short on forgiveness as permission.

'How long will it take?'

'These old pieces can't be rushed and they are heavy as lead. I've got extra men coming in about an hour, but it's gonna take time to move most of the pieces.'

With the graveyard relocation suspended, it didn't much matter. 'Sounds good.'

'We'll do an extra, extra good job for you, Adrianna,' Ben said.

Adrianna returned his smile. 'You always do.'

Ben grinned and lumbered into the house.

Dwayne watched his son move up the stairs. 'He's good at heart but he's not the brightest star in the sky.'

'He's always been polite and respectful when Wells Moving has worked for Barrington Designs.'

Adrianna had suspected Ben had slight developmental delays but had never asked.

'That's good to hear. Marie and I are always drilling into him that he's got to be polite. The guy is as strong as an ox and doesn't have much common sense.'

'He lives with you? I thought he'd gotten his own place last year.'

'He did. It's the apartment in our basement. He's doing real well with it.' Pride shone in his eyes.

The old man loved his son. It was one of the traits that drew Adrianna to Dwayne. 'He's lucky to have you.'

A hint of color tinted the older man's cheeks as if he wasn't accustomed to compliments. 'We'll load the pictures this morning and deliver them to the auction house. If we're lucky we can take our first load of furniture today as well.'

Knowing some progress was being made soothed Adrianna's nerves. 'And the auction house isn't giving you any trouble?'

'Nope. All the insurance paperwork cleared without a problem.'

'Great. At least I can check something off the list.'

He frowned. 'So what's the deal with those graves? Freaky stuff.'

She sighed. 'You're telling me.'

A bead of sweat trickled down his left temple and he swiped it away. 'It's going to cause a lot of delays.'

'Has news reached town yet?'

'No. Hudson's done a good job of keeping the lid on things. I was in the coffee shop in town this morning and not a word was mentioned.'

'Good.'

'It's real good. There could be trouble when word does leak out. Some feel like it's bad luck when you disturb the dead.'

The card on her windshield and the scent of Craig's aftershave still had her unsettled. 'Are you sure no one knows? Someone put a card on my windshield yesterday. It was an anniversary card and signed *Craig*.'

Dwayne frowned. 'Damn. I'm sorry. Bad joke.'

'And it's not funny. When folks do find out and start asking, make sure you tell everyone that I'm not going to be intimidated. I'm not backing down.'

I can't back down.

'Some folks are a little backward in these parts. They have a few drinks and then everyone is talking tough. They'll get over it.' He pulled off his cap and smoothed a gnarled hand over his bald head. 'I do wonder about that Dr. Heckman. If there ever was a nut.'

She was a bit surprised at Dwayne's appraisal. 'He's

passionate about his cause. And I do sympathize, but he's been ordered to stay off the land. If you see him, run him off.'

Dwayne sniffed. 'Consider it done. I'll tell Marie to do the same.'

Knowing Dwayne and Marie were behind her warmed Adrianna. These last couple of years, she'd been on her own. At times, she was terrified. But she'd grown up. Grown stronger. But when Dwayne or someone else offered help, she took it. Occasionally, it was nice not to carry all the weight.

'Marie called me and said the cops arrived minutes ago. They're digging into that second mound.'

'Did she say if they've found another body or not?'

'She says everyone's tight-lipped about it.'

'Right.'

'Marie says Hudson has arrived.'

'The guy gets around.' She tried to keep her voice neutral, but the mention of his name tipped her a little off balance.

'Hudson reminds me of a dog with a bone. He's not leaving this property or any one of us alone until he's squeezed out every answer.'

'I've no doubt.'

Tess had only been able to grab a couple of hours of sleep after she'd left the medical examiner's office. She'd been jazzed when she pushed through the front door of her small apartment, cluttered with books, magazines, and a couple of weeks' worth of laundry. Tidying had made sense but hadn't appealed, so she'd sat up until three a.m. watching an old John Wayne classic and eating rocky road ice cream.

Now the lack of sleep was biting her in the ass. Too bad she'd passed on the fourth cup of coffee.

She groaned when she saw the collection of cop cars. There had to be eight or nine. Crap. Didn't these guys have work to do?

Gage sat in his car, his phone pressed to his ear. He waved to her but didn't get out. She waved back, but couldn't scrounge a smile.

'Hey, Kier, what do you think you'll find today?' The question came from one of the cops. Brady somebody.

'Can't say, man.' She called half the guys on the force *man* because she couldn't remember names so well. She remembered the emotions cops showed at a crime scene. At a tough scene she could feel emotions rolling around her like the ocean, but the names were forgotten almost as soon as she heard them.

Dr. Alex Butler was one of the few she couldn't read. A cool blank slate that didn't give her a hint as to what was happening on the inside. She couldn't decide if that was a good thing or a bad thing.

'So you think it's another victim?' Brady said.

'Your guess is as good as mine.' That wasn't true. She was certain something or someone had been buried in the spot.

'Any word on cause of death on the first victim?' another said.

'Nope.' She didn't break stride as she passed them.

'Can we get a closer look?'

'Stay out of my crime scene.'

'Just a peek?' He was goading her to see if he could stir a reaction. 'Pretty please.'

'Bite me.' She'd learned long ago not to show any softness in this business.

Laughter rumbled through the cops until Gage got out of his car, and suddenly the men got quiet.

Gage moved toward her, his cowboy boots eating up the distance. Even in a suit, he always looked out of place here, like he belonged on the open range. 'You're in a sweet mood this morning.'

'Tell me what I don't know,' she said.

Gage cocked an eyebrow, clearly put off by her tone. Tess understood that she was a hard person to like. Abrasive was her stock in trade. But she'd decided long ago she'd rather be respected than liked. Nice people just got run over.

'Jesus, it's going to be a circus today,' she said.

'Hopefully, it'll die down soon. Everybody here has a job to do.'

'Just keep them out of my crime scene.'

'Yes, ma'am.'

'What about the press?'

'No sign yet. But that's a matter of time. Too many people know about this.'

'Right.'

'Dr. Butler is here.'

'I figured I'd beat him.'

'Not today.'

She nodded and turned toward the crime scene. The doctor was already at the second mound, oblivious to everyone else. He'd assembled his digging tools and laid them out neatly beside the site. He reminded her of a surgeon. Head bent, long fingers tucked into the pockets of his khakis as he studied the earth.

She pushed a loose strand of hair behind her ear and ducked under the tape. 'Dr. Butler.'

'Tess Kier.' He glanced up at her, his gaze accessing and critical. 'Did you sleep at all last night?'

Defenses rose. 'You saying I look bad?'

'Yes.'

His honesty caught her off guard. 'Boy, you know how to make a girl feel good.'

'I'm stating the obvious. You look exhausted.'

'Don't you ever sleep?'

'I don't need much sleep. Three hours seems to be my limit. You, I suspect, need six to eight.'

Nine was better, but it had been a while since she'd enjoyed a full night. She rubbed itchy eyes under her glasses. Too bad she wasn't a robot like the good doctor. She needed her Z's. That should have made her mad but instead she laughed. 'You always tell the truth?'

'Yes.'

'Can't say I always want to hear it, especially when it comes to my appearance, but if I had to choose between brutally honest and a guy who told me only what I wanted to hear, I'll take brutally honest.' Her ex had been a smooth number. Made her feel like a million bucks. And in the end had mangled the hell out of her heart when he'd started sleeping with one of his graduate students.

'Good. I think.' He shifted his attention back to the uneven ground and the spotty vegetation. 'Today is going to be long, the process as slow as yesterday.'

'I suspected as much. Did you identify the first skeleton?'

'Yes.' He knelt and checked his tools. 'Hudson was right.'

Knowing that one of the victims had been identified lifted her mood a fraction. 'That's something, at least. One step closer to catching her killer.'

'Let's hope.'

'Where do we start?'

'I start scraping the dirt. You sift. Just like yesterday.'

'Hold tight while I take a few more pictures.'

'You photographed yesterday.'

She raised the camera to her face and started clicking. 'You'd be surprised how the time of day can change perspective.' And honestly, she felt a little less intimidated by Dr. Butler hiding behind the lens of a camera.

Dr. Butler glanced at a tree that grew very close to the site. 'We may be in luck with this tree.'

'How so?'

'The roots. If the roots have grown up through a skeleton it may help us figure out how long the body was in the ground.'

She gave the guy points for that one. 'Clever, Doc.'

'You called me Alex the other day. Why the shift back?'

For most she kept it casual and had no problem with first names. 'I don't know. With you I think it should be more formal.'

'Why?'

'I don't know. Maybe because Alex makes you seem more human. And honestly, you're so smart it's, well, not all that human.'

He studied her, his gaze unreadable. 'I get that a lot.'

'What? The not human stuff?'

'Since I was a kid.'

Tess imagined him as a kid, fending off other children who had more mouth than sense. Kids like she'd been. She suddenly felt like a schmuck. 'You didn't like school?'

He picked up a trowel. 'I never really experienced normal school all that long. I was so far ahead of the normal curriculum that I transferred up several grades in the first year. When I found classes I loved, I was a good ten or twelve years younger than the other students.'

'How'd the older kids treat you?'

'Some nice. Some not so nice.'

Again just the facts, but they packed more emotion than any lament. 'Looks like you turned out all right.'

'I think so.'

She laughed. 'Modesty is another trait I'll have to add to your merits.' Shaking her head, she started to snap pictures. 'A few more shots and we can get to work.'

Alex offered a slight nod. Within fifteen minutes, Alex lay on his side beside the grave scraping soil from the surface. As he collected soil, he dumped it into her sieve. This process went on for over an hour. Each time he dumped fresh dirt into her sieve, he glanced at her as if he expected her to give up. As much as her muscles ached and as tired as she was, she wouldn't quit. Her instructor at the academy had said what she lacked in physical strength she'd always made up for with mental toughness.

When the silence became too much she heard herself asking, 'You strike me as a guy who is more suited for the library rather than field work.'

'I prefer being outside.'

'Play any sports?'

'Run. Swim to stay in shape. You?'

'Same.'

Again, they lapsed into silence. Both continued to work without complaint and within a couple of hours, they'd sifted through nearly ten inches of dirt. The other cops had lost interest. Most had realized the excitement wasn't going to happen immediately.

'So are you as smart as everyone says?' Tess never had trouble asking a question, even if common sense dictated that she keep her mouth shut.

'I don't know. How smart do they say I am?'

'Like Doogie Howser smart.'

'Who is Doogie Howser?'

'Didn't you watch television in the nineties?'

'I don't watch television.'

'Of course. Doogie Howser was a boy genius. Became a surgical resident when he was fourteen.'

'I was fourteen when I entered my residency.'

There was no hint of humor in his voice. 'You are Doogie Howser smart.'

He shrugged. 'Okay.'

'Doesn't it drive you a little nuts hanging around regular folk?' This question had chewed on her since the first day she'd met him.

Alex shook his head, never taking his eyes off the dirt. 'I don't follow.'

'When I hang out with my eight-month-old nephew Jack, I love it. He's sweet and good-natured. But after a few hours I start to want more adult conversation.'

'Reasonable.'

'Do you ever feel like that with the rest of us?'

'The rest of us?'

'The rest of the world that doesn't have a two hundred plus IQ?'

'Do you only talk to forensic people? Is that all you like to discuss?'

'No.'

'I'm not just interested in quantum physics and autopsies.'

She shrugged. 'I just think you'd get bored with someone who wasn't as smart as you.'

He looked up. 'What brought this up?'

She scraped a layer of dirt off the earth. 'I dated a guy back in California. He was kind of a mentor. So, so smart. I thought we'd be together forever.' She was amazed how the emotion still burned her throat. 'In the end he left me for a girl genius. Said I bored him.' Good Lord, why had she just admitted that? Even her family didn't know about Philip.

Alex shrugged. 'Maybe the guy wasn't as smart as you give him credit for. Frankly, I can't imagine you ever being boring.'

For some reason that made her blush. 'Abrasive, loud, and sometimes funny, but you're right, I am never ever boring. I'm not sure if that's a good thing or not.' He didn't comment, frowned as if he were thinking. What the devil was going on in that computer brain?

Gently, she sifted more dirt.

Then his trowel hit something hard. She glanced down and her heart jumped into high gear. This moment made the backbreaking work seem unimportant. He set down his trowel and picked up a paintbrush. He started to dust the dirt away.

'You've found something,' Tess said. There was no missing the excitement in her voice.

'I think so.' He started to brush dirt very gently. Slowly the earth melted away and the shape of a skull emerged. 'A cranium.'

He nodded. 'Front section.'

He continued to brush away the dirt and within another twenty minutes the entire face of the skeleton was revealed. Open eye sockets stared up at them. A slack jaw with rows of even white teeth appeared to be laughing. A root twisted up through the mouth opening.

'Female,' Alex said. 'And I see a gunshot hole in the left temple.'

'Any theories on how long she's been here?'

'I'm going to have to dig out more. But based on the soil staining on the bone, at least as long as the first victim.'

'Gage!' she shouted. 'Get your butt over here.'

Chapter Ten

Wednesday, September 27, 1 p.m.

Adrianna delayed going to the gravesite until the paintings were loaded onto the truck. She had no control over the police, and if Craig's illness had taught her anything, it was to focus on what she could control.

When Dwayne and Ben drove off with the paintings in their truck she drove the half mile to the gravesite. The place that had once unnerved her because it was so quiet. Now it buzzed with activity.

She parked and glanced toward the yellow crime scene tape and the people gathered around. Gage stood in the middle, his hands on his hips as if he were the captain of a ship.

Out here he appeared so stiff and cold, his emotions buried as deep as the bones in the ground. Adrianna sighed, unwillingly remembering the guy who liked to fish and tell jokes.

Four years ago he'd been anything but stone. It had been the summer. She'd just broken up with Craig. It had been a clean break and a fresh start. For the first time in years she'd felt happy.

The Saturday that came to mind had been a hot evening in June. She could feel the sweat stealing down her back and between her breasts. She and Gage had been on the edge of a pier that jutted into the James River. He'd been trying to teach her the finer points of fishing. She'd been bored beyond tears.

A large white floppy hat shaded her eyes and hid most of her face from the sun. She'd been staring at a rock in the water when he'd said, 'I can see I've got you wrapped around my finger.'

A smile lifted the edge of her lips as she kicked the edge of the cool water with red manicured toes. 'I wish I could say yes.'

His eyes danced with amusement. 'How long have you been faking it?'

She chuckled. 'Thirty minutes after we sat down.'

'Two hours.' He started to reel in his line. 'Sorry. I thought you'd like this.'

'I did at first. It's lovely here. And I want to care about catching fish. But I just can't find it in me. Especially when I know there is a lovely seafood shop on Patterson. Their stuff is so fresh you can smell the sea.'

He cocked his head toward her. 'Doesn't get much fresher than this.'

'I agree. Just seems like a lot of work.'

Gage grabbed his hook from the water and fastened it to his rod. 'The fun part is the hunt.'

'I've heard fishing is a Zen kinda thing.'

His gaze dipped to her white T-shirt, now damp and translucent with perspiration. He set the rod down and leaned toward her, his face so close she could feel his breath on her face. 'I don't know about Zen. I just know fishing.'

She moistened her lips, her gaze dropping to the V of his shirt. Dark chest hair curled on tanned, glistening skin. Her heart beat faster. They'd been dating all of two weeks and her vow not to jump into another relationship suddenly didn't seem so important.

'Ms. Barrington, if I didn't know better I'd think your thoughts are a bit tawdry.'

Up until now they'd shared polite kisses. Hand holding. He'd treated her like fine china. She'd appreciated that at first but now didn't want him to handle her with kid gloves. She moistened her lips. 'I'm afraid they are.'

'I'm shocked.' His deep accent dripped from each word. He leaned closer. 'Mind if I kiss you, Ms. Barrington?'

Words stuck in her throat. She nodded.

Gage pulled her hat off her head and watched as her hair tumbled around her shoulders. He cupped her face in his hands and kissed her on the lips. He tasted salty and though his lips were soft, the stubble on his chin rubbed the smooth skin of her face.

A sensation of emotions and desires made her body throb. Her hand rose to his chest. His heartbeat hammered under her fingertips.

A groan rumbled in his chest and he leaned forward, pressing her back against the hard pier. His erection pushed against her thigh and all rational thoughts scampered away like a band of traitors. She threaded her fingers through his hair and kissed him back, surprising him with her intensity.

This wasn't what she'd expected, but still she heard herself saying, 'Make love to me.'

The fading light caught the intensity of his gaze. 'You sure?'

Now or never. Jump or dive. 'Yes.'

'I'm happy to oblige.'

He kissed her on the lips but soon his kisses roamed lower to the hollow of her neck and then to the hardened peak of her breasts, which pressed against the thin white cotton of her shirt. He sucked her nipple through the fabric, dampening the cloth more and sending thousands of jolts through her body. Her body softened, moistened, and soon his rough hand slid up her thigh under the short Madras skirt. He'd touched her panties, teased her before he pulled them down past her ankles. Whatever control he'd nurtured had vanished and the raw desire burning in him blazed.

He mounted her and with unsteady, fevered hands she undid the snap on his shorts. She was hardly a virgin. She knew what was what, but still had never felt such a longing for a man.

She slid her hand over his erection and he groaned.

'You are too much for me.'

'In a good way?'

'In a very good way.' From his back pocket he pulled out a condom and ripped the foil package.

'Am I that obvious?'

'No, ma'am. Not at all. This was just wishful thinking.'

He slid on the condom. In the next moment he was poised to enter. He hesitated as if to give her one final chance to change her mind and then he pushed inside her, filling her and overwhelming her with a delicious intensity. She wrapped her legs around his waist.

In the fading light, they'd matched each other stroke for stroke, finding their release in a blinding jolt.

*

Now, as if Gage sensed she was thinking about him, he turned. The lines on his face deepened with his frown. He moved toward her in even, unhurried strides.

She held her ground. 'Did you find anything else?'

He stopped less than a foot from her and the breeze caught his masculine scent. 'I can't really say at this point.'

'Which means you have found something.' She held up her hand to silence any rebuttal she knew would follow. 'I know you can't say anything. I remember that part of your job.'

Gage rested his hands on his hips, revealing the gun holstered to his side. 'Then why are you here?'

To say I'm sorry. To tell you I shouldn't have allowed Mom and Frances to persuade me to leave. She heard herself say, 'How long will you all be out here?'

Cynicism sharpened his gaze. 'Worried about your money?'

'Yes.'

He pulled in a breath, his nostrils flaring. 'Always looking out for yourself.'

The accusation hit hard. 'I don't believe Craig killed that woman.'

Gage leaned toward her a fraction. 'Or that you married a murderer?'

'I wasn't that wrong about him.'

'Hey, we all misjudge people.' Bitterness sharpened the words. 'I've been known to get it wrong before.'

'Meaning you read *me* wrong.'

'Now that you brought it up, yeah. I always figured I was good at reading the signals, Adrianna. But you faked

138

me out better than anyone ever has, and that includes my ex-wife. Which is saying a lot.'

I'm sorry. 'Are you going to hold that against me during this investigation?'

Gray eyes narrowed. 'The only thing I care about is solving this case.'

'You sure about that?'

'Yeah. I'm damn sure.' Anger rolled off him like heat from an inferno.

Adrianna raised her chin. 'Good. Do us both a favor. Solve this case so I can get on with my life.'

On legs about to give way, she turned and moved back to her car. Feeling his gaze on her, she didn't dare look in the rearview mirror. Eyes fixed on the road ahead, she drove back to the city in a daze. She arrived in time for the two scheduled meetings with only minutes to shake off her mood and get organized.

The next few hours buzzed with client comments as she presented her designs. After those meetings, it was a mad dash to a scheduled visit to a furniture maker to discuss why several orders had fallen behind schedule. More calls and text messages on the upcoming charity auction kept her brain humming for several more hours.

By the time she was driving home it was after seven and she felt as if she'd gone several rounds in a boxing ring. Nothing would please her more than to go home and retreat to a hot bath with a glass of wine.

But as she pulled off the interstate onto Broad Street, her mind drifted to the conversation she'd had with her mother last night. *When are you coming? Soon.*

Every muscle in her body screamed for silence and rest and still she found herself turning off Cary Street to the side road where her mother lived.

The homes were old Richmond. Brick, compact manicured lawns, and oak trees. She turned into the crushed stone of her mother's driveway. Her keys jangling, she felt her stomach knot as she got out of the car and moved to the front door. When she'd been a kid, she'd walk in the front door and shout to Estelle, the housekeeper, who had been a fixture in Adrianna's life forever. Estelle was usually the first to greet her. Afternoons for her mother were generally filled with charity meetings and she didn't arrive home until five or six. And her father was always at the office. She wanted to believe her parents loved her in their way, and they were just busy people who were naturally reserved. Adrianna had been anything but reserved like her folks. Loud, full of energy, she could exhaust her mother and father in minutes.

Now, as Adrianna stood on the front stoop, the sunlight fading in the distance, she couldn't bring herself to push through the front door and waltz in as she had a million times before. This didn't feel like home anymore.

Since she'd learned of her adoption, everything had just felt wrong. She felt like a visitor here. This might have been her home as a kid but it wasn't anymore. She rang the bell.

Seconds later she heard the thud of footsteps. The quick purposeful sounds signaled that Estelle was answering the door. Relieved, she stood a little straighter.

The door snapped open, and Estelle frowned as if expecting a salesman or trouble. As Estelle had always said, friends and family came to the kitchen door. Everyone else was a stranger.

Estelle wore her gray-streaked black hair in a tight bun. The style, which she'd worn for as long as Adrianna could remember, accented a round face free of wrinkles.

The older woman's anger quickly switched from annoyance to confusion to kindness. 'Why on earth are you ringing the front bell, child? I thought it was one of those kids who sells magazines and candy.'

Adrianna leaned into Estelle's embrace. 'How are you?'

'I'm just as right as rain. Get in here before you get a chill and get sick.'

Estelle always associated chilly weather with illness. As a kid, Adrianna rarely got out of the house without a sweater. 'What's brought you here tonight?'

'I came to see Mom. She called.' A lifetime of worrying about her mom wasn't so easily dismissed.

Estelle met her gaze. 'You know she'd not have gone to the emergency room the other night if it hadn't been my night off. She always tries that foolishness when I'm gone.'

'I know. I know. How's she doing?'

'Fine. What set her off the other night?'

'I asked about the adoption again.'

Estelle patted Adrianna's arm. 'I didn't always like or agree with what your folks did, but I know they did love you. They wouldn't ever have wanted to disappoint you.'

'Sure.' But they had. Deeply.

'If I'd known about that adoption, I'd have found a way to tell you.'

'I know. I know.' She struggled to keep her voice even.

'Well your mom is doing better,' Estelle said quietly.

'More consistent with her medicine. No more hiding it in her chair when I'm not looking.' Margaret Barrington's delicate hold on sanity could easily be tipped out of balance by stress.

'Is she still awake?'

Relief softened Estelle's face. 'Sure is. Go on into her room and see her.'

Adrianna's stomach knotted. 'Thanks.'

'Can I make you a sandwich?'

'I'm good.'

'How about some banana bread? Made a batch today.'

'I'm good.'

'A cookie? I got cookies.'

Adrianna laughed. 'Still good.'

Estelle shook her head. 'You're too skinny.'

Adrianna grinned. 'You've been saying that for as long as I can remember. I'm eating. If anything, stress makes me eat.'

'Well, you don't seem to gain weight.' Estelle chuckled. 'Which as far as the rest of us are concerned ain't fair. You must get that skinny from your other parents.'

Adrianna rarely talked about her other parents. Kendall wanted to talk about them and dig up every detail she could, but Adrianna hadn't been interested. Good or bad, she was linked to the Barringtons by a lifetime of memories. They felt more a part of her than the people who had given her life.

Adrianna climbed the center staircase and made her way down the long hallway. She knocked and opened her mother's door, knowing that at seven thirty at night she'd be watching *Wheel of Fortune*.

Margaret sat on a couch in a small sitting nook. The light from the television made her face look pale and accentuated the gray roots rimming dull blond hair.

'Mom?'

Margaret Barrington looked up, startled from her show. She grinned. 'Adrianna.' She patted the spot next to her on the couch. 'You came to see me.'

Adrianna sat down. So much anger and confusion had burned through her these last few months. 'How are you doing?'

Margaret made a point to straighten the collar of her flannel nightgown. 'Good, dear, good.'

'Estelle said you're taking your medicine.'

'I want to get well and come back to work with you.'

Adrianna glanced at a painting of Margaret on the wall. She was holding an infant, smiling so lovingly down at her. Adrianna had always loved the picture. Now as she stared at it she didn't know if that was her in her mother's arms or not.

A sudden urgent need to know more sliced through her. 'I always liked that picture.'

Margaret followed her line of sight. 'I did, too. It was a chore getting that done, but well worth it.'

'Why was it a chore?'

'Oh, you cried and cried. You had terrible colic when you were that age. I would sing to you and sometimes you'd stop crying. That day you smiled and it felt like a miracle.'

'I didn't know I had colic.'

'Yes. Terrible case of it. I was always on the phone with the doctor. I didn't think I'd ever sleep again.'

'How old was I in that picture?'

Margaret frowned. 'I don't remember. One or two months.'

The time span was small. And yet in that month's time, one baby had died and one had been brought in to replace her.

It wasn't right that Baby Adrianna rested in an unmarked grave, forgotten. Six months ago, Adrianna had spoken to Dr. Moore, who'd testified to police that the child had died of crib death. He'd told her much the same. But for reasons she couldn't name, it didn't ring true.

'How are you doing, honey?'

Adrianna felt like she was drowning. 'I'm good. Don't worry.'

Margaret smiled. 'It's what mothers do.'

'Right.'

Adrianna kissed her mother and promised to return. On the way out, she found Estelle in the kitchen watching a small television as she fried up eggs and bacon for dinner. Adrianna loved this kitchen. She'd spent more hours than she could count sitting on a stool talking to Estelle. Here she'd learned to cook. 'Hey, I just wanted to say good-bye.'

Estelle shook her head. 'Let me make you some eggs before you go. Won't take but a minute.'

'I'm good, really. Hey, I have a question for you.'

'Shoot.'

'Did I have colic?'

'No, honey, you didn't have a bit of it. You were the easiest, sweetest baby I knew. Why you asking?'

'Just curious.' The child in the portrait wasn't her.

Estelle frowned. 'You're thinking about that other baby.'

'Yes.'

'Your mama has done a good job of rewriting history. She's blocked a lot out.'

'Did Dad hire you to take care of me?'

'Yes, I know for a fact it was you. You've got that birthmark on your butt, and if anything had happened to you I'd have known it wasn't you.'

'Why'd he hire you?'

'He said your mama wasn't well and you needed consistent care. You were a fussy baby those first few weeks. Not colic, but needy. Cried every time I put you down. I had a devil of a time getting you down for naps. I thought it might be your clothes – they were all brand spanking new. Itchy.'

'Really?'

'You wouldn't take formula either. Had a hard time with the bottle.'

She swallowed. 'Kendall told me our birth mother breastfed us.'

Estelle shook her head. 'That would make sense. She tell you anything else about your real parents?'

Real. 'They were simple folks. Loved the Bible. Our names were Eve and Sarah.'

'Good names.'

Nine months ago when Adrianna realized she'd never been legally adopted, she had had her attorney Reese Pearce quietly change her name from Sarah Turner – the name she'd been born with – to Adrianna Barrington. She'd made the name change for legal reasons but also because she didn't know Sarah Turner. Had no connection to the Turner family. Legally she was Adrianna Barrington, but that also felt a bit like a fraud now. She was trapped between the life she'd been born to and the one thrust upon her.

'Do you know if there are any snapshots of Mom's other baby?'

'If there were I never saw them. But I could have a look around in the attic. If there are pictures, they'd be there.'

'Thanks.'

Estelle frowned. 'You might be opening some nasty wounds, baby.'

Her thoughts tumbled back to Gage's dark expression when she'd left him today. 'It seems to be the theme of the day.'

Craig clicked on the television and settled back into his favorite chair. It felt good to sit down. His back ached. His head throbbed. The day had been riddled with more problems than he could count. Clients were either bitching at him or demanding his attention.

But that was all behind him now. He was home. Here he could be himself and drop the façade he now detested.

Remote in one hand, he held a whiskey in the other. He hit PLAY on the video.

The grainy picture snapped on the screen. The image featured a woman standing by a brick wall, her hands bound by a chain that threaded through a hook on the wall above her head. She wore a pink slip that skimmed her long pale legs and hugged small perky breasts. Sweat glistened from her body. Long blond hair tumbled down her shoulders.

'How are you doing?' His voice was a whisper from off-screen.

Her desperate gaze shifted toward him. 'Can I go now? My son is waiting.'

'Not yet. Not yet.'

She moistened damp lips. 'Hey, if you want to do it again, I'm game.' She offered a weak smile that transmitted more fear than joy. 'I just want to go home.'

'I mailed off your postcard today.'

She shook her head. 'Postcard?'

'To your sister. The postcard from San Francisco. I didn't want her or your son to worry.'

'Why should they worry? You said I could leave if I behaved.'

'Do you love me?'

She closed her eyes and cringed slightly as she recalled the lessons they'd had over the last seven days. 'Yes. I love you, Craig.'

'And I love you, too, Adrianna.'

He pulled the .38 from his waistband and shot her in the head. Blood splattered the wall behind her. Her body went limp.

The screen turned to static.

Craig turned off the television, ready for the next hunt.

Chapter Eleven

Wednesday, September 27, 8:58 p.m.

Gage had called Dr. Heckman's phone number a couple of times but hadn't gotten him or an answering machine. The phone just rang. Tomorrow he would track the man down.

He dropped his keys on his kitchen table. The second body had been excavated and transported to the state medical examiner's office. They'd suffered a grim setback when Dr. Butler had told Gage he didn't think the body was Jill Lable's. This victim hadn't been Craig's teenage girlfriend and was at least a decade older.

Now the process of identifying the second victim would begin.

He shrugged off his coat and tossed it on the table, went to the fridge, and pulled out a cold beer. A few years ago, Gage had bought an old house on Richmond's north side. The place had large rooms, plaster walls, and a big back-yard. And it had six bedrooms, which meant he'd been able to offer a roof to his three brothers and his sister when she wasn't in session at the University of Richmond.

Two of his three brothers, Travis and Kevin, had taken him up on the offers. Both were firefighters for the city and both were looking to save money and pay off college debt. His third brother, Tommy, lived with his girlfriend.

Gage popped the top and took a long sip. He loosened his tie and moved to the open newspaper that he'd been reading this morning. The paper was open to the society section. Normally, he skipped this part altogether but he'd had a few extra minutes to kill today.

The paper was still open to the page highlighting Adrianna's charity auction. Her picture was front and center. She was standing next to a couple of other women he didn't recognize. All were as young as she, all just as well bred. But she stood out from the rest. Vibrant, full of energy.

Gage sipped his beer as he lifted the picture and stared. He'd wanted to touch her so badly today that his fingers had ached. He'd figured he'd gotten over her and moved on but seeing her twice in twenty-four hours had proven he'd not gotten over shit.

'Fuck,' he muttered as he gulped down more beer.

The back door banged open and Travis appeared in the kitchen door. He wore jeans and a Richmond Fire Department T-shirt. He smelled of smoke. Dark circles hung under his eyes.

Grunting a greeting, Travis went to the fridge and pulled out a beer. He took a liberal pull before he sighed.

'Rough night?' Gage said.

'Yeah. Fire in Blackwell. We pulled out a couple of kids with third-degree burns.'

'I'm sorry.'

Travis shook his head. 'That kind of shit just shouldn't happen.'

Gage didn't respond. What could he say?

Travis shoved long, soot-stained fingers through his hair. 'There are days when I hate my job.'

Gage held the neck of the bottle, pausing with the top close to his lips. He glanced at the picture of Adrianna. 'Tell me about it.'

'Did Jessie get by the other night?'

'Yeah. Did some laundry and spent the night. Left most of the laundry behind and promised to return. Looks like she put a dent in the food in the refrigerator.'

'Good.' Travis pushed calloused fingers through his dark hair. 'She's doing okay?'

'Seems to be.' Gage took a long pull on his beer.

So did Travis.

A heavy silence hung between them. They didn't talk about Jessie's abduction much. But it was always there. Always weighing on the brothers.

'Do you think that she's forgotten?' Travis said.

'I don't think she remembers much. The drugs he gave her took care of that.' His throat felt tight with rage.

'She doesn't seem to let it get in the way of her life.'

'I can't say the same.'

Travis picked at the label on the beer bottle with his thumbnail. 'Me, either.' He sighed. 'She's told us it's not our fault.'

Gage shook his head. 'That's nice, but it's shit. It's my fault and I'll never forgive myself.'

Craig stood in the shadows outside of the church. Though it had been warm during the day, the temperature had turned cold and he was sorry now he'd left his blazer in the truck. As much as he wanted to leave, he knew the Alcoholics Anonymous meeting was breaking up and if he left now he'd miss her.

He rubbed his chilled arms and tapped his foot on

the ground. Another five minutes passed before the church doors opened and the group of six or seven men and women emerged. Four paused outside the doors and immediately lit up cigarettes. The other, a man, headed for a minivan parked in the church's lot. The woman he waited for was one of the smokers.

She stood in the halo of light holding a cigarette to her lips. Her hands trembled slightly and her shoulders hunched forward. The last two years had been hard ones. She looked like she'd aged a decade. But then he doubted she'd ever gone that long without a drink.

He watched as she puffed on the cigarette. 'Come on, bitch, wrap it up,' he sneered.

Slowly the other smokers finished and moved to their cars. One paused to ask, 'Hey, Tammy, are you coming?'

Smoke puffed from her mouth in wispy rings. 'Yeah. Just want to finish my smoke. I've half to go and don't want to waste it.'

The other woman shrugged. She wore a T-shirt that said Smartass. 'Maybe I should stick around until you're done. It's kind of dark.'

Tammy shook her head. 'Don't worry.'

The woman hesitated. 'Are you sure?'

'Yeah. Thanks, Jeannie.' Tammy sounded annoyed, as if she wanted a few minutes to herself. 'I'll just finish this up and go.'

The others in the group said their good-byes and drifted to their cars.

Tammy remained alone in the dark but didn't seem to mind. He knew what she was thinking: *Good neighborhood. I can take care of myself.*

For several more minutes, she inhaled deeply on the filter tip, holding the smoke in her lungs an extra beat before she blew it out. She savored every moment. Finally, she dropped her butt to the ground and smashed it into the ground with her sneaker. Her gaze scanned the horizon before she moved to her car. He sensed she wanted to postpone leaving and returning to her mother's small tri-level house on the south side of town.

Craig waited as Tammy slid behind the wheel of her mother's wood-paneled station wagon and cranked the engine. It rumbled but didn't turn over. Under the light he could see her frown and then swear. She tried again and again, pounded the wheel once, but the engine didn't respond.

Smiling, he pulled his hand from his pocket and strolled over to her car, careful to come up from behind so that she didn't see his approach. He knocked on her window and took pleasure from her startled expression.

'Can I help?' he said. 'Looks like you're having trouble.'

Tammy shook her head, her eyes dark with suspicion. Two years of doing time had made her wary. 'Thanks, I got it.' To prove she was fine, she cranked the engine again. Nothing happened.

Craig was in no rush. She wasn't going anywhere. He'd loosened wires in the engine. 'You're going to wear out the battery if you keep cranking. Stay in the car and pop the hood. Let me have a look.'

That seemed to ease her wariness enough to roll her window down a fraction. She unlatched the hood. He opened it, pretended to scan the interior and wiggle some of the wires and tubes. He peered around the side of the car. 'I think you've got corroded spark plugs. Happens a lot with the older models. Might take me a minute, but I think if I clean them off and put them back the engine will fire.'

'Thanks, I appreciate it.' The gratitude in her gaze was palpable. She fumbled in her purse for another cigarette and lit the tip. 'Are you sure you can get it started? I just bought the car and I need it to run.'

'Shouldn't be a problem. With any luck you'll be out of here in ten minutes.' He fiddled with the engine, taking his time. He knew from the trial transcripts that the confined space of her car would soon feel restrictive. She didn't like small spaces.

'Thanks.' Smoke trailed out the cracked window.

'How did you like the meeting tonight?'

'It was fine.'

'I'd planned to attend but had to work late. Crap like that always happens on meeting nights.'

'Yeah.'

'Almost got it.' He glanced around. 'You look stressed.'

'I am.'

He returned his gaze to the engine. 'When I'm stressed I dream of Fiji. I've always wanted to go there.'

'Yeah.'

'What about you? Where's your dream vacation?'

'Hadn't thought about it.'

'Come on, there must be somewhere?'

She puffed her cigarette. 'Maybe Arizona. I've always liked the desert.'

'Good choice.'

When he heard her car door open and her footsteps

move toward him, he swallowed a smile. He slipped his hand into his pocket and wrapped his fingers around a stun gun.

A gentle breeze didn't diminish the acrid cigarette smoke smell. 'Hey, thanks for doing this.'

He started to lift the Taser from his pocket when he heard someone else come out of the church. He stopped, smiled. 'No problem.'

'My name is Tammy,' she said, offering a trembling hand.

He accepted her cold hand. 'Nice to meet you, Tammy. I'm Bill.'

'How long have you been coming to the meetings?'

'About a year. I haven't seen you before.'

'It's my first time.'

'You'll like it. Good group of folks.'

Behind her he saw the church maintenance man move toward his white truck. Craig tilted his head to the side so shadows obscured his face. His palms sweated as the maintenance man paused and looked toward Tammy. Every muscle in his body tightened as he waited for her reaction. When she waved the maintenance man off, he let out a breath, knowing he'd have to act fast.

When the maintenance truck's brake lights vanished around the corner, he yanked the stun gun free from his pocket. The snap of electricity was Tammy's first warning that something was wrong. Her smile faltered as she glanced down toward the stun gun.

Before she could react, he jabbed the electric probes into the soft flesh of her neck. The electric shock had her eyes rolling back in her head and her limbs convulsing.

Craig caught Tammy as her knees buckled and her

body went limp. He turned the Taser off and tucked it back in his pocket.

'Hey, Tammy.'

She searched his face and mumbled an inaudible sound that sounded like, 'Why?'

'Do you remember Craig Thornton?'

Her eyes darkened with pain and remorse at the mention of the name. Tears welled in her eyes.

Laughing, he hefted her up and put her in the trunk of his car. Quickly, he bound her wrists and put a piece of duct tape over her mouth. 'You do remember him, don't you?'

She nodded as tears rolled down her cheeks.

'You murdered him with your car and now you have to be punished.'

Chapter Twelve

Thursday, September 28, 8:15 a.m.

Gage and Vega moved into the conference room. Sergeant David Ayden had asked to see Gage for an update on the case. Ayden had agreed to let Gage run the case but had stipulated he wanted frequent updates. The entire homicide team was there: Jacob Warwick, the broad-shouldered ex-boxer, his lean, rawboned partner Zack Kier, and Vega's usual partner, the only female, C.C. Ricker.

'Good morning,' Ayden said. A crisp red tie set off a white shirt fastened at the collar and cuffs.

'Morning,' Gage said.

Ayden nodded toward the chair opposite him. 'So give me the rundown.'

Gage sat down with Vega on his right. Ayden wasn't one for chitchat. He expected his detectives to cut to the chase. And Gage was glad for it.

'As you know, two skeletonized remains, both female, were found on the Thornton estate. Dr. Butler and Tess Kier finished excavating the second grave yesterday. Both females were in their midtwenties when they were shot in the head. No bullet was found in the first grave, but as Tess was sifting through the dirt on the second site she found a .38 slug.'

Ayden nodded. 'Did they find anything else other than bones?'

'Dr. Butler also found trace fibers on Jane Doe. Might be silk. Tess is not sure, but promises to report back. Dr. Butler also found synthetic hair fibers on Rhonda Minor.'

'You said the first body found was Rhonda Minor's?' Ayden said.

'Yes. She was the first uncovered but she was not the first victim. We've yet to identify the other body. I had a theory about the other victim but it didn't pan out.'

C.C. leaned back in her chair. Her red hair and freckles made her look younger than her thirtysomething years. 'That was a quick ID on the first body pulled from the ground.'

'I worked Minor's missing persons case a couple of years ago. Craig Thornton was Minor's boss. When I spoke to him, I suspected he was holding back information, but I couldn't prove anything. When Dr. Butler said the victim was female and midtwenties, I pulled Minor's dental records. They were a perfect match.'

Warwick nodded. 'What about the other victim? You said you had a theory that didn't pan.'

'I'm waiting on Dr. Butler's analysis of the bones. I'm also pulling missing persons records of women who disappeared in the last decade. I'd thought it might have been a girl Craig Thornton dated in high school. Jill Lable. But the bones are that of an older woman, not a teenager.'

Warwick flexed calloused fingers. 'What was Craig Thornton like?'

Gage kept his voice even. 'Old Virginia money, only

child, and spoiled. Georgetown grad. C student. Joined the art gallery his grandfather founded. Thornton Galleries. The gallery enjoys a good reputation but I don't have financials on the business. Never arrested.'

'And what did Minor do for him?'

'She was a student at VCU, majoring in art history and art preservation. She worked at the gallery as a secretary, but told family and friends she wanted to be an artist.'

Warwick shook his head. 'You never requested his financials?'

'I had no cause to get the warrant. But I do now and I have one waiting for a judge's signature. I've asked for access to both his bank records and his phone records now.'

'Good,' Ayden said.

'Thornton does have an alibi for the week Rhonda disappeared. He was on his honeymoon.'

'Do you think Minor and Thornton were having an affair?' Kier said.

Gage met the detective's direct gaze. 'Yes.'

'Any evidence to support that?' Kier challenged.

'None. Just a gut feeling.'

'God,' C.C. said. 'Adrianna Thornton's old man cheated on her? She's stunning. What hope do the rest of us have?'

'Show me a beautiful woman,' Vega said, 'and I'll show you a man who's already bored with her.'

C.C. glared at Vega. 'When did you get so cynical?'

Vega shrugged and winked.

'Hudson,' Ayden said, 'have you told Minor's family that you found her?'

'I will this morning. I wanted a firm confirmation from Dr. Butler before I spoke to them.' Gage tapped his thumb on the table and shifted his gaze to Warwick. 'I met your wife Tuesday at the estate.'

'Really?' He frowned. 'She didn't tell me.'

'She'd come to pay a visit to her sister and saw all the cop cars. Ms. Barrington told her about the bodies.'

Warwick steepled his fingers. 'As far as I know, no word has leaked to the press.'

'I asked her to keep quiet and Ms. Warwick agreed for the sake of her sister.'

That didn't seem to please Warwick. 'My wife is determined to make a connection with her sister. She'll do whatever it takes to salvage her family.' Warwick rubbed the back of his neck with his hand. 'What do you know about Adrianna Barrington?'

Gage recited the facts about her without revealing their past. He and Adrianna were history. This was about closure for the families. It wasn't personal. 'I did interview Ms. Barrington three years ago, right after the car accident. Her husband was in a coma and she'd suffered a miscarriage because of the accident.'

C.C. lifted a brow. 'You chose then to question her?'

Gage sighed, ignoring her annoyance. 'I hoped her husband might have said something to her about Minor.'

'And?' Warwick said.

'She said she knew nothing.'

'Do you think she knew where Minor was?' Ayden said.

'I don't think so.'

Ayden sat back in his chair staring at Gage as if he were fishing for the missing piece of the puzzle.

'There's something else to consider,' Gage said. 'I know the second Jane Doe's dental records didn't match Jill

Lable, but I still think it would be worth it to talk to her family. Jill went to prom with Craig and both landed up in jail that night on drug charges. She'd provided Craig with pot. His attorney got him off. But the girl did sixty days in juvenile detention. It was her third offense. Two days after she was released from detention she vanished. No one saw her again. I did a quick check last night. Her parents still live in the city.'

'If she's not our Jane Doe, then why talk to the parents?' Ayden said.

'Just a gut feeling.'

Ayden tapped his finger on the table. 'C.C., talk to the parents. See if their daughter ever turned up. Hudson, you have an address?'

Gage wrote it on the legal pad and tore off the page for C.C. 'Thanks.'

She folded the paper and creased the seam with her fingernail. 'No sweat.'

Ayden leaned forward. 'Hudson, keep digging in Adrianna Barrington's life. If I've learned anything, it's that nothing is what it seems.'

The gray sky was ripe with rain clouds when Gage and Vega arrived at the sleek office complex in the western end of the county. Gage and Vega had learned at the offices of Minor Landscapes that Fred Minor and his landscape crew were at this office location. It was easy to spot the three large green trucks and the collection of mowers and weed eaters.

Gage parked behind the last of the three trucks and they got out. Most of the workers were dark-skinned

Mexicans; however, one man in the front truck was taller, had a stock of sandy brown hair. His skin was weathered, making him look older than his early thirties.

Several of the men glanced up from rakes watching closely as if they couldn't decide to run or stay. Vega spoke briefly in clear Spanish and the men nodded. They didn't run but gazes remained wary.

'You tell them we aren't here for them?' Gage said.

Vega nodded. 'Yeah.'

Gage set his sights on the sandy-haired man. He wore pants and a matching shirt with a name tag that read FRED. The news he was about to break made his stomach churn. He'd never gotten used to this part. 'Mr. Minor.'

Minor glanced up from a clipboard. The lines in his sun-etched face deepened. 'Detective Hudson. It's been a while.'

Gage extended his hand. Minor's grip was strong and his hands deeply calloused. 'Yes, sir.'

'You have news about Rhonda?'

'I do.'

Minor nodded solemnly. 'Let's have it.'

'We found a body in a shallow grave near here. It's Rhonda.'

For a moment Fred Minor said nothing. His jaw tightened and released as if he struggled with emotions. He swallowed. 'Can't say that I'm surprised. All this time – it would have been a miracle if she'd been found alive. Still, I've lit a candle for her in church every week.' He smacked the clipboard against his thigh, pursed his lips as tears threatened. 'How'd she die?'

Gage remembered the feelings that had brewed when

his own sister had gone missing. If Jessie had died . . . 'I can't say now.'

'Why not!' Sadness and anger propelled the words forward. 'She was my sister and I have a right to know.'

'I don't want to release information now. I'm sorry and I'd tell you everything if I could. But I'm trying to identify her killer.' Gage spoke softly, understanding Minor's pain. He remembered the man's frantic words during the initial interviews three years ago. 'I really want to catch the killer.'

The words penetrated Minor's anger and almost immediately, it crumbled. His eyes glistened with unshed tears. 'What else can you tell me about what happened to her?'

'Not much. The remains, well, there wasn't much left. We're going to have to do some digging to piece together the story. We don't know much beyond the cause of death.'

Minor blinked, trying to hold on to the pooling tears in his eyes. 'At least tell me that she died quickly.'

The bullet that sliced through her brain had ended her life in a blink, but the days, maybe weeks leading up to her death . . . 'She died quickly.'

A sigh shuddered through the older man. 'Thank you for that much, Detective.'

Gage wanted answers. He wanted to know what had happened to Rhonda. 'You've had time to think over the last couple of years. Any idea who might have done this?'

'I always think about Craig Thornton. Rich, spoiled. Rhonda thought he was the best. She was always talking about him. Craig this. Craig that.' His voice cracked.

'Anyone else?'

'No.' A sigh shuddered through him. 'She wanted to be an artist. She wanted to paint. And Thornton played on that by going on and on about her talent. If she was so damn good, why did she just file papers for him?'

The man's pain grew with each syllable. Softly, Gage said, 'You know about his accident?'

'Yeah. The son of a bitch died on December second. I read the obits every day since his accident. I even went to his funeral.'

Gage had seen the same obit and had toyed with the idea of going. In the end, he'd stayed away because he'd not wanted to see Adrianna. 'Why?'

'I don't know. I just needed some kind of closure. I knew Rhonda wasn't coming back but I tried to take some satisfaction in knowing that if Thornton had hurt her, he was dead and burning in hell.'

'You think Thornton killed your sister?'

'Now more than ever.'

'What happened at the funeral?'

'I sat in the back. The service was packed with acquaintances and friends. Thornton's wife sat at the front of the church. She didn't move. Looked like marble. Ice. Didn't show any emotion at all.'

'Her husband had been in a coma for a couple of years at that point.' The surprising urge to defend Adrianna was automatic.

'Yeah, I guess she had it rough. But there was something cold and hard about her and I just didn't care about her feelings.' He pulled the air into his lungs and let it out slowly. 'At the end of the service I got in the receiving line because I wanted to shake her hand. I don't know why. I guess I just wanted to make some kind of contact.'

Gage frowned. 'You exchanged words with her?'

'She was nice enough. Thanked me for coming. I hadn't planned to introduce myself. I just wanted to see her up close.'

'And?'

'Standing next to her was her mother. The old lady looked upset. Eyes red and blotchy. The mother looked like she was all emotion and drama – the complete opposite of her daughter.'

'The mother's name is Mrs. Barrington.'

'Whatever. The longer I stood there, the madder I felt. So I told Adrianna that my sister Rhonda had worked with Craig at his gallery. Her eyes locked on mine and she asked me if I'd ever found my sister.'

'Did she?'

'Yeah. Surprised me. When I told her no, she said she was very sorry.' He shook his head. 'I thought for a moment she really meant it. It deflated some of my anger.'

'Anything else?'

'I was a few steps away when I heard the mother say, "They both hurt you. I hope they both rot in hell."'

'Really?'

'I turned back and saw Adrianna whisper something to her mother. The lady shut right up.'

'Why didn't you call me?' Gage said.

'And tell you what? That I thought I heard something? Rhonda's case was cold.'

He was right. There'd have been nothing he could have done with such scant information.

'I'll tell you one thing about that Adrianna woman.'

'What's that?'

'Never play poker against her. She can hide her emotions better than anyone I've ever met.'

Gage and Vega arrived at the Thornton Gallery located in the historic section of Richmond called Shockoe Bottom. The building had once been a tobacco warehouse but had been converted twenty years ago. Black paint covered the exterior and large picture windows gave a view into large white rooms that showcased works of art ranging from modern to classic. Pine floors with a heavy lacquer finish glistened.

The detectives were greeted by a large bronze sculpture of a ballerina. 'How much you think it's worth?' Vega said.

'Hell if I know. My tastes run to beer signs and football posters.'

'I hear ya.' This place, this world of art and fine pieces, eluded him. 'A lot of money for stuff.'

A twentysomething woman appeared from a secret door that blended seamlessly into the wall. She was dressed in a black pencil skirt, white blouse, and red high-heeled shoes. Red hair pulled back in tight curls highlighted the sharp bones of her face. One glance at them and her eyes turned from boredom to annoyance. 'May I help you?'

Gage pulled out his badge and showed it to her. 'We're here to see Janet Guthrie. I have a few questions about her late partner Craig Thornton.'

The receptionist managed a smile. 'Let me just tell her you're here.' She vanished back through the invisible door. Seconds later, she reappeared. 'I'll show you to her office.'

As they followed, Gage said, 'Did you know Rhonda Minor?'

The woman hesitated mid-step. 'We went to art school together.'

'What can you tell me about her?'

'Ambitious. Smart. Talented painter.'

'What did she like to paint?'

'Everything.'

'Any of her stuff still around?'

'Maybe. In storage.'

He pulled out a card and handed it to her. 'Do me a favor and look.'

'Why? She left the area. Her sister said she moved to Europe, I think.'

'We found Rhonda Minor's body two days ago. She was murdered.'

The girl's face paled. 'Oh.'

'Find those paintings.' He managed a smile he suspected was more like a snarl.

Her gaze flittered away. 'Sure.'

They followed the receptionist down a carpeted hallway to an office in the back corner. After a quick knock and introduction they were seated in front of Janet Guthrie. Late thirties, she wore her long dark hair loose around her shoulders. Her suit was a deep blue, designer no doubt, and diamond stud earrings winked from her earlobes.

After brief introductions, Janet Guthrie held out a manicured hand. 'Detective Hudson. What can I do for you?'

'I was here a few years ago.'

'Craig mentioned it. I was away around that time.' She

acted like this was a social call. 'You have questions about Craig.'

Gage noted her grip was firm, her gaze direct. 'Just a few.'

She gestured toward the two chairs in front of her desk and moved behind her desk. 'Please have a seat.'

The trio sat. Once fortified by the desk, she relaxed.

'Do you remember Rhonda Minor?' He was careful to keep his tone even.

The woman grimaced. 'How can I forget? She's the one you were looking for a couple of years ago. Craig told me everything about your visit.'

'As I remember, you were in Europe?'

'Good memory.'

He flipped through the pages of his notebook as if he couldn't remember. 'Thornton said Rhonda took off a lot and missed work.'

Janet lightly touched the diamond earring on her right ear. 'She missed some time but not an excessive amount. I don't think it was all that bad. Did you find her?'

'Yesterday, as a matter of fact.'

She leaned back in her chair and crossed her legs. 'Don't tell me. She was sunning herself on a tropical beach.'

Vega's gaze skimmed and catalogued the room. 'Not exactly.'

'Then where did you find her?'

'It appears she was murdered shortly after she vanished.' Gage watched Janet's face pale.

Janet drew in a sharp breath. 'That's awful. Where was she found?'

He leaned back in his chair. 'That's the puzzling part.'

'Why is that puzzling?'

'Can't really go into detail about that now.'

'Why not?'

'Not ready to tip my hand.' Gage noticed she kept touching her earring. He wondered what she was hiding.

'How did she die?'

'Shot.'

'Okay. What can I do?'

'Last time I was here, Craig Thornton was adamant that he and Rhonda had only a professional relationship.'

Her smile faltered just a fraction. 'Okay.'

Vega crossed his legs and straightened the cuff of his pants. 'Is that true?'

Janet traced a manicured finger around the bottom edge of her pristine blotter. 'I kept my nose out of Craig's personal life.'

Gage flipped a page in his notebook. 'Ms. Guthrie, the man is dead. What good would it do to protect him now?'

She brushed an imaginary strand of hair from her forehead. 'I'm not protecting Craig.'

Vega adjusted the cuff on his pants. 'The press hasn't sunk their teeth into this story, but the clock is ticking. When they do get a hold of this story, they'll put two and two together and then you'll have an ex-partner gallery linked to murder. Knowing how conservative folks are around here, that can't be good.'

Anger and fear darkened her eyes. 'Craig wouldn't have killed Rhonda.'

'Because . . .' Gage prompted.

Janet spoke carefully, deliberately. 'Craig was very, very fond of Rhonda.'

'They had a sexual relationship?' Vega said.

'Yes.' She lifted her chin. 'They'd been sleeping together for about a year before she went missing.'

The news didn't shock Gage. The outrage he felt for Adrianna did. 'Craig was engaged to Adrianna Barrington during that time, wasn't he?'

'He and Adrianna had dated since college. Everyone thought they were the perfect couple. And they were in many, many ways.' A bitter smile lifted the edge of her lips. 'Look, I liked Craig. He was a good man. But he grew bored very easily. Even with Adrianna. Rhonda offered him a distraction.'

'You think Adrianna knew her fiancé was cheating on her?' Vega said.

'He was discreet but I've no idea. She was a bit naïve in those days. But I can tell you that Craig did love Adrianna. He drew strength from her and he never would have left her.'

'But he liked to cat around with lots of different women,' Vega added.

'Those women meant nothing to him,' she said.

Vega leaned forward. 'The guy makes a habit of screwing around and Adrianna didn't know?'

'She married him, didn't she?' Janet retorted.

'Maybe she's the forgiving type,' Vega said.

'Adrianna wouldn't have tolerated that kind of behavior. I think Craig's mother understood this. Those last years she was alive she kept him on a short leash. Threatened to cut him off a couple of times.'

Gage kept his expression stoic. He switched the conversation's direction. 'Rhonda knew Craig was getting married.'

'Yes. Craig and Adrianna announced their engagement in September.'

'And she was okay with that?'

'Rhonda fancied herself in love with Craig. She wanted him to marry her, not Adrianna. About a week before the wedding she tried to force the issue. Craig told me later that she threatened to go to Adrianna if he didn't break off the wedding. He offered her money if she'd go away.'

Gage sat back, silent. He wanted Janet to do all the talking. Silence generally made people uncomfortable and he used that to his advantage.

'Two days before the wedding, Craig came into my office. He said Rhonda had taken the money he'd offered her and had agreed to leave town. Crisis averted. End of story.'

'He paid her off,' Vega said.

'Yes. And it worked. She didn't want him. She wanted his money.'

'What makes you think she left town?' Gage said.

Janet shrugged. 'Craig told me she did.'

Gage watched her face closely. 'Never occurred to you that he might have killed her?'

'No. Craig wasn't like that. He was a charming, funny man, but in so many ways he was weak. He wouldn't have the stones to kill someone. If there was a tough decision to be made, I made it. His mother made it. Adrianna made it. Not Craig.'

Her appraisal offered little solace. Many underestimated killers before the cops tallied the body count. 'What if he thought he could lose Adrianna? Would that drive him to murder?'

'He didn't have the balls. Didn't like to get his hands dirty.'

'Would you have killed for Craig?' Vega asked.

'No.'

'What about this business? Your reputation?'

She arched a plucked eyebrow. 'Ask me any more questions like that and you can ask them through my lawyer.'

Janet's unblinking gaze revealed nothing Gage could use in court. 'You've cleaned up your share of Craig's messes.'

'Sure.'

And he'd bet she'd bent laws to do it. But did loyalty include murder? 'Do you still have Rhonda Minor's personnel file?'

'It's most likely in storage by now, but I'm sure we can have it sent to you.'

'I'd appreciate that. Your receptionist also mentioned you had some of Rhonda's paintings in storage?'

'She's mistaken. I cleaned the room out about eight months ago.'

'Mind if I look?'

'I do. We've got delicate pieces down there that I don't want disturbed by cops mucking about.' Janet's fingers curled into fists. 'You're looking in the wrong place, Detective.'

'That so?'

'Craig wouldn't have hidden anything on the property that was incriminating.'

'Where would he have kept it?'

'An apartment that Adrianna didn't know about. Moondance Apartments. It's a modest complex in the west end.'

This valuable nugget of information hadn't been tossed to him out of kindness. 'I know it.' It pissed him off that this information didn't come up three years ago. 'Was the apartment leased under his name?'

'I doubt it. Most likely he leased it through a dummy corporation. He didn't want a paper trail connected to him.'

'That where he met Rhonda?'

'Among others. I didn't pay much attention to his love life as long as he pulled his weight at the gallery.'

'He didn't always pull his weight here?'

'Like I said, he could be easily distracted. Daily routines were a bore.'

Vega leaned forward. 'You two are an unlikely pair. How'd you two hook up?'

'His father hired me.'

'That would be Robert Thornton,' Gage said.

'Yes. He hired me about fifteen years ago. I interned here and he saw potential. When he offered me a paying job, he made no bones about my duties. I was to keep an eye on Craig.'

'You were his babysitter?'

She shrugged. 'It started out that way but as time passed I learned the ins and outs of the business and got to know the movers and shakers in the art world. I *am* Thornton Gallery now. Through my guidance it's become one of the premier galleries on the East Coast.' She lifted a brow, clearly pleased. 'Not bad for a girl from a small town in southside Virginia.'

The raw determination burning in her eyes mirrored Gage's. 'The Thornton name carries a lot of weight in the art world.'

'It certainly does. I never would have achieved the success I did if not for the Thornton family. But they would have failed several years ago if it weren't for my management.'

'Who received Craig's portion of the gallery when he died?' Gage said.

'Adrianna. I bought it from her last year.'

'Before he died?'

'Yes. She had power of attorney and sold me Craig's interest in the gallery.'

'Why?'

'She needed the money.'

'For what?' Vega asked.

'Medical expenses, I'm sure. That nursing home was eating her alive.' She shrugged. 'The doctors told her last November that even though Craig's brain was irrevocably damaged, his body was strong. He could live another twenty-five years.'

'She told you that?'

'Yes. That news prompted the gallery sale. Adrianna hides her feelings well, but that day she was shaky and scared. I made her an offer and she took it. If I'd waited a few more weeks, she might not have sold. Craig finally did something that helped her.'

'How so?' Gage said.

'He died.' She seemed to realize how harsh her words sounded. 'Look, I don't want to sound callous. But let's face it, Craig died the day that drunk driver slammed into him. He was just pulling Adrianna down. The woman visited him almost daily in the nursing home. She's a young, beautiful woman and she deserved better.'

'Where was she when he died?' Vega said.

Janet shrugged. 'At a design show in Alexandria. It was

a day trip, from what I hear. And honestly, by waiting until she was out of town, he spared her the trauma of watching him die.'

'Thank you for your time, Ms. Guthrie,' Gage said.

Neither Gage nor Vega spoke until they'd reached their car.

Vega put on his dark glasses. 'She rolled over on Craig pretty fast when you suggested she might have killed Rhonda.'

Gage fired up the engine. 'Janet Guthrie does what is best for Janet Guthrie.'

Vega relaxed back in his seat. 'Odd Craig died at a convenient time.'

Gage blew out a breath. 'Yeah. Might be a good idea to talk to Craig's doctor and get his theories on Craig's passing.'

'You think he was murdered?'

'Let's just say I don't like convenient deaths.' He pulled into traffic. 'I'd like for you to get a warrant for the gallery's basement. I want to see if any of Rhonda's paintings still exist.'

C.C. Ricker arrived at the upper-middle-class home in the far west end of the county an hour after her meeting with the homicide team. The streets were quiet, the lawns and flowerbeds neatly manicured, and the homes all had a similar Williamsburg kind of colonial feel. They were expensive, nice but too Stepford Wives for C.C.'s tastes. She preferred the quirky and mismatched.

She climbed brick front steps and rang the bell. Before she'd come, she'd called Sandra Lable and asked for the appointment. The woman had been hesitant at first, then agreed.

Footsteps echoed in the house, curtains by the front door fluttered briefly, and then the door opened. The woman standing there was short, petite and just as manicured as her lawn. Short hair dyed brown. French nails and toes. Dressed like she was headed to the gym.

'Mrs. Lable?'

A plucked eyebrow arched. 'Detective Ricker.'

'Yes, ma'am. I have a few questions about Jill.'

'Your call surprised me. Jill has been missing for over fifteen years. Have you found something?' No hint of emotion seeped into her words.

'Ma'am, do you mind if we don't have this conversation on the front porch.'

'Why not? Jill had no problem airing dirty laundry in public. Have you found something?' The woman radiated a hard, brittle energy as if one tap and she'd shatter.

'We're working another case that might be linked to your daughter's disappearance.'

'You mean death?'

'No body was found, from what I understand.'

'She's dead. I know it.'

'When was the last time you saw Jill?'

'Two days after she was released from detention. June fifteenth. She'd missed the last two months of school and we were arguing about getting her into summer school. She didn't want to go back. She stormed off. I thought she'd come back when she cooled. She always did. But she never came back.'

'Did you see her with anyone unusual?'

'No.'

'What can you tell me about Craig Thornton?'

She frowned. 'Her prom date? He died last year.'

'I know, but about the time he was dating your daughter.'

'They went out just a couple of times. Prom night they got arrested. Drugs. I remember seeing him at the police station. He looked shook up.'

'His parents came and got him?'

'No. Was a friend of the family. Whoever he was, Craig was thrilled to see him. The guy bailed him out. Family lawyer spun it so that it looked like it was all Jill's fault. That's why she did time and he didn't.'

'Anything else you can think of?'

She sighed. 'I try not to think about Jill. We failed each other so many times. I find it's better not to remember.'

'Anything else?'

'I pulled her scrapbook out from the attic. The whole book is about prom night. She worked on this while she was in detention.' Mrs. Lable leaned to the left and picked up the book. It was decorated with large flowers and hearts.

C.C. took it. The spine creaked when she opened the book full of fading pictures, napkins, and a dried corsage. 'Funny she'd want to remember that night so much.'

'She really liked Craig. I think she thought they'd get together when she got out.'

'Did they?'

'No. He was in Europe that whole summer.'

'They never saw each other again?'

'No.'

'Did you show this to Detective Hudson when he spoke to you four years ago?'

'No. I didn't think about it.'

'What made you think about it today?'

'My niece went shopping for a homecoming dress this past weekend. Reminded me of when Jill and I shopped for her prom dress. I don't know, the dots just connected.'

C.C. glanced at the book so full of young smiling faces. What a damn waste. As she turned the pages, a postcard fluttered to the floor. C.C. picked it up. It featured a picture of Texas wildflowers, was addressed to Mrs. Lable and from Jill. *Moving to Texas. Luv you! Jill.*

'That arrived a few days after she left,' Mrs. Lable said.

Rhonda had sent a postcard. Italy. 'Mind if I hang on to this?'

'I'll want it back. It's all I have of her.'

Adrianna's gaze sightlessly skimmed the dozen wallpaper books piled open and waiting on her workbench. She'd been flipping through the books for an hour looking for the right paper that would enhance but not overwhelm a retired admiral's study. The job's excitement had waned in the shadow of fatigue and nerves, which waged a tug-of-war match with her thoughts.

Adrianna reached for her coffee and took a sip. Cold. She rose and moved to the front of the shop where she kept an espresso machine for clients. The corner coffee shop's five-dollar lattes had prompted the machine's purchase. The machine had paid for itself in one month.

White muslin furniture samples were draped with hand-loomed chenille, linen-cut velvets, and rich tapestries. Antique French country end tables sported odd collectible accessories including a hand-painted rooster, blue and white vases, and inlaid china boxes. She'd learned early on to supplement her design work by selling unique antique store finds to her clients. Now she was selling it all at a forty percent discount.

Adrianna loaded fresh espresso into the machine when a knock on her door had her turning. Her assistant Phyllis Gentry waved to her. In her midfifties, Phyllis sported a khaki skirt, a crisp white polo shirt and a pink headband to hold back bobbed brown hair. A former math teacher, Phyllis had whipped Adrianna's accounts receivable into top shape with brutal efficiency.

Phyllis shouted through the glass front door. 'I lost my keys.'

Adrianna's annoyance wiped the welcoming smile from her face as she moved to the door and opened it. 'What do you mean, you lost your keys?'

Phyllis looked equally annoyed and frustrated. 'I've looked everywhere for them. All I can think is my husband took them accidentally when he went on his fishing trip. I've got backups to get me around, but I don't have an extra store key on that ring.'

'When will Harry be back?'

'Two weeks.' Phyllis smelled like magnolias. 'I've tried to call him but he's out of cell phone range. But he's promised to call from a landline mid-week.'

Adrianna sighed. 'I've got an extra key. But you need to let me know if Harry doesn't have those keys. I've got too much in the store to risk having a key floating around.'

'I promise.' She set her Vera Bradley purse on the front counter before she leveled her gaze on Adrianna. 'Did you sleep at all last night?'

'A couple of hours.' She retrieved her coffee and sipped it. 'Hey, can you mind the front? I've got to finish my sketch for tomorrow's presentation.'

'For the admiral?'

'Ahoy.'

Phyllis laughed as she tucked her purse under the front counter. 'Don't worry. Unless fire or blood is involved, I will leave you alone.'

'Thanks.' Adrianna retreated back into her office and just as she sat down the phone rang. 'I've got it, Phyllis!'

She picked up the receiver. 'Hello?'

For a moment there was only silence.

'Hello?'

'It's Craig, babe.' The voice sounded just above a whisper.

The hairs on the back of Adrianna's neck rose. She gripped the phone. Her breath grew short and shallow. The voice sounded exactly like Craig's. 'This isn't funny. Who is this?'

'It's Craig,' he whispered. 'I just wanted to call and tell you how much I love you. I've been thinking about you a lot lately.'

'Is this some kind of sick joke?' The card, the after-shave flyer, and now a call. 'You are cruel and twisted.'

'I love you, babe.'

'Damn you! Who is this?'

'Your husband. Did you get the flowers?'

'What flowers?'

'They'll be there soon.'

'Leave me the hell alone.' Adrianna slammed down the phone so hard her wedding rings dug into her finger. Her pulse thundered in her neck. 'Damn it. This has got to stop.'

Adrianna stared down at the phone, wondering what she could do to stop these pranks.

Suddenly, the nerves in her spine tingled anew. She spun around half-fearing she'd find Craig there, knowing it was likely Phyllis.

It wasn't Craig. Or Phyllis.

It was Gage.

Wide shoulders filled the doorjamb and fury radiated from him. 'Mind telling me what that was about?'

Chapter Thirteen

Thursday, September 28, 1:00 p.m.

Adrianna's face flushed with anger and worry. Her hands trembled at her side. He'd never seen her so truly rattled. 'What are you doing here?'

Gage moved into the room, ignoring the question. 'What was that all about?'

Her back as stiff as wood, she lifted her chin. In an instant she seemed to rally and the veil of ice cooled her expression. 'A prank call. Someone pretending to be Craig.'

The room was neat, organized, and filled with more decorating books than he ever knew existed. Disorganization and out-of-control clutter could have overwhelmed the space, but didn't. Like Adrianna, the area was neat, organized, and stylish. 'Someone who says they're your dead husband. That's some prank.'

Adrianna shoved long, trembling fingers through her hair. 'Funny, right?'

He moved to her phone, picked up her receiver, and dialed star sixty-nine. Within seconds an automated voice came on the line and gave him the number of the last incoming call. He picked up a Montblanc pen from her desk and scratched the number on a blue Post-it note.

'What's that?' she said.

'The number of the person who just called you.' He hung

up and dialed another number. When the police department communications officer answered, he gave her the number and asked for a quick back trace. On hold, he let the phone slip below his ear. He towered over her. 'Should be just a second before I have a name to go with the number.'

She clasped her hands so tightly her knuckles whitened. 'It's that easy?'

'Sometimes.' She looked perfect, as always, dressed in a lemon-colored wrap top, black form-fitting slacks, and a gold necklace that looked expensive. Long hair draped her shoulders and accentuated a high slash of cheekbones and long neck. Gone were the glasses, and make-up covered the freckles on her nose.

He glanced down at the sketch on her desk. It was clearly a man's study. Deep blues, khakis, and whites set off the deep tones of a large wooden desk and two over-stuffed club chairs in front of a fireplace. He thought about his own den painted antique white and stocked with a couple of La-Z-Boys and a wide-screen TV. Practical and no frills, just the way he liked it.

'You don't have to do this. It was just a bad joke.' Adrianna's perfume had changed since they'd been together. Flowers had been replaced by spice.

'Won't take but a minute.'

'Detective Hudson,' the communications officer said.

Adrianna opened her mouth to protest.

Gage raised a finger. 'Do you have a name? Thanks.' He hung up the phone.

'Well?' Adrianna looked at him hopefully.

It dug at him that he didn't have an answer for her. 'The number's no good. Untraceable cell.'

She shoved out a breath. 'Great.'

'Have you been getting a lot of calls like that?' He watched her closely, finding he learned more from her body language than he did her words.

'No. That was the first phone call.'

A hesitation in her voice had him asking, 'What else happened?'

She paused, unclasped her hands, and then dropped them to her side. 'I found a card on my car windshield on Tuesday. It was an anniversary card.' A hint of color rose in her pale cheeks. 'Tuesday would have been Craig's and my third wedding anniversary.'

'Where was your car parked?'

'In my driveway.'

He frowned. 'What can you tell me about the card?'

'Standard anniversary card. But it was signed on the inside. *Love, Craig.*'

'Where's the card?'

'I tossed it in my garbage can. And the trash man came yesterday, so it's gone.'

'Do you know who could be doing this?'

'I know there are a lot of people who hate to see the Thornton estate being sold. Lots of tradition in that area. The Thornton family was a big part of that county's history. And now I'm selling the land to a man who's going to build thirty homes on it.'

Gage reached in his coat pocket, pulled out a business card, and scrawled his cell number on it. 'If it happens again, call me.'

She took the card, frowning down at it. Accepting his help clearly didn't set well with her. 'What are you doing here?'

'I just came from a meeting with Janet Guthrie. She told me Craig and Rhonda were having an affair.' He watched her reaction closely.

Disbelief mingled with anger. 'She's lying.'

'Why would she lie?'

'She resented Craig. I think she'd do anything to ruin his reputation.'

Gage folded his arms. 'My ex-wife said she'd never cheat on me. Twenty-twenty hindsight revealed just how paper thin her tales had been.'

'I know it sounds like I'm being foolish. But I'm not.'

'You broke up with him once before. Was it over a woman then?'

'No. I broke up with Craig because he needed to grow up. I refused to marry a boy when I needed a man in my life.'

'So you left him to teach him a lesson?' Resentment crept into his voice.

'When I left him it was for good.' She held his gaze. 'When I was dating you, I didn't plan to return to him.'

'But you did.'

'Yes.' She adjusted the bracelet on her wrist. 'Even you have to admit that things had soured between us by that time. You were working that case. You never had time for me.'

Gage refused to apologize. He had been working the case of a missing child. Yeah, he'd been moody as hell. He'd taken it out on Adrianna. She'd started pulling away from him but he'd figured he could make it up to her later. He'd been wrong.

'Did Craig do anything that might have made you think twice?'

'He wasn't having an affair with Rhonda. Craig knew what my father's infidelities did to my mother and how I resented him for all the pain. I wouldn't have tolerated that kind of marriage.'

He believed her. The question was, had Craig fooled her? 'Any time that made you think twice about his actions? Something he said or did that didn't fit.'

She huffed out a breath and for a moment he thought she'd not answer. And then her brow wrinkled as if a memory elbowed its way to the front of her mind. 'There was one time. At our wedding reception. Something had really rattled him but he wouldn't say what it was.'

'Was he upset before the wedding?'

'No, he seemed fine. It was about midway through the reception. He was laughing one minute and the next he looked ready to jump out of his skin.'

'He get a call?'

'Honestly, I don't know. There was so much going on. Brides don't get much time to think on their wedding day. Do you think Rhonda called him?'

'According to Janet, Rhonda was blackmailing Craig. Rhonda wanted to marry him, but ended up with cash instead.'

A bitter smile tipped the edge of her lips. 'He never would have married her.'

'Why?'

'He wouldn't have married a nobody over a Barrington. The fact that we'd grown up in the same world was so important to him. He liked the connections my family brought.' A bitter smile twisted her lips. 'Looks like I got the last laugh after all.'

'What do you mean?'

'I'm not a real Barrington. I'm adopted.'

'Do you really think Craig wouldn't have married you if he knew you were adopted?'

'He might have dated plain old Sarah Turner, but he'd not have married her. Bloodlines were very important to Craig and his mother. He could be a bit of a snob.'

'Sarah Turner is your birth name?'

'Yes.'

Sarah. The name didn't fit her. Adrianna did. Her upbringing more than genetics had molded her.

'I can assure you Janet is wrong about the affair. He'd have had no reason to kill her.'

Gage pulled a notebook from his pocket and flipped through a couple of pages. 'What was the name of the nursing home that took care of Craig?'

'Shady Grove Estates. Dr. Henry Gregory was his attending. Why?'

'Just curious. His medical bills must have cost you a fortune.'

'Insurance barely covered half of the first year. He'd downgraded his policy. After that it was a real struggle.'

'Didn't the sale of the gallery help with the bills?'

'Janet paid half of what the gallery was worth.'

Gage shook his head. 'I know critical care is expensive, but so expensive that you sold your home, the gallery, and now the estate? What am I missing?'

'It wasn't just the medical bills. There was quite a bit of debt before the accident. Craig made a lot of bad investments. I learned shortly after we married that the Thorntons had been living on credit for over a decade. I've sold everything they owned and I'm barely breaking even. If Mazur wants his money back . . .'

'You don't have it.'

'No. And no doubt he'll take my house, my mother's house, and my business.'

'Why your mother's home?'

'Dad left everything to me with the understanding I take care of her.'

'You're on the edge?'

'Couldn't get any closer without falling.'

He felt for her. Wanted to help her. And a week ago, he might have seen his way to do that. Despite their history, she was in trouble.

But he couldn't help her now. If anything, he needed to maintain the distance between them to solve this case. 'Why didn't you tell me Rhonda Minor's brother came to Craig's funeral?'

'Honestly, I didn't remember it. That whole time is a blur.'

'Now that I've jogged your memory, what do you recall?'

'I asked if he'd found his sister. He said no.'

'Do me a favor and start thinking about that whole time. Real hard.'

'Jerk.'

Adrianna flung her pencil on the drawing board. Gage's visit had rendered her creatively dead in the water.

Elbows on the table, she cradled her head in her hands. Gage was a smart detective, tenacious at times. He was not going to give up on this case until it was solved.

The chime on the front door rang. She checked her watch. Rising, she moved through the curtains separating her office from the retail space, half-expecting Gage.

Phyllis had just signed for a stunning bouquet of white roses. She turned toward Adrianna. 'Have you ever seen flowers so lovely?'

The blooms drove her deeper into her sour mood. 'Who sent them?'

Phyllis searched through the blooms and found a small white card. 'Here it is.'

Adrianna opened the envelope and glanced at the bold script on the card. It read: *Love, Craig*. 'Damn it.'

Phyllis's eyes widened. 'What is it?'

She grabbed the bouquet, wincing when one of the thorns pricked her finger. Blood bloomed on her thumb. 'A really bad joke.'

'It's a stunning arrangement of flowers. How could it be a joke?'

Adrianna handed her the card. 'Read it.'

'Oh, Adrianna,' Phyllis said. 'This is awful.'

Flowers in hand, Adrianna stormed out the front door of the shop and down the sidewalk toward the Dumpster out back.

'Hey, Adrianna.' The sharp tone of Kendall's voice had her pausing in mid-stride.

Adrianna turned to see her sister stride toward her. Kendall wore a chocolate pantsuit with a tailored jacket that skimmed her hips and a cream-colored silk blouse. Her dark hair was woven into a twist. Dark sunglasses and pointed black high heels completed the look.

'What are you doing?' Kendall asked.

'I'll be right back.' High heels clicked on the asphalt. 'I'm headed to the Dumpster.'

'Tell me you aren't tossing those flowers.' Kendall's long legs ate up the space between them and she caught up to Adrianna as she reached the Dumpster.

'I am.'

Kendall touched a blossom. 'Good Lord, why? These flowers are stunning.'

Adrianna lowered the vase, swallowing sudden tears that threatened. 'The card reads *Love, Craig*.'

Kendall's gaze sharpened. She took the flowers from Adrianna and tossed them in the Dumpster. The glass vase shattered on the Dumpster's metal floor and white roses scattered across the filthy bottom.

Adrianna stared at the splay of flowers. 'I carried white roses in my wedding bouquet because of their poetic meaning: *I am worthy of you*.'

'Let's go have coffee.'

Adrianna swiped away a tear. 'I felt anything but worthy that morning.'

'Honey, why?'

'I loved Craig, but not like a wife should have.' She tried to smile. 'I never told anyone that.'

Kendall touched her shoulder. 'Coffee. Now.'

'I can't. I've got a design to finish. And I've got to get out to the estate and oversee the furniture removal.'

'Take five, Adrianna. You need it more than you realize.'

The softness in Kendall's tone caught her attention. 'Okay. Just a few minutes.'

They walked down the row of shops to the coffee shop located three stores down from Barrington Designs. The place smelled of cinnamon and fresh roasted coffee. The half dozen round tables were empty. Kendall moved to the counter and ordered an espresso. 'What's your poison?'

'I forgot my purse.'

'Please. I've got this. What do you want?'

'Cappuccino. Extra cream. And a muffin.'

Kendall smiled and placed the order and in less than a minute both were sitting at a table by the window. Outside they had a grand view of the eight lanes of Broad Street and the large mall across the street. 'Not exactly a view of the Seine, but I suppose it will do.'

Adrianna dumped two packets of sugar into her drink and stirred. 'It's fine.'

Kendall sipped her espresso. 'You look stunning, by the way. I love that blouse.'

'Thanks. You look pretty great yourself.'

'The more I get to know you, the more I see your design work, the more I realize how much we are alike.'

Adrianna couldn't deny the strong tug of genetics. 'I never gave much thought to the nature-versus-nurture debate until all this stuff that came up between us. It is odd how much alike we are.'

'So why aren't we better friends?' Candid sadness underscored Kendall's words.

Adrianna shook her head. 'Friendship and family take time, I suppose. We share blood, but no history. And we're different in a lot of ways.'

Kendall sipped her coffee but her gaze was like a laser. 'What do you mean?'

'You are so direct. You cut to the chase. You ask for everything you want, whereas I scramble around trying to please everyone and keep the peace. I can't imagine you in my kind of mess.'

Kendall laughed. 'I've made my share of mistakes. Just ask my husband. And the wanting-to-please-others thing is very common in adult adoptees.'

'I didn't know I was adopted. My parents lied, remember?'

Kendall dropped her voice a notch. 'Oh, come on. Are you telling me you didn't know on some level that you weren't born to the Barringtons? I bet you can look back and find a few moments when you stopped and thought: I just don't fit here.'

Adrianna pinched a piece from her muffin, hesitant to voice this long-held secret. 'Maybe. A couple of times. Okay, more than a few times. But doesn't every kid think she was dropped off by the gypsies at some point?'

Kendall ignored the joke. 'When did you feel like you didn't belong?'

The words tightened around her throat like a noose. 'I can see why you became a reporter.'

Kendall shrugged. 'You're dodging the question.'

'I know.'

Kendall waited, letting the silence do her coaxing.

Adrianna met her gaze. 'Nothing ever felt right when Mom was in one of her depressions. I just couldn't imagine how I'd come from her. On my worst day, I couldn't understand Mom's moods. And I was so much taller than Mom, even taller than Dad. And Dad was so sick with his diabetes. I never had any of their health problems.'

Kendall nodded, satisfied. 'Anything else?'

'I was about twelve and needed a stapler for a project I was working on. I went into Dad's home office and opened the front desk drawer because I knew that's where he kept it. That's when I found a picture of Dad standing by Mom. She was holding a newborn. He looked so happy and so did she. I never ever remembered seeing them that happy around me. It was as if a different couple raised me.'

'Their baby's death changed them.'

'The other Adrianna.'

'Jacob investigated the death himself. The family doctor confirmed she died of crib death.'

Adrianna tapped her finger on the side of her cup. 'You ever suspect there was more to a story even when the evidence was to the contrary?'

Kendall's lips tipped into a smile. 'Sure.'

'That's where I am with this. I just sense something happened.'

'Do you want me to talk to Jacob?'

'And tell him what? That I have a feeling? No. There's no reason to tell him anything.'

'There's got to be someone in that house who knew about the switch.'

'The housekeeper, Estelle, who just about raised me was hired when I was three months old.'

'After the switch?'

'Yeah.'

'What about neighbors? My parents' old neighbors helped me with my search. You'd be surprised what people in the neighborhood know.'

'I could ask Estelle again.'

Kendall tapped a manicured finger on the side of her cup. 'If you need help doing a little unofficial digging, I'm your girl.'

'I appreciate that. I really do. But this is something I've got to do for myself.'

'I get that.'

Adrianna shook her head. 'My whole life is based on so many lies.'

'Your mother should have told you. You had a right to know about your past, your biology. But I do believe she loves you. My own adoptive mother kept secrets, but I realize now she did it out of love for me.'

Anger burned in her belly. 'Mom didn't keep her secrets out of love. Fear motivated her. And regardless, I should have been told.'

'Agreed.'

Adrianna sat back in her chair. As furious as she was, she maintained a deep loyalty to her mother. A full-blooded sister still didn't trump a lifetime of memories. 'This conversation has gone a little deeper than I'd planned.'

Kendall opened her mouth to speak and then closed it. She laughed. 'Sorry. It is hard to turn off the reporter in my brain. Speaking of which, how goes it at the Thornton estate?'

'It's not. All work has stopped for now.'

'Jacob's not saying a word on this one.'

'Why not?'

'Our connection.'

'I'm sorry.'

'Don't be. We all have priorities.'

For the first time Adrianna heard a hint of sadness in her sister's voice.

'I don't want this to get in between you and Jacob.'

'It won't. We're stronger than that.'

'I envy you. Your marriage.' Adrianna fiddled with her muffin but didn't eat it.

'You'll find it one day.'

'Thanks.' Adrianna thought she had at one time with Gage. But she'd been wrong. 'Detective Hudson just informed me that Craig was having an affair with his secretary.'

Kendall shook her head. 'I'm really sorry.'

'I don't believe it.'

Kendall arched a brow.

'Yeah, that's the same look Hudson gave me. But I'm not wrong about this. Craig was a fool when it came to money, but he did love me.'

'Okay.'

'You want to hear something really crazy?'

'Sure.'

'I dated Hudson four years ago.'

Kendall's mouth dropped open, her shock undeniable. 'Say that again.'

'It was the summer I broke up with Craig. We dated that whole summer.'

'Wow.'

'Yeah.'

'Why'd you break up?'

'He worked a great deal of the time. Kind of obsessed with his cases. As much as he wanted to spend time with me, he wanted to work more.'

'I can see that happening. Cases can get under their skin.'

'He called last minute one Friday. Cancelled so he could keep working. It was the third time in a row and I'd made a gourmet meal. I was so mad. So hurt. I was tired of being last on the priority list.'

'You let him have it?'

'No. And I should have. Maybe if we'd had a knock-down drag-out fight I could have cleared the air. But I didn't say a word. And then Craig called. He was so sweet it was easy to forget why we'd broken up. I invited him to dinner. I broke up with Gage a few days later.'

Kendall sat back in her chair, her amazed shock palpable. 'That couldn't have been easy.'

'No.' Gage had been so wrapped in anger and frustration he'd barely been able to talk. She could barely finish what she had to say before she bolted from his office.

Gratefully, Kendall didn't ask for the details. 'And now he's investigating a murder on Thornton land.'

'Small world.'

'Gage is a fair man,' Kendall said. 'He'll do the job right.'

'I know.'

'Do you still have feelings for Gage?'

Adrianna all but stuttered out a forced, 'No.'

Kendall studied her a beat. 'You sure?'

'Yes!'

'I saw the sizzle in the room between you two at the estate.'

'I've no feelings for him.'

'Okay. But if you want to talk about him or any of this, know you can and it will stay between us.'

'Thanks.'

'It's what sisters do.'

'You know, I have no idea what being a sister entails.'

'Frankly, neither do I. But I hear from friends that it involves borrowing clothes, gossiping about men, and having the occasional fight.'

Adrianna smiled. 'I've heard a sister is the one person you can tell to go to hell in one breath and then ask to borrow a quarter from in the next.'

Kendall flashed even white teeth. 'I'll add that to the list.'

'List?'

'I've been reading up on sisterhood and keeping a list of bits of wisdom.'

If her own mother had been honest about her adoption, then maybe she might have sought Kendall out years ago. 'I'm afraid I haven't given us a lot of thought.'

'You've been up to your neck in bigger problems. I get that. And I don't want to add to your problems, like I'm one more person you have to worry about.' Kendall sounded as if she genuinely meant it.

'Thank you.'

'For what?'

'Just being here. Talking. It's nice to sit down and just talk.'

They chatted for a few moments and when it came time to leave, Kendall paused. 'Do you think you should tell Gage about those flowers? This is the behavior of a stalker.'

Adrianna grinned, determined to convince them both there was nothing to really worry about. 'I don't have a stalker.'

'Don't be so sure about that.'

Chapter Fourteen

Thursday, September 28, 2:00 p.m.

'Just have Dr. Gregory call me,' Gage said. He parked on East Broad Street in front of an old building that had been divided into small offices.

'No doctor?' Vega said.

'He's with a patient. Nurse said he'd call back in a couple of hours.'

'Why do you want to talk to him? It's not a great shock that Thornton died.'

'Adrianna said the doctors expected him to live another ten years. And then he just died in his sleep.'

'You think she had something to do with it?'

'No. But someone else might have.'

'Who?'

'The million-dollar question, my friend.'

Vega glanced at the building beside them. 'This is the address Dr. Heckman gave?'

'Yep.' They crossed the street and into the old building that smelled of must and garbage. The lobby floor tile was cracked and coated in years of grim and the overhead lights were dead or dying.

Vega punched the elevator button, but the car never came. 'Figures it doesn't work. What floor is he on?'

'Fifth.'

'Damn.'

In silence they climbed the dim staircase and followed the numbers on the wall until they found 504, the suite number on the card.

Vega brushed his hands as if trying to rid himself of the place's filth. 'I can't believe he works in a place like this.'

'Fitting, if you ask me.'

Dr. Heckman's voice echoed from the office. 'Have him call me at once. You have my number? I left it the last few times I called. Good, right, well, tell him to call. It's urgent.'

Gage pushed open the door and they found Dr. Heckman sitting behind an old desk piled high with papers, journals, and books. Behind him were signs that read SAVE THE DEAD. The room smelled of pastrami.

The old man glanced up and peered over his glasses. 'Detectives.'

Gage wondered if the guy had ever had a visitor in this office. 'Had a few more questions.'

'Sure. Would you like to sit?' A large mustard stain darkened the lapel of his jacket.

Gage glanced at the rickety chairs filled with more books, papers, and trash. 'We'll stand.'

Dr. Heckman knitted his fingers together in a tight hold. 'Have you moved the graves?'

'No, sir, everyone's where we left 'em.'

Some tension eased from the old man. 'Thank goodness. Why the visit?'

'Wonder if you could tell me a little about Frances Thornton and the folks closest to her son Craig.'

'Mrs. Thornton was a wonderful woman. Graceful. Beautiful. Dedicated to her family and the Thornton legacy.'

'How'd you two meet?'

'We've known each other for years. We met through the historical society. I also knew her late husband, Robert.'

'So you kept up all these years?'

'No. Separate paths and lives. I only came back into her life a few years ago.'

'Why?'

He adjusted his glasses. 'We met at a museum function by accident. We struck up our old friendship. We both love history and family legacies.' Dr. Heckman rattled off mundane facts about their meetings. The common thread was history.

Gage wondered how accidental Dr. Heckman's meeting with Frances Thornton had been. 'Frances Thornton cared a lot about the Thornton name?'

The old man's eyes glistened. 'It meant everything to her. Everything.'

'She'd have done just about anything to protect it?'

Dr. Heckman blinked, considered the question. 'She would have done what was necessary to save that grand family.'

Did necessary mean murder? 'What about Adrianna? She as dedicated to the family?'

Dr. Heckman's eyes lost their momentary spark. 'She has proven to be a poor steward of the land. All you have to do is look at the house to see she doesn't care.'

'Her hands have been mighty full these last couple of years.'

'A place like the Colonies needs love and attention, just like people.'

'What's it cost to run the Colonies?'

'Money shouldn't be a factor.'

Vega lifted his gaze from a pile of old magazines. 'It is when you don't have it.'

Dr. Heckman shrugged.

'So you're not happy about Mazur buying the place.'

'He's going to ruin it all.'

Vega sniffed. 'He's restoring the house. Gonna cost him some real money.'

'Adrianna Thornton could have found a way to save that house. She could have kept it in the family.'

'She's not a Thornton anymore.' Gage delivered the words with an unintended force.

Vega tossed him a quick glance, then focused on Dr. Heckman. 'Got any pictures of the Thorntons? I keep hearing names but can't picture anyone.'

He frowned, turned to a pile of random papers, and started to dig. After a few minutes of searching, he found an old black-and-white. 'It was taken on Frances and Robert's wedding day.'

Gage studied the picture. The image caught him off guard. Frances was a stunning woman, as regal as Adrianna. Robert, however, was a short man, with a stocky build. He studied the wedding party and a woman on the right caught his attention. 'This Margaret Barrington?'

'Yes. But her last name was Young then. The Youngs and Thorntons went way back. Margaret and Frances went to school together. Margaret introduced Frances to Robert.'

'They stay friends?' Gage said.

'All their lives. Margaret was at Frances's side when she passed.'

Gage studied the crowd of smiling faces behind the

wedding couple. The Wellses stood in the background. 'Mind if I keep this for a while?'

'If you return it.'

'Oh, I will.' Gage carefully slid the picture in his breast pocket. He thought about the tail end of Dr. Heckman's call. Gut instinct had him saying, 'You realize I'm trying to keep this quiet. I don't want a bunch of curiosity seekers in that crime scene.'

The old man raised a bearded chin. 'Do you realize what you are asking? Those graves are about to be desecrated. People have a right to know.'

Gage moved to the edge of Dr. Heckman's desk and stared down at him. 'I'm advising you to keep quiet.'

The old man rose on trembling legs. 'You have a job to do and so do I.'

Gage tightened and released his jaw. 'Remember what I said.'

The two detectives left and as they climbed down the stairs, Vega said, 'He's gonna talk to the press. Just a matter of time.'

'I know. At least he doesn't know who we found.'

Gage and Vega arrived at the Moondance Apartments twenty minutes later. The apartments had been built in the seventies and the heavy wood paneling on the outside of the ten large apartment buildings had been painted sometime in the eighties. But the place still looked dated and run down. The rental office was located on the second floor of one of the apartment buildings in a converted unit.

'Not exactly first class,' Vega said. 'Odd that Thornton would keep an apartment here.'

'It's the last place I would have looked for him.'

'It's also the last place his fiancée/wife would look.'

Gage pushed through the front door, which opened onto a living room setup. At the far end by a large bay window a young woman sat behind a desk. In the center of the desk were papers and on the edge a large fishbowl filled with colorful jellybeans.

The girl looked up at the detectives, her smile bright. 'Can I interest you two in an apartment? We have a special this month. Rent now and we'll give you your last month's rent free.'

Smiling, Gage pulled out his badge. 'We're with Henrico Police. I'd like to see the manager.'

The girl's eyes widened. 'Oh yeah, sure. I'll be right back.' She rose and disappeared down a shag-carpeted hallway that led to a back office.

Vega reached in the candy jar and scooped out a handful of jellybeans. 'Be a minor miracle if anyone remembers Craig Thornton. Employee turnover in these places can be pretty quick.'

'We'll see.'

Vega popped the jellybeans in his mouth.

Seconds later a petite woman with reddish hair and large glasses appeared. She wore a pale green pantsuit and glossy pink lipstick. 'My name is Wanda. I'm the manager. Can I help you?'

Gage explained the reason for the visit. 'I'm trying to track down a former tenant of yours. Craig Thornton and Rhonda Minor.'

Wanda rested a petite hand on her slim hip. 'When did they live here?'

'Would have been about three or four years ago.'

'If I saw their faces I might be able to help. I get to know people's faces when they drop off their rent checks. But I'm not so good connecting faces and names.'

Gage pulled out a picture of Craig and Rhonda. 'Do they look familiar?'

She studied the picture. Her glasses magnified her blue eyes, making her look a bit like an owl. 'I sure do. It's been a few years since he and his wife moved out.'

'Wife?'

'Yeah. A cute little brunette. Fact, I remember her more than him. She dropped off the rent check. He kept to himself. She liked the summer pool parties but he didn't.' She shook her head. 'Funny the things you remember about people.'

'What do you remember about her?'

She handed him back the pictures. 'She was a pain in my backside, if you know what I mean.'

'No, I don't.'

'She paid her rent on time but she was always playing her music too loud. Her next-door neighbor was always complaining to me. She in trouble? Wouldn't surprise me got into a fix.'

'She's dead.'

'Oh. Sorry. What happened?' She pushed up her glasses with her index finger.

'We're still working on that,' Gage said. 'I'd like to see your files if you have them.'

'I got my dead files in a storage room at the clubhouse.' She blushed realizing what she'd said. 'No pun.'

'Right. Can you show us?'

'Sure. Susan, hold down the fort.'

The girl smiled. 'Sure, Ms. Wanda.'

Wanda opened Susan's desk and pulled out a thick roll of keys. 'Follow me.'

Gage and Vega trailed behind Wanda, whose quick steps reminded him of a hummingbird. He doubted she ever slowed down for a breath. They crossed the parking lot and went into the complex's clubhouse. Unlike the rest of the property, it looked as if it had been renovated in the last five years. Grays and mauves were featured in the furnishings and patterned wallpaper. In the center of the room was a pool table and outside sliding glass doors a swimming pool, sporting its winter cover.

Wanda moved to a door, opened it, and flipped on a light. Rows of filing cabinets filled the room. She moved to a section on the right, pulled open a drawer, and flipped through dozens of manila folders and pulled out a thick file.

'As you can see, she cost me a good deal of paperwork.'

Gage nodded. 'What's the name on the file?'

'The Starlight Corporation.'

'Corporation?' Gage said.

Wanda opened the file. 'I remember it was printed on her checks.'

Gage nodded. They'd leased the apartment under a corporate name, which explained why his searches three years ago hadn't turned up this place.

Wanda glanced at her notes in the file and then pulled out two photos. She handed the pictures to Gage.

Rhonda and Craig's unattractive identification pictures stared back at him. 'You keep pictures of all your residents?'

'The ones that want a pool pass. We went to picture IDs about ten years ago. Folks kept trying to sneak non-residents into the pool. I remember he didn't want his picture taken, but she insisted. I don't think he ever did come to the pool.'

'What can you tell me about her?'

'Perky. Smiled a lot.'

'Where'd she go after she left?'

'Said she and her husband were moving to Florida — that he'd gotten a new job. And she paid the three-month balance of her lease in advance. Normally, she paid her rent a day or two late. Always said she forgot. She paid this balance in cash. I was shocked enough to underline *cash* three times.'

He glanced at the notation, which she'd punctuated with an exclamation mark. 'Did she give a forwarding address?'

'She did. But it turned out to be no good — a fact I found out when maintenance crews went to flip the apartment and discovered it was a disaster.'

Vega raised a brow. 'Flip?'

'Paint, clean, inspect. We do it on all units.'

'Right.'

'What did the maintenance people find?' Gage said.

'The crew found that she'd left a lot of her furniture and a good bit of trash: paint, brushes, and a ripped canvas.' She pulled out a couple of color photos, which documented the damage and mess.

Gage studied the pictures. His attention settled on a large carpet stain. 'What was this?'

'Nasty stain in the back bedroom.'

'What kind of stain?' Gage said.

'Brownish, red. One of the guys thought it was blood, turned out to be paint. They had to pull up the carpet and padding and replace both. I took that out of her security deposit.'

'Didn't you have to mail the balance to her?' Vega said.

'The carpet and padding replacement ate it up. In fact, my notes say the girl owed me six dollars more after it was all said and done. I called her cell but didn't get an answer. I mailed an invoice to the address she gave me but when it was returned *Address Unknown*, I wrote the six bucks off. It would have cost me more in phone calls to track her down.'

'Did you mark the date she paid you the last three months' rent?'

Wanda glanced at her pad. 'September twenty-fifth, three years ago. Almost to the day. Imagine that. So if she's dead, where's her husband?'

'He's of no help,' Gage said. 'You ever note any visitors to the apartment?'

'I notice when people pay and when they use the amenities. Beyond that I don't track my residents. I've got one hundred and fifty units.'

'Any of her old neighbors still around?'

She glanced at the file. 'Rhonda was in building six, second floor, apartment five.' She closed her eyes as if mentally running through the building. 'Apartment seven was living across the hall about that time. He'd remember Rhonda. I heard they got into some real fights over her music.'

'Do you have apartment seven's contact information?'

'Sure.' She held her walkie-talkie to her mouth. 'Susan,

this is Wanda. I need some info on building six, unit number seven.'

'Ten four, Ms. Wanda.'

Wanda's pert nod reminded Gage of his third-grade schoolteacher – Mrs. McCormick. As he remembered, he was always in trouble for making triangular footballs out of his worksheets.

Minutes later, Susan's voice squawked over the radio. 'Man's name is Mark Benton and he works for the power company.' She gave them his cell and work numbers.

Gage scribbled down the information as it came over the radio.

'Thank you, Susan. Over.' Wanda looked at Gage. 'You got that?'

'Yes. Thanks.' Gage handed her his card. 'If you think of anything else, call me.'

She held up his card. 'I'll put my thinking cap on and if I come up with something I'll call.'

'Thanks.'

Gage and Vega walked over to Rhonda's apartment building and knocked on the door of unit seven. Several seconds passed and no answer. Gage was reaching for a business card when he heard footsteps inside.

Vega stood back, hands on hips.

The door snapped open to a large man dressed in sweats, a stained T-shirt, and flip-flops. Black hair stuck up as if he'd just gotten out of bed and under thick dark chin stubble a sallow complexion suggested the guy was home sick. 'Yeah?'

'Mark Benton?' Gage introduced them and each showed their badges.

'Yeah?' Suspicion changed the entire tone of the word.

'We have questions about a former neighbor of yours. Rhonda Minor.'

He turned and coughed. 'What's she done now? Or what does she want?'

'Nothing. We just have a few questions about what kind of trouble she made for you.'

'Crazy bitch. She played that damn music of hers all the time. When I asked her to turn it down she would for a while but within an hour it was cranked again. Said she couldn't paint without the music. And then that idiot husband of hers sideswiped my car.'

'When was that?'

'Oh, I don't know. It was fall that last year she was here. They were having a fight and he tore out of here like a bat out of hell and hit my bumper.'

'Did he stop?'

'Damn right, he did.' Benton smelled of chips and beer. 'He was all attitude until I threatened to call the cops. Then he softened right up. Paid for the damage in cash.' He grunted. 'Rhonda even tried to be nice for a few days after that as if her boyfriend told her to keep quiet and stay out of my way. She offered me one of her paintings as a peace offering.'

'You take it?'

'Yeah.'

'You still have it?'

'Naw. It was a landscape. I gave it to my mom.'

'I'd like to see it.'

Mark shrugged. 'I'm seeing her in a couple of days. She

lives in Roanoke. I'll take a picture with my phone and e-mail it to you.'

'Thanks. Did Rhonda ever have any other visitors?'

'Not too many. She was either painting or playing that damn music. Not much of a life.' He snapped his fingers. 'She did get a visit from a woman late one night right before she left. I remember because they got into a fight, too. And don't ask me what about because I couldn't hear the words only the tone of their voices.'

'Can you describe the woman?' Vega said.

'She wore a hat. Blond. She looked rich and fancy.'

Gage held up a picture of Adrianna. 'Her name?'

'I couldn't say.'

Gage handed Mark his card. 'If you think of anything else, would you call me?'

'Yeah, sure.' He glanced at the card. 'So what did Rhonda do?'

'She was murdered shortly after you last saw her.'

His face paled. 'Well, I sure as shit didn't kill her.'

'I didn't say you did,' Gage said. 'But I do want you to keep thinking about those last days she lived here. Any detail will be helpful.'

The guy looked flustered. 'Yeah, yeah, sure.'

'Thanks.'

After Benton's door closed and the two descended the stairs, Vega said, 'Three years is a long time. He must have been some kind of mad to remember Rhonda.'

'Mad enough to kill her?'

'Another million-dollar question.'

'So what's next?'

'Alex thinks the other victim was dead four or five years.' That had been the time he and Adrianna had dated. 'I should have financial records for Craig by now. Hopefully, there are some credit card receipts that show us what he was up to about that time. We'll also do a check on Mark Benton.'

'You heard what Benton said. Blond. Well dressed. Icy. Janet says Craig was having an affair. Think he's talking about Adrianna Barrington?'

Gage measured his words and tone carefully. 'We've got two victims, not one. And you're assuming the victims both knew Thornton and his wife.'

'Both were female. Both on Thornton land. Come on. There has to be a connection to the guy. And I don't care what Adrianna Barrington said about her man not having an affair, I'd bet a paycheck he was and she knew about it.'

'I don't buy it.'

'Who wants to tell their friends at the country club that their old man's been doing the secretary at the office? Or that her zillion-dollar wedding might be off? She'd have a lot of humiliation to deal with if he dumped her.'

Gage drew in a breath. 'Let's see what Dr. Butler has to say.'

Tammy Borden's head pounded like she'd been on a three-day bender. Her mouth was dry and her limbs felt like they were covered in lead. Her first thought was that she'd fallen off the wagon. She'd been struggling to stay sober since she'd gotten out of jail. The booze was everywhere.

She remembered buying the bottle of vodka before her meeting. She'd prayed the meeting would straighten out her thinking but when she'd walked out of that meeting she'd been determined to kill it.

She not only craved the buzz but a blissfully numb mind that would let her forget that she'd murdered a man and his child.

Tammy glanced around the room. Dark and dim and windowless, the room had a dank smell. She sat a little straighter and ran a trembling hand through her hair.

As the seconds passed she realized she wasn't drunk or coming off a bender. Her heart started to race a little faster as memories flooded back. The parking lot. That guy and the stun gun.

Tammy tried to stand and then realized a chain bound her to the floor. She jerked at the chain but it was a good inch thick and made of galvanized metal. She screamed, 'Help!'

Her voice echoed off the concrete walls and bounced back like a rubber ball. She screamed again. After nearly fifteen minutes, her voice was hoarse and scratched. And no one had heard her.

Over the last three years she'd wished for death often enough. Now she feared she'd finally landed in hell.

'Oh God, oh God.'

A light rain ushered in the evening as Gage and Vega arrived at the medical examiner's office. They moved through the antiseptic hallways at a brisk pace and found Dr. Butler in his windowless small office. Shelves, jammed full of books and papers, lined the small space from floor to ceiling. In the center was a government-issue desk where two laptop computers hummed between towers of more papers and books.

Dr. Butler looked up from his computer, seemingly unaware of the chaos in his office. 'Good. You got my text message.'

Gage nodded. 'So what do you have?' There were two chairs in front of the desk but both were filled with files. He wondered how the guy could breathe in this kind of space.

Dr. Butler turned from one laptop to the other and with the few clicks of his mouse opened a document. 'I've reviewed the bones carefully. Took x-rays, searched for birth defects, injuries both old and new, job-related anomalies, and anything that might set her apart.'

'And?' Gage said.

'Rhonda Minor had two fractures on her face. The left cheekbone and the bottom right jaw. The fracture on the left was just a hairline whereas the blow to her right jaw had enough force to break teeth. The injuries hadn't fully healed, but the healing process had begun. Bone knitting begins immediately but takes time. It was the same with the other victim. Fractures to the face. Partial healing.'

Gage's lips flattened. 'Any guesses on how long he held them?'

'It would be a very, very rough guess.'

'I'll take it.'

Dr. Butler rubbed his eyes. 'Four or five days, a week maybe.'

Gage clenched and unclenched his jaw. Four or five days. A lifetime for a victim. Four days Jessie had been missing. Shit.

'How long has the other victim been dead?' Vega said.

'Based on the tree roots that had grown through and

around her bones, I'd say she's been dead about four or five years.'

'You can determine time of death by tree roots?' Vega said.

'Factoring in the average growth rate of an oak tree as well as rain we've had over the last couple of years, I can estimate how much the roots would have grown each year.'

Gage was impressed. 'You said you were searching for job-related anomalies.'

'Right,' Dr. Butler said nodding. 'If you work one part of your body more than another, over time muscle builds up. Increased muscle size is reflected on the bone.'

Gage nodded. 'The bone grows to support the muscle.'

'Exactly.' Dr. Butler had an IQ that bumped two hundred yet could break any complex issue down to the simplest terms. 'A horseback rider would have well-developed adductor magnus muscles and femurs. Butt and leg. A trumpet player builds up the cheek muscles and thus the lower jaw changes.'

'And what did you find on Jane Doe?'

'The tibia – lower leg bone – suggested strong calf muscles. And the outer edge of her right shoulder showed signs of a strong deltoid, suggesting she consistently carried heavy objects with her right hand.'

'Strong legs, one arm stronger. A waitress?' Gage said.

'That would be my guess.' Dr. Butler glanced at his notes. 'Jane Doe also had shin splints, suggesting a high-impact sport. Maybe even high heels. The pounding of the feet while wearing high heels is murder on the frame. She had the beginnings of bunions on her feet. Whatever shoes the victim wore didn't fit her feet so well. And her bones showed signs of malnutrition. When she was grow-ing up, she didn't eat as well as she should have and it left a mark on her bones. And changes to her pelvis tell me she gave birth at one point.'

'Supposing she was a waitress,' Gage said. 'And let's assume for the moment she knew Craig Thornton. Two and two equals . . .'

'A cocktail waitress,' Vega said. 'They carry heavy trays, they do wear high heels, and they can make a lot of money in tips, which would appeal to someone who didn't grow up with money and had a kid to support.'

Gage played devil's advocate. 'Why not a waitress who worked in a family restaurant who liked to play soccer or tennis?'

Vega grimaced. 'All good theory if she weren't found on Thornton land, the family home of our rich playboy. Four or five years ago, Thornton would have been in his midtwenties.'

Gage blew out a breath. 'Thanks, Doc.' He turned to Vega. 'We are going to need his financial records ASAP. Chances are if Thornton was a regular anywhere, he put the expense on plastic. Find the venue and we just might find Jane Doe.'

Chapter Fifteen

Friday, September 29, 9:00 a.m.

'And now I'd like to introduce Adrianna Barrington, the spokesperson for Virginians for Safer Roads. Let's give her a warm welcome.' The brief introduction from Charles Norton, the principal at Goodman High School, sounded more like an order than a request. As he applauded he scanned the auditorium full of tenth-grade students, searching for any signs of trouble.

As the students clapped Adrianna moved toward the podium and smiled. She'd given this speech dozens of times in the last couple of years and now rarely used her notecards. However, each time she stepped in front of a crowd she couldn't shake the sense that she was betraying Craig, the Thorntons, and her own family. Secrets, mistakes, even successes weren't shared with the public.

Shoving aside the guilt, Adrianna laid her hands on the podium. 'I had my last conversation with my husband on November twenty-first three years ago.' In the audience three cell phones rang at once and giggles erupted. Adrianna paused, not surprised by the interruption, which went with teen territory. Texts, IMs, and Facebook reigned in their world. It was her job to make drunk driving and death real.

However, the principal had less patience. He moved

behind her, his arms crossed. When the room settled down, she continued. 'Nearly three years ago,' she continued, 'my husband and I were driving to a restaurant. We were talking about when and where we were going to have dinner.' When she'd first started giving the talks she didn't mention the baby. It had been too painful. Lately she talked about her pregnancy. 'I was three months pregnant and I still had morning sickness, so I wanted a restaurant that had good bread and tomato soup to settle my stomach. That is the last thing I remember thinking until I woke up in the hospital a day later.' She pressed a button and behind her a screen dropped. An image of Craig's twisted and mangled BMW appeared on-screen. And as expected, the crowd grew silent. 'What I later learned was that a drunk driver had run a stop sign and plowed right into the side of my husband's car. I lost my baby. My husband survived the accident, but his head injuries were massive. He fell into a coma.'

She pushed another button and more images of the car appeared. Front. Side. Rear. In the background lights from the police and fire vehicles cast a deadly glow on the twisted metal.

The next slide was of Craig taken on his favorite sailing boat. His grin spread across his face. Wind swept through his thick blond hair. Blue eyes flashed. She clicked the button again to the picture taken of Craig lying in his hospital bed. A stunned hush fell over the room. 'His head had been shaved for the initial brain surgery. The doctors were trying to reduce the pressure on his brain. As you can see, his face is so swollen he is almost unrecognizable.' The police had taken this picture after his accident in the hospital. They were trying to make a case against the drunk driver who had been arrested on the scene. 'Craig was pronounced brain dead a day later by his doctors. They told me to take him off life support. After three days of praying and crying, I did. But he didn't die for another two years.'

Adrianna spent a little more time talking about Craig's injuries. She tossed in statistics about drunk driving as she clicked through more pictures of Craig, healthy and young and then again in his coma. The auditorium was silent. All eyes focused on her. 'Now I'd like to answer any questions.'

It took a moment for the first hand to go up. A young girl. Perky, perfect skin and hair, polo shirt and khakis. 'What can you tell us about the person who hit your husband?'

'She was thirty-two at the time of the accident. Pretty, smart, and a nurse at a local hospital. She was liked and respected by friends, many of whom spoke at her sentencing hearing.'

'Why would a hospital hire a drunk for a nurse?' the girl challenged.

'She always prided herself on showing up to work sober. The night she hit my husband's car, she'd just come off an eighteen-hour shift in the emergency room. She'd managed to save the life of a fourteen-year-old who'd almost died from a fall out of a tree house. She was so proud that she'd decided to stop at her favorite bar and have a drink. She ended up having ten. By the time she got into her car, her blood alcohol was twice the legal limit. She ran a stop sign that she'd later swear she never saw.

She hit my husband's car going forty miles an hour – the force of several sticks of dynamite.'

The principal stepped up to the podium. 'What happened to the driver?'

'She received three years in jail. It turns out she'd driven drunk before. This was her third offense. If Craig had died at the scene, she could have gotten ten years. That would have been vehicular homicide. But Craig had the misfortune of lingering and was still alive at the time of her sentencing.'

More questions followed. *What do you do for a living? How old are you? Do you think about your husband a lot?*

Afterward, everyone in the room stood and gave her a round of applause. She knew they were moved by the moment. By her story. And hoped they remembered it past lunch tomorrow. Most wouldn't. But one or two would. And that's all she could hope for.

When her time ended, Adrianna walked into the bright sunshine escorted by the principal. He was her height but his body was soft, fleshy. 'Thank you, Ms. Barrington. That was great.'

She always felt drained after talks like this one. It forced her to relive what she wanted to let go of but couldn't quite. She slipped on her sunglasses. 'Thank you, Principal Norton. I appreciate the opportunity.' She reached in her purse and pulled out two tickets. 'Two tickets to our benefit next week. We're auctioning off some very unique paintings. Please come as my guest. All proceeds benefit the new Thornton Neonatal Unit at Mercy Hospital.'

He accepted the tickets and smiled broadly. 'Thank you.'

'See you then?' The wind blew. Gold bracelets on her wrist jangled as she brushed hair from her eyes.

'I will.' He hesitated. 'Ms. Barrington, can I ask one question?'

'Sure.'

He glanced side to side as if he wasn't sure he should be asking this question. 'The woman who hit your husband, what's her status?'

Her spine was ramrod straight. 'She gets out of prison this month, I believe.'

His frown deepened. 'Do you know if she's stopped drinking?'

How many times had she been asked this question? 'She tells me she has quit.'

As always, her frankness shocked. 'You've spoken to her?'

'She's written to me several times and I've responded.'

His mouth dropped open in shock before he quickly snapped it closed. 'What could she say to you?'

She was grateful her sunglasses cloaked her eyes, which no doubt reflected sadness. 'She wanted my forgiveness.'

'Did you give it to her?' The personal question struck into the heart of so many *what ifs* that stalked her and kept her in a constant state of tension these days.

Adrianna repeated what she told everyone. 'It's a process, Mr. Norton. It's a process.'

In the light of day, she could embrace the idea of forgiveness. But the truth was when thoughts of her baby came to mind – his due date, his first birthday, his first steps – she realized she'd not forgiven Tammy Borden at all.

*

Tess tucked her motorcycle helmet under her arm and pushed through the main door of the medical examiner's office.

It was her first day off in two weeks. And if she were in her right mind or had any semblance of a personal life she'd be doing something fun like wandering through the historic shops in Carytown, getting a manicure or massage, or maybe having lunch with a friend.

But she'd never developed the knack of having fun. That explained her lacking wardrobe, shorn nails, and tense muscles. Work was pretty much her life. The only place she felt right. All the Kiers were defined by their work. Her brother Zack, a reformed work junkie, had gotten better about putting in the long days since he and his wife had had their son, but she and her brother Malcolm were hopeless workaholics. It had cost them relationships, friendships, and too many hours of sleep.

But she'd stopped fretting over her work obsession years ago. It was what it was.

And she had a new case that was eating into her life. Last year she'd collected evidence on three other murdered women. Nightmares had plagued her on those cases for months. In her sleep she heard their screams. She felt the breath being choked from their bodies as they'd been strangled. He had been stopped. Warwick had been the one to break the case.

Last night she'd had dreams, not of killers, but of missing a key piece of evidence. What evidence linked these two bodies that she wasn't seeing?

Tess pushed through the swinging doors of the medical examiner's office in search of Alex. The guy had enough work to do without her hanging around and prodding him with questions, but she'd come this far and as her mother used to say, 'Faint hearts never win.'

Tess found him in the autopsy room at the head of a chrome exam table studying the brain of a sixtysomething male cadaver. Across from Alex was his assistant, a short plump woman with lots of red curly hair peeking out from her surgical cap. Dee something. Both were dressed in scrubs, wore plastic gloves and splashguards to protect their eyes.

At the sound of the door whooshing open Alex and Dee looked up. Even through the thick protective glasses she saw Alex's ice blue eyes darkened with curiosity. 'Tess, what brings you here?'

With both of them staring at her, she felt just a little flat-footed. *I've no life.* 'I came to ask you a couple of questions about the Jane Does.'

Alex straightened to his full six feet. 'I performed a very thorough examination. What more do you want to know?'

'You've already looked at the bodies?'

'Detective Hudson seemed anxious for information. What do you need?'

Something about the remains bothered and pestered her but she couldn't put it into words. 'I just keep thinking that I need to see both side by side.' She glanced at her empty hands, wishing now she'd bought donuts or something. Wasn't that what you were supposed to do when you asked for favors? Instead she just tucked them in her jeans pocket.

'I'm just wrapping up this case and then I was breaking for lunch.'

'Oh right, I know I came without calling and that you have a full schedule. You don't have to stick around. I could just look at the bones alone.'

His gaze dropped to the body. 'Chain of custody makes that impossible in this situation.'

He was right, of course. The bones were in his possession. Chain of custody couldn't be broken. Coming here had been a bad idea. 'Oh, yeah, right. I should have thought about that. I'll leave you to your work. I know you're logging a lot of hours.'

Alex shrugged. 'Part of the territory.' His gaze skimmed her worn jeans and polo shirt. 'You didn't work today.'

'No. Day off. And like I said, I was just curious.' She should have turned and left, but she didn't know where to go. It felt odd, sad even, not to know what to do with her spare time. So she lingered as he finished the autopsy.

Minutes later, Alex glanced up at Dee as he pulled the sheet over the corpse. 'I think we're finally done here. Why don't you head on out to lunch.'

Dee stretched her back. 'You don't have to tell me twice. Unlike some people, I can leave this place behind and have a little fun.'

The barb hit its mark with Tess, but she shrugged as if it didn't matter at all. 'Stop, Dee, you're going to make me cry.'

Dee grimaced. 'Please. You're bulletproof, Tess Kier.'

'I'm Super Girl, baby.' Tess lingered, not sure if Dr. Butler had asked her to stay or go. She opted to stay, figuring he'd toss her out if and when she wore out her welcome.

Alex had stripped off his gloves, goggles, and gown. He turned toward the sink when he spoke. 'Okay, Tess, we can have one more look at the bones.'

'Don't you want lunch?' She wanted to give him an out, to be polite, but honestly, his stomach didn't concern her.

Alex's direct gaze held no hint of emotion. 'Buy me a sandwich after.'

'Sure.' It was a straightforward transaction: food for information.

'All right.' He washed his hands in the sink and removed his outer surgical gown.

'I'll leave you two lovebirds alone,' Dee said.

Both Tess and Alex ignored the comment. Neither needed to say *that* they were about the most non-romantic people in town.

'So what are you looking for with the bones?' His voice lacked inflection.

Sometimes she had the sense that he viewed her as a novice. 'I just know these women deserve better.'

He raised an eyebrow. 'I've been careful with the specimens. I've conducted x-rays, extracted DNA from the teeth, and studied each bone very carefully.'

'I know you've nailed the science stuff, but you see them as specimens.' Irritation crept into her voice.

'Exactly.'

'To me they are more than specimens. They were women.'

Alex shook his head. 'Their humanity is long gone.'

'How can you be so callous?' She'd been looking for a fight since she got up this morning and realized she might just have found one.

'It's not callous. It's logical. Humanity is more than bones. And I deal in facts, Tess. Not emotions. Period. If you're wise you'll do the same.'

The force behind the words surprised her and stoked

her temper. 'I can't just deal in facts. Who the victims were, how they lived, who they loved plays a part in how they died.' She squared her shoulders.

'Reasonable. But you are listing facts.'

'It's more than facts. What did they want from life? What were their dreams? Likes? Dislikes? All that makes up their humanity.'

'All I have are bones.' He sounded so damn reasonable.

'I know.' She sighed. 'It's very important to me that Jane Doe is identified.'

'Why is this so personal to you?'

Jesus, didn't the guy have any feelings? 'There might be people looking for her, worrying.'

He cocked his head a fraction. 'Yes, but why is that important to you?'

'There were no clothes on the body. Not a shred. Even a few years in the ground aren't enough time to eat away at most fabrics. She was naked when he buried her. No man who takes a woman to the woods and strips her naked is doing good things. Her last hours must have been terrifying.'

'Perhaps he stripped the body postmortem so there'd be no identifying bits of clothing.'

'That's always a possibility, but I don't think so. Who-ever did this is a sadist.'

'No facts to support that, but your theory isn't without merit based on what the bones reveal.'

Tess ran long fingers through her hair. 'I really want to catch this guy.'

He nodded. 'Our goals are the same, Tess, but I realize that odds are minimal after the passage of so many years.'

'Alex, don't you ever go on your gut instinct?'

'No.' His voice held no hint of emotion. 'I either have the facts or I don't.'

Tess could feel her frustration growing and knew she needed to get a handle on it. Dial it down a notch or she just might burn another bridge. 'So can I see the bones?'

A silence settled in the room and she half thought he'd tell her to get lost. He didn't. 'Follow me.'

She trailed him into another, smaller tiled room. There were two tables in the room and laid out on each was the completely assembled bones of the victims. The guy must have been up all night for a couple of nights in a row assembling them. Suddenly, she felt bad about what she'd said. 'I can be a bitch when I've got an unsolved case.'

'Understandable.' Alex looked tired. His face was pale and dark circles smudged the soft skin under his eyes.

'You didn't sleep last night, did you?' Tess said.

'No.'

Tess leaned in, noting the bones smelled of mold and musk.

Curiosity brightened Alex's eyes. 'What are you doing?'

'Trying to imagine her last day.'

'Why?'

She walked around the table studying the earth-stained bones that had once supported the bodies of two young women. 'You think I'm crazy.'

Alex shrugged. 'I'm reserving judgment.'

That made her smile. 'Me, too.'

She stared at the hands, the arms, the face, and the legs. 'He didn't kill her in the woods. Because he needed privacy for what he wanted to do. He didn't want to be disturbed.'

Alex shook his head, genuinely frustrated. 'This is not a person on the table. It's a case. It's evidence. If you want to catch the killer, these bones can't be a person.'

Tess tempered her voice. They could go round and round forever. 'Please, just humor me. Your brain is not going to short-circuit if we just toss out theories.'

'Theories.' He seemed to like the sound of that word. 'I can do theories.'

'Theories. Stories. Let's see what she can tell us.' His frown had her smiling. 'What the evidence can tell us.'

Alex picked up the skull. 'Caucasian female. Late twenties. Five six or seven. Dancer or waitress. Had at least one child. Slight hyperextension in her spine. Four cavities. No fillings or signs of dental work.'

'Single mom becomes a waitress to support her child. It's hard to get out and date, but she wants to. The best place to meet a guy is at work.'

He ignored her. 'Victim number two identified as Rhonda Minor. Working-class family. Art student. Painting. Petite. Brunette. Knew Craig Thornton. Student at VCU.'

'He liked the artistic types.'

'Thornton owned an art gallery. He had an appreciation for art.'

Tess studied the bones. What was wrong? 'We didn't find them this way in the ground.' She reached in her satchel and pulled out pictures of the skeletons as they lay in the graves. 'Do these bodies looked posed to you? Note the way the left hand appears draped over victim one and two's chests. Number one is looking to the right. Two might have been if Miller's crew hadn't sliced into the skull.'

Alex raised a brow.

'He's posed them like models.'

'The killer thinks of himself –'

'Or herself. We've no evidence to support the fact that the killer is a man.'

He nodded. 'Point taken. Herself.'

'As an artist. The question is what or who is his inspiration?'

The call from Tess had detoured Gage's morning plans. *The killer considers himself an artist.* Far-flung, but then he thought about all the paintings in the Thornton house. The gallery. It wouldn't hurt to look at them. He'd intended to go through Thornton's financial records but instead had pulled Vega along with him to the auctioneer's warehouse, which now stored all the Thornton paintings.

Vega slid his hands into his pockets. 'So what are we looking for?'

'Don't even have a clue.'

Vega shook his head. 'This artist theory is a stretch.'

'Agreed. But it doesn't hurt to look at the paintings.'

'You know anything about art?'

Gage laughed. 'Could fit what I know in the eye of a needle.'

'Even if this art theory holds true, it just points more to Thornton as the murderer. Thornton made his living by brokering art.'

'Yeah.'

'We're busting our humps to prove a dead man killed these women.'

'Maybe. But I want to prove it.' And he wasn't naïve enough to believe solving this was all about justice. A small part of him wanted to prove to Adrianna that she'd chosen wrong when she'd left him four years ago.

The appraiser, Mr. Kingston Willard, greeted them. Though he couldn't have been more than thirty, the auctioneer was clad in a gray suit, white shirt, bow tie, and tortoise-shell glasses. 'Gentlemen, the Thornton paintings are in the back room. We've been reviewing them and getting them ready for next week's sale.'

'This a big auction for you?' Gage said.

'Mid-sized. None of the works are hugely valuable. But we do have some early works of Thomas Cole and John Singleton Copley. Both their pieces should fetch a nice price.' He opened the door to the storage room.

'Who are Cole and Copley?' Gage said.

'Early American mid-nineteenth-century painters. Best known for portraits and landscapes. They went on to create some very valuable works, but what's in the Thornton collection represents some of their earliest, less valuable pieces.'

'Break it down for me,' Gage said. 'How much is this stuff worth in dollars?'

'Assuming the whole collection sells and it's a good night?'

'Sure, why not?'

'A million dollars.'

Gage whistled. 'Damn. That's a nice chunk of change.'

Willard adjusted his glasses as he took them down a

row of paintings explaining each one's history and potential value. None held any real interest for Gage and he didn't see why they were such a big deal. However, when they reached the last portrait he stopped. It was of Adrianna and it looked to have been done about four or five years ago. She wore a light blue dress, her long blond hair draped over her shoulders, a pearl choker wound around her neck and matching pearls dangling from her ears.

The sight of her made him catch his breath.

'She's stunning, isn't she?' Willard said.

Gage felt foolish for being caught staring. 'Why's she selling this?'

'Said she had no need for it. Apparently, she sat for the picture as a favor to her late mother-in-law. It was traditional for the new Thornton wife to sit for her portrait.'

'You think it'll fetch much?' Gage said.

'It will do well. Twenty thousand, maybe. The artist is up and coming and Ms. Barrington is stunning. I'd be tempted to buy it myself.'

Gage didn't like the idea of someone else gawking at Adrianna. But twenty grand was too damn rich for his blood. 'You find anything unusual after you transported the pictures?'

'No. The entire move went like clockwork. But it always does with Wells Moving. They are very professional.'

'Nothing taped behind a painting?' Vega said.

That seemed to amuse Willard. 'Like a secret message? No.'

Gage stared at the painting. And then it hit him. Adrianna's face was turned to the right and her left hand was draped over her chest. 'Vega, look at Adrianna's portrait.'

'Pretty.'

'Look at her hands and face.'

Willard studied the painting. 'That's a very traditional pose. Hand over the heart symbolizes love and affection.'

Vega nodded, seeing the connection. 'The pose is the same as . . .' He stopped short of saying *bodies* in front of Willard.

Gage's jaw tightened.

Adrianna's pose mirrored the position of the two murdered women.

Chapter Sixteen

Friday, September 29, 12:19 p.m.

'You alluded to problems at the estate?' The question came from Adrianna's attorney, Reese Pearce, who sat across from her in the Grove Avenue restaurant. Reese's sharp gray eyes suited his hand-tailored shirt, dark suit, and red silk tie. Thick dark hair, cut short, emphasized skin tanned by hours spent sailing, his one passion when he wasn't practicing law. Reese was in his early fifties and he'd been the Thorntons' and Barringtons' attorney for two decades.

Adrianna gave Reese a recap of events.

With each new detail his frown deepened. 'I haven't heard anything in the news.'

'It's just a matter of time before this gets out. And when it does I'm afraid the estate is going to be overrun with curiosity seekers.'

'This isn't good.'

'It gets worse.'

'What's that supposed to mean?'

'One of the victims – Rhonda Minor – worked for Craig at the gallery.'

Reese leaned forward and dropped his voice. 'What kinds of questions are the cops asking you?'

She traced her finger around the rim of her water glass. Soft piano music drifted in through hidden speakers. 'Like if I knew about Rhonda Minor's affair with Craig.'

He lifted a brow. 'Did you know about the affair?'

Tension twisted around her heart. 'Frankly, I don't believe there was an affair.'

Pearce raised a brow. 'Adrianna, Craig could be impulsive.'

'I know. I've seen his stock choices. But I just don't believe he was an adulterer or murderer.' She shook her head. 'Just weeks before the accident I'd had a major discussion with Craig about all the time he was putting in at the gallery. He told me he'd just made a big sale that he'd been working on for weeks. He said we were set.'

Reese's expression remained neutral. No shock. No surprise. 'What do the cops know?'

'I told them what I told you.'

'Adrianna.' Her name sounded like a painful groan. 'Never ever talk to the cops without talking to me first.'

'I saw no reason to lie to Detective Hudson. I do want the killer caught.'

'Detective Gage Hudson?'

'Yes.'

'A few years ago, he was the detective who wanted to search the estate for that woman in Craig's office. I was able to prevent it.'

'Why would you do that?'

Pearce shrugged. 'Better safe than sorry.'

'Craig didn't kill those women.'

'I didn't say he did, but the cops are thinking it. Going forward, I don't want you to give them a weather report without talking to me first.'

'Don't you want this murder solved?'

'My priority is to protect my client, and until those graves are moved, you are my client.' He picked up his Scotch and swirled the amber liquid. 'Adrianna, I'm not as convinced of Craig's innocence. The firm assigned me to the Thornton family twenty years ago. In that time I've cleaned up a few family messes.'

'For Craig?'

He avoided the question. 'Do you know who that other woman might be?'

'I honestly have no idea.'

'And if you did, would you tell me?'

A half smile tipped the edge of his lips. 'Doubtful.'

'Why not? I think the last couple of years have proven that I'm not the naïve bride who married Craig.'

His gaze settled on her. Appreciation flashed. 'You've grown into an amazing woman. But if I tell you what I knew, then you couldn't claim innocence when the cops asked more questions.'

Suddenly, her stomach turned with fear and disgust. She glanced down at the garden salad she'd barely touched. 'Why would Janet tell the cops they were sleeping together?'

'Janet has a big mouth and not enough brains. She likely has her own agenda.'

'What could she possibly want? She owns the gallery outright.'

He raised his glass. All his nails were buffed perfectly, except the thumb on his right hand, which was blackened. No doubt caught in the rigging of his sailboat. 'Who knows with Janet?'

She sipped her iced tea. 'Reese, I'm worried about the

land sale. If Mazur wants his money back I won't be able to pay him. It's all gone to bills.'

'Mazur wants the land. He's made that clear. Going forward, let me handle him. And let me see what I can do about getting the cops to proceed with the excavations. I know a judge.'

'I don't want to interfere with their investigation.'

'Neither do I.' Sunlight caught the gold on his Harvard class ring. 'Don't worry.'

'Reece, let's give the cops a few more days. I've got the time.'

'Sure. If that's what you want.'

'Thanks.'

'How's your mother doing?'

'Okay, not great. We had another trip to the ER the other night. She's fine, as always. She still won't discuss the adoption with me.' She swirled the half-full cup. 'I've been thinking about Mom's first daughter a lot these last couple of months.'

'Why? Don't you have enough on your plate?'

She shrugged. 'My plate is always full. That's par for the course. But no one ever seemed to give that baby a second thought. It's as if she never lived. That bothers me.'

Reese laid a hand on hers. 'The only thing that should be on your mind now is planning your new life. Have you found an apartment in Paris yet?'

'I haven't had the time to look.'

'You can always use mine.'

'Thanks, but that is too generous.'

'Not at all. It sits empty most of the time.'

'Thanks, Reese.' She pulled her hand free and glanced

at her watch. 'I've got to go. There are boxes at the Colonies waiting for me.'

'Boxes?'

'Up from the basement at the estate. I've got to go through and determine if they're trash or treasure.'

'Adrianna.' His expression grew serious. 'I am here for you, not just as an attorney but a friend.'

Reese's hold on her gaze had her running nervous fingers through her hair. 'Keep your fingers crossed and hope there are no more surprises.'

'Hey, Gage, it's Jessie.' A wave of relief washed over Gage as he listened to his sister's voicemail message. 'I've still got the mountain o' laundry at your place. I think some of it might be alive. Anyway, I'll be swinging by Saturday to finish. If you and the bros are there we can order pizza. Ciao.'

Gage hung up. He'd make a point to stop by late Saturday night or early Sunday morning to catch up with her. He clipped his phone back in his belt holster and dropped his gaze back to ten years' worth of Craig Thornton's phone bills. From the stacks of paperwork, it was clear Craig had lived on his phone.

Vega pushed through the conference room doors, his arms loaded with more boxes of paper. 'I've picked up the missing persons files. Five to ten years ago, Caucasian females who were over fifteen and under fifty.'

'Good.'

'You work a lot of these cases?'

Gage nodded. 'A good many.'

Vega glanced in the box. 'So many missing. I can't imagine what the families must go through.'

Gage pinched the bridge of his nose. 'It sucks.'

Vega picked up on the anger tangled around the words. 'Sounds personal.'

'It is. Was. Long story.' His tone left no room for more discussion. 'Let's start digging.'

As Gage glanced at the box of missing persons files, a familiar tension rose in his chest. 'Let's hope we have a match.'

As Adrianna pushed through the front door of the estate, the sound of hammers greeted her. Shoving her sunglasses on top of her head, she let her eyes adjust to the dimmer light. The main parlor was filled with a few dozen barrels, each with a round metal latch at the top.

The hammering grew louder and she moved toward the kitchen. When she rounded the corner, she found Ben standing on a ladder, hammering at the side of the old cabinets.

In between whacks she shouted, 'Ben!'

He started and turned. 'Adrianna. Good Lord, you scared the pudding out of me.'

She smiled. 'Sorry. What's going on? I thought you'd be gone by now.'

He climbed down off the ladder and tucked the hammer in the pocket of his coveralls. 'Mom tells me that the new owner is fixing to gut the kitchen.'

'That's right.'

'Well, it just seemed a shame to me that these cabinets were going to waste. The new owner was by earlier and said I could take whatever I wanted.'

'Mr. Mazur was here?'

'Walking the property,' he said. 'Wants his surveyors in soon.'

'Right.'

'I figured I'd salvage the fixtures and cabinets for you, along with some of the bathroom gear. I know you like old fixtures.'

'That's kind of you. But I have no real use for them. They're all yours.'

'Oh, no. These should be sold. You could make money.'

'It's a nice thought, but I just don't want them.'

He pulled out a pad from his pocket. He smelled of sweat and hard labor. 'Well, I did some calling around. The cabinets, bath fixtures, and paneling could fetch ten grand. I could take it to a buyer and have a check cut for you.'

That was about right. 'Only if you charge me fifty percent. I'll donate my half to the charity auction.'

'Oh, I wasn't fixing to charge you.'

'I won't let you remove a single item if you don't.'

He frowned, turning over her proposal. 'Okay. But I'm going to make the buyer give me top dollar.'

The front door opened and closed with a bang. Marie appeared, looking breathless. 'Sorry about that. The wind must have caught the door. Forgot my cell phone.'

Adrianna smiled. 'No problem. I was just visiting with Ben.'

Marie fiddled with the button on her blue sweater. 'I hope he's not bothering you.'

'Not at all.'

Ben smiled. 'Just taking down cabinets Mazur doesn't want. I'm gonna sell them and split the proceeds with Adrianna. She's donating her share.'

'That's good thinking, Ben,' Marie said.

Adrianna glanced at her watch. 'The more for the charity, the better. Hey, I've got to start going through those boxes if I hope to be done today.'

He wrinkled his nose. 'They're all moldy and nasty.'

Marie glanced at the bins. 'I'd expect no less. Lord only knows how many years they've been in the basement.'

'Sorting them is the last job I have to do, other than moving the graves,' Adrianna said.

'That must be a relief,' Marie said. 'When are the police going to get back to work on that?'

'Soon, I hope.'

'And speaking of work.' Ben nodded to them. 'Best get back to those cabinets.'

'Thank you, Ben. See you at home tonight,' Marie said.

'Will do, Mom.'

'Thanks, Ben,' Adrianna said.

Marie followed Adrianna into the living room. She quickly spotted her phone on the windowsill. 'Honestly, I should wear it around my neck.'

'I couldn't live without mine.' She stared at the few dozen storage barrels. She chose a barrel at random, unlatched the ring that held the round top in place, and pried it open. The smell of must and old house rose up. She sneezed. 'Great.'

Marie shook her head. 'Why don't you leave those to me?'

'No, I really need to do this.'

From the kitchen, Ben's hammer started banging again.

Gingerly, Adrianna started to pick through what looked like old linens. 'Vintage. Nineteen thirties. Handwork was lovely.'

'Pity moths have eaten through some of the fine fabrics, but others might be salvaged.'

'I think you're right.'

As Adrianna dug through the linens, Marie stood close, her hands tracing the smooth line of her phone. 'What are you looking for?'

'I don't know.'

Marie glanced back toward the kitchen and then lowered her voice a notch. 'You're looking for something that belonged to the baby?'

Adrianna glanced up. For a moment she just stared, not sure if she'd heard Marie right.

'I know your mother and Miss Frances were friends. I remember the night . . . well, the night the baby died.'

Adrianna blinked. Never would she have expected this. 'What do you know about the baby?'

Marie moistened her lips, swallowed. 'Only that I was working the night your father called. I heard Miss Frances talking to him. From what I heard, the baby had died. Frances argued with your father. Said Margaret loved the baby and that she never would have hurt her.'

'What happened next?'

'Miss Frances went straight to your parents' house. She didn't come back until morning.'

Adrianna was grateful for the pounding hammer that forced her to pause a moment. 'She knew I wasn't my parents' biological child?'

'Yes.'

'Did Craig know?'

'No. She never told anyone and swore me to keep quiet. I did until just now. Never even told Mr. Wells.'

'Do you think there could be something in these bins?'

'Maybe.'

'Is she buried on this land?'

'I don't think so. Miss Frances was heartbroken over the loss of the child. She'd have wanted a proper burial for her.'

'I'll dig through every barrel.'

'Let me help.'

Adrianna laid her hand on Marie's and squeezed. 'Thank you. But I've got to do this.'

'I'm here if you need my help.' She took a step back. 'Let me collect Ben and leave you to your privacy.'

Adrianna waited until the two left before she started digging deeper into the bin. It took a half hour just to go through the one bin and sort trash from treasure.

She dug a red pen from her purse and wrote TRASH on the side of the empty bin. The next bin emptied would say KEEP. 'This is going to take forever.'

But just knowing Frances might have information locked in one of these barrels about Baby Adrianna gave her the resolve to keep digging.

A lungful of dust from the third bin had her coughing as she pried the lid off. This bin was filled with baby clothes. Made of soft yellows and pinks, the clothes looked to be about twenty-five or thirty years old and were suited more for a girl than a boy. Gingerly, she picked up a sleeper and held it in her hands. Her heart constricted and for a moment tears threatened as she thought about the baby she'd carried and lost.

These must have been Baby Adrianna's clothes. She rubbed her fingers over a sleeper still downy soft and stained with milk.

Adrianna swiped a tear away and sat back on her heels. For months she'd been trying to get information out of her mother about the baby. Good Lord, could the answer really be on the estate?

Adrianna carefully placed the clothes in the KEEP box and set her sights on the next bin. Anxiety churned in her stomach as she peeled the next lid off. But the next bin was stuffed full of yellowed newspapers, dating back to the thirties. Under the papers were molded books.

The next barrel latch proved to be stubborn. She gave it a hard shove but her hand slipped and her nail caught on the rim. It tore to the quick. 'Damn.'

She was studying the jagged edge of her nail when she heard footsteps.

'Ms. Barrington?' The voice belonged to Dr. Heckman.

His sudden appearance startled her. 'Dr. Heckman. What are you doing here?'

'The police came to see me.'

'Really?'

'They asked all kinds of questions about the Thornton family.'

She placed the sleeper back in the bin. She rose. 'What do you want?'

He slid his hands into the pockets of his dark slacks and moved a couple of steps closer. 'I came by to check on the graves.'

Something about his demeanor bothered her. 'You are trespassing, Dr. Heckman. I need you off my land.'

'It's not your land. It's Mr. Mazur's.'

She was sorry now Ben and Marie had left. 'You need to leave.'

His eyes lighted with fervor she'd not seen before. 'Your mother-in-law wanted me to protect the Thorntons.'

'Did she, or do you just believe that?'

His lips flattened. 'Your mother-in-law was a grand lady and you are a pale substitute.'

A bitter laugh escaped her. 'And I've said before, Dr. Heckman, I'm used to it.'

'What's going on in the cemetery is unholy. The bodies and spirits should be left alone.'

Where was her purse? Her phone? 'I'll keep that in mind.'

'No, I mean it, Ms. Barrington. These woods are alive with spirits. This land is not at peace. The bodies deserve to stay in their final resting place.'

Suddenly a question she should have asked days ago came to mind. 'Have you been sending me cards, Dr. Heckman?'

'What cards?'

He looked genuinely baffled, but she wasn't wholly convinced. 'If I receive anything like that again, I will call the police and file charges.'

'I haven't sent any cards.'

Maybe. Maybe not. 'Leave.'

His gaze narrowed and for a moment she thought she'd have a problem on her hands, and then he turned on his heel and left.

She stood alone in the center of the room, surrounded by remnants of a past that would not release her.

'Craig is dead,' she whispered. 'Gone forever.'

And still a chill snaked down her spine and her breath came fast and shallow.

*

Craig stared at the woman sitting on the floor. Her head bent forward, sending her red curly hair cascading over her face. She wept quietly. 'Please don't hurt me. Please. I don't want to die.'

'What's my name?'

She glanced up at him with hopeful, mascara-smudged eyes. 'Craig. And I'm Adrianna.'

So eager to please. Almost too eager. There was no fight, no challenge in this one. And the hair was wrong, he thought bitterly. It needed to be blond. And the freckles on her face didn't fit his image.

But the wig would fix the hair and hopefully would be enough to let him present that he and his Adrianna had been reunited.

'Don't you want to leave here?'

She averted her eyes. 'Yes. Yes. I do.'

'You don't seem willing to fight for it.'

'I'll do whatever I have to do to get out of here. Just tell me.'

He wanted her to fight, to rail against him so that he could break her bit by bit.

Craig checked his camera, made sure that the green light flashed on when he clicked RECORD. 'I want you to put on this wig. And then I want you to fight me.'

'Fight you? I don't understand.'

How could he explain? This was all wrong! There was no challenge. What was the point of taking something – someone – that no one else wanted? 'Damn it!'

'Tell me what you want! And I'll be it!' She grabbed the wig and with trembling hands placed it on her head. Her own hair escaped the sides and framed her face.

243

'Fix your wig.'

She did as he bade.

'Turn your face away from me.'

Again, she obeyed. He dimmed the light and if he blurred his vision he could almost . . . almost believe it was her.

Anticipation slowly, slowly warmed his blood and he felt his erection harden. 'It's so good to see you again, Adrianna.'

Tammy had never been more terrified in her life. She tried to distance herself from what was happening but couldn't quite blot out her attacker's hands pawing at her body. 'Why are you doing this to me?'

His eyes darkened as he shoved into her with such force that the pain took her breath away. 'Call me Craig when you speak to me.'

She forced herself to look into his eyes. 'Why? I don't understand.'

He shoved her face to the left, forcing her gaze away from his. 'That's my name. I am Craig Thornton.'

'He's dead,' she whispered. 'He's dead.'

Her attacker started to move inside her with a sharp violence. Her insides felt like they were on fire. Finally, she cried out and begged him to stop. Her pleas seemed to excite him more and soon he found his release. He collapsed on her, his body sweaty and hot. His heartbeat, alive and strong, pounded against her chest.

Could she be mistaken? Could he be Craig? It had been a long time since she'd seen his picture in the newspaper.

And there was something that reminded her of Craig. Was it his jawline? The eyes?

The newspapers' obituary had said the accident she'd caused had put him in a two-year coma before killing him. But what if the papers had gotten it wrong? Papers weren't always right. What if Craig Thornton was still alive?

A half hour later, Craig was finished with Tammy and getting dressed. She lay on her side, tracing circles on the concrete floor.

Craig handed a postcard of Tucson to Tammy. 'You said you always wanted to go to Arizona.'

She stared up at him with vacant eyes. 'Where?'

'Arizona. You said you wanted to go there.'

'I guess.'

He handed her a pen. 'Write your mom. Tell her we're going to Tucson.'

'We're leaving?'

'That we are, and real soon. Now write that postcard like I asked.'

She took the pen. 'What should I say?'

He smiled. 'Dear Mom . . .'

With a trembling hand, she wrote down what he dictated. When she'd finished she handed him the card. He smiled as he tucked it in his back pocket.

As she glanced back to the floor he pulled the gun from his pocket, raised it to her temple, and fired.

Chapter Seventeen

Monday, October 2, 8:00 a.m.

Gage and Vega spent the better part of Sunday plowing through Craig's phone records. There'd been little time to spend with Jessie or his brothers. Just a quick trip home late Sunday to shower and grab a few hours of sleep before he headed back to the office.

After tedious review of financial statements a picture of Craig Thornton emerged. The guy played the market like an addict and in the few years he had had control of the family fortune, he pissed away ninety percent of it.

No wonder Adrianna had been desperate to sell the land. This kind of financial mess coupled with the medical expenses was crushing.

It was past two a.m. when Gage found the bit of information he needed.

Now as Gage and Vega stood in Warwick's office, he recapped their find. 'Craig had twenty-one credit cards and was an expert at juggling debt, payments, and balances. The guy liked to live well. Trips to Europe. Nice jewelry. Handmade suits. Restaurants not even on my radar.'

Warwick's chair squeaked as he leaned back. 'No real surprises.'

The muscles in the back of Gage's neck bunched painfully. 'He was consistent with his spending until about four years ago. He started taking a series of cash withdrawals. In the past if Thornton wanted something, he simply charged it. But no more. He seemed to be dealing in cash only. Two hundred dollars here. Five hundred dollars there.'

Vega cradled his cup. 'Our boy didn't want anyone to know where he went or what he spent his money on. This went on for several months.'

'Why the secrecy?'

'He'd broken up with his fiancée,' Gage said. 'He was trying to prove to her and his mother he was a good boy.'

'Only he wasn't so good,' Vega added. 'In late August there were a couple of charges to a place called Doxies.'

Warwick nodded. 'A strip joint/gentleman's club in the city.'

'Closed about three years ago after the owner was arrested for sleeping with a minor,' Gage said.

'And?'

'Dr. Butler had said the second victim could have been a waitress or dancer.'

'You're thinking at Doxies?'

Gage nodded. 'Yes.'

Warwick tapped a long finger on his desk. 'The owner of Doxies has a new place. A bar, no stripping, out near the airport. His name is Rex Jones.'

Gage checked his watch. 'When does the new place open for business?'

'They start setups in the afternoon.' Vega stretched his back, looking relieved to be moving. 'As soon as he opens we'll have a chat with him.'

'Okay. What about Thornton's cell phone records?' Warwick said.

'They show nothing out of the ordinary. If he was calling someone, he didn't use his cell, work, or home phone.'

'Would he have used his fiancée's phone?' Warwick said.

'I've already requested Adrianna's cell phone bills. They should be here this afternoon.'

'I'll have Ricker or Kier go through them.'

'Good.' But a part of him was afraid of what they'd find.

Adrianna had spent the weekend working at the estate going through the last of the bins. Beyond the baby clothes she'd found on Friday, there'd been nothing else of import.

The open house her realtor had hosted Sunday afternoon went well. Catherine had hinted they might be getting offers. While she'd been out of the house and at her office, she'd continued to go through Frances's ledgers. She'd found nothing. As she'd slipped through the dusty pages, her cell had rung constantly. Mazur. Dr. Heckman. Kendall. But thankfully no one who claimed to be Craig.

Just after ten Adrianna arrived at the Madison Hotel to discuss the final details of the charity auction. She'd had mixed feelings about this site. Her primary concern was the transport of the art from the auction house to the hotel. Each time art was transported from one venue to another, insurance costs and security concerns rose. In an ideal situation, the sale would have been held at the auction house. But several ladies on the committee didn't like the auction house's downtown location on East Broad Street. Too gritty. Too urban. They'd wanted to hold the event in a nice hotel. They'd all gone round and round about the venue until one committee member had announced the

Madison Hotel would give them a tremendous discount and another agreed to pay the additional transport and insurance costs. Adrianna had relented.

Now as Adrianna moved over the cobblestone entry-way, she was unexpectedly blindsided by memories of her September wedding day. Hot temperatures. Rose petals scattered on the main entrance's brick circular drive. The shiny limo decorated with a glittery JUST MARRIED sign. Morning sickness.

Adrianna blew out a breath. 'One step at a time. One step.'

Inside, marble pillars and a stunning chandelier greeted her as she moved across oriental carpets. Standing next to the front desk was the woman she'd come to see. Cary Winters, the banquet manager, was dressed in a plain dark maternity dress that covered a large, low-slung belly.

Adrianna smiled and extended her hand. 'Cary, good to see you.'

Cary grinned. 'And you, too, Ms. Barrington.'

'How are you feeling? You look wonderful.'

'Thanks. I feel like Orca.'

Adrianna laughed. She'd barely been showing when she'd miscarried. 'How many more weeks?'

'Two.' Cary glanced at her clipboard. 'Ready to discuss last-minute details?'

'Absolutely.'

The two moved across the lobby and down a flight of stairs to the main ballroom. Cary pushed open the door to reveal dozens of round tables dressed with white linens, china, and center flower arrangements. At the far end of the room the floor space was open and the staff was putting final touches on the bandstand.

'I wanted you to see the setup because this is how we are going to set up the ball. Of course the color scheme will be different and in place of the bandstand we'll have the art hung on the walls.'

'You'll have a podium for the auctioneer?'

'Yes. And we've arranged for low-level lighting on the paintings as you requested.'

'It sounds like you've got it all covered. As I remember, your staff is very efficient.'

Cary lifted a brow. 'I didn't realize you'd been with us before.'

Adrianna's wedding day setup had featured white and gold linens. Tall crystal vases with long-stemmed white roses. 'For my wedding day. Three years ago.'

Craig had arrived at the church a half hour late that day. The sanctuary had been packed and her mother a nervous wreck. She'd known the instant Craig had taken his place by the minister because relieved whispers had whisked through the room. Relieved and sick to her stomach, she'd never thought to ask what had been the delay.

Now all she could do was wonder why he'd been late. Had he been with Rhonda? Was she that wrong about him?

Cary frowned as if she could have kicked herself for not remembering. 'Barrington. You married Craig Thornton.'

'That's right.'

'I knew you looked familiar. At weddings I often don't look past the bride's white dress.' She stammered and searched for the best thing to say. 'I was sorry to hear about your husband's accident and passing.'

Adrianna made an effort at a genuine smile. She wondered when the day would come when Craig's accident didn't shadow her life.

Cary hesitated as if she debated what she was about to say. Adrianna braced for another platitude.

'I do remember your reception very clearly. I'd never seen so much food, and the champagne flowed endlessly.'

'My mother knows how to throw a party. And my mother-in-law wanted a big splash.'

'I can't believe I didn't connect the dots immediately. The event was a huge deal for the hotel. I was head waitress then. It was all hands on deck.'

'You all did a nice job that day. Everything went smoothly.'

They started to walk toward the door. 'We pride ourselves on handling problems that could ruin a bride's big day.'

Something in the tone of her voice had her saying, 'Were there problems on my wedding day?'

'You don't know?' Cary looked surprised.

'I heard that the bandleader got into a bit of a scuffle because he thought the horn player was ogling the wedding singer or something.'

Cary laughed. 'He did. But that's not what I'm talking about. It involved your husband.'

Adrianna stopped, her hand poised on the ballroom door. 'Really.'

Cary's face turned red. 'I thought you knew.'

'No.'

'Oh, well then, just forget about it.'

Adrianna didn't move. 'I'd like to know. Did Craig get into a fight or cause a problem?'

'No, it wasn't Craig exactly. It was that woman who snuck in through the kitchen entrance and tried to get into the reception.'

'What woman?' She thought about Rhonda Minor and her affair with Craig.

'I don't remember. But she looked very upset. She wore jeans and an old T-shirt. She was insistent on talking to you and your husband. Wouldn't take no for an answer. We ended up having to call the police.'

She'd been completely unaware of the drama. 'She was arrested?'

Cary's eyes widened. 'Oh, no, a guest from your reception intercepted her first. He escorted her off the property.'

'I had no idea about any of this.'

Cary shook her head. 'She kept saying, *If she only knew . . . If she only knew.*'

'Knew what?'

'She never did say.'

'Was her name Rhonda?'

Cary thought for a minute and smiled. 'I don't remember her name.'

'Dark hair. Petite. Pretty.'

'Yes. How did you know?'

'Just a guess.'

Reese stared into his Scotch as he swirled the amber liquid in the crystal glass. 'So why do you want this meeting?'

Janet sipped her Chardonnay. 'We have a problem.'

He sighed, weary of yet another Thornton-related problem. 'Don't tell me. Something Craig did.'

She arched a brow. 'Isn't it always?'

'That was why the firm hired you. To take care of Craig and his little problems.'

Janet tapped a manicured finger on the edge of the glass. 'This one is not so little.'

'Worse than the others?'

'Yes.' Color rose in her face. 'It involves that damn girl.'

'Rhonda Minor.' The name sounded like an expletive.

'That little bitch was far more trouble than any of us ever anticipated.'

A silver pin on her red suit caught the light. 'I hoped she'd been taken care of and forgotten.' He glanced at his drink. 'What do you want from me?'

'Do what you do so well. Make the problem go away.'

Reese was silent for a moment. 'You're on your own this time, Janet. I bailed you out the last time.'

'You can't ditch me now.' She gripped her glass. 'We're both in this neck deep.'

He shook his head. 'There's no paper trail connecting me to any of this. You and Craig screwed this up all on your own.'

'I didn't know what he was doing.'

His gaze turned menacing. 'It was your job to know.'

Anxiety heightened the intensity of her eyes. 'As far as I'm concerned we can lay the whole entire mess at Craig's feet. The cops suspect him already. Maybe if I spoke to the media.'

'No press, Janet. No more scandal.'

'Then if I could talk to Adrianna, I could get her to –'

His lips rose into a sneer. 'I want you to leave Adrianna alone.'

The protective tone in his voice made her smile. 'Why, do you want Little Miss Sunshine for yourself?'

'That's none of your business.'

She laughed. 'You do. You do want her.' She shrugged. 'I don't blame you. She's a beautiful woman. I've seen the way men stare at her.'

The idea that other men looked at Adrianna like that angered him. If it were up to him, no man would look at Adrianna like that ever again.

Rex, the former owner of Doxies, had a new place called Buddy's, a sports bar located in a strip mall about a mile from the airport.

It was after three when the two detectives got out of their car and pushed through the front door of the bar. There was a large bar to the left and a couple of dozen round tables in the dimly lit room. A large-screen television mounted on the wall showed highlights from an old football game and a loudspeaker blared the audio. This early on a Monday night it wasn't a surprise that the place was quiet.

Gage walked up to the bar and showed his badge to the bartender, a thirtysomething woman with bleached white hair, nose ring, and a tight shirt that said Red Sox. 'I'm looking for Rex.'

'Rex doesn't come in on Monday nights.' She popped her gum.

'Where can I find him?' Gage's irritation shone through in his tone.

The woman didn't look intimidated as she filled a beer mug from the tap. 'I don't know. I'm not his mom. At his home, I guess. What's this about?'

'What's your name?' Gage said.

'Peggy.'

'Peggy, I want to talk to him about a dancer that worked at Doxies about four years ago.'

She stopped snapping her gum. 'Why?'

Normally, he didn't explain himself but he had the sense if he did now, he might get more information. 'I'm trying to ID a Jane Doe at the morgue.'

She handed the beer to a man at the end of the bar. 'I worked at Doxies about that time. I was a bartender and a dancer once in a while.'

Gage reached in his breast pocket and pulled out a picture of Craig Thornton. 'Ever see this guy?'

She took the picture and studied it. 'Yeah. He was in a lot during one summer a few years ago. Big tipper.'

'You sure?'

'Yeah. Whatever name he gave, I don't think it was his real name. Saw his picture in the paper once. Different name, but I don't recall.' She lifted a brow. 'Most men who went to Doxies didn't use their real names.'

'Did he have a favorite dancer?'

'Yeah,' she said. 'Sapphire.'

'That her real name?'

Frowning, she seemed to search her memory. 'Kelly Jo?'

'Kelly Jo got a last name?'

'Honestly, I couldn't tell you.'

He shoved out a sigh. A first name was something to run through missing persons. 'Tell me about them.'

'The guy was like obsessed with Sapphire. See, the way it worked, the girls would parade out on-stage several times a night. They were decked to the nines. And the guys would choose which ones they wanted to come to their table for a private dance. This guy always chose her. He would sit and watch her for hours.'

'What did she look like?'

'Tall, thin, blond.'

'How'd she feel about his attentions?' Gage said.

'Oh, she loved it. Said he was real nice and had given her lots of jewelry. Said he promised that he'd take her away from all this.' The bartender rolled her eyes. 'She was young and fell for his bullshit hook, line, and sinker.'

'They dated outside of the club?' Gage said.

She nodded. 'Sure. That summer they were inseparable.'

'And what happened after that?'

'Sapphire's guy stopped calling. She was real hurt by it. That's life in this kind of business. Nothing lasts forever.'

'Did Sapphire quit?' Vega said.

'Sure did. Gave her two weeks' notice and said she was moving on.'

'No unexpected vanishing act?' Vega said.

'No. Fact, I remember her leaving because most dancers don't bother to give notice. They just take off. She worked her two weeks. Figured she needed the money for the kid.'

'Kid?'

'Had a five-year-old boy.'

Kelly Jo had a child just like their Jane Doe. Gage pulled out a business card. 'Know anything about Kelly Jo's upbringing?'

'Most girls who strip don't come from money.'

'If you think of anything else, call me. And tell Rex to call me. I want Kelly Jo's last name.'

They left the bar and got into Gage's car. 'We need to

check those missing persons files for a Kelly Jo as soon as we get back to the office.'

Vega rubbed his eyes and yawned. 'I read them all, but the name doesn't ring a bell.'

'Could have been a nickname.'

Vega nodded. 'So you think rich boy was doing the stripper?'

Gage shook his head as he pulled onto the road and into traffic. 'Looks like it.'

Vega stretched out his legs and folded his arms over his chest. 'I tell you what, Adrianna is a fine, fine-looking woman. I'd think twice before cheating on her.'

'You said she was like ice.'

Vega grinned. 'Heating her up wouldn't be a problem for me.'

Irritation burned Gage. 'She's out of your league.'

Sensing he'd hit a nerve, he grinned. 'My friend, she is out of both of our leagues.'

That rankled Gage. 'Let's see if Kelly Jo is our Jane Doe. Then we'll take it from there.'

Chapter Eighteen

Tuesday, October 3, 5:00 a.m.

Gage had always risen early. Even on his days off he couldn't sleep late. It all went back to the days when he was a kid and his dad would wake him as he left for the coal mine. He expected Gage, rain or shine, to run six miles. *Conditioning, boy, conditioning. You're not the most talented football player, so you're gonna have to work harder.*

There'd been a lot of days between then and now when he could have slept in, but somehow he couldn't shake the notion that if he did, he'd lose out. On what, he didn't know.

Besides, he'd dreamed of Adrianna last night. It had been the last time they'd made love.

They'd not seen each other in a week – his work had kept him away. He had felt things were off between them but he'd been too busy to find out what was happening.

Adrianna showed up at his house late on a Thursday night. She was coming from a client meeting and took the chance he'd be home. He barely registered her words. All he could think about was being inside her.

Adrianna wore a sleek green wrap dress that hugged her narrow waist and accentuated her tanned breasts. The instant he saw her, he got hard as a pike. He pulled her inside, cupping her face in his hands and kissing her. He kicked the front door closed, savoring her soft skin and the way her scent swirled around him.

They didn't make it as far as the bedroom before he unwrapped her dress. A black silky lace bra and matching thong made his mouth water.

He lowered her to the couch, struggling to pull his own pants off. He shoved inside her seconds later. She'd wrapped high-heeled feet around his waist and taken all of him. They'd come in a matter of minutes.

If he'd only known it would be the last time they'd make love. *If only* . . .

'Damn it.'

Gage shoved aside the memory, dragging a shaking hand through his hair. He'd showered and dressed in black slacks and a white shirt, a red tie hung loosely around his neck. He was just pouring his second cup of coffee, irritated that there'd been no match in the missing persons files. Kelly Jo was a nickname and until they got a last name from the bar owner, he was dead in the water.

As Gage sipped his coffee, his phone rang. He glanced at caller ID and then shoved out a breath. He picked up the phone. 'Dad.'

'I knew you'd be up. You're like your old man. Can't sleep.' His voice was made gruff by years of cigarette smoke.

'Mom okay?'

'Yeah, yeah. She's still sleeping.'

His father had retired from the coal mines a couple of years ago but still rose at four. These days, though, he napped around two. 'What's up?'

'I was watching the ESPN highlights last night and

they were doing a recap of the past twenty Sugar Bowls. They showed the game you played in.'

'That so.' When he'd first torn his shoulder, he'd watched the old game films to keep himself motivated and focused. However, he'd found second-guessing old decisions put him in a foul mood and reliving dumb-ass plays painful.

'That was your best game ever. You were at the top. Never understood why you gave it all up.'

His father knew. He'd told him enough times. But the old man never listened. 'I'd like to think I am at the top of my game now.' His dad had been a celebrity at work when Gage had been playing ball. Gage's fall from grace had landed his dad back amongst the ranks of the ordinary.

His dad ignored the comment. 'Fourth quarter, you're down by three and you throw a fifty-five-yard pass to your receiver. It was a sweet moment. Still makes my palms sweat.'

Gage sipped his coffee and found it tasted bitter now. 'Dad, I'm just about to leave for the office.'

'This early?'

'Working a case.'

'Right.' His dad never asked Gage about his cases. His father had never held the police in high regard.

'Have you called Jessie lately?'

'Your mom talked to her a couple of days ago.' He rarely talked to Jessie. He'd kept a distance since the days she'd gone missing.

'She's doing real well in school.'

'So your mother tells me.' The sound of a beer tab opening popped through the phone. 'Before I let you go, I saw someone you knew yesterday.'

They lived in a small town. Everyone knew everyone. 'That so? Who?'

A cough rattled in his dad's throat. 'Susan.'

'Ah.' His ex-wife. They'd not spoken in a decade. Gage's dad had hated seeing them split almost as much as he'd hated seeing Gage leave the pros.

'She was asking about you.'

Gage sipped his coffee.

'She got married again. Has a couple of kids.'

He didn't miss Susan or mourn the loss of their marriage. But mention of kids reminded him of that moment in the hospital when he'd seen Adrianna standing next to the nursery. The nurses had told him about her miscarriage. And it had been an unexpected kick in the gut. He remembered when *they'd* talked about having children. 'Good for her.'

Gage's old man puffed on a cigarette. 'Don't you want to know how she looks?'

'No.'

'She looks great. A stunner like always. I told her you were doing well. She said that was real nice.'

'Did she?' He bet that must have made her laugh. She'd hated the idea of him being a cop. 'I've got to get going, Dad.'

'Yeah, yeah, sure. Your mom wants to know when you, the boys, and Jessie are coming home.'

He set his mug on the counter. Going home meant reliving football days and his marriage to Susan. 'Why don't you two come this way, visit us?'

'Ah, you know me. I'm no good with travel.'

There was a heavy silence. He loved his old man and

knew the guy loved him but they'd never said the words. It was his mom that always conveyed feelings. *You know your father loves you.* 'Think about coming east, Pop.'

'I will.'

He wouldn't. 'Okay. Got to go.'

'Bye, son.'

Gage hung up the phone and restlessness churned inside him as he moved to the bathroom and stood in front of the mirror. He adjusted his tie under his collar and with sharp, quick moves began to tie it. He'd not thought about Susan and their life for a long, long time. Hell, he knew he didn't love her.

So why did he feel a sense of loss?

Gage's thoughts turned to Adrianna. If he were honest he'd admit how much he wanted to thaw the ice and hold the woman who'd once been so warm and willing in his arms.

A sickening realization hit him. Gage still wanted her in his life. Even after she'd torn out his heart and handed it to him.

Shit.

Who was he kidding? He'd never stopped loving her.

At her office, Adrianna glanced down at her to-do list wishing it were half as short. Refusing to wallow in might-have-beens, she checked her watch. Wells Moving was scheduled to deliver furniture from a mini warehouse to the home of one of her clients. The client's home interior had been completely repainted and the hardwood floor refinished. The client would return from vacation in a week and the furniture needed to be reinstalled.

Before she could head out to the job site, she had to

review and sign dozens of checks that Phyllis had prepared. Time. When was there going to be more of it?

A knock on the front door of her shop had her irritation rising. Annoyance changed to shock when she saw Janet Guthrie standing there. Adrianna had not talked to the woman in almost a year. Janet rarely did anything without a reason and Adrianna wondered why she had come now.

Adrianna crossed to the door, unlocked and opened it. 'Janet.'

Always stylish, Janet wore a pale peach pantsuit, a David Yurman gold and silver necklace, and her short dark hair in a French twist. She smiled warmly. 'Adrianna.'

Adrianna's body stiffened at the touch. Janet could be friendly and open when Craig had been around but when they'd been alone the women could be cold and distant. 'I'm in a huge rush. What can I do for you?'

As if Adrianna hadn't spoken, Janet moved into the shop. 'I love your taste, Adrianna. I still can't believe you're selling.'

'I can run Barrington Designs anywhere.'

'But you're doing so well here.'

'I will do well somewhere else.'

Janet nodded, approving. 'I always told Craig he was lucky to have you.'

'Why are you here? I have an appointment in fifteen minutes.'

'I won't take long. I just came to check on you.'

'I'm fine.' Adrianna's back stiffened. 'Now you can go.'

Janet didn't budge. 'Adrianna, I know you've been under so much stress.'

She held on to the door. 'Janet, not a good time.'

Tension rippled through Janet's body. Outside a car

horn honked on the main street. Adrianna, realizing Janet wouldn't leave until she said her piece, let the door close.

Janet smiled. 'I know the discovery of Rhonda's body has to be upsetting. Probably raises a lot of hurt feelings.'

'Ah, so there it is. The reason for the visit.'

'I don't understand.'

'You want more dirt?' Bitterness dripped from each word.

'No, I don't.'

'Come to tell me how long Craig and Rhonda had been sleeping together?'

'Didn't take that detective long to share.' There was no hint of apology from Janet. 'I'd hoped Rhonda was just an amusement for Craig and that it would all pass. But she held on to him tight.'

'I don't believe it.'

An amused eyebrow arched. 'They were.'

'You have evidence?'

'I know what I saw.'

'Do you think Craig killed her?'

Janet shook her head. 'Craig made messes, he didn't clean them up.'

The callousness wasn't unexpected, but even from Janet sounded so harsh. 'Killing Rhonda was cleaning up?'

Janet shrugged. 'Let's face it, Rhonda's death was timely. And it stopped her from making a good deal of trouble for Craig and you.'

'Honestly, I wish Rhonda had made her trouble. I wish she'd had the chance to drag every dirty little secret into the open. Then we wouldn't be standing here guessing what they did or didn't do.'

'Be careful what you wish for. You loved Craig. You wanted to marry him.'

She'd had so many nagging doubts about the wedding. But she was pregnant and wanted her child to have a happy family. 'Why'd you come here, Janet?'

'Like I said, just to see how you're doing. And to see if I could view that art collection you're selling a little early. My customers are asking about it and I know there are pieces I'd buy.'

'The paintings are sealed in storage right now. I can't move them. Insurance.'

'What about the catalogue? Surely I can peek at that.'

'It's not finished.'

'I would have thought it would be done by now.'

'The printer is donating the print job so it keeps getting pushed back.'

'What about proofs?'

'Nope.'

'No bending the rules for an old friend?'

'Sorry. But we'll see you at the auction?'

'Oh, you can count on it.'

'Why the sudden interest in the paintings, Janet? A year ago, they were of no interest to you.'

'Markets change. The art world can be fickle.'

Janet grinned. 'See you at the auction on Friday.'

Adrianna stood by the glass storefront watching Janet slide behind the wheel of her Mercedes. 'What the devil are you up to?'

As much as she wanted to know, she didn't have time to waste. She began signing checks.

At exactly eight o'clock the Wells Moving van pulled up in front of her shop. *Always punctual*, she mused.

As she quickly signed the last check and placed it in the *Process* folder for Phyllis, Janet's words played in her head.

Let's face it. Rhonda's death was timely.

She thought about what Cary had said about the woman who'd shown up at her wedding reception ready to make a fuss. Why hadn't Rhonda found Adrianna later to say what was on her mind? She and Craig hadn't left until Monday for their honeymoon.

Let's face it. Rhonda's death was timely.

A pink message slip waited for Gage on his desk when he arrived at the office. Rex had called. Immediately, he picked up the phone and returned the call.

A gruff voice barked, 'What?'

'Detective Gage Hudson. You called.'

'What? Oh, yeah, right.' A lighter clicked open, flint struck, and Rex inhaled. 'Peggy said you were asking about Kelly Jo.'

'That's right. What can you tell me?'

'Last name was Morgan. Kelly Jo Morgan. Lived with a sister on south side. Her legal name was Colleen Morgan.'

'You got an address?'

'Thought you'd ask. I pulled her personnel card.' He rattled off an address off of Courthouse Road. 'Sister's name is Brenda Davidson.'

'Thanks. Have any idea what happened to her?'

'Heard she moved to New York.'

Another faraway place. 'Thanks.'

Fifteen minutes later, Gage and Vega were in his car

headed south. Morning traffic was backed up on the Willey Bridge thanks to a fender bender so he diverted a few miles east to the Huguenot Bridge. While Gage drove, Vega got on the car computer and searched Colleen Morgan's name. A rap sheet appeared on-screen and he printed it off.

'Looks like Kelly Jo/Colleen got into some trouble. Bad checks. Identity theft. Some drugs.'

'She do time?'

'A few months.'

Once they crossed the James River, traffic opened up and in another quarter hour they arrived at Davidson's small white rancher. The aluminum siding needed a good cleaning and the grass in the front yard was seven or eight inches tall. A cracked cement sidewalk led to three front brick steps.

Inside the house they heard the loud clamor of feet and a dog barking. Next came a woman's voice shouting, 'Get your asses in gear!'

Vega chuckled. 'Sounds a little like my mom back in the day. Mom should have been a marine.'

Gage rang the bell. 'I can't imagine what kind of shit you put that poor woman through.'

'More than any woman deserves.'

The front door snapped open and standing there was a trim woman who looked to be in her late forties. She'd swept dark hair back in a barrette, wore jeans and a large blue sweatshirt. Behind her stood two boys who looked middle school age. Backpacks slung on their shoulders and brown-bagged lunches dangled in their hands. One had dark hair, one light.

'Can I help you?' the woman said.

Gage showed his badge. 'I'm Detective Gage Hudson.'

The boys glanced at each other and then the woman. Confusion turned to worry.

The woman winked at the kids. 'Boys, don't worry about this. Just hustle on out the door or you'll miss the bus.'

'Bye, Mom,' they said. They glanced sharply at the detectives as they left.

When the boys were out of earshot, Gage said, 'We're looking for Brenda Davidson.'

'That's me.' She waved at the youngest boy when he glanced back. 'Hurry up, Trey.'

'We'd like to talk to you about your sister, Kelly Jo.'

Brenda pushed open the screened door. 'Come on in.'

'You don't sound so surprised to see us,' Gage said.

'I'm not. I haven't heard from Kelly Jo in almost four years, but I figured she'd turn up again. Bad pennies always do.'

The living room was neat though the furniture was older and well worn as if teenaged boys had plopped all over them a million times. On the walls were pictures of the boys, but by the looks of the gap-toothed smiles, the photos had been taken a couple of years ago.

'When was the last time you saw your sister?' Gage said. They followed her into the kitchen. Coffee brewed in a pot and she offered them both a cup. They declined, so she poured herself one. Her hands trembled.

'Like I said, over four years ago. It was late August or early September. She was in a great mood.'

Gage detected censure in her voice, but let her keep talking.

'Kelly Jo had big dreams but she wasn't willing to put in the work. She was always taking shortcuts.' She sniffed.

'That's how she got into stripping. Said she could make more in one night than she could in two weeks of waiting tables.'

'How long did she strip at Doxies?'

'About two years.'

'Did she have anything to say about the patrons?' Gage glanced at the kids' school pictures on the refrigerator. One had dark hair. One light.

'She loved the attention.' She sipped her coffee. 'She used to say a few got a little handsy, but overall they were just businessmen looking to blow off steam.'

'Anyone in particular pay attention to her?' Vega asked

Brenda set her cup down on the counter. 'Okay, boys, I've answered a couple of your questions. Before I say anything else, tell me what this is all about? Has Kelly Jo resurfaced? Has she been stealing from someone?'

'Two bodies have been found. They've been in the ground a few years. We have identified one victim. And we suspect the second might be your sister.'

'I haven't heard anything in the news about it.'

'So far, we've kept it quiet.'

For a moment she just stared at him, her eyes blinking slowly. There was no sign of sadness or grief. 'I suppose I'm not surprised she came to a bad end. She was a handful since she was a kid.' She released a long breath. 'Those boys you just saw leave – the dark-haired one is hers. He was just about five when she vanished. I've been raising him since. I always figured she'd taken off with that boyfriend 'cause she'd gotten tired of taking care of Max.'

Gage rubbed the back of his neck. 'What boyfriend?'

'Honestly, I never paid much attention when she talked

about him. I figured he was just a jerk from the bar and she was reading more into the situation than was really there.'

'What did she say about him?' Vega asked.

'That he really loved her.' There was no missing the bitterness in her voice. 'That he wanted to marry her. That they would be together forever.' As the news of her sister's death sank deeper, she seemed more unsettled. 'She believed he would marry her if she was going to have his baby. So she went out of her way to get pregnant.'

'Was she?'

'No. Kelly Jo had problems after Max was born. Collapsed tubes or something. She couldn't have had anyone's baby. But she refused to believe that. She just knew she could get pregnant if she wanted it enough. At one point she really thought she was pregnant and she told him so.'

Craig had been trying to get back together with Adrianna at that point. An unplanned baby couldn't have been welcome.

'After she left, did she send you a postcard?' Gage said.

'Yeah. San Francisco's Golden Gate Bridge. But I didn't hang on to it. I was pissed.' Her lips flattened. 'I wish I had it now. Would have been something for Max.'

'Do you have any pictures of your sister or maybe even the boyfriend?'

Brenda frowned. 'I got a couple of pictures. I saved them for Max, seeing as he might ask about her one day. Wait just a second and I'll go look.'

When she left the room, Vega looked at Gage. 'How much you want to bet the boyfriend is Craig?'

'Let's not jump to conclusions right now.' They heard

Brenda rummage through a closet and then minutes later her heavy, purposeful steps returning to the kitchen.

'Here you go,' she said. She held out a handful of pictures.

Gage took them and started to flip through each slowly. Kelly Jo had been a lovely woman. Bleached blond hair, rich brown eyes, and large breasts – nothing like Rhonda Minor. The last picture was a group shot taken at Doxies. Kelly Jo was in the center and around her were several other dancers and patrons. On the back row and to the left was a familiar face. Gage handed the photo to Vega.

Vega studied the picture just a moment before saying, 'Craig Thornton.'

'Who?' Brenda said.

Vega showed her the picture. 'This man on the back row. He's not standing next to her but he's smiling at her.'

'Yeah, he's the one. Her boyfriend. But his name isn't Craig. I think she said his name was Tim.'

'And you are certain he was her boyfriend?'

'Very. She showed me the damn picture enough.' The quiver in her voice robbed the words of intended anger. 'Do you really think that body is Kelly Jo?'

Gage hadn't come here expecting to make a death notice. But there was no getting around it. 'We have to make a positive identification first. Did Kelly Jo have dental x-rays made?'

'A couple of times. She saw my guy, Dr. Dawson.' The woman turned to the refrigerator and pulled off an appointment card for the boys. 'Here's his number.'

Gage jotted down the full name and number. 'Can we keep the photos?'

'Yeah, but I'll want them back eventually. Like I said,

Max will ask questions one day.' She accepted the card back from Gage and put it back on the refrigerator under a magnet. 'Do you think this Tim guy killed her?'

'We don't know. But you might as well know, the guy died about ten months ago.'

'You're chasing a dead man?' Bitterness coated the words.

Craig didn't have the balls. He made messes, didn't clean them up.

The more Gage learned about Craig, the less convinced he was that he was the killer.

'I don't know. I'll keep you posted.'

'Promise.'

'Yes.' He handed her his card.

Gage and Vega left and as he slid behind the wheel his phone started to ring. 'Hudson.'

'It's C.C. Ricker. I got an update on Adrianna Barrington's phone records.'

'Okay.'

'I cross-checked against Rhonda Minor's name and Colleen Morgan's name.'

'Let's hear it.'

'We have a hit.'

'When?'

'Four years ago. September second.'

Gage gripped the phone. 'She called Colleen Morgan?'

'That she did.'

'Shit.'

C.C. sighed. 'I'd have thought you'd be happy.'

Gage wasn't happy one damn bit. Adrianna had kept information from him yet again. 'I am.'

Chapter Nineteen

Tuesday, October 3, 3:00 p.m.

Brett Newington, station manager for Channel 10, adjusted the cuff of his hand-tailored shirt as he reviewed the copy the new evening anchor had written. He didn't like the text. It was sloppy and wordy.

He pulled off his glasses and rubbed his eyes. Plus she was too fat for his tastes. She didn't have a spark and she wasn't quick on her feet. Basically, she was no Kendall Shaw.

Kendall. He got pissed every time he thought about her. He'd offered her everything and she'd turned him down flat to open that damn PR firm and marry that cop. Ungrateful bitch. Whore.

A hard, frantic rap on his door had him looking up sharply. Standing in his doorway was a rumpled old man who smelled of dust and age and looked like he'd been plucked out of the stacks of a dusty library.

'Who the hell are you?' Brett asked.

'Dr. Cyril Heckman.'

'How'd you get in here?'

Dr. Heckman eased into his office and closed the door. 'I snuck in.'

Brett rose, lifting the phone receiver as he did. 'I'm calling security.'

'No, don't. I have a great story for you.'

Brett started to dial. 'I doubt that.'

'Have you heard of Adrianna Barrington? Kendall Shaw Warwick's sister?'

She'd had a press conference last week. It had been about selling land and moving graves. He'd not covered it because he'd be damned before he did a favor for Kendall's sister. Still, he was curious about Dr. Heckman's visit.

When security picked up Brett said, 'Never mind.' He set down the phone. 'Keep talking.'

'I've been trying to get to you for days.'

'You've got thirty seconds to tell me why you're here.'

Dr. Heckman blinked as he tried to collect his thoughts. 'Adrianna Barrington has got trouble on her land.'

'What kind of trouble?'

Dr. Heckman recapped the story of the bodies. He didn't have many details, only that one had been female and the cops suspected murder.

Brett threaded manicured hands together. 'I've not heard anything about this.'

'The cops are trying to keep it quiet. They don't want the coverage.'

All the better. 'What else do you know?'

'Nothing really. But I suspect you can figure out what's happening.'

'Why are you telling me this?'

'Adrianna Barrington is trying to destroy that property. If enough people know what she's doing, the land sale could fall apart. Nothing on the estate would change.'

Brett's heart raced. An unmarked grave. Murder. Fucking over Kendall's sister. Stories just didn't get any better.

*

274

It was late in the evening and Adrianna was less than a mile from home when her cell rang. She hit the hands-free option as she turned down a side street. 'Adrianna Barrington.'

'This is Brett Newington.'

'Who?'

'I'm the station manager at Channel 10.'

She gripped the phone. 'Yes.'

'I hear you've had a bit of excitement out at the Colonies.'

She smacked her hand against the steering wheel and swallowed a curse. 'I don't know what you've heard.'

'I've heard a lot. Care to comment on the discovery of two dead women?'

'No.'

'I've been doing a lot of digging in the last couple of hours. No one's telling me the identity of the bodies. Care to comment?'

She hung up. 'Damn it!' This wasn't going to be good.

The phone rang again and she nearly didn't answer it but on the third ring picked it up. 'Adrianna Barrington.'

'Hey, Ms. B. You called?'

Dwayne Wells. She shoved out a relieved breath. 'Yes. Just was checking in for Friday. You and Ben set to move all the art to the hotel?'

'We are set.' Papers flipped in the background. 'And as I understand it, we also have art to collect from the Renfo, Medina, and Schenley family collections.'

'Correct. You anticipate any problems?'

'Not a one, but if we hit a snag I'll call.'

So nice to have someone do their job without her having to chase after them. 'Thanks, Mr. Wells.'

'Will do.'

'Dwayne, have you or Marie heard from a reporter from Channel 10?'

'No, we haven't.'

'One just called me.'

'We won't be talking to no reporters, Ms. B. Secrets are safe with us.'

'Thanks. I appreciate that.'

'You call me if you need me.'

'Thanks.'

She hung up, still troubled about the call from Newington and debating whether she should call Gage or Mazur. Both needed to know. From what Kendall had told her about Brett, he was capable of causing big problems.

Gage first. Mazur second. As she dialed Gage's number and rounded the corner of her street, she spotted the cop car parked in front of her house. She didn't have to look inside the car to know who it was. Gage Hudson, but there were no signs of his partner.

Stomach clenching, she pulled into her driveway, shut off the car, and grabbed her purse. She marched straight toward him.

'Ms. Barrington.' Gage sounded annoyed.

Good. She wasn't in such a stellar mood herself. 'Detective. I just got a call from a reporter, Brett Newington. Channel 10. They know about the graves.' She didn't bother to turn but focused on unlocking the deadbolt on her front door.

Shadows from the post light sharpened the angles on his face. 'What did you tell him?'

'Nothing.'

'Don't talk to him. He'll do whatever he can to get the story.'

'I can handle it myself.'

Gage shook his head. 'He's not a good guy. Nasty stories have surfaced about him. Nothing has been proven, but he's trouble.'

The hint of genuine concern smoothed out her frayed nerves. 'Okay, I'll be careful. What are you doing here?'

'I have a few questions for you.'

She opened the front door and clicked on the foyer light. Grabbing the mail from the box by the front door, she shifted through it, half-expecting a card laced with aftershave or a creepy endearment. There was nothing. She wavered between being disappointed and relieved because with Gage here, she'd have a witness. 'What kind of questions?'

His gaze dipped to the mail in her hand and then back up to her face. 'About your cell phone bill.'

'It's late and I've had a long day. Can we do this another time?'

Even white teeth flashed. 'We need to do this now.'

'Or you're going to drag me downtown?'

He slid his hands into his pockets. The casual gesture oddly made him more intimidating. 'Basically.'

She pursed her lips. 'Ask away.'

He stood at the bottom of the stairs, one foot resting on the second step. 'You want to do this on your front porch?'

Adrianna glanced up and down the street wondering who was watching. 'Fine, come inside.'

She flipped on lights as she headed down the center

hallway toward the kitchen. Gage closed the front door with a soft click and followed her, his purposeful steps never wavering.

In the kitchen, his gaze meandered around, absorbing every detail. He seemed a bit surprised by what he saw. The room was scrubbed clean but the stainless equipment's well-used patina reflected lots of use. Batter stains discolored the pages of an open cookbook on the counter. A cherry print apron dusted with flour draped over a chair at the table. It was a cook's kitchen.

'Why do you want to know about my cell phone?'

'You called a woman named Kelly Jo Morgan in September four years ago.'

'Four years ago.' They'd just broken up about then — a fact she doubted was lost on him. 'I barely remember what I had for lunch yesterday. Who's Kelly Jo, anyway?'

'According to your records, you talked to her three times on September second four years ago. Each call lasted between five and fifteen minutes.'

'Okay. Who was she?'

'She was a stripper at a bar called Doxies,' Gage said.

She'd have laughed if he didn't look so serious. 'Now why would I be calling a stripper?'

'We believe she was dating Craig Thornton during that summer you two were apart.'

Adrianna shoved a hand through her hair. She'd heard from Craig's mother he was mixing with a different crowd. 'I was dating you that summer. I didn't care who Craig saw.'

He tightened and released his jaw. 'You sure about that? In the end you couldn't let him go.'

'When I left Craig I thought it was for good.'

'You went back to him.' Accusation coated the words.

'It was complicated.'

A bitter smile tipped the edge of his lips. 'Black and white where I'm sitting.'

A bolt of sadness shot through her body. Those days had been so painful. As much as she'd told herself she was doing the right thing when she'd left Gage, she'd felt awful. 'I didn't call her.'

'The calls were made on September second.'

'I didn't call her.'

Gage laid the records on the granite counter. He pointed to the lines highlighted in yellow. 'This is your number?'

She tucked her hair behind her ear and leaned forward to study the sheet. 'Yes.'

'This Kelly Jo Morgan's number?'

A frown furrowed her brow. 'I don't know what to tell you. May I look at the printout?'

'Absolutely.'

She picked it up and studied it. More memories swirled in her head. Slowly the day trickled back. 'Mom and Frances were giving a party that weekend. It was a celebration of sorts.'

'You and Thornton had reunited.' He ground the words out as if he had cut glass in his mouth.

'Yes.' Uneasiness had made her feel like a fraud that day. That summer with Gage had changed her and she didn't feel as if she belonged in her old life anymore. 'I remember that night was a whirlwind. Lots of catching up after having been out of touch all summer. I saw so many people that night I didn't have time to go to the restroom, let alone have three telephone conversations with a strange woman.'

'It's easy to slip away in the middle of a party and make a call.'

'Not for fifteen minutes, like this last call. My mother was glued at my side almost the entire night.' She shot him an annoyed look.

'Where was your phone?'

'I don't know. I left my purse in my mom's bedroom. Anyone could have gone in and used it.'

'Did Thornton know the purse and phone were in that room?'

'Yes.' She dug long fingers through her hair. 'Why was he calling her?'

'Kelly Jo told her sister she was going to have Craig's baby.'

Color drained from her face. Hot tears sprang into her eyes. 'Was she?'

'No.'

She swiped away a tear and turned away. 'Sorry.'

Gage slowly collected the printouts and closed the file.

Adrianna cleared her throat. 'She's the other woman found on the estate?'

'We think so.'

She sighed. 'You said she was a stripper.'

'Kelly Jo and Craig dated the summer you two were broken up.'

'Okay.' She felt no anger or jealousy.

'Did Craig own a gun?'

'His father owned a lot of rifles. Robert loved to hunt. So did my father. Dad and Mr. Thornton used to hunt together.'

'What about handguns?'

'I don't know. Mom sold all of Dad's guns after he

died.' She drew in a sigh. 'Craig sold all his father's guns just before we were married.'

'Do you have a record of the sales?'

'I wouldn't know where to look for them. They were all private sales.'

'I'll check.'

To keep her hands busy, she started to make coffee. 'I just can't imagine Craig as a killer.'

Tension rippled as he collected the printouts. 'Who do you think could have killed those women other than him?'

'I don't know. I just don't know.'

'Have you received any more cards or phone calls?'

'After you left my shop, someone sent me flowers.'

'Why didn't you call me?'

Her reasons felt a little childish now. 'I was annoyed and angry with you.'

He shook his head. 'Anything else?'

'It's ridiculous.'

'Tell me.'

'The other night I got a postcard in the mail. Just a plain advertisement for aftershave – Craig's old aftershave.'

'Damn it. Adrianna, I don't like this one damn bit.'

'I've got to admit, each incident has really spooked me.'

'Never ignore a gut feeling, Adrianna. If you sense danger, then get the hell out of wherever you are and call me.'

'I know. I know. You're right.'

He flatted long, calloused hands on the countertop. 'Anything else?'

'No.'

He pulled a business card from his breast pocket and scribbled a number on it. 'This is my cell number.'

She glanced at the number. Color rose in her cheeks. 'I still have it on my phone.'

'Right.'

She pulled two mugs from the cabinet and poured coffee into both. She set a mug in front of him, remembering he always took it black.

Gage stared at the cup, as if lost in thought.

'I remember that look,' she said.

'What look?'

'That look. Your brow creases when you're upset. You're worried.'

'I haven't changed much.'

'No.' She stared into the dark depths of her cup. 'I have.' She wasn't sure what had triggered her to say that or to feel like she needed to say something more to him.

He let the silence hang between them.

Adrianna traced the rim of her cup, cleared the tightness from her throat, but didn't raise her gaze, which settled on her wedding band that now felt tight and awkward. 'I wasn't fair to you. I mean, back then. I expected a white knight to wipe away my confusion about my life and make me happy. I can see now that saving me was my job, not yours.'

The silence felt heavy and uncomfortable. After a long tense moment, she lifted her gaze.

Gage's gaze pinned directly on her. Hot and intense, his expression was neutral and only the tightness in his jaw hinted at a reaction. A couple of feet separated them but it might as well have been a million miles.

There'd been a time when she'd have settled into his arms and he'd have held her close. The world would have felt right.

As if sensing her thoughts, he straightened his shoulders. 'I'm starting to wonder if all this is about Craig.'

The case. Work. He had retreated to safe territory. Maybe it was for the best. 'What do you mean?'

'Maybe those women weren't killed to protect Craig. Maybe the killer was protecting you.'

'Me? Why?'

'Someone who didn't want your reunion ruined by a pregnant stripper. Someone who didn't want your wedding canceled by another of Craig's mistresses.'

'My father was dead. And my mother doesn't have it in her to do something like this.'

He didn't look convinced. 'I'd like to talk to your mother. No one knows you better than her.'

'Talking to Mom isn't such a great idea. She's often confused and, frankly, can be difficult.'

'Difficult never bothered me. I want to talk to her.'

She sighed, relented. 'You can try. But I should be there with you when you do. She's been fragile.'

A half smile tugged his lips reminding her of the man that she'd loved four years ago. 'I can be subtle if I try.'

She arched a brow. 'Like a Mack truck.'

'I'll keep it in low gear.' Gage cleared his throat, 'I'll meet you in the morning at your mother's house. Say nine?'

'You really don't think she can be of much help, do you?'

'Your mother hid the death of a child for over twenty-seven years. There's no telling what else she's capable of doing.'

Gage arrived at Craig's former nursing home just after ten p.m. He'd learned that Dr. Gregory, Craig's attending

283

physician, pulled the three-to-eleven shift this week and could be found in his office.

He moved down the hallway carpeted in a plush blue and painted a soft antique white. Soothing landscapes hung on the walls. Side tables sported decorative bowls with brass fruit. The place could have passed for a swank hotel if not for the beep, beep of unseen machines and the antiseptic smell.

As much as Gage had not liked Thornton, he couldn't help pity the bastard. This was one hell of a lonely place to die.

Gage found the last door on the right as the reception-ist had directed minutes ago and knocked. The brass nameplate read DR. HENRY GREGORY.

Gage knocked and entered.

A willowy man with gray hair and heavily rimmed glasses glanced up from a chart. 'Detective Hudson?'

Gage pulled out his badge and showed it to the man. 'Yes. Thank you for seeing me.'

'Certainly. Have a seat.'

Gage sat in one of the overstuffed club chairs in front of the desk. Diplomas and citations peppered the wall behind the doctor and on a credenza were dozens of fam-ily pictures. 'As I said on the phone, I wanted to ask you about a patient of yours. Craig Thornton.'

Dr. Gregory folded his long hands in front of him. 'That was a tragic case. Always tough when you see some-one young struck down.'

'Can you tell me about his case?'

The doctor leaned back in his chair. 'Irreversible head trauma. He never would have woken up.'

'I understand he could have lived for years.'

'That's what we thought.'

'Was his death unexpected, then?'

Dr. Gregory shook his head. 'The human body isn't meant to lie in a coma. After prolonged inactivity over time, it starts to break down. Craig Thornton had a strong constitution and he surprised all his doctors every step of the way. But his death wasn't out of the realm of possibilities.'

'How so?'

'The accident alone would have killed most people.'

'Were you shocked when he died?'

'Yes. I'd examined him myself that day. His heart sounded strong. Blood pressure was good. And there were no infections. All was fine. Then just after ten that night the nurse called and said he'd coded. There was a DNR on his folder — Do Not Resuscitate — so she didn't try and save him.'

'What do you think caused the death?'

He pulled off his glasses and rubbed his eyes. 'I suppose his heart just gave out.'

'You didn't do an autopsy?'

'No.'

'His wife didn't request one?'

'She mentioned it but I advised her to let it all go.'

For over two years Adrianna came to this place. He wasn't sure if he could claim that kind of strength. 'Mr. Thornton have any visitors that last day?'

Dr. Gregory leaned forward and glanced at the papers on his desk. 'When you called earlier, I had the office manager pull the logs for December second. Turns out he had three visitors that day.'

'Who was that?'

'Fred Minor. Janet Guthrie. Margaret Barrington.'

Gage released the breath he'd been holding. Deep in his heart he'd feared Adrianna hadn't been in Alexandria and had come to the nursing home. 'Does the log say how long they stayed?'

'Yes. Mr. Minor clocked in at twelve that day and was out by twelve twenty.'

'Minor come often?'

'Very regularly. Fact, I spoke to him many times. He said he was a friend of the family.'

'And Guthrie? She was here around four and left around four ten. She rarely came.'

'That so?'

'She said this place gave her the creeps. We get that a lot. No one likes to face their mortality, and this place is full of once-healthy people gravely injured or ill.'

Gage shifted in his chair. Languishing in a place like this was worse than death. Buried alive. 'What time was Mrs. Margaret Barrington here?'

'About five. She also didn't stay long.'

'And Thornton died around ten that evening?'

'That's right.'

'Did Mrs. Barrington also visit often?'

'As a matter of fact, she didn't. She came some in the beginning with her daughter, but it seemed too upsetting for her.'

Had someone hurried Thornton's death along? All three visitors had a reason. 'No one visited around ten?'

'Not according to the log.'

'Can I see his room?'

'Sure. It's vacant right now, as a matter of fact.'

Gage followed the doctor down a carpeted hallway to room number 102. It was first floor and next to the emergency exit. 'That door locked all the time?'

'An alarm sounds if it's opened.' Dr. Gregory slid his hand into the pocket of his white coat. 'Why are you asking these questions now?'

Gage shook his head, not sure himself. 'Just checking a couple of loose ends regarding another case.' He pushed open the door to the room and turned on the lights. The bed was neatly made and beside it were two nightstands, shaded lamps, and a chair with a small desk in the far right corner. Behind the bed, heavy-duty electrical outlets waited for the next life support machine's cables. The room had four large windows. 'All the rooms have windows like this?'

'No. It's a corner room. So there's an extra window. Ms. Barrington wanted a sunny room.'

'She pay her bills on time?'

He hesitated as if he were revealing something he shouldn't. 'For the most part. We're the best in the area and we're expensive. She was struggling those last couple of months.'

'How often did Thornton's wife visit?' Gage said.

'She was here four or five times a week. Always stayed for at least an hour. She often read to Craig.'

'A devoted spouse.'

'It's a hard thing to stick by someone for the long haul. In the emergency room family is pumped up with adrenaline and everyone is committed to doing what it takes to help the patient. Then when the emergency passes and the realization of extended long-term care sinks in, many fade. She didn't. She's one of the strongest people I know.'

'Thanks.'

Gage left the place, not taking a real deep breath until he stood in the parking lot outside awash in moonlight. He took a moment to enjoy the cool night air and being away from that building before he climbed into his car.

Margaret Barrington had visited Craig. She'd made a scene at his funeral. She'd hidden the death of a child.

Gage remembered the one time he'd met Margaret Barrington. He'd been dating Adrianna for about a month and they'd been having lunch. Margaret Barrington had happened upon them. Adrianna had been shocked by the unexpected appearance, risen quickly, her face flushed. Gage realized then that Adrianna hadn't told her mother about their relationship. He'd shrugged off the disappointment and watched as the woman had wrapped her daughter in a warm embrace. When Margaret had turned to him, she'd made no effort to hide her disapproval. Her comments to him had been curt, cutting, and cold.

Adrianna might think of her mother as fragile but he wasn't so sure. A stripper trying to steal Craig from Adrianna. A mistress threatening exposure at the advent of Adrianna's wedding. A disabled husband draining Adrianna's energy and life. Could Margaret have killed them?

Adrianna stood in the center of her kitchen pouring herself a glass of wine. She took a liberal sip, closing her eyes as the cool liquid moved down her throat. 'Craig, did you kill those women? Was I that wrong about you?'

She'd always prided herself on good judgment. But now suspected it was faulty to the core.

The kitchen window creaked and strained against the

growing wind outside and prompted her to retreat down the hallway to her bedroom. Painted a pale blue, the room was her sanctuary. A two-hundred-year-old four-poster bed and canopy that had been hers since she was a kid dominated the center. The sleek white comforter and dozen or so eyelet pillows gave the antique an updated, clean feel suited for a woman, not a girl. Sleek bedside tables complemented the bed, sheer curtains pooled on the floor and a painting by a local artist hung over the bed. Fresh daisies filled a vase on her bureau.

She set the wineglass on the bedside table next to a half-read design book and started to pull the pillows from the bed, which she neatly stacked on a chaise in the corner.

Her limbs felt heavy and the day had finally caught up with her. It took all she had to wash her face and hang up her clothes before slipping on a nightgown and sliding in between the covers. The bed felt so good. And right now all she wanted to do was fall asleep and let this day go forever.

She closed her eyes and let her thoughts trip through her mind.

Craig's handsome face flashed in her mind. His long fingers touched her face and caressed her cheek, yet it wasn't his name she muttered. 'Gage.'

Craig grabbed a clumpful of her hair and twisted painfully. Her eyes were so heavy with sleep, she couldn't open them as his hot breath brushed her ear.

'Bitch. Whore,' he said.

Clumsily, she pushed at his hands, unable to focus or to wrestle away from him. 'Go away. You're dead.'

His laughter radiated around her. 'You wish.'
'You're dead.'
'I am not. And if I could I'd kill you now.'
'No!'
'But soon you are going to pay for your unfaithfulness.'

Adrianna sat up in bed, her body drenched in sweat. She raked a shaking hand through her long hair. 'Craig is dead. He's dead!'

Craig cut off his headlights and pulled off the main road. Darkness had him slowing to a crawl as he followed the dusty road that wound a mile through wooded land toward the county landfill. The facility was closed but that didn't really matter. He hadn't planned on driving up to the gate. Instead he stopped halfway between the road and the landfill attendant's gatehouse.

He thought about the body in the bed of his truck under the worn blue quilted blanket. He was anxious now to get rid of it. In all honesty, she'd been a disappointment. There'd been no real fight in her. And when she'd died, he'd not felt the sense of loss as he had the others.

Still, he'd kept her for four more days.

Craig put the car in PARK. Turning off the engine, he pocketed the keys and got out. The cooling fall air made his hip ache and he knew without weather forecasters saying so that it would rain soon.

Craig pulled the blanket off the woman. She lay curled on her side, her hands bound behind her back. The thick scent of death clung to her. Disposing of the bodies wasn't pleasant and already he was anxious to be done. Gritting his teeth he picked her up, finding that she felt heavier and more unwieldy.

Her head flopped on his shoulder as he carried her away from the dirt road into low-lying underbrush. He didn't walk as far as he should and he wasn't going to dig a hole this time.

He wanted her to be found. He wanted people to see his handiwork.

Carefully, he laid her on her back and folded her left hand over her chest. He turned her face to the right. The postcard would arrive at her mother's house by tomorrow. *Enjoying Tucson.*

He pushed the hair from her eyes. A swell of pride rose up in him. Finding her was really going to fuck with Hudson. 'Figure this one out, asshole.'

As he got back into his truck, his thoughts turned to Adrianna. He dug her assistant's keys out of the cup holder by the driver's seat. He'd copied the whole set and needed to return the keys.

Craig tightened his grip on the keys until the metal edges dug into his skin. His set would give him access to her house or business anytime he wanted.

He thought about the wine in her refrigerator. He'd spiked it. And if she drank it, she'd sleep hard. Dream hard. The thought made him smile.

Craig dropped the keys and pulled out a bottle of hand sanitizer from the glove box. Liberally he squirted it on his hands. He rubbed and rubbed until all traces of the gel and woman's scent vanished. He would ditch the truck until the smell of the body faded and then he would take a long, cleansing shower.

He flipped open a cell phone and hit speed dial. The phone rang once, twice, and on the third ring the call was picked up.

'Is it done?'

'Yeah, I took care of her.'

'You went deep into the woods?'

He glanced toward the stand of trees not twenty feet from him. 'Yeah, I went deep into the woods.'

'You're sure?'

He didn't like being questioned as if he were a child. 'Yeah, I took care of it just like you said.'

'Let's hope, because you managed to botch the other two.'

Craig had known for weeks that his girls would be found. The more he mulled over their discovery, the more he was pleased about it. 'That wasn't my damn fault. Shit, what were the chances that those bodies would be found?'

'You shouldn't have buried them in the cemetery. That was stupid.'

'I never thought the land would be sold.' For the first time he let his anger bleed through.

'What's with your attitude?'

Craig ran his fingers through his hair. 'What do you mean?'

'You're sounding full of yourself. And I don't like it.'

'Why shouldn't I?'

'Don't forget your place.'

His place. Shit. 'Don't take that tone with me. I'm doing your work.'

'And you're enjoying it, too, so don't act like you've done me any great favors. If you do your job right we won't have any issues.'

Craig pounded his fist softly against the steering wheel. 'Fine.'

'And this one is the last one. No more. We've done what we set out to do.'

Craig didn't want this to be the last one. He wanted another one. Just one more. One with fight. One he could remember for a long time. Maybe he'd take Jessie and Adrianna.

Still, he said, 'Yeah, sure.'

Something in Craig's voice caught the ear of the caller. 'I mean it. This one is the last.'

'I agreed with you. What more do you want?'

'I just know if this could get screwed up, you'd be the one to do it.'

Craig had heard this bullshit all his life. Never good enough. Never smart enough.

But he was *good* enough. Instead of arguing, though, he kept his thoughts to himself. 'I won't mess this up.'

Without another word the caller hung up on him.

Craig closed his eyes, picturing the detective's face when news reached him that his sister Jessie and his beloved Adrianna were missing. He smiled, savoring the detective's pain.

Chapter Twenty

A small cry escaped Adrianna as she started awake and bolted up in her bed. The digital clock on her nightstand blinked 12:00. Sometime during the night the house had lost power.

Adrianna clicked on the side lamp and scrambled for her watch. She blinked twice trying to register the correct time. Six a.m. She'd slept the entire night, barely moving in her bed.

Sliding her feet from under the covers, she stood and immediately regretted it. Her head spun and she felt as if a brick pounded against her skull. She lay back on the pillow and closed her eyes. The room spun and for an instant she thought she'd be sick. She bolted to the bathroom and knelt in front of the toilet. Seconds went by and then thankfully the nausea passed. She glanced back at her bed, not sure if she was annoyed or grateful to be away from it. The remnants of a dream fluttered on the edges of her mind and she thought about Craig.

For some reason, she half-expected Craig to come waltzing in the room and wish her a good morning. Her heart hammered in her chest.

Of course, Craig did not appear. He was dead. Gone. Buried.

And still her gut screamed, *Trouble*.

Call Gage.

He had told her to call him if things didn't feel right. But she'd had a nightmare. Or her wine hadn't agreed with her. Gut or no, she had to be overreacting.

With a trembling hand, she rose and flipped on the bathroom light and every other light between her bedroom and the kitchen. She clicked on the coffee machine, grabbed a couple of slices of whole wheat bread, and popped them in her toaster oven. Normally, she made an egg white omelet but today her stomach felt unsettled.

She clicked on the small television on the counter and then grabbed juice from the refrigerator. As she poured, the reporter's voice blared over the screen.

'A gruesome discovery was made last week on the Thornton estate known as the Colonies. Sources say the remains of at least one woman have been unearthed. Police refused to comment at this time.'

No victims had been named but there were suggestions of a coverup as footage of the estate, her, Dr. Heckman, and Gage flashed.

'Crap,' she moaned.

Seconds later her phone rang. It was Kendall. 'Are you watching television?'

'Yes.'

'Brett's a jerk.'

'I know.'

'It'll blow over.'

'Do you really believe that?'

'He's going to dig and eventually the cops will make a statement. It might get bumpy for a while but in the end it will go away. All of us end up as yesterday's news eventually.'

'Let's hope sooner than later.'

'You ready for the auction?' Kendall had deliberately changed the subject.

'Yes. See you there?'

'Wild horses couldn't keep me away.'

'Thanks.'

'And don't worry. This too shall pass.'

She laughed. 'See you.'

As Adrianna hung up the phone, the morning light caught the diamond in her engagement ring. She stared down at it a long moment, realizing it no longer belonged on her hand. She'd worn it out of love and loyalty. But the time had come to take it off.

She yanked the rings off her finger and stared at the impressions they left on her skin. She massaged the ridges away.

No matter what came with the press or the investigation, she would get through it all. She would.

Adrianna ate her toast and drank a couple of cups of coffee. Within a half hour she felt like herself.

She glanced at the clock. She agreed to meet Gage at her mother's house. Gage had said this was routine. Instinct egged her to believe him but logic refused. This was a police investigation. The gloves were off. And she needed to be smart. If her time with Gage had taught her anything, it was that Gage was a cop first and foremost.

Adrianna picked up her phone and dialed her attorney's number. The call went to voicemail. 'Reese,' she said. 'This is Adrianna.' She quickly explained what was happening and when she was meeting the cops at her mother's. Reese had been her parents' attorney for years and if he could be present, he would.

She turned on the shower and let the water heat up. Sliding off her silk shorts, she tossed them on the floor. Next came her top. She stepped into the shower and dunked her head under the hot spray. The heat soothed the tension in her muscles and settled the last bits of unsteadiness in her body.

She got out, quickly toweled off, and set about the task of drying her hair. Within a half hour, her hair was straightened and her make-up applied. Naked, she moved into her bedroom.

As she opened the closet, the phone rang. She hesitated, then snapped it up. 'Hello?'

'Adrianna, this is Catherine. We have a great offer on the house.'

For a moment she said nothing as the information sank in.

'Did you hear me?'

'I did. That's great. What's the offer?'

Catherine rattled off the details.

'All right. Sounds good. Let me have a look at the contract before I commit.'

'I'll drop it by your house today.'

'I've got to go out but will look at it this afternoon. Just leave it on my kitchen counter. And make sure you lock up. Last week you left the front door open.'

'Doll, I always check locks. I'm obsessed with leaving my properties locked.'

'Just double-check.'

'Will do.'

Adrianna hung up and stared at the rumpled bed. She'd made her bed almost every day of her life and had never questioned the chore.

And now in the grand scheme, worry over something so trivial seemed stupid. She left the bed as it was and got dressed. Fifteen minutes later, she left the unmade bed and got into her Land Rover.

A string of long days was taking a toll on Gage's body. His shoulder ached and his back felt as stiff as a coach's sideline bench.

As he drank his coffee and watched the morning news, anger boiled inside him. Where the hell had Brett gotten his information? He'd kept a tight lid on the investigation, which explained why Brett didn't have names for the victims. But it was a matter of time.

His attention was pulled from the television when he heard the key in the lock. He was relieved to see Jessie push through the door with a basket crammed full of dirty laundry. 'I thought you were coming home last night?'

A ponytail held back long dark hair and she wore jeans and a University of Richmond sweatshirt. 'Good morning to you, too.'

'I left you a message last night.'

'I know. And I must say, bro, I appreciate your restraint. Only one message.' Jessie kicked the door closed with her foot.

'Sue me. I worry.'

'Too much.' She matched him stare for stare. One of the things that comforted and frustrated him about Jessie was that she rarely apologized. 'The hotel called and asked if I could work a banquet event. Money was too good to say no.'

Gage respected Jessie's work ethic but didn't like her

working so hard. He wanted her to be a kid. 'I wish you'd told me you had a party or a hot date.' He sipped his coffee. 'Want a cup?'

'God, yes. In fact, make it a double.' She set her basket down by the kitchen counter bar stool. 'I like working, helping out with expenses.'

'I told you I'd take care of school.' He took a fresh mug from the cabinet, poured her a cup, and handed it to her.

'Even with my scholarship, the tuition is so steep.'

'That's what my football signing bonus is for.'

'I'd rather you spend that on yourself.'

He shrugged wide shoulders. 'Now what on earth would I need?'

'I don't know. A new car. That truck of yours has to be a hundred years old.'

'Not quite.' He shifted the subject back to her. 'Late night?'

'Two a.m. It took forever to clear the wedding party out.' She rubbed red eyes with long fingers. She'd been biting her nails again. Had the nightmares returned?

'How are the grades looking this semester?' He got the milk, eggs, and whole wheat bread he'd picked up last night at the market after work. He set the milk on the counter in front of her and the eggs by the stove.

'Good. Real good.' She poured milk into her coffee, and then sipped it. 'If I can ace this paper I've got due next week, I'm exempt from the mid-term exam.'

Pride had him nodding as he pulled out a skillet from the cabinet. 'I always said you were the one with the brains in the family.' He'd worked his ass off for his grades, so had his brothers, but Jessie's grades came with little or no effort. 'How you feeling?'

'Good.'

He cracked six eggs in a bowl and started to mix. 'What's good mean?'

'I'm making friends. I'm eating well. I'm exercising.'

Jessie had listed off all the hallmarks of a healthy person, according to her therapist. 'You're dodging, Jessie.'

She sipped her coffee, her gaze down. 'No, I'm not.'

'Jessie.' The warning note in his voice said in no uncertain terms that he'd press if need be.

'I've just been getting the creeps lately. Like I used to after the abduction. You know, when I imagined shadows in every corner.'

Worry lines creased his brow. 'Why do you think this is happening?'

'Honestly, I think it's just stress. I'm burning the candle at both ends. But it's okay. I'm certain this too shall pass once I get this paper done.'

'You'll tell me if it doesn't?'

Her grin reached her tired eyes. 'I promise.'

Gage shoved out a breath, knowing as much as he wanted to create a worry-free world for his sister, he couldn't. 'Okay. I'll back off.'

She leaned forward, her gaze turning assessing. 'So why do you look like the wrath of God?'

'A case.' He put the bread in the toaster and then with a wooden spoon started to scramble the eggs in the pan. He could make three different meals fairly well: eggs and toast, hamburgers, and steak.

Jessie loved hearing about his cases. 'What's the scoop on this one?'

As he buttered the toast, Gage gave her the rundown.

'Adrianna Barrington? Not the same chick you dated about four years ago?'

In a moment of weakness he'd told Jessie about Adrianna. Not all the details but enough so that he could get his sister's take. 'One and the same.'

'Damn, bro. You couldn't have planned it better.' Jessie was ten years younger but possessed wisdom beyond her years, which made it easy to forget she was a kid in college.

'Tell me about it.'

'She got anything to say about what happened between you two? Ever explain why she broke it off?'

'Last night she apologized.' He was still processing that one.

She sat on a stool and scooted to the edge. 'And?'

'Nothing. I didn't say a word.'

'She ever say why she left you?'

'I knew the answer to that one. She went back to the guy she'd been dating before we met. They'd been together for years. Her family approved of him. I suppose she just realized she couldn't live without him.'

'What a twit.'

He laughed and it felt good to let go of some of the seriousness weighing him down. 'It wasn't all her fault. I was working a lot then. We were starting to have our own issues.'

'She should have talked to you.'

'Yeah, maybe. But I've realized I need to cut her a break. She's had a rough couple of years. That guy she left me for died in December after two years in a coma.'

'Yeah, I read something about that.'

'She's different. Steadier. Seems to know what she wants.'

'Who're you trying to convince? Me or you?'

'Just stating facts.'

Jessie shook her head. 'You're slipping, bro. She apologized and your heart is melting.'

'I'm just making an observation. Giving credit where it's due.'

'You said it yourself years ago. Trailer park doesn't mix with Virginia blueblood.'

'You remember everything?' His estimation then still held water, but it annoyed him to think about it.

'Hey, don't shoot the messenger.'

'I'm not.' He plated eggs and toast for the both of them.

'But you're pissed.'

'No.' He got forks and paper towels.

'If you want to rekindle something, then do it. I don't care if you date Miss Blue Blood as long as you're happy. You spend way too much time alone.'

Embarrassment rose up in Gage. He stabbed the eggs on his plate with a fork. 'She's part of this investigation and I've got to deal with her. When the case is done, we are done.'

'You sure?'

'Yes.'

'Another growl? I think you're done, bro.'

'I think you need to stow it.' He dropped his fork on the plate, his eggs untouched. 'I'm late.'

'For?'

'A meeting with Adrianna.'

She barked a laugh. 'You're kidding.'

'When was the last time I kidded about anything?'

'Point taken.'

He shrugged on his jacket and tightened his tie. 'I'm meeting Adrianna at her mother's. I've got questions about the case for Mrs. Barrington. The Thorntons and Barringtons go way back.'

She shuddered. 'Sounds like fun.'

'Yeah. And make sure you eat all those eggs. Protein is good for you.' He pulled his gun from a locked drawer and tucked it in the holster on his hip. Then he snatched up his keys. 'Call Mom and Dad while you're here.'

'I just talked to them a week ago.'

The sudden shift in her tone from playful to sullen caught his attention. 'What's wrong?'

Jessie pushed eggs around the plate with her fork. 'Dad drags me down. I never seem to be good enough. Dad barely speaks to me.'

'You are good enough, Jessie. Don't let Dad make you think otherwise. And Mom, well, she just worries.'

Jessie met his gaze. 'What happened to me happened a long time ago. I've moved beyond it. And I just wish everyone else would get past it.'

Gage leaned forward and kissed her gently on the head. 'The problem isn't you, Jess. It's us. It's hard to forgive our mistakes.'

'You and Dad and Mom told me a million times not to talk to strangers. I did. I screwed up.'

'We were the adults. It was our job to see that you didn't screw up.'

She shook her head, her eyes as clear and bright as a star. 'Let it go. Let it go.'

A half smile tugged at the edge of his lips. 'I'll give it a shot.'

*

Dumping trash in the woods would earn Lester Doyle a hefty fine if he got caught. But, fuck it. The risk suited him better than waiting until the dump opened at eight. His shift at the restaurant started in less than a half hour and if he didn't get this trash dumped and to work on time, his old lady was going to bust his balls.

Lester parked his car on the side of the road and got out. Hurrying to the back of his trunk, he popped open the lid of his camper top and grabbed the three plastic bags stuffed full of garbage. He half carried, half dragged the bags off the side of the dirt road into the woods that separated the landfill from the interstate. Drop the garbage in his favorite spot and be on the main road within five minutes. No one would be the wiser.

The underbrush had grown thick in the last couple of weeks. It tangled around his feet, forcing him to take precise steps so he didn't trip. And the unwieldy weight of the bags, coupled with his hangover, didn't make the trek any easier. But he kept trudging forward, half carrying, half dragging the bags.

Twenty yards into the woods, a smell hit him like a ball-peen hammer. A sick sweet smell, it coiled around him, choking the breath from him. It reminded him of death.

'Fuck.' Some animal had died. Or worse, that vet had dumped more dead dogs again. His stomach lurched and he feared he'd upchuck.

Lester dropped his bags and glanced into the woods, hoping to avoid what reeked. In the growing light, he saw an object. 'What the hell?'

He moved closer, dragging the bags.

The smell got stronger.

He squinted. Searched the green foliage.

And then he saw it. The body of a woman. She lay on her back, her face turned to the side.

'Holy shit! Holy –' This time his stomach lurched and before he could think, he vomited right on his feet.

Adrianna parked in the half circle of her mother's driveway and got out of her car. The morning air was fresh and a slight breeze off the river cooled her skin.

Gold and orange leaves rustled, a reminder that fall weather was weeks away.

This was the time of year Adrianna hated the most. A month and a half from now would be the anniversary of Craig's accident, the loss of the baby, and after that the holidays. There'd been a time when she'd adored the holidays. But for the last few years they'd been quiet and lonely times. Friends had told her to leave town and head to a warm beach, but with Craig in the nursing home, it hadn't felt right. And last year there'd been the funeral to plan. This year would be the first holiday season where she'd truly be free to do whatever she wished. Free. She had no idea what to do with her freedom. But she was anxious to find out.

Adrianna walked around to the back of the house and pushed through the kitchen door to find Estelle at the stove pulling muffins from a tin. 'Estelle.'

The woman dried her hands on a blue apron and grinned. 'I knew if I cooked these muffins you'd show. You never could say no to them when you were a kid.'

Adrianna felt her blood pressure drop. Tall windows let bright southern light into the room, making it the cheeriest spot in the house. Adrianna grew up in this kitchen. Often she'd climb up on a footstool and stand beside Estelle and the two baked cookies or peeled potatoes for dinner.

Estelle pushed the plate toward Adrianna. 'I saw the news this morning. That why the police are coming to talk to your mama?'

Adrianna had called yesterday and explained the situation. 'Seems Mom went to see one of the murdered women just days before she vanished. The police want to find out what Mom discussed with her.'

Estelle frowned. 'No telling. You know your mama has a temper.'

'I know. I know. I wanted to get here before the cops did to prepare her.'

'Your mama is a little bit confused this morning. Last night was bad. She had lots of dreams. Even caught her sleepwalking again.'

'Is she taking her medications?'

'She sure is. I stand and watch her and check her mouth afterward. She's giving me a devil of a time.'

'Thanks.'

The front bell rang. 'Well, I suppose that's those policemen you were talking about.'

Adrianna straightened. 'I called Reese, but I haven't heard from him. Hopefully, he'll make it.'

Estelle wrinkled her nose. 'I don't like him.'

Adrianna hadn't understood Estelle's dislike of the man. 'He's helped me out a lot these last couple of years.'

'The question is why?'

'It's his job.'

306

'That man goes way beyond the call for you.'

That she couldn't argue with. 'Check on Mom. I'll get the door.' Adrianna glanced toward the front door and through its glass planes she could see the blue Crown Vic.

Adrianna walked toward the door and opened it. Gage stood there and on the bottom step Vega.

Both wore sunglasses and dark suits. Gage turned part-way from the door, studied the yard as if trying to get a read on her mother. He wore no aftershave but the scent of Dial soap lingered.

Vega, staring at the front door, had his hands slid casually in his pockets but his jaw muscles were clenched.

Adrianna straightened. 'Detectives.'

Gage pulled off his glasses as he turned toward her. Energy radiated from gray eyes. 'Good morning.'

Vega nodded. 'Ms. Barrington.'

She slid a nervous hand down her thighs. 'I've not seen my mother yet, but Estelle tells me that she's not having a good day.'

'Who is Estelle?' Gage said.

'She takes care of us – Mom. Has since I was a baby.'

Gage seemed to absorb the information. 'I'd still like to talk to her.' Even disguised as a request, she recognized an order when she saw it.

'Of course.'

At that moment a Jaguar roared into the driveway. It parked behind Gage's car. Its gray exterior glistened in the morning sun. The driver's side door opened and Reese got out. He wore khakis, a golf shirt, and a gold Rolex.

Reese passed by Vega and Gage without a word and strode directly up to Adrianna. He kissed her on the cheek and immediately she was struck by his scent. Armani. Craig's scent. Unsettled, her heart beat faster.

'Adrianna, I got your call and came as soon as I could.'

Adrianna shook off memories triggered by the scent. 'Thank you for coming, Reese.'

Gage stiffened a fraction. 'I'm Detective Gage Hudson with the Henrico County Police.'

The two men – the junkyard dog and the Doberman purebred – faced each other.

'So what is this about, Detective?' Reese said. He sounded bored.

Gage looked amused by Reese's haughty tone. 'We've got two homicides. Mrs. Barrington was seen speaking to the second victim just before she vanished. She also visited Craig Thornton the day he died. I'd like to ask her a few questions.'

That last bit of news caught Adrianna by surprise. 'Mom visited Craig?'

Gage kept his gaze on Reese. 'Yes.'

Reese didn't show any emotion. 'You're reaching at straws.'

'Maybe. I still want to talk to her.'

'Margaret won't be able to tell you much,' Reese said. 'Her delicate frame of mind is common knowledge.'

'I still want to talk to her.'

'No,' Reese said.

Since she was a child, Adrianna and her father had united in a silent conspiracy to deceive the world about Margaret's mental health when she was like this.

Now, letting Gage see the truth felt like a betrayal. But two women had been brutally murdered. And they deserved justice.

'They can talk to Mom,' she said. 'But I should be there.'

Reese raised a brow. 'Are you sure? You don't have to do this.'

'Their questions need to be answered.'

Gage kept his gaze on Reese. 'Come in, too, if you like, Reese.'

The attorney glowered. 'Oh, I will be there.'

Oddly, of all people, Adrianna didn't want Gage judging her mother. 'She might not respond at all.'

Gage's gaze shifted to her. 'I'll take that chance. But we do this together.'

The Barrington house was all Gage expected and more. First class, money made generations ago, it typified old Richmond. And it was a universe away from the trailer park.

As they climbed the stairs, he glanced at a painting on the wall. Another portrait of Adrianna, but this one appeared to have been done when she was about sixteen. She wore a pale blue dress with a scooped neckline. A pearl necklace rested in the hollow of her neck and accentuated the ivory paleness of her skin. Jessie would have a field day with it. The princess jokes would fly like bullets.

Gage followed Adrianna and Reese to the second-floor hallway, decorated with watercolors. Landscapes. The third door on the right was ajar and he could hear a woman talking in hushed tones. He frowned, wondering if Estelle had been sent up here to coach Margaret.

Adrianna knocked softly and pushed open the door. Margaret sat in an overstuffed chair by a large window that overlooked the river. The view was spectacular but Margaret wasn't looking at the view. She stared down at her tightly clenched hands. She wore a thick, white robe and her silver hair was pulled into a neat twist. No doubt Estelle's doing. The lack of make-up added a decade to her sixty-some years.

Adrianna paused, stiffening when she stared at her mother. He couldn't decide if the reaction was anger, fear, or protectiveness. Likely, it was all three.

Estelle passed Adrianna, patting her on the shoulder as she left the room.

Reese touched Adrianna's arm lightly. 'Do you want me to talk to her first?'

'No, thank you,' Adrianna said.

She crossed the room and knelt beside her mother. She cleared her throat. 'Mom, it's me, Adrianna.'

Margaret's eyes cleared. 'Adrianna?'

'Yes, Mom.'

The woman raised a shaking hand and cupped her daughter's face. 'You came to see me.'

'Yes. I wanted to talk to you about that girl who worked for Craig. Rhonda.'

'Rhonda?'

'You remember. She worked at the gallery. Dark hair, big eyes. She was a painter like you.'

'Right. Right. I remember. She preferred oil paints to my watercolors.'

Adrianna took her mother's hand in hers and held it. 'Did you go and talk to Rhonda at her apartment?'

Margaret stared at her, clearly confused. 'Her apartment?'

'At Moondance Apartments.'

Margaret thought for a moment. 'Yes. Yes I did.'

The honesty surprised Gage.

Reese shifted and opened his mouth to speak when Adrianna shook her head, signaling him to be silent.

'How did you find her, Mom?'

Margaret tucked Adrianna's hair behind her ear. 'I followed Craig. I thought he might be sneaking around. Thought he might be up to something.'

'Where did you follow Craig from?'

'From the gallery. I waited in the lot across the street and watched as he put a package in his trunk. When he started to drive, I drove. You know, following people is so easy.'

'Where did he go?'

'To that girl's apartment. He didn't stay long. When he left, I went upstairs to talk to her.'

'What did she say?' Gage said.

Adrianna glared up at him, annoyed he'd interjected.

Margaret didn't shut down as Adrianna suspected. She smiled. 'The stupid girl said Craig owed her money. That she wasn't leaving until he paid it.' Margaret suddenly looked stricken. 'I told her to leave Craig alone. I told her Craig was marrying Adrianna. Whatever they had was over.'

Adrianna leaned toward her mother. 'What did Rhonda say?'

'She was brazen. Said she'd ruin the wedding if Craig didn't pay her.'

Adrianna sighed. 'We had our reception at the Madison Hotel, which is also where the auction is going to be held. The banquet manager remembered my wedding and a woman who tried to get into the reception through the kitchen.'

'Did this banquet manager remember what the woman looked like?' Gage said.

'Like Rhonda.'

Margaret's gaze jumped between Adrianna and Gage. 'Did I do something wrong?'

'No,' Adrianna said. Gage saw the subtle tightening in Adrianna's jaw. 'I just wish you'd told me you visited Rhonda.'

Margaret frowned. 'I didn't mean to hurt you. I thought I was protecting you.'

Gage pulled a chair up in front of Mrs. Barrington so that they could look at each other eye to eye. He was so close he could feel the heat from Adrianna. 'Did you go see Craig the day he died in the nursing home?'

Margaret's gaze narrowed. 'I know you.'

'We met a few years ago.' Gage didn't elaborate.

'You were having lunch with Adrianna.'

Aware that Reese and Vega were listening, he nodded. 'That's right.'

'You were holding her hand.'

'Yes, ma'am.'

Margaret frowned and dropped her gaze to the fringe on her shawl. 'I wasn't happy about that.'

He let that comment drop. 'Did you go see your son-in-law the day he died?'

Adrianna stiffened, but didn't interrupt.

'Why does it matter?' Margaret said. 'I visited him at the home a lot.'

'According to Craig's doctor, you didn't visit often,' Gage said.

'I rarely signed the log. The receptionist was always busy and it was easy to slip by.'

'Okay,' Gage said. 'Tell me about your visit. How'd he appear?'

'Like always. He was just there. I talked. He didn't talk back.'

'What time did you leave?'

Margaret picked at the threads of her shawl. 'I didn't stay long.'

'How long?'

'I don't know.'

'And what did you talk about?'

'The gallery. And Janet, I think.'

'I think she's had enough,' Reese said.

Gage didn't budge. 'What did you say about Janet?'

'I don't recall.'

'That's enough, Detective,' Reese said.

Gage wondered what information was locked in Margaret Barrington's head. Whatever it was, he wasn't going to get at it here, in front of this group. 'Thank you.'

Adrianna kissed her mother and promised to return soon. Everyone left together. No one spoke until they were all downstairs.

'I told you she wasn't up for visitors, Detective,' Reese said.

Gage slid his hands into his pockets. 'She seemed all right to me. Remarkably clear.'

Adrianna didn't comment. Clearly, she'd been dealing with her mother's issues for a very long time.

This house reminded Gage of the nursing home. 'Buried alive' came to mind and he itched to be in the sunlight.

He had even more respect for Adrianna's strength. The princess had a backbone of steel.

Gage and Vega walked outside and he savored the morning sun and fresh air.

'You and Adrianna dated?' Vega said. No missing the surprise in his voice.

'Four years ago. Before she married Craig.'

'Shit. What happened?'

Gage stared at the house. 'Didn't work out. She ended up reconciling with Craig and marrying him.'

'And you decided not to share this?'

'It has no bearing. Ancient history.'

Vega shook his head. 'That's crap. You sizzle when she's close. I just figured it was her looks.'

Gage looked past Vega, his gaze narrowing when Adrianna emerged from the house. Reese was at her side, his hand resting on her lower back like there was something between them. After a few brief words with Reese, she allowed him to kiss her on the cheek and she moved toward her car.

'Ssss-izzle,' Vega said.

'Shut up.' Gage caught up to Adrianna as she slid behind the wheel of her car. He tapped on the glass and when she lowered it he said, 'Where are you headed?'

Dark glasses tossed back his reflection. 'Work.'

Gage's gut urged him to take her somewhere private and just talk. So much needed to be said. 'Do you have a few minutes?'

She hesitated. 'Sure.'

'We need to talk.'

His cell phone rang. Damn. Straightening, he said, 'Sorry,' as he unclipped the phone. 'Hudson.'

'It's Warwick. We've got a homicide. Body was found near the landfill in the western part of the county.'

The homicide detective wouldn't have wasted time or the call on something that didn't matter. 'Go on.'

'She was shot in the head. Body was nude. Her hands were draped over her chest.'

'Like the others?'

'That's what Tess thinks.'

Shit. He'd thought all along that the killer had been Craig Thornton. If ballistics matched, then he was right back at square one.

'I'll be right there.' He closed the phone. 'I've got to go.'

'Sure.' The softness had left her tone. Just like four years ago.

'Do me a favor. Lock your doors and be careful.'

'Why?'

'Just as a favor to me . . . do it.'

Adrianna arrived at her shop. Phyllis had opened up the shop and she was showing a vase to a well-dressed man by the counter. Adrianna opted not to stop, only waved as she made a beeline to the back.

The man turned as she passed. 'Adrianna Barrington?'

She stopped. 'Yes?'

The man was attractive. Tall, trim, blond, and very well dressed. His suit was tailored and his linen shirt monogrammed. 'You're a hard woman to catch up with.'

'Excuse me?'

'I'm Brett Newington with Channel 10. I wanted to ask you a few questions about those graves found on your land.'

'Like I said before, I have nothing to say.'

'See our story today?'

'Yes.'

He moved toward her, smiling, and unmindful of what she'd said. 'I want your reaction. Do you know who is in those graves?'

'Leave my store.'

'People want to know your thoughts, Ms. Barrington.'

'Go away.'

'I'm running with a story tonight at six with or without your comments.'

'Without.'

'Do you think your husband killed those women?'

'Go away.'

'My sources tell me he has connections to both women.'

He was fishing. 'Phyllis, call the police.'

The wide-eyed woman moved to the front desk and picked up the receiver.

He held up his hands in surrender. 'No need for that.' But instead of leaving he moved toward her. 'You're selling this store?'

'That's right.'

'Because of the murders?'

'Phyllis. Dial.'

Phyllis started dialing.

'Hold that call, Phyllis.' He leaned a fraction toward her. 'You look so much like your sister. It's quite remarkable.'

'Nine-one-one, Phyllis.'

Brett shook his head. 'And you're just as cold a bitch as Kendall.'

'Cops are on their way,' Phyllis said.

Adrianna smiled. 'Thanks, Brett. That's just about the nicest thing I've heard today.'

Chapter Twenty-One

Wednesday, October 4, 11:00 a.m.

The sun hung high in the sky when Gage arrived at the county landfill road. Warwick stood at the edge of the crime scene, his back to the road, hands on hips. Around him, police lights flashed.

In the woods beyond the yellow tape, Tess squatted next to the body as she covered the victim's hands with paper bags. The bags protected evidence that might be trapped under the nail beds. The breathable paper prevented moisture buildup, which led to the destruction of biological evidence.

Gage moved toward Warwick. 'When was she found?'

Warwick released a breath. 'A few hours ago. Tess arrived at the scene before me. She's the one that thought there might be a connection.'

'Why?'

'Go have a look.'

Without a word, Gage moved toward the yellow tape. Twenty yards beyond he glimpsed the victim. Red hair. Slim build. Nude. She lay on her back but he couldn't see how her face and hands were positioned.

'Tess, you told Warwick that this one reminded you of the other two victims,' Gage said.

Tess straightened, moving her head from side to side.

She walked toward the edge of the tape billowing gently between them. 'The method of death is the same as the other two victims. Shot point-blank in the head. Looks like a .38 but ballistics will confirm if we have a match.'

'People are shot in the head all the time. Why link this to the other two?'

'Look at her left arm. Notice how it's draped over her chest. The other two were positioned the same. Her head is askew but appears to have been turned to the right. Animals chewed the face up pretty good, which messed with the positioning.'

His gaze followed her outstretched hand. 'You're right.'

'Blows the theory that Craig is our killer,' Tess said.

For too many years Gage had held on to the theory that Craig was his killer. Letting go of it wasn't easy. 'What have you learned here that we didn't know before?'

'She appears to have been restrained by a chain around her waist. Judging by the chafing on the skin, the killer held on to her for a while.'

Gage looked closer at the victim. Red hair. Slim build. What was familiar about her? 'Rigor mortis has left her limbs.'

'Right,' Tess said. 'That takes around seventy-two hours.' She seemed to struggle with her anger. 'And based on some bruising on her thighs, I think she was sexually assaulted. But the ME can tell you better than I.'

'Any identifying marks?' Gage said.

'She has three tattoos on her body: an eagle on the base of her spine, barbed wire on her arm, and stars on her ankle.'

Gage tightened and relaxed his jaw. 'What can you tell me about her?'

'First glance, I'd say she was a heavy smoker based on

the yellowing around her nail beds.' Her voice softened. 'Back in the day, I'll bet she'd been an attractive woman, but no more.'

What was it about her? He dug into his memory.

'And why dump her here?' Gage said. 'Why not bury her like the others?'

'Think he's getting sloppy?' Tess said.

Gage shook his head. 'I don't think so. I think he wanted us to see her.'

'Why?'

'He's proud of what he did. He wants us to know he's still out there and active.'

'Getting chased makes the game more fun,' Tess said.

Gage agreed with her. 'We need to figure out who this woman is. I've seen her somewhere.'

'I'll roll prints as soon as we get to the medical examiner's office,' Tess said. 'If she's in the AFIS system, we'll find her.' AFIS was the automated fingerprint system and it had millions of prints in its database. The system was quick and could make matches in a couple of hours.

'Do you have anything else?' Gage said.

'I've got tire tracks by the road. Maybe six or seven different prints. I've made casts of them all and will let you know what I find out. I've also pulled hair and fiber samples.'

'Thanks.'

Gage returned to Warwick.

'You still think this victim knew Craig Thornton or Adrianna Barrington?' Warwick said.

'I'd bet money on it.'

*

Tess was bone tired when she arrived at the medical examiner's office. At Gage's request, she'd followed the hearse carrying Jane Doe's body here. Gage wanted to make sure there were no glitches or any questions regarding chain of custody.

No one was saying it yet, but three murdered women who were all killed in the same way. One missing and unaccounted for. They had a serial killer.

She parked her vehicle behind the hearse in the underground garage. She got out of her car, closed and locked the door.

Tess waved to the body removal attendants. Dean, the first guy, was short with a stocky build. He wore dark clothes like his employer required, but diamond studs winked from his ears. The other attendant, Tony, was a tall black man with muscled arms. The only extra jewelry he wore was a cross around his neck.

'Hey, Tony and Dean,' she said. 'We got to stop meeting like this.'

Tony opened the back of the hearse. 'I hear ya, Tess. I hear ya. Too many bodies.'

'Three.' Dean sensed the tension radiating in her. 'We can take it from here, Tess. Why don't you call it a day?'

'Wish I could go. But I gotta follow Jane Doe all the way to Dr. Butler's office. Gage and Warwick insisted I stay put until the doctor arrives.'

Unbothered, Tony shrugged. 'Gage sure does play it all by the book. Kinda overdoes it as far as I'm concerned.'

'He's a tight-ass, but he's a good cop.' She didn't always like the guy but respected his work. Her brothers vouched for him so she was willing to put up with the occasional inconvenience.

Tony and Dean pulled the gurney out and lowered the wheels. The three moved to the elevator and when the elevator door closed, they rode it to the sixth floor in silence.

'Yo, Tess, I have a friend who likes you and wants to ask you out,' Tony said.

Tess glanced up at her reflection in the elevator's reflective doors. Ebony wisps stuck out from under her ball cap and dark mascara now smudged shaded the skin under her eyes. Toss in the shapeless blue jumpsuit covered in dirt and blood and scuffed steel-tipped boots and she looked ready for the asylum. 'What's wrong with him?'

Tony surveyed her appearance. 'I don't know. Must be a little messed up.'

Tucking a stray strand behind her ear, she couldn't remember the last time she'd put on high heels and make-up. 'Seems to be the kind that likes me the best.'

Dean grinned. 'Good money says the doctor's got a thing for you.'

She rolled her eyes. 'Please.'

The two guys exchanged amused glances. 'Be straight with us, Tess. We've got money riding on a bet.'

'You got a bet on my love life?'

'I'd bet you never go out with him,' Tony said.

'Why?'

'You're a bitter woman, Ms. Kier,' Tony said. The amusement in his voice didn't soften the words as much as he'd intended.

'I'm not bitter.' To prove it she tried to soften the muscles in her body. 'I'm in the middle of a case, which I don't want to screw up.' She *wasn't* bitter. Intense, yes, but *not* bitter.

That managed to wipe the grins from their faces.

The doors opened and she followed the gurney down the long tiled hallway toward the autopsy room. Tony pushed the body through the swinging doors and immediately she was hit by the smell of formaldehyde and alcohol. Without thinking, she started to breathe through her mouth.

Standing in the corner of the autopsy room was Alex, who leaned against a metal counter, his head bowed over a clipboard.

Her stomach churned. Tony's comment about the bet goaded her.

'We've got your Jane Doe, Doc,' Tony said.

Alex raised his head from the clipboard. His brown gaze skittered over her first before landing on Tony. 'Thanks, Tony, Dean. I appreciate it.' He glanced back toward Tess. 'You look tired.'

Did tired mean *tired* or did it mean *you look like a wreck*? Crap. 'Thanks.'

Alex looked confused. 'It wasn't a compliment. It was an observation.'

She shoved her hands in the pockets of her coveralls. 'Right.'

Dean grinned. 'Gals don't like to hear they look tired or fat.'

That seemed to surprise Alex. 'I don't think she looks fat at all.'

Tony shuddered. 'Never even mention the F-word in front of a woman. When I was first married, my wife asked me if a dress made her look fat. I said it wasn't the dress but her ass.'

Dean laughed. 'He slept on the sofa for a month.'

'Tell me about it.'

Alex watched the interplay between the two men. 'I just think she looks like she can use a break.'

'I told her on the elevator she looked a little rough,' Tony said.

'Can we stop analyzing my appearance?' Tess said. She dropped her gaze to her clipboard. The sheets Alex needed to sign were on top but pretending to rummage gave her something to do.

'So, Dr. Genius,' Tony said with a smile. 'I got another puzzler for you. Saw it in the paper on Sunday.'

A smile lifted the edge of Alex's lips. 'Shoot.'

Tony pulled a rumbled piece of paper from his pocket and started to read. 'What timepiece has the least number of moving parts?'

Tess rolled her eyes. 'What does that have to do with anything? I thought you guys had another body to pick up?'

Tony shrugged. 'He ain't going anywhere. Besides, I like to try and stump the doc.'

Alex pretended to think but she sensed he knew the answer before Tony had finished the question. 'A sundial.'

'Right. I have one more.'

Alex's face was a study in patience. 'Shoot.'

Tess thought she'd jump out of her skin. 'Look, Tony, I need paperwork signed so I can get back on the road. I still have two robberies to process.'

Tony looked disappointed. 'So what's got you in such a foul mood?'

'I'm always in a foul mood,' Tess said. 'Hadn't you noticed?'

Tony and Dean laughed. They transferred the black body bag to the metal table in the middle of the room before moving toward the doors.

'We'll see you two later,' Tony said. 'We got another customer waiting.'

Folks from the outside wouldn't have understood such callousness in the presence of death. But all cops quickly learned that if you didn't blow off some steam, you'd go nuts.

'Wise guys,' she muttered.

They left and suddenly the room took on a different air. Anyone else and she'd have made small talk: inquired about weekend plans or asked about the kids or hobbies. But with Alex she didn't know what to say. So, she moved toward him and held out her clipboard. 'I need your John Hancock.'

From a pocket protector he pulled out a pen. He glanced at the pages and scanned them. She'd heard he was a skilled speed-reader. After another moment, he signed the paper, his signature bold and firm, before handing the clipboard back to her.

'Thank you,' he said. He tucked the pen back in his pocket protector.

'That pocket protector standard issue at MIT?' she snapped before she thought.

He looked at her, his expression unreadable. 'No.'

'Sorry, that didn't come out right. Way too bitchy. I just don't see guys who wear those things that often.'

He didn't seem bothered. 'No problem.'

The guy was being nice and still he annoyed her. God, she needed to check the calendar and make sure her period wasn't due. 'Gage and Vega will be here soon. They asked that I wait until they got here.'

Alex held her gaze. 'So tell me what you have.'

Thank God there was always business to discuss. 'White female, midthirties. Gunshot wound to the head. I suspect sexual assault.'

He frowned. 'Based on?'

'Bruising on the hips and thighs. She was also restrained, I think, based on raw marks around her waist. My gut tells me it's the same guy.'

'Your gut?'

'Yeah.' She felt defensive. 'Remember. Illogical emotion?'

'Right.'

Her ego bristled, but she let it go. 'I need to roll her prints. Gage is itching for an ID.'

'Sure. I'll do it now.' It took less than ten minutes before Dr. Butler had pressed the dead woman's fingers into an inkpad and rolled the prints on a fingerprint card.

He handed it to her. 'There you go.'

'Thanks.'

'You really don't look well, Tess.'

'I'm just not sleeping well. Cases like this drive me a little nuts.'

Worry crept into his gaze. 'That's not good.'

'I know. I know. Don't worry, I'll keep it together for the sake of the case.'

'How about for your own sake?'

Was it his words, his soft, determined tone, or just the moment? Tess didn't know which had her raising her gaze to his, and for the first time she felt a sense of calmness as if she'd reached the eye of a storm. 'Thanks. I'll be fine.'

An odd electricity shot through her body. Crap. What the hell was that about?

Gage and Vega pushed through the door. They had grim faces and both sported thick five o'clock shadows. Chances were neither would see their homes for days. Cops went nonstop until cases like this were solved.

Tess moved toward them and felt the tension in her muscles return. 'We just arrived. I was filling in the doctor.'

Gage extended his hand to Alex. As Alex accepted Gage's hand, the sinew in his own arm tightened. Alex might have been the brainy type but the guy could hold his own. She wasn't sure why that mattered.

'Doc,' Gage said, 'I'm hoping you can tell me something about Jane Doe sooner rather than later.'

Alex nodded. 'I just rolled the prints. I'll get to the autopsy as soon as I can.'

Jaw tightening, Gage swung his gaze on Dr. Butler like the barrel of a gun. 'How soon?'

Alex didn't flinch. In fact, he seemed anything but intimidated. Behind the calm she sensed steel. 'Just as soon as I can.'

Chapter Twenty-Two

Thursday, October 5, 8:00 a.m.

When Gage arrived at the county's forensics lab, his shoulder felt as if it were filled with rocks. He'd spent most of the night sharing his notes with Warwick on the other two missing women. It had been a long, grueling session. He'd had time to go home, shower, and brew a strong pot of coffee before heading back to the county forensics lab.

More than a couple of times during the night Adrianna's name had come up. He'd thought about her alone at her store working late into the night.

Shoving aside the gnawing worry, Gage pushed through the door of the examining room. Tess leaned over a microscope, adjusting the focus dial.

She didn't glance up. 'I think I know who your Jane Doe is. I'm just double-checking to be sure.'

'Give me what you have.'

'Tammy Borden.' Tess shifted the fingerprint to check another marker.

Energy shot through Gage. 'Are you sure?'

'Ninety-nine percent. You know her?'

'Shit. I should have seen it yesterday. I knew she looked familiar.'

'Who is she?'

'She's the drunk driver that hit Craig Thornton.'

Tess straightened. 'Crap.'

Gage muttered an oath. 'Another connection to Craig Thornton.'

'And Adrianna.'

Gage shook his head, shoved his hands in his pockets, and started to pace. 'Damn.'

Warwick pushed through the doors. He'd showered and changed but looked as if he'd not slept. 'What do you have?'

Gage gave him the update.

Warwick rested his hands on his hips. 'You were right. Whoever is killing these women is connected to the Thorntons.'

'I want to release the gravesite and let the excavation continue. I'd bet money we'll find Jill Lable there.'

'Nothing showed up on the radar earlier, correct?'

'We're missing something. It's in that graveyard. I'm certain.'

'All right. Dig away.'

Gage couldn't find Adrianna at her shop or her mother's. He'd left her several voicemail messages for her to call, but she'd returned none of them.

'Where the hell are you?' he said into the voicemail of her phone.

Gage slid it back in its holster as he climbed the stairs to the parole offices. The large room was filled with cubicles filled with officers and their parolees. He found Ethan Martinez's cubicle in back of the room. Martinez, a heavyset guy with a white shirt and a loose black tie, leaned back in his chair, his phone pressed to his ear. When Gage knocked on the side of the booth, Martinez turned. Gage held up his badge and Martinez ended his call.

The springs on Martinez's chair groaned as he pushed his bulk forward and up. 'Yes, sir?'

'Gage Hudson, Henrico Police.' They shook hands.

'What can I do for you?'

'A question about one of your parolees.'

Martinez frowned and retook his seat. 'Have a seat and tell me who's done what to whom.'

Gage sat next to the desk piled high with files. There was a half-eaten jelly donut on a napkin next to a cup of black coffee. 'Tammy Borden was found murdered yesterday. She'd been shot.'

Martinez turned to the folders in front of him and thumbed through the tabs until he found the right one halfway down. 'She just got out two weeks ago. What happened?'

'She was found in a dump site off the access road to the landfill in the western part of the county. We know she was held for a couple of days, sexually assaulted, and shot.'

He opened the file, glanced at her picture, and then turned the file toward Gage. 'Damn.'

Gage glanced at the sunken features of the woman, whose eyes were downcast. 'What can you tell me about her?'

'She checked in with me as she was supposed to on Tuesday. She was shaky. Chain-smoked. She was finding it hard to stay sober now that she was on the outside. I suggested an AA meeting near her house.'

'Did she make the meeting?'

'Yeah. I called and checked behind her. Her meeting

leader said she seemed committed to the program. Stayed for the whole thing.'

'Where was the meeting? And where does her mother live?'

Martinez rattled off names and numbers for both. 'If she was in trouble, she never said a word to me. But then they don't all see me as the good guy.'

Craig sat in the lobby of the Madison Hotel in a discreet corner, his back to the wall. He sipped an iced tea. Adrianna was late. She should have been here fifteen minutes ago and it wasn't like her to be late. He'd been too busy today to keep tabs on her, but he'd not worried knowing she'd had a seven o'clock meeting here.

As he sipped his tea, his mind drifted back to the tape he'd made of his latest girl. A disappointment from the moment he'd taken her. Skinny, weak, almost too cooperative, she reminded him of a wounded animal. At least the other two had had some fight in them.

At least the other two had been more like Adrianna.

A waitress approached him with a pitcher of tea. 'Fill up?'

He smiled and held up his glass as he glanced at her name tag. 'Thanks, Jessie.'

Jessie smiled and filled up his glass. 'Can I get you anything else?'

'Just the check when you get the chance.'

'Sure.'

'Appreciate it.'

He watched as she walked toward another table and spoke to another guest.

Jessie Hudson. She had fire. She had spirit and he'd bet

anything she'd keep him entertained for days. Just the thought of her sent tremors of desire through him. He was under orders not to kill again. But he was starting to resent the rules and being told what to do.

He pulled a twenty out of his pocket and tossed it on the table. As he grabbed his keys and prepared to leave, Adrianna rushed through the front door of the hotel.

Smiling, he watched her vanish around a corner. Yes, sir, he was starting to really resent the rules.

Gage and Vega tracked down the group leader for the local AA meeting. He worked out of a church on Northside in a small office crammed full of books, pamphlets, and papers. 'Dr. Stewart?'

A pale skinny man with reddish hair and glasses glanced up at them. 'Yes?'

Gage and Vega pulled out their badges. 'We'd like to ask you a couple of questions about the AA meeting you ran last week.'

Frowning he rose. 'Which night?'

'Wednesday. One of the women who attended that meeting was found murdered. Tammy Borden.'

Shock gave him a ghostly pallor. 'My God. What happened?'

'Can't say right now, but I just need to know who was at the meeting.'

He glanced down as if trying to recall who had been there. 'We had about eight people that night.'

'About?'

Dr. Stewart frowned. 'Yes. We had eight. Tammy, of course, and seven others.'

'Men versus women?' Vega said.

'Four men and four women that night.'

'Anyone new?'

'Most of them, in fact. A couple of regulars, but the others, including Tammy, were first-timers. That happens a lot with that group. We get folks newly released from prison. Many start out gung-ho about sobriety but many fade away.'

'Tell me about the newcomers? Names, descriptions,' Gage said.

'We only ask for first names. Privacy is important in what we do.'

'Any first names?'

'John. Bill. Lois. Susie.' He shook his head. 'I don't remember the others.'

'Did anyone pay any particular attention to Tammy?' Gage said.

'No. In fact, she was very quiet. She smoked her cigarettes and listened as the others spoke. Most of our conversation was dominated by Bill, a regular. He has a tendency to go on and on about his ex-wife.'

'No one else said anything.'

'Lois talked about staying sober around the anniversary of her son's death. John didn't say much. Susie commented she'd reached her one-hundred-day mark. We congratulated her.' He gave descriptions of the others including a big guy and a short spindly woman.

'Who'd Tammy leave with?' Gage said

Dr. Stewart slid his hands into his pockets. 'She left by herself.'

'Anyone see her drive off?'

'Now, that I don't know. I left right after the meeting because I had to get home. The maintenance man always closes up the building. Let me ask.' He picked up the phone and dialed a number. After brief words, he hung up. 'Clarence will be right here.'

'Great. And you meet here every Wednesday?'

'Yes.'

'At six?' Gage said.

'Yes.'

'Do you have names or phone numbers for anyone who were there that night?'

'No. Again, privacy is important.'

'And they'll meet next Wednesday?'

'At six. No guarantees who will be there.'

'I understand.' Gage would attend the meeting.

Dr. Stewart shook his head. 'This is just awful about Tammy. I did visit with her once or twice while she was still in prison.'

'Really?'

'She wanted to make amends. She was particularly interested in gaining the forgiveness of the widow of the man she killed. I know they corresponded a few times.'

Gage lifted his gaze from the notepad. 'What was the widow's name?'

'I don't remember. But it sounded rich. Tammy commented that the man she hit came from a wealthy family.'

'Did the widow ever give Tammy her forgiveness?' Vega said.

'The woman had lost a husband and a child. That kind of grief is hard to lose.'

Clarence, a willowy Asian man, appeared in the doorway. 'Dr. Stewart, you wanted to see me.'

Dr. Stewart explained the situation. 'Did you see anything?'

'I saw a woman in her car and the hood was up. She waved me away. Said not to worry. And I was late for my next job.'

'Is the car still in the lot?' Gage said.

Dr. Stewart shrugged. 'I'm not sure. Let's go see.'

As they walked out to the parking lot, Vega kept glancing at Gage. Finally, Gage lost patience. 'What?'

'It's bothering you, isn't it?' Vega said.

'What?'

'Adrianna has a motive to kill all three victims.'

'She didn't kill them.'

'You sure you're objective?'

'Yes.'

They found the car parked under a tree. It was an old beater, rusty red, with a black interior. Gage tried the door handle. It was unlocked. He glanced inside the car but saw nothing other than a couple of fast-food wrappers. The ashtray was full.

'Why didn't you have it towed?' Gage said.

'We had a couple of church mission trips leave out of here last week. They're not due back until Saturday and I thought it might be one of their cars.' He shook his head. 'I didn't realize it was Tammy's.'

Vega moved to the front of the car. 'Pop the hood.'

Gage opened the driver's side door and pulled the latch. Keys dangled from the ignition. 'Anything?'

Vega lifted the hood. 'Loose wires.'

Gage turned the keys. The radio came on but the engine didn't turn. 'Not clever, but effective.'

Robbing Peter to pay Paul – stealing time from one part of her life to give to another. It had been the theme of Adrianna's life for the last three years. Today was no exception. She dashed between two job sites today – a furniture installation and a house that needed design changes so that it could be sold.

There'd been a couple of messages from Gage but she'd not bothered to call him back. They did need to talk but she just didn't have the time now.

She rushed to the front desk and asked the clerk to buzz Cary. The woman appeared minutes later and soon they were reviewing the last of the auction particulars.

By the time the meeting wrapped and the final details were set for tomorrow night's auction, she was tired, hungry, and her nerves shot. As she moved across the lobby of the hotel, the laughter from the bar caught her attention. God, it had been so long since she'd laughed. So long since she'd been around people.

Clutching her purse, she stopped short of the revolving doors and turned back around. She'd have a half glass of wine and dinner. It wasn't so much that she wanted the food or the wine, but she wanted to be around the living.

Adrianna moved to the chrome bar and took a seat. The place was crowded, not so unusual, she supposed, on a Friday night. Most of the patrons wore dark suits, white shirts, and red ties, a sign they'd all just arrived from an office somewhere close. Her deep aqua wrap dress, a thick, gold manacle bracelet, and shoulder-length blond hair made her the odd splash of color in the sea of gray.

She raised her hand for the bartender, who crossed immediately. A note of appreciation flashed in the bartender's eyes as he set a bowl of nuts down in front of her. 'What can I get you?'

'White wine.'

The bartender nodded and placed a clean cocktail napkin in front of her. 'Will do.'

She picked a cashew out of the bowl. It tasted good and reminded her she'd not eaten much today. She ate a few more bites, feeling her nerves calm. Seconds later, the bartender set a chilled glass of wine in front of her. She sipped it, enjoying the taste. In the last two years, she'd had no time for pleasures like this. Perhaps she'd have a good steak dinner. *Just take care of yourself.*

'I've never seen you before.' The male voice came from behind her.

She sipped her wine but didn't turn in his direction, hoping he was talking to someone else.

A tall, lean man slid onto the bar stool beside her. He had a crop of blond hair and wore a nice suit. He grabbed a handful of nuts from the bowl in front of her and popped a few in his mouth. 'My name is Vince.'

Adrianna smiled. 'Hey, Vince, I've had a long, long day. I'm not looking for conversation.'

Vince ordered a Scotch, settling into his spot. 'How do you know? Maybe conversation is what you need.'

The moments of calm faded. She sipped her wine and ignored him.

'So why are you here?'

'Just having a drink by myself.'

Vince accepted his Scotch from the bartender and put a ten on the bar. 'I'm good company.'

'No, thanks.'

'You sure about that?'

She glanced at the bartender. 'How much do I owe you?'

The bartender glanced at her nearly full glass of wine and frowned. 'Four bucks.'

Vince raised a bushy brow. 'Hey, what's your rush?'

She didn't make eye contact as she dug a twenty out of her purse. 'Like I said, I've had a long day.'

'Maybe you should loosen up and spend time with someone like me,' Vince said.

'No, thanks.' She snapped her clutch closed.

'What's with you?' Vince said. 'I just want to have a little conversation. Maybe buy you some dinner.'

She pushed the twenty toward the bartender and glanced at her wine, which she'd barely touched. 'And I said no to both.'

Vince rose and blocked her exit. 'A woman dressed like you in a bar does not want to be left alone.'

'Maybe that's exactly what she wants.' Gage's deep voice came from behind her. She glanced over her shoulder, discovering he was so close she could feel his body heat.

Vince glanced up at the guy. 'Who are you?'

Power radiated from Gage. He didn't look down at her but kept his gaze on Vince. 'The guy that's telling you to leave.'

Vince's gaze flickered between Adrianna and Gage as if

338

debating whether she was worth the trouble. Vince hesitated only a fraction and then opted to snatch up his drink and move to a corner table.

Adrianna glanced at Gage. 'What are you doing here?'

'Looking for you.'

'How did you find me?'

'Phyllis. She said to tell you she found the keys.'

'Good.'

'Keys missing?'

'Hers. Not mine.'

Gage put a long, tapered hand on the bar. Waiting was something he'd never been very good at. He ordered a seltzer and lime and dropped a five on the bar. 'Your friend is persistent.'

She glanced toward Vince, who still kept glancing in her direction. 'He's not my friend. But he doesn't look ready to give up.'

'It's okay. 'Cause I have a few questions for you.'

She sipped her soda. 'About?'

'Tammy Borden.'

She paused, the chilled glass by her lips. 'I haven't seen her since the trial.'

'You wrote to her while she was in prison.'

'She wrote to me. And yes, I did respond. My emotions were still pretty raw when I wrote those letters.'

'She's supposed to be released soon.'

'So I've heard.'

'How do you feel about that?'

'As long as she leaves me alone, we'll be fine. She did a lot of damage in my life and I don't know if I'll ever be able to let that go. I wish I were a better person, but I'm not.'

He sipped his seltzer. There was more behind his calm expression but she couldn't guess what it was.

'Why are you asking me about Tammy Borden?'

'She's dead.' He studied her closely. 'Murdered.'

'What?'

'Evidence links her murder to the women found on Thornton land.'

A cold shiver slithered through her body. 'I don't know what to say.'

'Tell me who would care so much about your late husband that they'd kill her.'

She released a deep breath. 'At one time, I've have said his mother. Frances adored Craig. So did his father. They'd have done anything for him. But they're dead and he had no siblings.'

'Close friends? I hear his funeral was packed.'

'Lots of acquaintances. Everyone knew Craig. But none were close. Only a few ever visited him in the nursing home. None kept up with me after the funeral.'

'Why did you have Miller sweep the entire cemetery with radar?'

They were beyond secrets now. 'I was looking for my mother's first daughter. Mom and Miss Frances were very close. Frances could easily have buried the child on her land. The cemetery seemed a logical place.'

'What else has your mother told you about the child?'

'Nothing. I can't get anything out of her. I even spoke to Dr. Moore – he testified that the child died of crib death.'

'You don't believe that?'

'I don't know. Maybe. I just think the child deserves to be remembered.'

'Miller is moving the graves on Saturday. I'll be there supervising.'

'Why the change?'

'The rest of the puzzle pieces are in that cemetery. Figure that out and I'll find my killer.'

'How do you know you'll find anything?'

'Hunch.'

'That's not saying a lot.'

He lifted his glass. Droplets dripped down the chilled side. 'Rarely steers me wrong.'

'So one way or another, this will all be over soon.'

'It's not over until we find the killer.'

Adrianna left Gage in the Madison Hotel parking lot just before seven. He waited in his car until she started hers up and pulled onto Main Street.

While they'd been in the bar, a rainstorm had swept across the city and left the air dewy and cooler. The streets glistened under the streetlights.

Tammy was dead. As angry as she'd been, she'd never have wished such a cruel ending for the woman.

When she hit her first red light three blocks later, she dialed the number for her message center and hit Send. An automated voice asked for her password as she stared blankly out the windshield. She was just about to key in her password when a flicker of movement caught her attention.

To her left was a man walking between two cars. His back was to her but his gait, jacket, and hair color reminded her so much of Craig's. Mesmerized, she watched him move toward a black BMW.

Her mouth felt dry and her heart raced faster. She

didn't have a good view of his face, but she watched as the man checked his reflection in the rearview window just as Craig always had done.

Any other time, she'd not have thought much about the man. Everyone had a lookalike. She and Kendall were proof of that.

But the events of the last few days had left her vulnerable and feeling frightened, and that combination now made her mad. Craig was dead. And someone was screwing with her and trying to throw her off her game.

She'd had enough of feeling out of control.

The beep of her phone service startled her. But instead of keying in the password, she snapped the phone closed. As the BMW pulled out of its space, she followed him. No plan in mind, she didn't know what she'd say to this guy when she caught up to him. But for now, she'd follow him until she figured out something. If he was the one messing with her, she wanted to know.

As the BMW passed under the light at Belvedere and Main, the light turned yellow. Adrianna tapped her brakes but realized if she stopped now, she'd lose sight of him.

Adrianna made a quick decision. Looking left and right for an all clear, she ran the light, determined not to lose this guy. She needed answers.

The light ahead would turn red by the time he reached it and she'd get her first chance to see him face-to-face.

However, she'd gone only a half a block when blue lights flashed behind her. She looked in her rearview mirror and saw a patrol car's flashing red light.

'Damn.' With no choice, she pulled to the side of the road.

Helplessly, she watched the BMW brake at the light and then take a right on red. In seconds he was gone and a cop was standing at her door, asking for license and registration.

'Officer, there's a car up ahead that I'm trying not to lose.'

The policeman didn't show any expression as he glanced up Main Street. He sighed as if he were in no mood for any excuses. 'Why?'

She tightened her grip on the steering wheel. 'Long story. I just need to go.'

'I'll bet.' He appeared in no rush. 'What did the other driver do?'

'Do? Nothing. Not really. He just looks like someone I know and haven't seen in a long while. I wanted to talk to him.' She smiled, hoping she didn't sound too flaky.

Stoic features glared. 'That's why you ran the red light?'

Damn. This was going poorly. 'Yes.'

'Driver's license and registration.'

'But I really need to go.' The car had vanished around the corner.

'And I really need to see your license and registration. *Now*, please.' An uncompromising tone silenced all arguments.

Her smile widened as she dug her wallet out of her purse. She'd charmed her way out of tickets before. And she didn't want to end up in driver's school. 'Can't you just give me a pass this time?'

'No.'

Adrianna's home phone was ringing when she came through the door just after nine. She dumped her keys on the entryway table and reached for the phone. For a moment, she almost didn't answer it, thinking maybe it was better that the machine got it. After her Craig sighting and the ticket, she didn't need any more trouble.

'Don't be a weenie,' she muttered and before she thought twice she snapped up the phone. 'Hello?'

'Adrianna? It's Estelle.'

Relief that it wasn't a crank quickly gave way to worry. 'Is everything all right? Is Mom okay?'

'Oh, yes, she's fine, darling. She was a bit flustered today but she didn't give me trouble about taking her medicines. She's sleeping like a baby now.'

Adrianna shrugged off her jacket and switched the phone to her other ear. 'What can I do for you?'

'Well, I was thinking about what we talked about yesterday. You know, the other baby.'

'Yeah, I remember.'

'I couldn't find any old pictures in the attic. I checked every box. But then I got to thinking. You should talk to Dr. Manny Davis, not that doctor who delivered you . . . er, her.'

'Who's he?'

She dropped her voice a little as if she were afraid she'd be overheard. 'He was one of those general doctors. You know, they take care of all kinds of complaints.'

'A general practitioner.' She'd never heard the guy's name.

'That's right. Right after I started work, he and his wife lived next door. They came over and would check up on you fairly regularly. Until one day Mrs. Davis and your mom got into a fight. I remember your mom saying she could take care of you just fine. They had some angry words and Mrs. Davis stormed out. Soon after they moved out of the neighborhood.'

'They would have known Mom and Dad and the first Adrianna.'

'And they might have an idea of what happened. If my baby got into trouble, I'd sure call the doctor next door to come and have a look.'

Adrianna would have done exactly the same. 'Thanks, Estelle. I'll see if I can find Dr. Davis or his wife.'

There was no missing the worry in Estelle's voice. 'You be careful, you hear?'

'Why the worry? I'm just going to ask a couple of questions.'

'Just be careful, baby. I've been worrying something awful about you lately.'

'I'll be fine.'

When Adrianna hung up, she called Information and got Dr. Manny Davis's number and address. His office was on Monument Avenue. General practitioner. She'd left half a dozen messages for Moore and it had taken weeks for him to return her call.

This time she'd not leave any messages. This time she'd just show up and start asking questions.

Tendrils of smoke rose from Janet's cigarette as she sat at her office desk.

Janet laid her cigarette in a crystal ashtray as she held her cell phone to her ear. When Reese Pearce answered, she said, 'We've got a problem.'

'What?'

'Adrianna wouldn't sell me the painting.'

'Not surprising. I don't think she likes you very much.'

Janet bristled. Resentment burned. Adrianna had been given every advantage in life and yet she couldn't have given Janet this one thing. Bitch.

But Janet was careful not to say that. Instead, she kept her voice even. 'I'm going to try to buy the painting at the auction. And if I can't, I'm calling the press and telling them what Craig was doing. He'll take the fall.'

There was a long silence on the other end. She could almost hear the wheels turning in his mind. Reese might have been hired to protect the Thorntons and Barringtons, but he also knew when to cut his losses to save himself. 'I don't want Adrianna implicated at all.'

She'd sell the bitch out if she could. But to say that to Reese risked too much. 'She'll come out of this smelling like a rose.'

'Make sure of it.' He hung up.

Janet heard the bang of a back door down the hallway. She hung up, rose from her desk, and went to the door of her office. 'Is anyone there?'

There was no answer.

The hairs on the back of her neck rose and she moved down the darkened hallway and checked the back service door that fed into the lobby. It was unlocked.

Janet drew in a shuddered breath. She turned and standing in the shadows was a man. Her fists clenched. 'Who the hell are you?'

Brett Newington stepped out of the shadows. Even white teeth flashed. 'I got your call.'

Janet blew out a tense breath. 'So I see.'

He moved close to her, stopping just inches away. 'Said you have information about the bodies found on the Thornton land.'

'Yes. But before I tell you what I know, I want to make a deal.'

His gaze dropped to her breasts before rising again. 'What kind of deal?'

'I might have a sticky PR problem, and I want a story that shifts the blame from me to Adrianna Barrington.'

Brett grinned. 'Why don't we have a drink and talk?'

'My office is this way.'

The screen turned to static. Craig turned off the television, ready and anxious for the next hunt.

'You look pretty in pink. It suits you. But your wig. It's crooked.'
The girl glanced up at him with dazed, drugged eyes and watched helplessly as he tenderly adjusted the wig and tucked the wisps of brown hair out of sight.

Craig had saved this tape because she had been his first. And the first time was always special.

He'd been young when he'd made this tape. The quality of the picture was awful. The lighting a mess. If he'd not been such a terrified novice, he'd not have drugged her. But he'd been afraid of the trouble she might cause. The trailer where he'd kept her hadn't been soundproof.

But this first one had taught him so much about what he liked and wanted. This one had shown him how exciting the hunt could be.

And despite the mistakes he'd made, he'd learned. After

this one he'd started building his special room. Kelly Jo and Rhonda had been to his room, but even then it wasn't finished. Just a single, unfinished concrete room.

Now as he looked around the underground space, he felt pride. Now his special place was a suite of rooms. A bedroom. Small kitchen. Bathroom. A dining table. Down here he could keep a woman for years. No one would hear her screams. No one would find her.

'I see from the note in your backpack you're running away from home. That's nice that you told your mother. She shouldn't have to worry about you. I'll be sure to mail it.'

Her eyes drooped and she moistened her lips. 'I want to go home. Please.'

'Sure. Sure. I'll send you home.'

The gunshot shattered the silence and she slumped forward, dead.

Upstairs a door opened and closed. Footsteps sounded on the steps.

Craig shut off the tape and turned off the television, moving toward the door and closing it behind him.

As he turned the key in the deadbolt, he had to smile. Down here, no one was going to find the next one. No one.

Chapter Twenty-Three

Friday, October 6, 7:00 a.m.

Adrianna fought the butterflies in her stomach when she pushed through the front door of Dr. Davis's office. She should have been totally focused on the auction and getting ready for tonight but instead she was here chasing yet another ghost. She moved past the waiting patients and tapped on the receptionist window.

The woman peered up at her over half glasses. 'Yes?'

'I'd like to see Dr. Davis. My name is Adrianna Barrington.'

'Miss, he has a full schedule today and he's already running behind because of an early morning emergency.'

'It's very important.'

'I'm sure that it is. But he can't see you today.' She glanced at a computer screen and punched a couple of keys. 'He can see you on October twenty-ninth.'

'Not good.' Adrianna turned, but instead of leaving pushed through the door separating the reception area and the back office.

The nurse scrambled to her feet. 'Ms. Barrington. You are not allowed back here.'

'I want to see Dr. Davis.' Raising her voice flew in the face of all she'd been taught but she couldn't let this go. If she waited she could very well lose her nerve. 'I'm not going.'

At that moment exam room two's door opened and a distinguished white-haired man stepped out. He wore glasses. He was fit and wore khakis and a polo shirt under his white lab coat. 'What's going on?'

Adrianna faced him. 'My name is Adrianna Barrington. I need to speak with you. You used to live next door to my parents.'

The slight widening of his eyes told her that he knew who she was. 'It's okay, Ms. Beemer. I have this.'

Dr. Davis pulled off his glasses and extended his hand in invitation. 'Ms. Barrington, won't you come into my office.'

The muscles bunched at the base of her spine. 'Thank you.'

Seconds later she found herself sitting across from him in his small office. The shelves were packed with journals, the wall crammed full of diplomas.

'I'll get right to it,' she said. 'I want to know about Baby Adrianna.'

He frowned. 'You know, don't you?'

'Yes.'

'How long?'

'Nine months.'

He nodded. 'Have you talked to your mother?'

'She's not very helpful.'

'No, I don't suppose she would be.'

A swell of sadness rose up in Adrianna. 'No one is asking about that baby girl, and it feels wrong. Please tell me what happened to her.'

The lines in Dr. Davis's face deepened. 'Your parents had been trying for a year to get pregnant. Your mother had been especially worried that she couldn't get pregnant. A good friend of hers had suffered with infertility for years and your mother feared she'd be in the same boat.'

'You mean Frances Thornton?' Frances often spoke about what a miracle Craig had been.

'Yes.'

The doctor seemed relieved to be talking about this now. 'Your mother did get pregnant after a year of trying, and the pregnancy was textbook. No problems. The delivery was long, difficult, and your mother had a hard time. But when it was all over everyone looked and acted just fine. Mother and child went home after just four days.'

Adrianna felt a tightening in her throat. 'So when did the baby die?'

'She was two months, nine days when I got the call from your father.'

'What happened?'

He glanced down, as his mind seemed to drift to the past. 'It was the middle of the night when your father called me. He was in a panic. He'd been out at a business meeting and he came home to find your mother in the nursery rocking the baby. Your mother was singing, but he realized very quickly the baby was too still. When he touched her she was cold. He panicked and called us.'

Time stopped for Adrianna as she listened. The noise outside the office doors faded.

'My wife and I raced over to their house. It was February and cold as sin. Your father met me at the door and took me right upstairs to the nursery. Your mother was still sitting in the chair rocking the child.'

Adrianna understood how fragile her mother had always been. The loss of a baby must have tipped her into a dark place. 'What had happened to the child?'

He wiped sweat from his brow. 'I was finally able to coax the baby away from your mother. She was cold and blue. She'd stopped breathing. I tried to resuscitate her but she was dead. Your mother became hysterical, as if she'd finally realized what was happening. Your father tried to calm her but she was inconsolable. She snatched the baby up and held her close. Finally your father asked me to leave. He said he'd take care of everything. I said the police needed to be called.

'Your father begged me not to. This was a painful, private matter and they didn't want the police taking their baby and autopsying her. He couldn't bear the thought of his child being cut into.' He pressed a trembling hand to his temple. 'It appeared like crib death. Your parents were my friends and I didn't want to compound their pain.'

'So you just left it alone.'

'At first I did. But I couldn't sleep that night. So I called your father a couple of days later. He said he was taking care of things. That afternoon my wife saw your mother with a baby.'

'Me?'

'Yes. She went up to your mother and asked who the baby was. Your mother said it was Adrianna. That she was all better now. My wife called me immediately. I went to your father and demanded to know what had happened. At first he didn't tell me, told me to butt out. When I pushed, he told me he'd found another baby. Margaret had been desperate, ready to kill herself. So he'd gotten another baby to save her.'

'Just like that?' Bitterness burned inside her to think that one child could be substituted for another.

'I asked about the first baby. And he said not to worry. She was at peace.' He shoved out a sigh. 'I told your father this was wrong. I told him I was calling the police.'

Folded hands in her lap were so tight her knuckles had turned white. 'But you didn't.'

'Your father knew some things about me. He was my attorney at the time. He said he'd expose me if I talked.' Tears glistened in his eyes. 'Secrets or no, I told your father to hire help, someone to take care of you. Margaret wasn't capable. I knew that. And I told him I'd go to the police if he didn't hire someone.

'He said he'd already hired Estelle to take care of you. I insisted on meeting her. When I did I sensed she'd keep you safe.'

'What happened to Baby Adrianna? How did she die?'

'I don't know. She looked fine but there was no telling without an autopsy. It was the secrecy around your adoption that set off the alarm bells. There'd have been no reason to hide a natural death.'

'Do you think my father really came home and found Baby Adrianna dead in my mom's arms? Could Dad have hurt her?'

'I've had a lot of nights to think about what might have happened and I think your mother or father was sleep deprived and frazzled. I think someone snapped. Maybe the baby was shaken too hard.'

'Where is she buried?'

'Your father never would tell me. He was afraid I'd really do that autopsy. But I don't think he did anything formal.'

'He just put her in the ground somewhere?'

'I don't think he would have put her just anywhere. He adored her. Her death was painful for him. He was never the same.'

'Maybe that explains why he always kept his distance from me. Why Estelle was my primary caregiver until I was in middle school.'

Adrianna's father had never hugged her, told her he loved her. He had been a distant, quiet man who rarely spoke to her. All those years she'd tried to get him to love her. All these years she'd thought it had been her fault. All those years of trying to be perfect so he would toss her a kind word.

And none of it had been her fault.

'That reporter won't leave me alone.' Fred Minor's voice blared through Gage's phone.

Phone to ear, Gage crossed the parking lot of police headquarters. Vega was at his side. 'Did he say how he found out that Rhonda was one of the victims?'

'No. But he's running with a story tonight about her affair with Craig.'

'You did the right thing by not talking to him. I promise you, we're working on it.'

Minor was silent for a moment. 'This is killing me. I'm trying to plan a funeral and I can't even get the medical examiner to release the body. Now the whole city is going to think Rhonda was trash.'

'She wasn't trash.' Gage gripped the phone. 'Give me just a little more time, Mr. Minor. We're working on this, I promise you.'

'Fine.'

'Fred, I didn't realize you visited Craig in the nursing home.'

'Yeah, I did. I wanted the son of a bitch to know I hadn't forgotten.'

'You were there the day he died.'

'I was.' There was no hint of apology in his words.

'Did you kill him?'

Fred laughed. 'I thought about it. But when I left him he was alive. And as it turns out Mother Nature did the job.'

Gage wasn't so sure it was Mother Nature. But instinct told him Fred hadn't killed Craig. 'We're gonna talk more about this, Fred.'

'Sure. I got nothing to hide.'

Gage hung up and he and Vega entered headquarters and made their way to the first-floor forensics section.

'What's going on?' Vega said.

'Someone is talking to Brett. He has Rhonda's identity.'

'Shit.'

'Yeah.'

At Tess's request, Gage and Vega arrived at the forensics lab. She had an update on the forensics evidence linked to all three victims.

In the center of the room stood a large galvanized table where Tess had laid out crime scene pictures of all three victims as well as shots taken when they were alive.

Gage slid his hands in his pockets as he stared at the women's faces. 'What do you have, Tess?'

She flipped through the pages of a notebook filled with her thick, scrawled handwriting as she dug dark-rimmed glasses from the breast pocket of her shirt. Before she could start, Warwick pushed through the lab door. He was dressed in a dark suit, white shirt, and tie.

'Look who's dressed up,' Tess said.

Warwick scowled. 'I'm headed to Adrianna Barrington's auction. Kendall is meeting me here in a half hour. I won't be gone more than a few hours.'

Gage had almost forgotten about the auction. 'Tess was just about to start.'

All gazes shifted to Tess.

'Same gun killed Tammy Borden and Kelly Jo Morgan,' she said. 'As you know, we never found the bullet that killed Rhonda Minor.'

'What about the tire tracks?' Gage said.

'I pulled five different sets. All from large vehicles. Trucks. Which isn't surprising near a landfill. I'm working on makes and models but it'll take some time. I also found trace evidence on Tammy Borden's body, including blue cotton fibers, which I'm guessing came from the blanket the killer wrapped around her body.'

'I also spoke to C.C.,' Gage said. 'She spoke to Tammy's mother today. The mother received a postcard a few days ago. It was from Tammy. She told her mother she was moving to Tucson.'

'Why send the postcard and then do such a sloppy job of dumping the body?' Tess said.

Gage shook his head. 'Maybe he wants us to know about his handiwork. He's gotten a lot of attention from the police and now the media is involved.'

Warwick frowned. 'Not good.'

'He's more dangerous now than ever,' Gage said.

Warwick muttered an oath. 'Any curiosity seekers at the gravesite? One could be him.'

'I've put extra patrol cars out there to question anyone who shows up.'

'Tess, what about the bandana?' Vega said.

'It's got stains on it, likely sweat and maybe blood. I'm running DNA but those results will take time.' She glanced at her notes. 'I also found a few blond hair fibers on Borden's body. The hair is human but has no traces of a root, which leads me to believe they're from a wig.'

'So he likes blondes,' Vega said. 'The killer is playing out a fantasy?'

'That's my guess,' Warwick said.

Gage's unease grew by the minute as he pictured Adrianna Barrington's long blond hair. 'Adrianna Barrington has received odd calls. Caller said he was Craig and that he loved her. She brushed it off and said it was someone who didn't want the land sale to go through. I traced the call to a disposable phone. She also said she received an anniversary card and it was signed "Craig." And someone delivered flowers to her.'

'Did you see the card?' Warwick said.

Gage shook his head. 'No.'

'Did Thornton have any family or friends who'd be very loyal to him?'

'No siblings. Parents are dead. As for Adrianna, her mother is alive but the woman doesn't appear to be in any kind of shape to hurt anyone.'

Warwick frowned. 'I'm not so sure. She and her lawyer provided enough evidence regarding the death of her first child to prevent charges from being filed, but I am not entirely convinced they weren't hiding something.'

Gage tapped his index finger on his belt. 'Are you saying she's not as sick as she pretends to be?'

Warwick shook his head. 'I've no doubt she's ill. But sick doesn't mean stupid and it doesn't mean they can't act.'

'Is Mrs. Barrington going to be at the auction?' Gage said.

Warwick shook his head. 'Not according to Kendall.'

'Vega and I could swing by and have a chat with her at her home.'

Warwick nodded. 'Why not?'

Gage and Vega arrived at Margaret Barrington's house an hour later. Without thinking, Gage adjusted his tie before he rang the bell.

Footsteps sounded on the other side of the door and seconds later it snapped open. Estelle stood in the entryway, her face the hard mask of a defender.

She dried her hands with a blue and white kitchen towel. 'What can I do for you two?'

'I'd like to talk to Mrs. Barrington,' Gage said.

'She's dozing right now.'

'This is about Adrianna.'

Worry knitted Estelle's brow. 'Everything all right with my baby?'

'For now. But I have questions that need answering.'

Estelle considered what he said for a few more seconds and then nodded. 'Come on in. I'll wake her up.'

They followed her up the stairs to the older woman's room and Estelle knocked. After a pause, Estelle cracked the door and peeked in before facing Gage. 'She's decent and watching TV.'

'You're not going to warn her that we're here?' Vega said.

Estelle shook her head. 'Won't hurt to shake her up a little. You might learn something if she's off guard.'

Gage nodded. 'Thanks.'

Estelle frowned. 'You take care of my baby, you hear?'

'Yes, ma'am.'

Estelle pushed open the door, then turned and walked away.

'Mrs. Barrington?' Gage said.

Margaret started and turned from the television. She looked at Gage, her eyes wide with surprise before narrowing. 'What do you want, Detective?'

There was steel under the veil. 'I want to talk to you about Adrianna.'

She sat straighter and adjusted her shawl. 'Why? Is something wrong with her?'

'No. Not yet.'

'Then what?'

Gage and Vega moved into the room. She didn't ask them to sit, so both stood.

'You were very close to Craig and the Thornton family, weren't you?' Gage asked.

'Yes. I went to college with Frances. We were best friends. She married Robert right after college. I introduced them.'

'Did you see much of them in the early days of their marriage?'

'Not so much. I moved to New York. I wanted to be an

artist. I met my husband Carter during a Christmas break at home. We married a few days before my thirtieth birthday.'

'The Thorntons were married about ten years before Craig was born.'

'Yes. Margaret often wrote me of their struggles to have a baby. It was a miracle she ever got pregnant.'

'Why do you say that?'

'Robert had a terrible case of the measles as a child.' She picked at the fringe of her shawl. 'I was there when she found out she was finally pregnant and there when Craig was born. I watched him grow up.'

'When was Adrianna born?'

Her brow wrinkled. 'Four years after Carter and I married. She was three years younger than Craig.'

He squatted so that he wouldn't tower over her. 'And Frances was there for you when Adrianna was born?'

Margaret's face glowed with happiness. 'Yes. We used to dream of Craig marrying Adrianna and of our families being joined.'

'Sounds like you looked out for each other.'

'We did.'

'You ever hear of Kelly Jo Morgan?'

She frowned. 'No.'

'She dated Craig the summer he and Adrianna were apart. She wanted to marry Craig. Said she was pregnant with his child.'

Margaret shook her head. 'He wouldn't have married her.'

'Kelly Jo was willing to raise Cain if he didn't.'

'Frances would never have allowed it. And Craig wanted Adrianna back.'

'And we both know you knew Rhonda Minor.'

360

'Yes. Why are you asking all these questions?'

'Both those women were murdered, Mrs. Barrington. Seems whoever killed them was either protecting Craig or maybe protecting Adrianna. I thought Craig might have been the killer, but I know now I was wrong.'

'How do you know that?'

'Another woman has died. Another woman who hurt Craig and Adrianna.' Gage decided to take a gamble. 'Tammy Borden, the drunk driver that slammed into Adrianna and Craig's car, was found dead.'

Mrs. Barrington fiddled with the fringe on her shawl. 'I remember her from the trial.'

He took another risk. 'I'm starting to think that maybe Adrianna might have had a hand in those murders.'

Mrs. Barrington laughed. 'She did not kill those women.'

'How can you be so sure? She had good reason to kill them all.'

'She wouldn't have killed to keep Craig.'

'Why?'

She let out a long sigh. 'I don't think she ever really wanted Craig. Frances and I talked her into returning to him. We pushed hard. She was young and feeling guilty about leaving him in the first place. Their reconciliation wouldn't have lasted if not for the baby. I could tell the day she married she was conflicted.'

Gage didn't speak as he threaded trembling hands together. Resentment churned as he thought about the effect this woman had had on his life. Who knew what would have happened to his relationship with Adrianna if not for her interference?

'She wanted you.'

His head snapped up. Resentment burned like hot coals in the pit of his stomach. 'Would you have killed to protect Adrianna?'

'Yes. Yes, I would have. But I didn't kill those women.'

'Who would want to protect her like that?'

She hesitated. 'I don't know.'

'You best think hard, Mrs. Barrington, because I think whoever is doing this just might turn on her.'

Chapter Twenty-Four

Friday, October 6, 7:00 p.m.

Adrianna had called Cary before she'd arrived at the hotel to make sure the press weren't waiting. There'd been a few reporters but hotel security had escorted them off the property. Adrianna had parked in the deck and come up the service entrance to the ballroom.

The setup for the auction was complete. The main exhibit hall had been draped in black. The paintings were placed around the room, suspended from wires that hooked into bolts on the ceiling.

Adrianna had chosen a silk black halter dress that clung to her frame. She'd selected a white choker pearl necklace and wore four-inch stilettos. She would tower over most. Good. Better for coaxing people to buy.

The crowds had yet to arrive, but auction staff was humming round rechecking each picture moved in by Wells Moving, stacking programs, and making sure everything was in its place. The auctioneer was warming up his voice.

She checked her watch. The doors would open in five minutes.

Three years ago, almost to the day, she'd stood in this same room. It had been packed full of people, some she knew, and most she didn't. The wedding planner hired by her mother had run the show, dictating every move she'd made. And she'd let her because she'd been overwhelmed. The day had been a blur.

This night would be different. She was in charge. This was her vision. She spotted Cary and moved across the room to her. 'It all looks wonderful.'

Cary's full belly pressed against the folds of her dark maternity dress. 'Simple. Elegant. Just as you requested. The bidding starts at eight?'

'Correct. That'll give time for our guests to mill before they come in here ready to buy.'

Cary pressed her hand to her belly. 'Oooh.'

'Everything all right?'

'All good. He's just a kicker. Hey, I might have to leave early tonight.'

'The baby?'

'I'm not sure. Could just be indigestion. But if I have to leave, I wanted you to know the head waitress tonight is great. She'll end up running this place one day.'

'Sure. We'll be fine. You just take care of the baby.'

'The name of the head waitress is Jessie Hudson.'

Jessie Hudson. Adrianna almost laughed. Small, small world. 'Thanks. Leave if you need to, okay?'

'Will do. I hope you raise lots of money tonight for the pediatric wing.'

Adrianna allowed herself a bright smile. 'I hope I do, too.'

As guests began to arrive, Adrianna greeted each at the door. If she'd learned anything from Margaret Barrington, it was how to make a party work. From the cradle she'd learned how to make charitable events a success.

Kendall and her husband Jacob arrived. Kendall looked

stunning in a white off-the-shoulder cocktail dress and Jacob looked handsome in a dark suit. She beamed. He looked bored.

Adrianna kissed Kendall on the cheek. 'I'm so glad you came.'

Kendall slid her arm into Jacob's. 'Wouldn't have missed it for the world.'

Adrianna glanced to Jacob. 'Thank you for coming.'

'It's a good cause.'

Kendall squeezed his forearm. 'Events aren't his thing.'

Adrianna smiled at Warwick. 'In all honesty, these kind of things were never to my taste. But I understand their purpose.'

Jacob raised a brow. 'To make me miserable.'

Adrianna laughed. 'You and every other man in the room. Keep telling yourself it's a good cause. It's a good cause.'

'Thanks.'

The moment of laughter died in her when she looked across the room and saw Brett Newington. 'Look what the cat dragged in.'

Jacob and Kendall turned. He frowned, his expression dark and menacing.

The trio watched as Janet Guthrie crossed the room toward Brett. She kissed him on the cheek.

'Look who've become such good friends,' Adrianna said.

'There's one of the sources of that news report.' Kendall arched a brow. 'Jacob, would you mind getting us something to drink? And maybe ask Mr. Newington to move along.'

Jacob smiled, the first spark of pleasure in his eyes. 'I would be glad to.'

Kendall winked at him. For just a split second his eyes softened before the wall rose up again. He moved across the room, like a panther on the hunt. In seconds he was beside Newington, leaning toward the man and saying something that no one could hear. Newington paled and within seconds departed.

Adrianna laughed. 'Jacob has a way.'

Pride glistened in Kendall's eyes. 'I don't think we'll be seeing Brett again tonight.' Her gaze settled on Adrianna. 'So it's going well?'

'So far so good.' Having Kendall here felt good.

'So what aren't you telling me?' Kendall said.

'Nothing.'

'Please. I can spot a cover-up with my eyes closed and one hand tied behind my back. Spill.' Hope sparked in Kendall's eyes. 'It's what sisters do.'

'I know. And I appreciate the offer. But tonight I don't want to get into it.' Adrianna did feel a connection to Kendall. 'I almost feel like we're sisters.'

Kendall frowned. 'We *are* sisters, Adrianna. We may not have the history but we're working on that part.'

Adrianna wanted a sister. Wanted someone with whom she could laugh or cry. Someone to talk about the baby that had vanished. 'After this. Let's do something. Something fun.'

Kendall nodded, seeing the opening but wise enough not to push. 'I'd like that.'

The band picked up its tempo and soon couples paired off and were on the dance floor. She felt a swell of satisfaction as she watched the movers and shakers of Richmond filling the space.

*

By the time Gage left Margaret Barrington's house, he didn't have time to drive home, shower, or change. So he headed to the auction as he was. As he parked across the street from the hotel, his phone rang. It was a text message from Mark Benton, Rhonda's neighbor. It read: **Found Rhonda's painting.**

Gage studied the image Benton had photographed and sent him. It was a landscape. Trees, rolling hills, the river in the distance. What struck him most about the painting was that it looked old, as if it had been done a century ago. Not something he'd expect a vibrant young woman to paint.

He closed the phone and moved inside. He'd attended enough of these swanky affairs when he'd joined the Falcons. He knew how to negotiate them, but didn't care for them. His ex, Susan, had loved them and had clung to his arm and grinned as if she'd landed the prized bull. She was all glitz, no substance, and he'd been too young to know better.

He stared into the room of tuxes, evening gowns, and glittering jewelry. *I am one fish out of water.*

Gage was half-tempted to retreat and wait in the lobby for Adrianna when he spotted her. Stunning was too lame a word to describe her. A black dress accentuated her creamy white skin and a pearl choker her slim neck. High heels made her taller than most and almost brought her up to his eye level. She wasn't wearing her wedding bands.

She was talking to a tall, distinguished guy. Tux, manicured hair, buffed nails. Her type. No. Not her type. She was more than these people.

As if sensing his gaze, Adrianna looked toward him.

Her smile faltered a fraction and he thought she'd turn away. But she excused herself and soon worked her way through the crowds toward him.

She was stopped several times along the way. Each time she was gracious, patient, and ready to cajole more money out of some rich patron. One elderly man she spoke to was one of the most powerful attorneys in the city. He had a reputation as a ball buster. And in Adrianna's hands he appeared to be Jell-O.

Damn, but the woman had the power of a witch.

Every man in the room knew it.

And no man cared.

Gage found himself impatient for her to reach him and started to resent the people who stood in her way. He started to weave into the room, meeting her halfway.

'Welcome, Detective. I didn't think you were going to make it.'

He wished he had a drink, or something to hold. 'Nice gig.'

Adrianna's smile was warm and her eyes danced. 'Thanks.'

He prided himself on reading people. Even his ex was an open book. Susan wanted it all and made no apologies. But with Adrianna, he didn't have any idea what she wanted. 'So you've managed to put together a dry party. And by the looks of the people you have here, that's no small feat.'

'You should have been here an hour ago. The auction had a few heated moments.'

'That so?'

'Janet went toe to toe with a local matron over a painting. Quite exciting. Janet won and paid twice what she'd intended.'

'I wish I'd been here.' Her smell was soft and elegant. 'Getting people to open their wallets while they're sober is no small accomplishment.'

'The trick is a gentle twisting of the arm. Not too drastic so that they try to escape.'

A couple, who were nicely but simply dressed approached. 'Ms. Barrington?'

Adrianna smiled. 'Dr. Norton.'

'This is my wife, Maureen.'

'It's a pleasure to meet you. I'm so glad you could come. Dr. Norton and Maureen, I'd like you to meet Gage Hudson. Dr. Norton is the principal of Goodman High School, where I spoke last week.'

Gage watched Maureen slip her arm possessively into the crook of her husband's arm. And the good Dr. Norton tried not too hard to gush over Adrianna. 'What did she speak about?'

'Drunk driving. I've got to tell you, Ms. Barrington, your talk made a real impression on those kids.'

She smiled. 'I'm glad.'

They chatted a few more minutes and Gage noted Adrianna made a point to bring both him and Maureen into the conversation.

When they left, another woman across the room raised her hand and called out to Adrianna. She smiled and raised her glass of ginger ale. 'Excuse me. Mrs. Welbourne spent a lot of money here tonight.'

'Don't let me stop you.' As she walked away his gaze traveled the length of her body. Perfect. Like her.

'Careful, Detective, your horns are showing.'

Janet Guthrie's crude remark had him turning. She

wore a red silk suit, lots of diamonds, and so much make-up it made her look like a caricature. 'Ms. Guthrie.'

Janet nodded her head toward Adrianna without looking in her direction. 'Watch how she twists that sour old maid around her little finger. I'll bet she has a check for fifty thousand dollars in her hand by tomorrow.'

Adrianna leaned in close to the older woman. He didn't see guile, but kindness in Adrianna's eyes.

As if reading his thoughts, Janet said. 'And she looks so genuine, don't you think? I think Craig was always in love with her. Even in his worst moments of debauchery, he worried that Adrianna would find out.'

Gage remembered what Margaret had told him earlier. Craig would never have cheated on Adrianna. 'And she never did?'

'So Adrianna says, but seeing her tonight I'm not so sure. She is quite the manipulator.'

Margaret and Janet painted different pictures of Adrianna. 'She seems to be the real deal to me.'

Janet laughed. 'No one is the real deal. We all have our masks on.'

'I hear you had an interesting bidding war tonight.'

'The piece I wanted was the most valuable in the collection. It stands to reason I'd have competition.'

'All for a good cause.'

She lifted a brow. 'Of course.'

'I hear you've been talking to the press.' The bluff dangled in the air like a worm from a fishing pole.

She arched a brow. 'What makes you think it was me?'

'I wasn't sure until now.'

She shrugged. 'It wasn't me.'

'Why'd you visit Craig the day he died?'

Surprise widened her eyes. 'To tell him I'd bought the gallery. That it was all mine now.'

'Nothing like kicking a guy when he's down.'

'It's the best time.' Someone called out Janet's name and she moved away from him.

Gage watched her vanish into the crowd. 'What the hell are you up to?'

Gage strode toward the wall of paintings that had just been sold. They were nice enough. Most were landscapes. Old. Nothing he'd ever bother to buy.

As he stared at one landscape, he was reminded of Benton's text. He flipped open his phone and started to walk down the row again comparing the phone image to what he saw. He was on the last painting when he had a match.

The version on the phone wasn't as good as the one in front of him. Still, he could see that she was doing her best to copy the painting down to each brush stroke and the artist's signature.

'New love for art, Hudson?' Warwick's voice held no hint of humor.

Gage turned to find Warwick and Kendall standing there. 'Have a look at this.' He showed them the phone picture. 'This was one of the last paintings Rhonda created.'

Warwick compared the two. Kendall studied them as well.

It was Kendall that spoke first. 'I'd say Rhonda was perfecting her techniques.'

'Her techniques?' Gage said.

'Forgery.' She nodded her head toward the SOLD sign. 'Look who bought it.'

'Janet Guthrie,' Gage said.

Craig stood outside the hotel, staring up at the glittering lights. His thoughts were on Adrianna. Blond hair. A fighter's spirit. He'd been thinking about her so much. And his body burned with anticipation.

He closed his eyes and focused on the hotel. It was a grand place, a place where he belonged. The people inside were his people and he should be there. But he was wise enough to understand that he had to bide his time.

Ducking his head, he crossed the street and moved down the sidewalk to the parking garage under the hotel near the service entrance. Adrianna had parked here earlier.

He strode up to her car, glanced around to make sure no one saw him, and then quickly and efficiently pulled a knife from his pocket and knelt by the tire. He slid the knife between the tire and the rim and sliced the rubber. Immediately, air started to leak out.

When she came out later, she'd see that her car had been disabled. And he'd be here waiting for her.

Tess cradled the six-pack under her arm and moved with quick efficient steps toward Dr. Butler's office. She didn't break stride, fearing she'd lose her nerve. The way she kept showing up here, she was starting to feel like a stalker. 'You are a mess, Kier.'

As expected she found him in his office, his head bent over papers. 'Are we the only two geeks on the planet who like to hang around the dead on Friday night?'

Alex smiled though he didn't glance up. 'Tess, I know I don't have a life, but I thought you would.'

She accepted that as invitation enough and moved into his office. 'I lost it somewhere along the way.'

Slowly he pulled his glasses off and looked at her. He was a good-looking man. Not stunningly handsome, but that was okay. She'd never gone for the pretty-boy types. She liked character, laugh lines, and intelligent eyes. She pulled a beer out of the bag and offered it to him. He nodded and accepted it. 'So what are you working on?'

'Reading my notes on the Borden autopsy.'

She twisted the top off her own beer. 'Why?'

'It bothers me. I feel like I'm missing something.'

'Any thoughts as to what?'

'None. But it's there. I know I've missed something.'

'I didn't think you missed much.'

'Not enough sleep, I guess.'

Tess leaned forward. 'How about tonight we let the work go. How about we do something radical.'

'Such as?'

'Have fun.'

'Fun?' A smile tweaked the edge of his lips. 'I've heard of that.'

So the robot had a dry sense of humor. 'It's been around for a long time, and people of all walks of life pursue it.'

'Really? Might be worth some study.' He had long, lean hands, neatly trimmed nails, and no rings.

She tipped the neck of her beer bottle toward him. 'That's the thing. You can't study it. It's just something that you do.'

'What do you propose?'

'Breaking bread. Dinner. Conversation that's not work related.'

'I'm game. When should we have this . . . what did you call it?'

She rose. 'Fun. It's called fun. And I suggest there is no time like the present. A bit of fun and you might find your mind clears and solutions present themselves.'

He stood and pulled his coat from the back of his chair. 'I know a place. Great food.'

'My parents own a restaurant, so I'm quite particular.'

'You'll like this place. I'll drive.'

'Normally, I drive.'

'Why not kick back for an evening and let someone else do something for you?'

His tone more than his words convinced her. No demands. No expectation. Just a statement. 'Okay, Alex Butler. You drive.'

Adrianna's feet felt as if they'd explode in her four-inch heels. Thoughts of comfort had been secondary when she'd slipped on the stunning shoes earlier this evening. Now comfort was all she could think about.

A satisfied smile tipped her lips as she thought about the evening. It had been a fabulous success. She'd raised over a half a million dollars tonight and the proceeds would go directly to Mercy Hospital's neonatal unit.

Somewhere along the evening, she'd lost sight of Gage. She'd meant to get back to him, had really wanted to, but she could never break free. So she'd shoved aside the disappointment and let herself be swept up by the night.

It was past eleven as she stood in the back of the ball-room, watching the waitstaff clear the dishes away, stack chairs, and vacuum the confetti off the floor.

She spotted Jessie and moved across the room. 'Did Cary leave?'

'Contractions.'

'She all right?'

'Doing fine, according to her husband's last report.'

Jessie looked tired. No doubt she'd been on the job fourteen or fifteen hours. 'Thank you. I know you really helped make this event a success.'

Jessie nodded. 'I was glad to help.'

'Do I need to sign anything?'

Jessie flipped through the pages of her clipboard and pulled out an invoice. 'Yes.'

Adrianna accepted the sheet and glanced down the itemized list of the night. She'd been over this list with Cary at least a dozen times. It was just as she remembered it. No extra expenses or hidden costs. Lord knew she'd worked hard to make sure she'd accounted in advance for the costs.

'It looks just right.' She signed her name and added the extra swirl to the *B*. 'Again, I couldn't have done it without you.'

For just an instant, a heavy silence hung between them and she thought Jessie would say something. Instead, she smiled. 'Think of us again for next year.'

Adrianna laughed. 'Next year.' All she wanted to do was get through tomorrow.

She left the ballroom and moved across the lobby of the hotel toward the bank of elevators.

'Looks like your evening was a big hit.'

At the sound of Gage's voice, she turned. He moved across the lobby. He'd lost the tie and unbuttoned the top couple of buttons of his shirt. He radiated a quiet strength.

'Your sister did a great job.'

'She runs a tight ship. I tried to keep my distance. She doesn't appreciate the hovering.'

'I thought you'd have left by now.' She was careful to keep the excitement from her voice.

'Thought I'd stick around. Where's Reese?'

'He had another appointment with a client.'

Gage frowned as if the answer did not set well. 'He left you.'

'No. I brought myself. I had to get here so early, it made sense for me to drive.'

He nodded. 'I'll walk you to your car.'

Even in her heels he was taller. 'Sure.'

The doors opened and they stepped inside the elevator.

The walls were lined with mirrors and the floor carpeted in a deep blue. However, the compartment shrank when the doors closed. All night she'd made small talk and now she struggled to find words. 'Thanks for coming. Was it what you expected?'

'Yes and no. You amazed me how you made some of the city's toughest weak at the knees.'

'Who did you have in mind?'

'Burt Kline, for one.'

'He was sweet.'

Gage looked at her as if she'd gone mad. 'He's a barracuda in the courtroom. Tried to do a number on me a couple of months ago.'

She could picture that. Burt was no one's fool. 'Really?'

'I testified against his client, who was on trial for murder. Kline tried to rip at my credibility.'

'I've seen his snaps of temper.' She shrugged. 'I know how to handle him.'

He arched an eyebrow. 'Is that what you do with people? Handle them?'

The doors to the elevator opened. 'Isn't that what you do?'

'Point taken.' They stepped out of the elevator and walked through the parking lot.

'Were you planning to walk to your car alone?'

'Sure.'

'Next time get an escort.'

'It's well lighted.'

'Don't be fooled.' He peered into the shadows.

As they walked to her car, the click of her heels echoed in the lot. Lord, but she longed to take the shoes off. 'Are you always looking for trouble?'

'It has a way of showing up.'

They reached her car and she unlocked the front door. She was sorry to see him go. She wanted to ask him out or something but realized how painfully out of practice she was when it came to this sort of thing. 'Thanks.'

He rested his arm against her open door. He lingered but didn't ask her for anything. She sensed that if something was going to happen it would have to come from her. But she didn't ask. 'Thank you again.'

He nodded and stepped back. When she swung her legs inside he closed the door, lingering.

She fumbled with her keys, managed to get them in the ignition and start the car.

Gage tapped on her window. She glanced toward him, surprised now to see the frown on his face. She rolled down the window.

'You have a flat.'

'What?' She shut off the engine and got out. The right front tire was completely flat. 'It was fine earlier today.'

'Do you have a spare?'

She frowned. 'No. I mean, I did, but I had a flat about a month ago and had to use the spare. I just never got it replaced.'

That answer didn't set well with him. 'I'll give you a ride home.'

'I can call a cab.'

He pulled his keys from his pocket. 'My car is right over here.'

She closed and locked her door. 'Tell me it's not too far. These shoes are killing me.'

He glanced down at her shoes. Appreciation sparked. 'They look great.'

She fell in step beside him. 'So the pain was worth it?'

'Yes.'

Craig watched from the shadows. His anger burned as Hudson escorted his Adrianna away from him. Tonight was supposed to be their night. Their time together. And now she was slipping from his fingers.

Hudson was taking something from her.

Maybe he should repay the favor.

Jessie.

She wouldn't leave the hotel for hours, but he could wait.

As he moved from the shadows back to his truck, his cell buzzed in his pocket. Annoyed, he snapped it open. 'What?'

'I have another job for you.'

'Really?' The day wouldn't be a total loss.

'Janet Guthrie.'

'Why her?' He wasn't so fond of the snooty bitch.

'She's been talking to the press.'

'So what if she talks to the press? They haven't talked about anything that can hurt us.'

'It's a matter of time before she starts talking about those paintings.'

'She wouldn't. That would hurt her.'

'We both know how the unexpected can change everything. If push came to shove, she'd turn on a dime.'

'I want something in return for this job.'

'Sure, you can take her to your little room. Keep her as long as you want.'

'I don't want her. I want another one. One I can keep for a really long time. Maybe forever.'

'I don't make bargains.'

'If you want Janet killed, then I get another one to keep.'

A long silence followed. 'Who?'

Adrianna. But knowing that wouldn't meet with approval, he said, 'Jessie.'

Another pause. 'I don't want any trails leading back to me.'

'None have yet, have they?'

'No.'

'Fine. Just do it. Tonight.'

Craig closed the phone and put it in his pocket. He only had to wait fifteen minutes before Janet emerged from the elevators. The sound of his footsteps had her raising her gaze from her open purse.

Janet paused for a moment, her expression tight and frightened. 'You scared the crap out of me.'

He liked seeing fear in her eyes. She needed to be brought down a peg or two. 'Sorry about that.'

'It isn't like me to be paranoid. What are you doing here?'

He shrugged. 'Why wouldn't I be?'

Janet's gaze narrowed. 'What are you doing here?' she asked again.

Her silk blouse draped open just slightly, revealing a hint of her white breast. Janet had a good body and she liked to flaunt it.

When he didn't answer, her annoyance grew. 'Answer me or get out of my way.'

The challenge in her voice said more than words ever could. *Wimp. Spineless. Twit.*

Janet moved toward her car and clicked it open with the remote. She'd dismissed him like he was nothing.

'Don't walk away from me.'

'Don't waste my time.'

Rage bolted through his limbs. She was just like everyone else. Always underestimating him.

Damn her! Damn her!

He pulled the .38 from his pocket. 'Don't walk away from me.'

She turned, glanced at the gun. Lifting her chin, she met his gaze. 'You don't have the balls.'

His throat constricted. For just a split second she realized she'd pushed the wrong button and fear washed away the arrogance. He fired. The bullet hit her in the side.

The shot was a quiet echo in the garage. For a moment Janet stopped, her body still. They both glanced down at her side as the bloom of blood blossomed and grew. 'What the hell?'

Excitement rolled through him. He fired a second and third time. These bullets struck her in the chest and she fell to the ground. She landed on her knees and then tipped sideways. She hit the ground hard.

Craig's hands trembled. He'd let his anger get the better of him. He'd made a mess. But he didn't care right at this moment. Later he would worry. 'Don't ever tell me I don't have the balls to kill.'

Janet stared up at him, eyes filled with pain and fear. 'Please.'

'Please what, Janet?' The fourth bullet struck her between the eyes and killed her instantly.

His rage deserted him and now only consequences rambled in his head. He had visions of Hudson coming after him. The guy was relentless and wouldn't stop until he was finally dead. He ducked down and pushed Janet's limp body under her car. Blood smeared his hands and shirt.

The deck's elevator doors dinged open. A group of hotel staff workers got out. Jessie was in the center, laughing with a coworker. One waiter lighted a cigarette.

Craig wanted to go after Jessie but with Janet's blood on his hands, he didn't dare.

He watched her and several friends get into her Jeep

and drive away. Damn. This wasn't fair. He'd earned her. He'd made a deal.

A car horn beeped and he glanced at his hands, dripping with blood.

The time had come to take care of Hudson, and then he'd go after Jessie and Adrianna.

Chapter Twenty-Five

Tess sat on the bar stool at the end of a butcher-block countertop. They were in Alex's loft condo located in the heart of the city. She sipped her wine and watched with fascination as he chopped an onion at lightning speed. 'So this is the best place to eat in town.'

'Absolutely. I generally don't have time to eat out. Half the time it's two in the morning when I do eat.'

'And you always cook?'

'Always.'

'Okay, so we've covered the food. And we could talk about the weather or we could discuss the elephant in the room.'

'What would that be?'

Alex's gaze locked on her. Suddenly, she felt oddly warm inside. And she wasn't thinking about him as Dr. Butler, Robo-Doc, or even Mr. Wizard. He was a man. A man who'd not be a rushed lover. A man who would move over her body slowly, carefully, inspecting every square inch of her.

Tess sipped her wine and worked to keep her voice steady. 'The case, of course.'

Alex smiled and she sensed he read her thoughts. Challenge sparked. 'What is it that's bothering you?'

You, you pencil-neck geek. You have no business making me want what I've sworn off of. 'The injuries aren't consistent.'

He stared at her for a moment and blinked as if the pieces of the puzzle just came together. 'The fractures on the faces of all three victims. The ones on the left were more pronounced than the ones on the right.'

'The bruising on Tammy's face really brings this home. And you can also see bruises on her arms. Again some much darker than the others.'

Blue eyes blazed with excitement. 'Two killers?'

She nodded, her heart racing. 'Yes. One killer is strong. The other weak.'

His gaze darkened. 'Or old and young?'

'Male or female.'

Gage noticed the FOR SALE sign in front of Adrianna's house had been changed to SOLD.

Frowning, he escorted Adrianna up to the front porch of her house. Soft pale light from the iron fixture above shone down on her, giving her skin a luminescent look. She'd slipped off her shoes and was now barefoot, making her a good four inches shorter than him.

Adrianna opened the front door. 'Want to come in for coffee? It's the least I can do.'

Gage wasn't ready to say good night. 'Sure.'

She flipped on the lights and led him through the house into the kitchen.

On a butcher-block countertop there was a crystal cake stand filled with cookies. 'So did you buy that to impress the buyers or did you bake them?'

Laughing, she dropped her shoes and purse in an over-stuffed chair by a dining table. 'They're real. I bake.'

'I would have taken a bet against that one any day.'

She moved behind the center island and clicked on a preset coffeepot. Immediately it started to gurgle. 'I bake when I can't sleep.'

He glanced at the pile of cookies and the cake on another counter. 'Not sleeping much these days?'

'I've had better months.'

'What's keeping you up?'

'You asking as a cop?'

'No.'

She looked on the verge of opening up, but then shrugged those golden shoulders. 'Doesn't matter.'

It did to him. 'You sold the house.'

'Just accepted the offer.'

'What are you going to do?'

'I don't know. For the first time in three years I have no ties. Maybe Paris. New York.'

'Faraway places.' Gage thought about the words she'd spoken to him here just days ago. *I'm sorry.* Simple words that had been rattling in his head since he'd heard them.

'So, what do you do when a case like this is solved?'

'Have a beer with my partner. Take a day off if I can and then get back to work on the next case.'

She removed cups from the cabinet and filled each with coffee. 'The work never ends.'

'No.'

Gage's fingers brushed hers as he reached for the cup. Energy shot through his body. He took her left hand in his and smoothed his thumb over her naked ring finger.

Suddenly, he saw himself at a crossroads. If he didn't choose wisely, he feared he'd lose more than he could put into words. He released her hand and moved around the island.

Adrianna stood still, staring at him as if she didn't know what to do. He moved to within inches of her, but not touching her.

He brushed a strand of hair from her shoulder. She looked up and moistened her lips. She made no move to touch him but didn't retreat either.

'I'm sorry,' he said.

'For what?'

'Four years ago. I made mistakes, too.'

'The past is gone.'

Slowly, he moved his hand up her arm, savoring the soft warmth of her skin. Fingertips skimmed over her shoulder and he cupped her face. Gage had never wanted a woman as much as he wanted Adrianna. He tilted his head down and kissed her on the lips. She tasted sweet, soft; and unable to resist, he leaned into the kiss. She wrapped her arm around his neck. Full breasts pressed against his chest.

Gage knew the point of no return approached like a runaway train. He wanted to make love to her. But the idea of loving and losing her again scared the shit out of him. He broke the kiss. 'I'd rather not start something that can't be finished.'

She stared at him a long moment, understanding he wasn't just talking about tonight, but tomorrow and the next day. 'I can't make any promises, Gage. I wish I could.'

He traced her jawline. 'At least you're honest.'

'I owe you fairness.' She placed her hand on his chest.

The simple touch made his heart beat faster. No promises. She was offering just now. God help him, he prayed it would be enough. With a groan he took her in his arms and refused to think beyond right now.

When they broke the kiss, he could barely think. His voice was a rough, dark growl. 'Where's your bedroom?'

She guided him down the hallway to her room. As they entered, he didn't notice lights or décor. He saw only the bed at twelve o'clock.

He slid his hand along her shoulders. Her skin felt like silk. Smelled of roses. He unfastened the halter strap behind her neck and let the dress fall. Her naked breasts glistened in the moonlight that streamed in through the window.

Gage cupped her breast in his hand and teased the tip to a hard peak as he kissed her on the lips.

Adrianna pushed his jacket from his shoulders and let it fall to the floor. He backed her up toward the bed and when the back of her knees pressed against the mattress, she fell back. She propped herself up with her elbows.

Breath caught in his throat. He lowered himself on top of her and kissed the hollow between her breasts. She moaned and arched as he kissed her flat belly.

'Gage, please.'

He smiled, liking the way his name sounded on her lips now. He wanted to tease her longer and savor this moment but he felt ready to explode.

Quickly, he shed his clothes and straddled her, savoring the sight of silk garters holding up silk stockings. Ripping her panties free, he pressed his erection against her moist center and stared down at her. She watched him with half-open eyes.

He pushed inside her and she wrapped her legs around him. She felt so deliciously tight.

They moved together in a frenzied dance. Soon their bodies glistened with sweat. And when they found their release, she called out his name as she arched her back. He collapsed against her and rolled on his side, spooning his body against her.

For the first time in a long time, he felt at home.

Chapter Twenty-Six

Saturday, October 7, 7:00 a.m.

Adrianna was in the shower when Gage's cell phone rang. The sound sent a bolt of irritation through him as he rolled on his side and checked the display on the phone. It read: **Nick Vega**. He flipped it open.

'This better be damn good,' he muttered.

'A video arrived at the station.'

Gage picked up his watch from the nightstand and checked the time. 'What about it?'

The sound of the shower turning on had him turning toward the bathroom. He imagined Adrianna's nude body under the water.

'It looks like a snuff film. A woman chained to a wall. Looks like Kelly Jo Morgan. She's crying into the camera and talking to someone.'

He swung his legs over the side of the bed. 'Who?'

'She keeps saying, "I love you, Craig."'

Jesus. Gage pressed fingers to his temple. 'I'll be right down.'

'Gage.'

'What?'

'The camera isn't on a tripod. Someone else is holding it.'

'Two killers.'

'Yeah.'

'I'll be right there.'

He dressed and moved into the bathroom. Adrianna was in the shower. Her eyes closed, she'd buried her face under the hot spray. He opened the shower door. 'Adrianna.'

She stepped back, pushing the water from her eyes. Without make-up, she looked so vulnerable. 'Hey. Join me.'

'I want to.' He shook his head. 'But I've got to go. Something's come up.'

'Bad news?'

'Yes.' He'd been called away so much when they'd dated the first time. 'I'm sorry.'

She leaned forward to kiss him. 'Don't be. Go.'

His lips touched hers but he didn't lean into the kiss. His thoughts were only to find the killer or killers and protect her. 'I'll call you.'

Her smile faltered. 'Sure.'

Gage knew if he kissed her again he wouldn't leave and they'd spend the whole weekend in bed. So he turned and left, praying like hell he'd not lost her again.

Adrianna stood in the shower letting the hot spray wash over her skin. She wiped the tears from her face. 'God, you are such a fool.'

Last night they'd made love a couple of times but there'd been few words. Neither had wanted to venture into the past or the future when the moment felt so good. For the first time in a very long time she didn't feel buried alive. She simply felt alive.

And now he was gone.

'Idiot.' She shut off the water, grabbed a towel, and

dried off. Her first venture into dating and she felt as if she'd landed on her face.

Outside the bathroom, the air felt cold and had goose bumps puckering her skin. Mechanically she started to brush the tangles from her hair. The clock ticked in the hallway. Had Gage just slept with her for kicks? To get back at her?

A deep sadness burned inside her. Had he been using her?

'Do not go there,' Adrianna muttered. 'Do not go there. No promises were made, so none were broken.'

The phone rang and she hurried down the hallway. Breathless, she picked up the receiver. 'Gage?'

'No,' Kendall's voice purred.

Adrianna felt a terrible letdown. 'Kendall. Oh.'

'I'd feel insulted if I wasn't so curious about why you were expecting Gage Hudson this early in the morning?'

Adrianna shoved long fingers through her wet hair. Water dripped around her feet. 'It's a long story.'

'I'm in no rush at all.' Subtle amusement wove through the words. 'In fact, there's nothing I'd like better than a bit of good, juicy gossip.'

'There's nothing to say.' And she realized with some embarrassment that there was nothing to say. Gage had slept with her and left. End of story.

'You sound sad,' Kendall said.

'I'm not sad.' She straightened her shoulders. She refused to be sad. There'd been too much of that in her life. She'd find a better, more powerful emotion to describe this moment. 'I'm just irritated. Maybe even a little pissed.'

'What did Hudson do?' Kendall's voice dropped a notch and adopted an air of aggression.

Adrianna glanced at the rumpled sheets on the bed. 'Nothing I didn't fully consent to.'

Kendall sighed into the phone. 'So where is he now?'

She turned from the bed where the rumpled sheets still held the imprint of his body. 'He just left without an explanation.'

'Cops have to do that sometimes, Adrianna. Jacob tore out of here early this morning.'

Adrianna straightened. 'Something has happened.'

'I think so. That's why I called.'

'If I find out anything, I'll call you.'

'I'll do the same.'

Adrianna hung up and glanced at the clock. Eight o'clock. Restless energy churned inside her and she couldn't sit still. She dried her hair, applied make-up, and dressed in jeans and a V-neck sweater. She was halfway down the hallway when the phone rang.

'It's Billy Miller. We're breaking ground in an hour. Cops gave the okay. Permit says you need to be here.'

'I'm on my way.'

'Mazur asked me to call him. He wants to see the graves removed with his own eyes.'

'Fine. Call him.'

Gage, Vega, and Warwick rewound the tape and watched it for the fourth time.

She wore a pink slip that skimmed her long, pale legs and hugged small perky breasts. Sweat glistened from her body. Long blond hair tumbled down her shoulders.

'How are you doing?' His voice was a whisper from off-screen.

Her desperate gaze shifted toward him. 'Can I go now? My son is waiting.'

'Not yet. Not yet.'

Rage boiled inside Gage as he watched Kelly Jo cower in the corner and the off-screen man prompt her to confess her love. He stiffened when the gun muzzle appeared and the killing shot took her life.

'See the way the camera shakes,' Vega said.

Warwick worked his jaw from side to side, as if he'd just absorbed a right hook. 'Two killers.'

Gage tightened his jaw. 'And note the way she keeps looking off-screen as if she's looking for help.'

'He insists that she use his name. "I love you, Craig."'

Gage's rage boiled. 'And he calls her Adrianna.'

'You think Thornton did this?' Warwick said.

'Maybe,' Gage said. 'But it doesn't explain Tammy Borden's murder.'

'That other someone might be carrying on his work,' Warwick said. 'His widow?'

Gage stared at the woman's face. The pain. The terror. The knowing death came soon. 'Adrianna wasn't a part of this.'

Warwick's scowl deepened. 'You sound sure of yourself.'

'I am.'

Warwick studied him and then, shaking his head, turned away. 'Then who?'

'Something Margaret Barrington said about Robert Thornton. She said he'd had the measles as a kid.'

'Yeah, so?'

'I'd bet money he was sterile. And according to

Dr. Heckman, Frances Thornton would do whatever it took to protect the family line.'

Warwick's gaze narrowed. 'Craig wasn't Robert Thornton's biological son?'

Gage shook his head. 'I don't think so.'

'So who's the daddy?' Vega said.

'That's the million-dollar question,' Gage said. 'It's time to let Miller finish that grave excavation. Once the bodies are out, we can do a DNA test.'

Warwick nodded. 'That's gonna take time.'

'I know. I know. And I don't think we have much.' Gage pressed his fingers to his temple. 'Tammy Borden's trial — it lasted two days.'

Vega nodded. 'I finally got a hold of her mother this morning. She recently received a postcard from Tammy in the morning mail. From Tucson.'

Gage rubbed the back of his neck, now tighter than a bow string. 'Was the mother at Tammy's trial?'

Vega nodded. 'She was.'

'She might remember someone at the trial. Someone who wanted to see Tammy dead.'

Vega snapped his fingers. 'I'll do you one better. I'll check the court logs and see who signed in during the trial or who requested transcripts.'

'Good. Good. There might be a connection.'

Tess pushed through the doors of the conference room. She stopped, a bit surprised by the crowd of detectives. 'Is this reception for me?'

Vega attempted a smile.

No hints of welcome softened Gage's granite features. 'I hear you have more information.'

'Cheerful as always, I see.'

Gage's patience, thin on the best days, snapped. 'Play the tape for her.'

Warwick hit PLAY.

Tess approached the television screen and watched as the gruesome scene unfolded. Pain constricted her features, but there was no hint of it in her voice. Only steel and determination. 'Someone is definitely holding the camera.'

'You said on the phone you had more information.'

'Yes.' She dropped her eyes to the manila folder in her hands. 'Dr. Butler and I have had a chance to study the injuries of our three victims. Each appeared to have been struck in the face on both the left and right sides, evidenced by fractures. Consistently, the fractures on the left are faint, almost hairline, whereas the fractures on the right are deeper, more pronounced.'

'The same injuries were on all three victims?' Gage asked.

'That's right.'

'So who sent the tape?' Vega said.

'Someone who has a conscience. Someone who is angry and wants revenge. Who knows?' Gage said.

Tess cocked her head as she stared at the woman on the screen. 'Do you hear that? He's whispering a name. "I love you . . ."'

Gage couldn't remain in the room any longer. 'I've got to find Adrianna.'

Chapter Twenty-Seven

Saturday, October 7, 12:15 p.m.

Gage tapped his index finger on the steering wheel as he drove down the interstate. On the fifth ring, he got Adrianna's voicemail. 'Call me. It's urgent.' Frustrated, he dropped the phone in his lap. 'Kendall said she was going to the estate. She's meeting Miller there.'

Something in Gage's tone caught Vega's attention. Vega muttered something in Spanish.

'What the hell are you saying?'

'You know damn well what it means. How long you two been going at it this time?'

Gage shot him a glare. 'Back off.'

Vega pressed his fingers into the bridge of his nose. 'Shit.'

'Save the lecture.' He pulled into traffic. 'The more I think about it, the more I think there's a nut out there who thinks he's Craig. I think these killings have been about roleplaying. All his victims have been Adrianna.'

'Why not just kill her?'

'Someone or something has been holding him back.'

If he hurried he could be at the estate in twenty minutes. He wouldn't relax until he saw Adrianna face-to-face.

The next few seconds played out slowly. For a brief second he glanced up at the overpass up ahead and noticed the dark truck parked in the middle. And then before he thought to question the misplaced vehicle, a bullet pierced his windshield and sliced into the seat just inches from his shoulder.

Gage slammed on the brakes. Another shot struck the front tire and the car fishtailed. 'What the fuck!'

The car skidded off the road and onto the grassy shoulder. He held on to the wheel as the car slammed into an embankment and air bags deployed. His head slammed back against the headrest and for a moment his brains felt like scrambled eggs.

He and Vega pushed the deflating bags away and stumbled out of the car. Gage glanced back to the overpass. The truck was gone.

Adrianna passed two news vans as she drove up to the estate's brick pillars. Police cars kept them at bay but she knew it was a matter of time before one made it onto the property. She paused, showed her ID to the police officer, and drove onto the estate grounds. In her rearview mirror she watched cameramen filming her.

She found Miller and his crew were at the gravesite. By the looks of the rumbling backhoe and the waiting flatbed, they were ready to proceed. There was no sign of Gage.

Adrianna had received his call saying his message was urgent. But when she'd called him back there'd been no answer.

She parked and moved toward the crew. Anxiety snapped through her body like electricity. More than ever she wanted to close this chapter of her life.

'Ms. Barrington.' Miller pulled off his work glove and shook her hand. 'We're ready when you are. We're just waiting on Detective Hudson.'

'Do we need to wait for him?'

'No. He's given us the all clear.'

'What about Mazur?'

'En route.'

'We're not waiting. Get started. The sooner this is over, the better.'

Miller nodded. He seemed anxious to finish the job. 'Will do.'

Less than a year ago she'd stood on this same ground and watched as Craig's casket had been lowered into the earth. Guilt, relief, and sadness had collided in her that cold, gray day. And oddly, the same emotions were reemerging.

Miller tossed a thumbs-up to his man on the Bobcat and the guy fired up the engine. Gray smoke puffed from the exhaust. Slowly he maneuvered the machine over to the gravesite and began to scrape the earth from the grave farthest from the flatbed. CRAIG ROBERT THORNTON IV.

Adrianna wrapped her arms around her chest and began to pace. Her connection to the Thornton family had seemed like it would last forever. There'd been a time when she couldn't imagine that the family wouldn't have been a part of her life. Since she was twelve her mother had talked about her marrying Craig.

And now it was ending.

The new life she'd dreamed of as she'd paced the halls of the nursing home was about to begin.

And as frightening as that was, she knew this was what had to be. Time to move on.

She kept glancing toward the main road expecting to see Gage's car. What could have held him up?

After a half hour of digging, the Bobcat driver backed off from the hole.

All the drama, and now the end would be quiet and uneventful. 'I'm sorry,' she whispered.

'Ms. Barrington.' Miller's deep voice was a welcome distraction from her thoughts.

Adrianna moved toward him. 'Yes?'

'We've got a problem.'

She felt as if the earth shifted under her feet. 'Please tell me it's not another body?'

He pulled off his ball cap and wiped the sweat from his forehead. 'No. That's exactly what is *not* the problem.'

'What do you mean?'

'There's no vault. No coffin. No body. Craig Thornton's body is not there.'

'What do you mean?' Adrianna felt sick, remembering the flowers, the card, and the scent of aftershave. 'My husband is dead. I saw him buried in that spot not a year ago.'

Miller shrugged. 'He isn't there now.'

'You swept the graveyard with radar.'

'I didn't bother with his spot or his parents'. I was only worried about the old graves.'

The too-familiar voice on the phone rang in her ears. *I love you, babe. I'll be seeing you soon.*

Adrianna's cell phone rang and the sound startled her. For a moment she didn't recognize the number and considered not answering. Refusing to cower, she picked up the phone. 'Yes.'

It was Marie Wells. 'I've found something at the main

house. Something to do with that baby you were looking for. I think I've found her.'

Adrianna's head spun. 'I'll be right up.' She closed her phone. 'Miller, get your radar out and start checking. This has to be a mistake.'

Minutes later, Adrianna parked in front of the main house and got out of her car. She was struck by the silence. There was no sign of Marie. Slinging her purse over her shoulder, she climbed the front steps and unlocked the front door. The entryway was completely empty. 'Marie!'

No answer. She walked into the house. The click of her shoes echoed through the empty rooms. There was no sign of anyone. She moved into the kitchen and found Marie lying on the floor.

'Marie!'

Adrianna dropped her purse and started to run toward her but in midstride, strong hands grabbed her. Before she could scream, a cold wet cloth that smelled of chemicals flattened against her face. She tried to hold her breath and she struggled, clawing at the hands that held her. Panic exploded.

Her captor laughed. 'Breathe, Adrianna, breathe. It's okay.'

Patiently he waited. Finally, she could hold her breath no longer and sucked in a lungful of air laden with chemicals. The drugs hit her system like a two-by-four and within seconds the room started to spin.

'That's it. Just breathe, honey. Just breathe.'

Strength seeped from her limbs and soon her knees buckled.

'Don't worry. I've got you.'

She collapsed and passed out.

*

Gage and Vega stood by a patrol car. The shooting had effectively shut off this part of the interstate. Lights from a dozen police cars flashed. Forensics was on the overpass searching for any evidence the shooter might have left behind.

'So when can we get out of here?' Vega asked as Gage approached.

'All we need is a car.'

Vega glanced toward an unmarked vehicle. 'Leaving now means there are going to be mountains of paperwork on this one, brother. Mountains.'

Gage didn't give a shit about paperwork. His top priority was Adrianna. He reached for the phone on his hip. It wasn't there. His phone was still in the car.

He moved to the wrecked vehicle and reached in the open driver's side door. He found the phone on the floor. **One new message.** It was from Adrianna. **I'm at the estate. Call me.**

He dialed her number, but didn't get an answer.

Something was wrong. 'Get me a car, Vega.'

'Will do.'

His cell phone rang. 'Hudson.'

'It's Warwick.'

'What is it?'

'City police called. Another body. Janet Guthrie. She was shot.'

'Where?'

'The parking garage near the hotel.'

'What kind of gun?' He and Vega got into the car and fired up the engine.

'Looks like a .38 but we won't know until ballistics can look at it,' Warwick said.

Gage put his phone on speaker and pulled onto the interstate. 'You think the killer is still protecting Craig Thornton.'

'I'll bet Janet knows about the forgeries,' Warwick said. 'My guess is that she found out about them when she bought the gallery from Adrianna last year.'

Vega nodded. 'Didn't she say she'd cleaned out the gallery's basement?'

'Right,' Gage said. 'If that kind of information became public, it would have shattered the family's reputation – Craig's reputation.'

'She was cozy at the auction with Brett,' Warwick said.

'Vega and I are fifteen minutes from the estate. I'll call back as soon as I've found Adrianna.'

Gage called Miller. 'This is Hudson. Is Adrianna with you?'

'She went up to the main house about a half hour ago. We got a problem. Craig Thornton's body is missing.'

'What?'

'No vault. No coffin. No body.'

'Shit.' His heart slammed into his chest. 'Do me a favor and go up to the main house and find Adrianna for me. Have her call me. I'm on my way.'

This was all turning to shit.

Gage and Vega arrived at the Thornton estate just after four. Gage parked his Crown Vic behind Adrianna's car in front of the main house.

Miller ran out of the house, his face a tight mask of fear. 'She's not there. But that old lady, Marie, is there. No pulse. I called nine-one-one.'

Gage and Vega unholstered their guns and ran toward the front door. They paused, checked to make sure no

402

one was in the house, and made their way back toward the kitchen. They found Marie.

Gage holstered his gun and rushed toward her. He checked for a pulse. Nothing.

Sticking out from her clutched right hand was his business card. 'She sent us the tapes.'

Vega was already on his phone calling for backup.

Gage spotted Adrianna's purse lying in the center of the room. Beside the purse were her keys.

'Shit, where is she?'

Chapter Twenty-Eight

Saturday, October 7, 5:00 p.m.

When Adrianna awoke, her stomach churned with nausea and her head felt like it was going to explode. Disoriented, she tried to shake the fog from her brain. What had happened to her? Had she passed out?

Eyelids heavy, she moistened her dried lips and tried to swallow but found the simple act made her stomach all the more unsettled.

Roll to your side. Put your feet on the floor. But when she tried to shift her position, she quickly realized she couldn't. She forced her eyes open only to be assailed by a bright spotlight that made her wince and turn her head.

Panic ignited and burned through the haze coating her brain. *Oh, dear God, where am I?*

Squinting, she allowed her eyes to adjust as she tried to remain calm and figure out where she was. With growing horror she realized she was tied to a bed. Her gaze darted around the room. It was large and made of gray cinderblock. There appeared to be no windows and a slight dank smell that mingled with cool air suggested she was in a basement.

Underground.

'Help!' Her voice sounded hoarse and rusty and her tongue felt as if it had been wrapped in cotton. 'Help!'

Her pulse thrummed in her neck as she listened and prayed help would arrive. For several tense seconds, she couldn't hear anything. 'Please. Someone find me.'

But no one came or spoke.

And then out of the silence arose an eerie sensation that made her skin crawl. She wasn't alone. Someone was watching her.

She forced herself to stare beyond the light. 'Who's out there? What do you want?' Her voice cracked, betraying her fear.

Silence.

Her skin tingled. 'I know someone is there,' she said. 'Help me get out of here.'

'It's okay, babe.' The familiar voice came from beyond the light.

She curled her hands into fists. 'Who is that?'

'Don't you recognize my voice?' Amusement dripped from the words.

The voice was familiar, but growing terror combined with whatever drugs she'd been given had rattled her. 'Just tell me.'

There was a long pause and she thought he'd not answer and then he said, 'It's Craig, babe.'

Craig. No, that couldn't be right. Craig was dead. And the voice didn't match. 'You are not Craig. Who are *you*?'

'Yes, I am.' The voice was a little like Craig's but the silhouetted figure that appeared at the edge of the light was too large to be Craig. 'You didn't find my body.'

The voice was familiar, but the speech pattern sounded stilted, as if forced. 'Who are you?'

Out from the shadows stepped Ben Wells. Ben. *Ben.*

Her brain couldn't process the information, which made no sense.

Adrianna tried to shake the fog from her head as she stared at him, a mixture of shock and horror shooting through her body. 'Ben. I don't understand. What are you doing here?'

Smiling, he walked up to her and gently stroked her hair. 'I've been waiting for you.'

Immediately, she was struck by the thick, coiling scent of his aftershave. Craig's aftershave. He'd replaced his faded jeans, work boots, and Wells Moving T-shirt with khaki pants, brown loafers, and a blue sweater with a white button-down collar underneath. And he'd cut his hair and slicked it back. The outfit and the hairstyle were identical to what Craig would have worn.

Oh, God, oh, God. What game was Ben playing?

'Ben, why are you dressed like that?'

Ben brushed his hand over his hair. A signet ring winked from his pinky finger. God, it looked just like the ring Craig's father had given him when he'd graduated from prep school. 'Like what?'

'Like Craig!' A rising hysteria underscored the words.

'I am Craig.'

Adrianna searched his eyes, looking for any hesitation, any hint of sanity, something that told her he didn't really believe what he'd just said. 'You're Ben.'

'No, I'm not,' he said easily. 'I'm Craig.'

His calmness frightened her more than if he'd ranted like a madman. She tried to keep her voice calm. 'You're Ben Wells. You're my friend. Craig, *my husband*, is dead.'

'The old Craig is dead.' Ben smiled as if to comfort her. 'It was his death that allowed me to step out of the shadows and take my rightful place.' He came so close she could feel the heat from his body. 'The old Craig was weak and foolish. And I promise you that you won't miss him. I am a much better Craig. You'll see.'

Tears pooled in her eyes. How could she not have seen that he was so insane? Ben Wells had always been so kind and so rational. She'd always relied on him to get the tough jobs done. And yet under all his calm smiles was a madman.

She softened her voice as if talking to a child. 'Ben, you aren't Craig.'

His smile didn't fade but his eyes hardened a fraction. 'You need to stop saying that. Of course I'm Craig. And I've proven time and again that I am more of a man than he ever was. He made messes while *I* cleaned them up.'

Adrianna thought about the graves. She didn't want to know what he'd done but knew she had to ask. 'What messes?'

Lightly he stroked her hair. 'There were women, evil women. They wanted to hurt you.'

His touch disgusted her but she resisted the urge to twist her head away from him. 'The women in the graves?'

'Yes.'

'What did they do that was so horrible?'

His eyes shone with pride. 'The first, Jill, was Craig's prom date. She got him into trouble – got him arrested for drugs. I knew you would have been so humiliated if you'd known. Even then I saw the way you looked at him – you liked Craig. So I made her go away. In fact, they've not even found her body yet.'

A tear rolled down the side of her cheek. He'd killed a teenager. A child. Dear God. She tamped down her terror.

'The next one was that stripper. Kelly Jo something. You and Craig were broken up then but I knew you'd get back together. But if that stripper-whore had her way, you wouldn't have. She even told Craig she was pregnant, which of course she wasn't. Faker. I was afraid when I killed that first girl, but not Kelly Jo. I liked it – even took my time with her a bit. And then I got the idea to bury her in the Thornton cemetery. So close and easy and I figured it would be the last place anyone would look. Plus I could visit her grave from time to time.' He winked.

She swallowed, doing her best not to get sick. 'And Rhonda?'

'She was making those forgeries for Craig.'

'Forgeries?'

'Craig was copying the best paintings in his collection and selling them overseas. He needed money just like he always did. And like always, Craig was taking shortcuts.' His nostrils flared with anger and for a moment he said nothing. Finally, when he seemed to get his anger under control, he said, 'Rhonda wanted more money and when he wouldn't pay, she threatened to go to the cops. You know she even showed up at your wedding? Came in through the kitchen. I spotted her and was able to take care of her. Then there was Tammy. The worst of all.' He kissed Adrianna lightly on her brow. 'She killed your baby.'

Tears welled in her eyes. 'Oh, Ben.'

'Shh. Honey, it's all right. She can't hurt you anymore

and you'll have more children one day.' His warm breath brushed her cheek. 'Maybe we'll have more children.'

She tensed. 'No! Ben. We can't do that. We can't have a child.'

As if she hadn't spoken he said, 'I also killed Janet for you. She hated you. She wanted to drag you through the mud and destroy you.'

Adrianna hadn't liked Janet but never would have wished such a grisly fate on her. 'Ben, please, let me go.'

'I've loved you for as long as I can remember.' His smile was gentle, as if he were her lover.

Adrianna had never looked into the eyes of insanity. Until now. 'Ben, I need to leave.'

'I can't let you go, Adrianna. There's so much we need to do together.' He leaned forward and pressed his lips to hers. He tasted of beer and cigarettes. 'We have our whole lives ahead of us.'

'Ben, please.'

'I'm Craig.'

'Why? Why do you want to be called Craig?'

'Everyone loved Craig. He was the star. The one people wanted to be with.'

She swallowed the bile rising in her throat. 'Your parents loved you.'

Ben shook his head. 'My father loved Craig more. My father always talked about *him*. How smart he was. How handsome he was. He never talked about me. Craig. Craig. Craig.'

She had always known that Mr. Wells had a fondness for Craig. She'd never realized his affection for the younger man would have bothered Ben so much.

In a flash, Adrianna remembered Marie lying on the floor. She'd been so cold and still. 'What about your mother? Did you hurt her?'

He shook his head, his gaze vacant for a moment. 'I thought she loved me, but she turned out to be the biggest liar of them all.'

'I know Marie loved you.'

'She betrayed me.'

Sweat pooled at the base of her spine. 'I know you loved her. I saw the way you looked out for her.'

'Of course I loved her.' Anger tightened his features. 'She turned on me.'

'What could she have done that was so horrible? She was your mother.'

His gaze grew vacant as if he'd gone to a faraway place. 'She took one of my tapes and sent it to the cops.'

As Adrianna strained against her bindings, the rope started to rub her wrists raw. 'What tapes?'

He glanced toward the bright light. 'I'm taping us now just like I taped the others.'

Adrianna glanced toward the light. Beyond the brightness she spotted the red glow of a camera's power button. *Oh, God. Think. Stay calm.* 'You filmed those women as you killed them?'

'That and other things I did to them. I didn't want to forget. I wanted to remember our special times together.'

Her thoughts turned to Marie, who must have been horrified as she watched the tape. 'She never knew about the women you killed?'

'Oh, she suspected. But she kept quiet out of her loyalty for Miss Frances and my father. She was always good at pretending problems didn't exist. For some reason, this time she decided to go to the cops.'

Her bindings hadn't budged. 'You've got to let me go.'

'I can't do that. I brought you here to keep you safe.'

She focused her gaze on his face. 'I don't want to be taken care of.'

'But I want to take care of you. Craig never appreciated what he had in you. He kept making such bad choices.' His eyes shone with admiration as he stared at her. 'I am going to look out for you. Forever.'

Fear clawed at her heart. 'What are you going to do?'

'We've got all the time in the world to get to know each other.' He glanced around the room. 'I built this room for us. No one will ever find us.'

The room. Cinderblock. Dark. Dank. Underground. Buried alive.

'Let me go. We don't have to do it this way.'

'It's the only way, Adrianna. Out there, people get in our way.'

'Ben, please.'

'I'm *Craig*!' he shouted.

Tears spilled down her cheeks. She wanted to close her eyes and shut out this nightmare but she didn't dare. 'You sent me those cards. You were in my home.'

'Yes.' Pride shone in his eyes.

'All those times I thought someone had been in my house.'

'It was me. I stole your assistant's keys, which had your house key on the ring. I made copies before I gave the keys back.'

He'd been stalking her. Watching her. For months or

maybe even years. Suddenly she couldn't contain her fear any longer. She screamed until her voice was hoarse.

Ben watched, partly amused, as if witnessing the tantrum of a small child. 'Scream all you want, Adrianna. It's not going to help. No one is going to hear you. I made certain the walls were soundproof.'

'Ben, please don't do this.'

'My name is Craig! Say it!'

Adrianna twisted her hands, trying to free them. She would not give him what he wanted. 'You're Ben. You're my friend.'

He snatched up a small handheld device and flipped a switch. Electricity snapped and popped between receptors. He moved toward her.

She tugged harder at her bindings and tried to roll away from him but there was nowhere to go. He pressed the device to the tender flesh on her side.

Jolts of energy shot through her and her entire body jerked with pain. 'My name is Craig.'

She gritted her teeth, realizing she was just as angry as she was afraid. 'You're Ben.'

'A fighter. Good.' He touched her again and she jolted again.

The door to the room banged open and she turned toward it, screaming before she even saw who it was. 'Help me! Help me!'

Dwayne Wells rushed in the room, his face flushed with anger. A quick survey of the scene had him zeroing his gaze on his son. 'Ben, what the hell are you doing?'

Adrianna twisted against her bindings. She'd never been happier to see anyone in her life. 'Mr. Wells, please help me.'

Dwayne moved toward them. 'Damn it, Ben!' He pushed his son to the side and reached for the binding of her right hand. 'Adrianna, it's going to be fine.'

Ben curled his hand around the stun gun. 'You can't do this. She's mine.'

Dwayne's face twisted with anger as he turned on his son. He grabbed Ben by the throat and squeezed so hard Ben coughed and sputtered. 'She ain't yours. She's Craig's and always will be.'

'Craig is dead,' Ben choked. 'I'm Craig now.'

Dwayne looked at his son. 'You are not Craig. You never will be half the man he was.'

'Don't say that!' Ben howled.

Adrianna's muscles burned as she forced her attention to the rope binding her right hand. Dwayne had untied it partly. If only she could get free.

'And Adrianna will always be Craig's wife.' Dwayne Wells spoke through gritted teeth. Eyes bulged with rage. 'I've always told you that she was off-limits.'

That infuriated Ben. He'd dropped the stun gun to his side but held it in a white-knuckle grip. 'I don't give a fuck what you want or what once belonged to Craig. Craig was a spoiled little shit who got what he deserved.'

'Don't talk about him like that,' Dwayne said. 'He was your brother.'

Adrianna froze. 'His brother?'

Dwayne nodded and some of the anger bled from his body. 'I was his father. No one knows, except his mother and me. I promised her I'd never tell. But Ben heard me talking to Frances once and figured it out. I made him swear not to tell.'

As Ben paced frantically back and forth, Adrianna kept her sights on Dwayne as she twisted under her bindings. 'I don't understand.'

'His mama came to me. Said she needed to give her husband a child. They'd been married so many years and hadn't had any children. She knew she could have children. She'd had a baby long before she'd met Mr. Thornton and given it away. She knew he was the reason they couldn't have children.' He tugged at the binding on her left leg and it came loose. 'I wasn't thinking long term that night when she stood in front of me. She was so damn beautiful. I knew I just wanted her.'

Adrianna's left leg came free and she watched with desperate anticipation as he started on the other leg. Her right hand was nearly loose. 'Did Marie know you were Craig's father?'

Dwayne nodded. 'She figured it out when Craig got older. Saw some similarities that Craig shared with Ben. But she never told.'

'I wish she had now.' Ben shouted an oath. 'After Craig was born, I just vanished. It was always about Craig from then on. He was your favorite son. All you did was talk about how smart he was, how handsome he was, how great he was. I got so damn tired of sweating my ass off working in your business while he sat by the pool at his damn country club pissing his life away.' He shoved his father's hand from Adrianna's bindings. 'You aren't taking her.'

Dwayne faced his son. 'You can't do this to her, Ben. You can't.'

'Why not? You let me have the others.'

'They were whores. Trash. And they wanted to hurt Craig. She's different. She was Craig's wife. She carried his child.'

Adrianna went very still. *You let me have the others.* 'Dwayne, you knew?'

Ben sneered. 'He knew, all right. He's the one that sent me to take care of them. He didn't care how or what I did with them as long as the problems they'd created just went away.'

'They wanted to hurt my son,' Dwayne said. 'They wanted to destroy his life. I couldn't let that happen.'

Ben shook his head. 'So you came to me to do your dirty work.'

The old man's gaze narrowed. 'You never complained. You were always glad to help.'

Ben shrugged. 'Lucky for me, that stupid little shit brother of mine kept getting into trouble with whores and you kept sending me after them.'

Dwayne nodded, his shoulders slumping a fraction. 'Maybe. Maybe Craig had some growing up to do. But I never sent you after Adrianna. Adrianna isn't like the other women. She was loyal to my boy.'

Ben shook his head, his face now contorted with hate and malevolence. 'She's a whore just like the others.'

Dwayne reeled around and struck his son in the mouth so hard that he split his lip. 'Shut your mouth.'

Ben wiped the blood from his mouth with the back of his hand. 'Ask her who she's sleeping with.'

'Shut up!'

'Ask her who she left Craig for that summer.' He laughed, revealing bloodstained teeth.

Dwayne shook his head. 'What the hell are you talking about?'

'Adrianna is sleeping with that damn Gage Hudson. The same guy who hounded Craig after Rhonda vanished. Look, she even took her wedding band off.'

Dwayne glanced at her hand and took in the naked ring finger. 'It's a lie. She'd not sleep with him. Not after all the hell Hudson put Craig through.'

'She did sleep with him. Four years ago and last night. I can still smell him on her.'

Dwayne looked at Adrianna. 'That true?'

Adrianna tamped down the panic rising in her throat. 'Mr. Wells, please let me go. I've done nothing wrong.'

'See, the bitch can't even deny it!' Ben shouted. 'She did sleep with him.'

Dwayne studied her eyes. And then slowly he shook his head. 'You did sleep with him.'

Adrianna shook her head. 'Mr. Wells, please let me go. Ben is insane. He killed his own mother – your wife.'

Dwayne shook his head. '*I* killed her when I realized she'd sent that tape to the cops.' Pain darkened his eyes. 'I never figured you of all people would have betrayed Craig with Gage Hudson.'

She tried to roll to the left and undo her other hand. 'I stood by his side all the time while he was sick.'

Dwayne shook his head. 'Do what you want with her, Ben. I wash my hands clean of her.'

Ben grinned.

Dwayne paused by the door, his shoulders slumping.

'Might as well know. Gage is dead. I shot him a few hours ago.' He left.

Adrianna's eyes flooded with tears. She screamed and clawed at the knot with trembling hands but couldn't get it loose. 'No!'

Ben moved toward her, as if he had all the time in the world.

Gage pulled up in front of the Wells home. He needed to find Dwayne or Ben now. Ben's age. His dedication to the Thorntons. *I was kinda like a Dutch uncle to Craig.*

'Dwayne is Craig's father,' Gage said.

Vega nodded. 'That's what I'm thinking.'

Gage climbed the front steps two at a time. Vega stood on the bottom step. Both had guns drawn. Gage stood at the side of the door and pounded on it. No one answered the door.

'Let's have a look out back,' Vega said.

The two ran around the side of the house and spotted a dirt road that snaked into the woods. Fresh tire tracks dug into the dirt. 'Look over here.'

'Someone just drove down there.'

Gage headed back to the car. 'Let's go.'

They got in the car and seconds later drove down the rough road. They'd driven less than a half a mile when Gage spotted Dwayne Wells's truck parked at a dead end.

'What the hell is he doing out here?' Vega said.

'Looks like he's gone into the woods.' Gage got out of his car. 'There are two paths.'

Vega's gaze narrowed. 'You go left and I'll go right.'

'Sure. Call it in and then head out.'

They split up and headed into the woods. Gage was halfway down the path with he spotted Wells around a bend. 'Wells!'

Wells glanced up at him. For a moment shock registered and then he smiled. 'Detective. What are you doing here?'

'I'm looking for Adrianna.'

He slid his hands to his waist. 'Adrianna? Why would she be down here?'

Gage pointed his gun at the ground but his finger slid to the trigger. 'Where'd you just come from?'

'Oh, just back that way.' Smiling, he reached behind his back.

'You were Craig's father.'

Dwayne tossed them an uneasy smile. 'What makes you say such a fool thing as that?' The old man dropped his gaze and kicked the dirt with his booted foot. 'I ain't Craig's father.'

'You know who is?'

The next seconds played out frame by frame. Wells pulled a revolver from his waistband. Gage raised his gun, pissed that the old man had fooled him.

Wells pointed his gun just as Gage lifted his.

But before either fired, a shot rang out from behind him. Wells stumbled back and a plum of blood blossomed on his chest. He dropped to his knees.

Without taking his gaze off Wells, Gage shouted, 'Vega!'

'Yeah.' The voice came from directly behind him. 'I've got him covered. Go find her.'

Gage ran down the path Wells had been traveling on. Dodging branches and thick brush, he came upon a shed that looked like new construction. He paused and glanced around the area, looking to see if anyone was lying in wait.

But when Adrianna's cry for help shrieked out from somewhere inside the shed, rational thought deserted him.

Adrianna refused to believe that Gage could be dead. It was too horrible, too wrenching to consider now. *Get out of here! Stay alive! Dwayne is lying!*

She repeated the phrases over and over again. Ben moved to the camera and checked its alignment. In one frantic jerk, she freed her hand, but quickly replaced it so he wouldn't notice.

Ben closed the door but didn't bother to lock it. He felt so sure of himself. God, she hoped she could use that to her advantage.

'I told you screaming won't help, Adrianna. No one can hear you out in the woods.' Ben moved toward her and sat on the edge of the bed. He ran his hand over Adrianna's breast and down her flat belly.

'I want to leave.'

'I made a mistake with the others. I didn't keep them very long. I was rushed. But now with this new room we will have years and years together. And with Gage gone there won't be anything to stop me.'

'You can't do that.'

'I sure can.'

Fresh tears threatened but she forced them back. 'It doesn't have to be this way. Just let me go.'

He reached for the clasp on her pants and unfastened it. 'I've waited so long for this. I've dreamed of loving you.'

No! She held on to the rope wrapped loosely around

her hand waiting for him to put down the stun gun. 'Ben, please, just talk to me.'

He traced a calloused finger around her belly button and she flinched. 'We have our whole lives to talk.'

Her brain scavenged for anything that would keep him talking. 'Craig's doctors said he'd live another twenty years and then suddenly he died. Did you kill Craig?'

A proud smile tipped the edge of his lips. 'I guess there's no need for secrets here.'

'No.'

'Yeah, I killed him. I got so damn tired of hearing everyone always talking about him. Craig is doing better. Craig looks good today. Craig this. Craig that. The guy was a damn vegetable. He was never coming back. And as long as he was alive, Pa would never see me. You would never see me.'

'How?'

'Just held a pillow to his face. Slipped in at night through the service entrance. You were out of town and he never had many visitors at night, so the time was perfect. Didn't hardly take any effort at all. He was just twisted bones by then.'

Tears slipped down her cheeks.

He wiped her tear away and raised the finger to his lips. 'I did it for you. That place was killing you. You deserved to live a real life.'

Thoughts tumbled. And this was the life he wanted to give her? The words begged to be screamed but she didn't dare. *Keep him talking about anything.* 'How old were you when Craig was born?'

He frowned, surprised by the question. 'Seven.' He set the stun gun on the table beside the bed.

'That is a hard age for a boy to lose his father's attention.'

He swallowed. 'It was.'

'What was it like before Craig was born?'

'Until then I had my father all to myself. It was perfect. We did everything together.'

His whole body seemed to soften as he talked about the days before Craig. She thought she might be reaching him when his face hardened suddenly. He traced his index finger over her belly and slipped it below the waistband of her pants. 'I know what you're doing. It won't work.'

Revulsion shuttered through her. She desperately wanted to slap his hand away with her free hand but held steady. She needed him to look away. 'The lens is crooked.'

He glanced back. 'So it is.'

She waited until he turned toward the camera before she allowed herself to look at the stun gun. She was ready to reach for it when she looked up and saw that he was watching her in the lens's reflection.

'You ain't going nowhere.' Ben turned and moved the gun out of her reach.

Adrianna curled her right hand into a fist and as he leaned forward to kiss her she mustered every bit of strength she could and drove her hand into his throat.

He choked, sputtered as he stepped back. 'Bitch.'

She rolled on her side and started to pull at the bindings on her left hand. Her fingers trembled. Her mind pushed through the fear that threatened to paralyze her.

Coughing and sputtering, Ben wrapped calloused hands around her neck and used his weight to flatten her on her back. He started to squeeze hard. 'You selfish, stupid bitch.'

Adrianna choked. She raised her right hand and clawed at his fingers. With no oxygen, her heart started to thunder. She could count the beats. One. Two. Three.

She was going to die.

The door burst open so hard it slammed against the wall. Gage stood in the doorway of the dimly lit room, the sun silhouetting his frame.

Ben released her and went for the gun in his waistband.

Gage fired as Ben whirled around. The bullet struck Ben in the chest and sent him tumbling back. He fell on Adrianna. Warm blood dripped from his wound and seeped into her sweater. He gurgled his last breaths.

Hysteria bubbled inside her and she started to scream.

Gage jerked Ben's body off her. He checked Ben's pulse as he flipped open his phone. 'He's dead, Adrianna. He can't hurt you.'

'Oh, Gage,' she sobbed.

'Are you all right, Adrianna?'

Terror shuddered through her. 'Yes.'

Raw anguish deepened the lines on Gage's face as he stared at her. 'Vega, we need an ambulance. No, I'm fine. Adrianna looks fine as well. Ben Wells is dead.' He closed the phone and shoved it in the holster.

With trembling limbs he undid the bindings that still held her. 'God, honey, I am so sorry.'

The tears and emotions she'd struggled to hide from Ben burst inside her. She stood and started to weep. 'Gage.'

Gage wrapped strong arms around her and buried his face in her hair. 'It's okay. It's okay. You're safe.'

Epilogue

Four months later

A light snow had fallen as Adrianna checked the last of the day's receipts and locked the cash in the safe under her counter in her store. Normally, she dropped cash at the bank's night drop box, but today she was in a hurry.

When Adrianna heard a knock at the front door she started. Four months had passed since Ben had held her captive in his basement prison, but she'd not shaken the wariness that likely would linger for a long time. She still kept her doors locked and still jumped at unexpected sounds.

She glanced up and saw Gage standing on the other side of the glass. He wore a dark leather jacket, jeans, and a black turtleneck. Snow dusted his wide shoulders.

Her smile came easily as she quickly tucked her receipts away and crossed the room. She unlocked the door and opened it. He came into the store and kissed her softly on the lips. 'Hey.'

Adrianna's nerves calmed. 'I'm just about done here.'

'Great.' He moved up to the counter and leaned against it as she moved back around it and finished counting her receipts.

'It was a crazy day,' she said. 'But crazy in a good way.'

He nodded, understanding. There'd been many nights

he'd held her when she'd awakened from nightmares that left her screaming and clawing to free herself from an underground coffin.

Ben had done so much damage. Not just to her but also to the families of the women he'd murdered. The grave excavations had continued but there'd been no sign of Jill's body. Ben had left no clues where he'd buried the teen and most had accepted that she'd never be found. Her mother had at least gotten some closure just knowing what had really happened to her child.

Craig's body was found, buried on the back edge of Dwayne Wells's property. The grave had been marked with a simple marble slab that had only read: MY SON.

Gage and the other detectives had pieced together as much as they could and now believed Dwayne had dug up Craig just after his funeral and buried him on Wells property as a final tribute.

DNA evidence had linked Ben to the sweat-stained bandana, and traces of Dwayne and Ben's DNA had been found on Tammy.

The father-and-son killing team had murdered six women. Jill was killed because she'd involved Craig in drug charges. Kelly Jo had said she was pregnant. Rhonda had been forging paintings for Craig, who was strapped for cash. When she demanded more and Craig refused, she'd threatened to ruin his wedding to Adrianna. Tammy had killed Craig Thornton and Adrianna's unborn child the day she'd driven drunk and struck their car. Janet had discovered the forgery when the fake painting came up for auction on the West Coast and had planned to go public. And Marie had tried to stop the two murderers.

The last few months had not been all darkness. Adrianna had opted to stay in Richmond and had found another house to buy after hers had sold. Her mother was improving, and though Adrianna longed to know what had happened to the Barringtons' first child, she'd stopped pressing the issue. She and her mother would never be as close as she'd have liked, but they were no longer at odds. Adrianna had grown closer to Kendall, who felt more and more like a sister each day.

'I should be finished here in just a minute. I don't want to keep Tess and Alex waiting,' she said. Tess and Alex had eloped to Vegas two weeks ago and had decided to hold a reception for friends and family to celebrate.

'No rush.'

His too-serious expression worried her. 'What's wrong?'

Gage never minced words. 'I found something.'

'I don't like the sound of that.'

He pulled a piece of paper from his breast pocket. Carefully he unfolded it. 'I found Baby Adrianna's grave.'

She released the breath she was holding. She felt some measure of relief but also an odd sadness. 'You did? How?'

'I thought about what your mother had said to me. She and Frances were like sisters. It didn't make sense to me that Frances would leave her best friend's child in an unmarked grave. So I searched area cemeteries.'

Margaret Barrington swore she'd never hurt the baby and had found her dead. It had been Frances and Margaret's husband Carter who had assumed the sleep-deprived new mother had accidentally harmed the baby that would never stop crying. Carter had also feared the death would ruin his career. However, he'd never banked on the fact that hiding the baby's death would eat at his soul. The anger and loss he felt over his child's death had been the reason he'd refused to get close with his second daughter.

'Where is she?'

'She's in a small church cemetery up in Ashland. I got a call back from the cemetery the other day, so I drove out there. I wanted to be sure before I told you. I met the caretaker, who took me to her place.' He handed her a picture of the grave.

She studied the picture. 'Oh, my God.' She traced the outline of the headstone, which read simply ADRIANNA. 'Poor baby girl.'

Gage slid his hands into his pockets. 'Didn't set too well with me seeing your name on the headstone.'

She stared at her name etched in stone. The image unsettled her as well. 'Thank you.'

'I'd do anything for you.'

She came around the counter and kissed him on the lips. He rarely spoke words of love, yet she knew he loved her deeply. 'I love you.'

The hardness around his eyes and mouth that always seemed to be there faded for just a moment. 'I love you.' Their relationship wasn't perfect. His work demanded so much of him, and there were times when she felt alone. But this time they were careful to talk through problems. Both were committed to making this work.

Gage kissed her. It was a long, lingering kiss that telegraphed more emotion than words ever could. Finally, when the kiss ended, he seemed reluctant to release her.

'We better get going.' Her voice sounded rusty.

He sighed and released her. 'Okay.'

Gage helped her on with her coat and shut off the lights.

She threaded her fingers into his and smiled, knowing she was right where she belonged.

Read on for an extract from
Mary Burton's next novel, *Senseless*,
coming soon from Penguin . . .

The Next to Die

'Did you hear about Lisa?' Eva asked.

A flicker of emotion darkened Kristen's eyes. 'It was on the news. So sad.'

'I came to talk to you about Sara Miller.'

'What about her?'

'Sara is dead, too. Killed. Murdered. I've seen pictures of her body.'

Color drained from Kristen's already pale face. 'Why are you telling me this?'

'I thought you might know what happened to her. Someone is killing people we know and branding them with a four-pointed star.'

Kristen lifted a brow. 'Is that someone you?'

'Drugs and pain aren't clouding my memory or thoughts. I see very clearly. The big question is am I looking at a killer?'

'Stay away from me or you'll find out.'

Eva shook her head. 'Be careful, Kristen. Two of the three girls who testified against me in college are dead.'

'Is that a threat?'

'No. I'm just pointing out a pattern to you, like when we were in college? I see a pattern and you and I are a part of it. . . .'

Prologue

Duct tape muffled the woman's hoarse moans as a hooded figure stoked the glowing embers in the basement hearth. She had been screaming and struggling, hoping to get her captor's attention since she'd started awake . . . was it an hour ago? Two hours? Down in this cellar prison, time leaked away like the *drip, drip* of water from an overhead pipe.

No amount of crying or rattling of chains against the stone floor diverted the shadowy figure's attention from the flames that hungrily danced and licked the logs in the ancient hearth. Twig by twig, her jailer tenderly fed the flames as a mother might nourish a child, never paying her a moment's attention. In this dank place, she was invisible, of no greater consequence than the three-legged chair leaning in the shadowy corner or the trash bags piled by the rickety staircase.

The hard, uneven stone floor dug into her back, cramping her muscles, numbing her skin and driving home the realization that there'd be no escape. She was going to die.

She closed her eyes, the thud of her heart mingling with the crackle of the fire and the clink of the andiron against the blackened grate cradling the logs. Since childhood, she'd been told she didn't deserve happiness or a full life. *Bad girl. You are a bad girl.* All her life, she railed against those messages, grabbing or stealing what she could to not only survive but also to prevail. Maybe the dark message funneled into her soul since the cradle was right. Bad girls always came to a bad end.

Despair rose up in her like a black storm cloud, wrapping around her throat and beckoning her to relent. It would be so easy to give in to her predestined fate. So easy just to close her eyes and let the darkness slide over her.

As she eased toward the mental abyss, ready to surrender to fate, a primal survival urge jerked her back from the edge.

No! You want to live! You deserve to live!

She opened her eyes and stared at her captor. He wasn't so large. He didn't look so strong. Or so evil. Perhaps she could wedge a bit of reason under his icy exterior and get him to take pity.

Drawing on what little energy remained in her limbs, she kicked and screamed, but he didn't shift his gaze from the fire.

God, what was he planning? What could he want with her? As her mind tumbled over increasing vicious scenarios, fear and panic reignited her struggles.

Please, God, get me out of this. A thousand promises, *I swears* and resolutions raced through her mind as she bartered with God.

And then a miracle came in the form of a loud thump from upstairs. The noise cut through the stream of *I swears*. She craned her neck toward the rickety staircase that led to the upper floor. Someone had arrived! Her heart pounded faster, harder and her stomach coiled like a tight spring.

She studied her captor's posture, searching for a sign.

Was the upstairs arrival good or bad? Did this creep have some sick friend who'd come to enjoy this party? Or did she have a savior?

His narrow shoulders stiffened and an abrupt jerk of his head toward the door told her that the guest was uninvited.

Hope exploded. Maybe someone had come! Maybe someone had figured out that she'd been kidnapped.

Oh, God. Oh, God. Please send someone to save me!

She jerked against her bindings and screamed muffled pleas, projecting her voice beyond the tape.

Sunglasses and a hood hid a great deal, but she caught traces of a scraggly beard as he carefully laid down his iron and climbed the stairs to the first floor. He unlocked a shiny new padlock on the basement door, opened it and vanished.

Her heart thundered in her chest as she strained to listen. Above, the ceiling creaked as her jailer crossed the first floor in search of the intruder.

Someone, please, save me.

Floorboards creaked with light tentative footsteps of the newcomer who moved about the upstairs freely. As the seconds passed, the footsteps grew more confident as if the new arrival wasn't expecting company.

Be careful! He's waiting for you!

She screamed until her throat burned, but the duct tape muffled her words, garbling all her warnings.

The intruder moved across the first floor. Her jailer remained still, lying in wait, like a snake ready to strike.

And then a loud scream, 'Shit!'

A scuffle followed. Bodies slammed against walls. Glass

435

hit the floor and shattered. A subdued groan and something large slammed the floor, as if a body had crumpled under its own weight. And then silence.

The woman's heart jackhammered her ribs so hard she thought bones would crack as she frantically twisted her hands and stared at the door, hoping for a miracle. Who had won the battle? She struggled against her bindings, willing the hemp to snap even as it cut into her flesh.

Oh, God, save me!

Her mind tumbled as she imagined police storming into the basement and cutting her bindings as they explained in soothing tones that she was now safe. They'd ask her what had happened and she'd calmly explain.

'The last thing I remember was sitting at the bar in Moments, a little upscale place on the Potomac. It's a good place to hang out. Normal people, like doctors, lawyers and bankers, drink at Moments. It's not the kind of place crazy people visit. It's safe.'

She'd be sure to mention that she'd only sipped a single white wine and had spent most of that night chatting with the female bartender, killing time until her blind date showed. This had been her Saturday night routine for over a year.

Toward the end of the evening, a guy had settled beside her on a bar stool. He'd worn sunglasses, had a neatly trimmed beard and a nice oversized dark suit. He was a strange still man who could hardly be classified as overly masculine. Her stepfather would have called him a 'Girlie-man.' He'd ordered vodka in a quiet raspy voice that had sent a chill whispering down her spine. But his drink had arrived and he'd sipped it without fanfare as if content to be alone. Ignoring him had been easy.

She remembered a woman walking into the restaurant

and shouting someone needed to fix her flat tire. The shrill voice knifed through the hum of conversation and soft jazz.

Distracted, she had turned to see who was making so much noise. She'd classified the woman as unimportant . . . some nobody from the street. She'd returned to her drink, forgetting the woman even before she'd swallowed her next sip.

And then . . . then she'd woken up here – a dank, dark basement, tied to the floor.

Oh, God, how she desperately wanted to tell that story. To be saved.

Seconds passed – then minutes and then the steady sound of footsteps. Steady. Not rushed. Cautious like a rescuer or unhurried like a madman? Impossible to tell.

And still she hoped. What if her savior was just being cautious? He didn't know what was downstairs. He had to be careful so he didn't get hurt himself.

Please hurry.

The door at the top of the stairs opened and a silhouetted form appeared. Who was there? He descended the steps, carefully and deliberately moving into the light generated by the fire.

Her captor.

No savior.

No rescue.

Fresh tears welled and streamed down the side of her face, pooling in her knotted blond hair.

As if she were invisible, he passed her, his attention transfixed by the fire. He stoked the embers, whistling as he lovingly coaxed more life from the flames.

Tears ran down her face. *Look at me, damn you! See me as a frightened woman!* She was a good girl. She was from a respectable family. Sure she liked to party. What girl didn't? She'd told a terrible lie years ago, but it had haunted her almost every day of her life and she'd prayed for forgiveness. She'd donated to an animal shelter at Christmas. She went to church at Easter. She laid flowers on her stepfather's grave even though the bastard had never deserved respect. Christ, she'd just turned thirty.

Good people didn't die this way.

She didn't deserve this!

Her head slumped back as she tried to block out the panic and focus on what might get her out of this horror.

Oh, Holy Mother of God, this had to be a nightmare. It had to be! This did *not* happen to regular girls. It just *didn't*.

But the raw skin on her wrists and pain in her spine said otherwise. This wasn't a nightmare.

Fear fisted in the woman's gut as she stared at the man. Was he the one from the bar who'd sat down beside her? She couldn't tell, but sensed he had to be the one. Who else would do this to her? The one man she'd known who could be this cruel had died years ago.

'Finding you was easy, you know.' His voice sounded like sandpaper rubbing against wood. 'You didn't move more than five blocks from your parents' house.'

She stopped struggling, searching her brain for any clue to his identity. But as much as she tried to cut through haze and confusion, she found no answers. Fear rose up in her and she couldn't suppress a moan that sounded like an animal caught in a trap.

The guy straightened and turned. He wore a large bulky

coat, making it hard to judge his size, maybe five-nine. As the figure moved toward her, his glasses reflected the firelight, which mingled with her terrified face. He pulled the tape from her mouth and the adhesive pulled bits of the skin on her lips. She tasted blood.

'Surprised to see me again?'

The raspy voice sent a chill snaking down her spine. In the dim light she could see that he wore a wig and his beard appeared fake. Smoky glasses obscured his eyes.

She winced, moistening her cracked dry lips with her tongue. 'You were in the bar.'

'Yes.'

If she hadn't been trying so hard to ignore him in Moments she'd have seen he was a freak. 'You drugged me.'

'Yes.'

'Why?'

'Makes you more reasonable.' With a gloved hand he pushed up her shirt, exposing her flat belly.

'What are you doing?' Her white flesh quivered with fear.

Gently, he smoothed his hand over the pale skin. 'So pretty and clean. But we both know that you aren't clean, are you?'

'I'm a good girl.'

'No, you are not.'

Her mind reeled. *Make a connection. Let this freak see that I'm a person.* 'I have a family. Parents. A child.'

He circled an index finger around her belly button. 'You haven't seen any of them in a very long time. None of them want you.'

The words clawed at her insides. He was right. She'd

lost contact with them all. She grasped for the right words that would cause delay. 'Someone was upstairs! Someone knows you are here. They know *I* am here.'

'He's trussed up like a pig for slaughter. I'll deal with him after you.'

Tears welled in her eyes. 'Please let me go.'

He arched an amused eyebrow. 'Can you imagine? A thief breaking into this house, tonight of all nights. Talk about timing.' A smile teased the edges of his beard. 'You can scream if you want.'

Her heart hammered so hard it rattled her ribs like a speeding freight train. Tears spilled down her cheeks. 'I'm not going to scream.'

The guy cocked his head. 'Why not? You've reason to scream.'

Oh, God. Please. 'I won't scream.'

The smile widened, revealing small yellowed teeth. 'We shall see.'

Words tangled with fear and caught in her throat. 'What do you want?'

'You.'

'Why? I'm nobody. You said so yourself. My family doesn't want me. I'm not worth the time.'

'No, you're special.'

Special. That's what her stepfather used to say. *My special little girl, it'll be our secret, won't it?* 'What do you want?'

'Not much really. All you have to do is lie still.' Gloved hands stroked her hair, the heavy-handed gesture pulling hard against her blond curls.

She winced. 'I want to leave.'

'No.'

440

Panic rose up in her throat. 'People will miss me.'

'No they won't.'

With quick, angry strokes, the guy jabbed a metal rod into the embers. Finally, he raised the tip out of the flames and inspected the glowing star-shaped tip. A four-pointed star.

Memories from long ago burned through her mind, forcing her to remember a time she'd worked hard to forget. 'What are you going to do with that?'

'You remember the star, don't you?'

'What are you talking about?'

'The star. And The Secret.'

Memories elbowed to the front of her mind. 'No, I don't remember,' she lied.

'Liar.'

'No, I swear.' She squirmed and tugged against her bindings but her struggling only tightened their hold.

He adjusted his sunglasses as he stared at the glowing red star. 'I promise you before I'm done, it'll be burned in your memory.'

Sobs fueled her hysteria. 'Please, I don't want to remember.'

He knelt beside her, the coarse fabric of his pants brushing her hip. 'Your job is to send a message to the others.'

The others. 'You don't know about the others.'

'I surely do. I surely do. And soon everyone will know of their betrayal.' The scent of hot metal wafted around her, stirring up the old sin buried under a decade of wine and denial.

'Please.' Her gaze locked on the red tip of the brand and every muscle in her body tensed with terror.

'Starlight, star bright; the first star I see tonight. I wish I may; I wish I might; Have the wish I wish tonight.'

And then he touched the hot brand to her stomach. The metal seared into her flesh. Instantly, pain robbed her of breath and she couldn't squeak out a sound. Every nerve in her body convulsed. When he pulled the brand away, the pain lingered. Her heart slammed the walls of her chest, as if trying to flee the agony.

Glasses hid her tormentor's eyes, but a twitch of his lips betrayed a euphoric joy as if this moment had been a pleasure long denied. 'When I'm done, they'll see you and they'll know it's time to atone.'

Her lungs contracted, sucking in air.

She screamed like a wild animal caught in a trap.

MARY BURTON

DEAD RINGER

SOME NIGHTMARES
Beside each body, he leaves a simple charm bearing a woman's name. Ruth, Martha, Judith. The victims are strangers to each other, but they have been chosen with the utmost care. Each bears a striking resemblance to Kendall Shaw, a local TV presenter, and each is brutally strangled by a madman with a life-long obsession . . .

DON'T FADE
In front of the cameras, Kendall is the picture of stylish confidence. But at night she's haunted by disturbing nightmares that feel like fragmented memories of a childhood she can't remember. Despite warnings from Detective Jacob Warwick, Kendall can't stop investigating the recent string of murders. She knows she holds the key to catching an obsessed psychopath – if he doesn't get to her first . . .

WITH DAYLIGHT
The deeper Kendall and Jacob dig into the victims' backgrounds, the more terrifying the discoveries. From the shadows of the past, a legacy of evil has resurfaced. Every murder, every moment has been leading to Kendall. And this time, nothing will stop the killer making her his final victim . . .

He just wanted a decent book to read ...

Not too much to ask, is it? It was in 1935 when Allen Lane, Managing Director of Bodley Head Publishers, stood on a platform at Exeter railway station looking for something good to read on his journey back to London. His choice was limited to popular magazines and poor-quality paperbacks – the same choice faced every day by the vast majority of readers, few of whom could afford hardbacks. Lane's disappointment and subsequent anger at the range of books generally available led him to found a company – and change the world.

'We believed in the existence in this country of a vast reading public for intelligent books at a low price, and staked everything on it'
Sir Allen Lane, 1902–1970, founder of Penguin Books

The quality paperback had arrived – and not just in bookshops. Lane was adamant that his Penguins should appear in chain stores and tobacconists, and should cost no more than a packet of cigarettes.

Reading habits (and cigarette prices) have changed since 1935, but Penguin still believes in publishing the best books for everybody to enjoy. We still believe that good design costs no more than bad design, and we still believe that quality books published passionately and responsibly make the world a better place.

So wherever you see the little bird – whether it's on a piece of prize-winning literary fiction or a celebrity autobiography, political tour de force or historical masterpiece, a serial-killer thriller, reference book, world classic or a piece of pure escapism – you can bet that it represents the very best that the genre has to offer.

Whatever you like to read – trust Penguin.